Phoenix

Redoubt

Book Six of the Outsider series.

by
Aiden Phoenix

Redoubt

Copyright © 2023 Aiden Phoenix

No part of this book may be reproduced in any form or by any electronic or mechanical means including information storage and retrieval systems, without permission in writing from the author. Except for the purposes of making reviews or other cases permitted by copyright law.

ISBN: 9798859014057

Cover created by Aiden Phoenix.

This book is a work of fiction. Names, characters, locations, and events are products of the author's imagination. Any resemblance to any persons living or dead, locations, or events are coincidental and unintended by the author.

Table of Contents

Prologue: Silver 5
Chapter One: Fortune 18
Chapter Two: Spoils of Victory 35
Chapter Three: New Arrivals 49
Chapter Four: Eagerly Awaited 67
Chapter Five: Timely Gift 89
Chapter Six: Haze 110
Chapter Seven: Arrival 128
Chapter Eight: New Position 146
Chapter Nine: Mingling 161
Chapter Ten: Petition 180
Chapter Eleven: Proving Grounds 197
Chapter Twelve: Lifetangled 220
Chapter Thirteen: Valor 241
Chapter Fourteen: Vigil 257
Chapter Fifteen: Adventure 278
Chapter Sixteen: Noble Knighthood 301
Chapter Seventeen: Going Home 318
Epilogue: New Adventures 338

Redoubt

Welcome to Collisa!

Collisa is a new world brimming with opportunities for adventure and growth. It is also brimming with chances for romance and fun. This is the story of Dare and the life he builds for himself with the women he meets and falls in love with.

As you can guess, it is a harem tale, with all that includes. Be aware that it features varied and explicit erotic scenes between multiple partners. It is intended to be enjoyed by adults. All characters involved in adult scenes are over the age of 18.

Phoenix

Prologue
Silver

Dare pulled out all the stops cooking dinner for Lily.

The best cuts from an epind, the small, cow-like creature with incredibly succulent and delicious meat, which he'd slaughtered that very day for the freshest possible steaks. The finest quality root vegetables, winter greens, and dried fruits he could find. All the best spices he'd been able to buy or gather, the amounts carefully tweaked over several attempts until he had the most nuanced flavor possible.

Since he knew that the bunny girl, unsurprisingly, preferred greens and vegetables, he focused mostly on salads, vegetable dishes, and fruit desserts. Although she'd told him at one point that her warren gathered root vegetables for the winter months that they cooked into a stew, which he planned to make.

As for the epind steaks, well, he could admit those were mostly for him.

Not just him, though. Given how easy the cooking ability made things, so it not only took less time but required almost no supervision while the food was cooking, he was able to make enough portions for all his fiancees. The plan was to have a quiet, romantic candlelit dinner with just him and Lily, but he wanted to cook for his other beloved as well.

And, as more than one of them had pointed out, also have individual romantic dinners with all of them. Which, given how their harem had grown, would take over a week if he devoted one full evening to each of his fiancees.

Much as Dare wanted to spend quality time with them, and much as they all deserved the pampering and special attention, at the moment his time was limited. Thankfully they were all understanding of that and supportive of his efforts.

He had to finish preparing to petition for knighthood on the first of the year, less than a month away now. In that time he wanted to get at least one more level, ideally two to bring him up to 38, and at this point each level took about 10 days of determined monster slaying. He also needed to find two more party rated monsters, as well as killing the high level one he'd already found, to finish his Protector of Bastion achievement.

Dare also had to account for travel, being there for when Pella gave birth to their children, and any more unexpected blizzards that might keep him from going out. Or worse, trapping him in the midst of a storm like yesterday.

In fact, the only reason he'd had time to take a personal day to fix things around the manor, and have a proper romantic dinner with Lily, was because yesterday's blizzard had dumped enough snow to make travel a pain.

He was hoping that a few days of warmth would melt some of that snow, but in the meantime he'd made a sturdy pair of snowshoes to help him get around. Although it was going to slow his normally superhuman travel speeds.

On the plus side, Ireni had talked it over with Lily and Linia and agreed he should have the Home Ward. The two lower level women had a ways to travel themselves to reach spawn points to farm monsters at, but not nearly as far now that Lily was Level 20. On top of that with three people it was awkward since the artifact could only transport two, which would leave Lily to run home on her own.

She certainly could, since as a bunny girl she could run even faster than Dare and was much less slowed by snow. But they weren't in such a rush that they wanted her to travel alone.

As for Dare, having the Home Ward to take him back to Nirim Manor at the end of each day, at a speed of 120 miles an hour, was a huge boon. A lot of his time was spent scouting the mountains for party rated monsters, taking him great distances over rough terrain, and having an extra few hours to search was huge.

Phoenix

For tonight, though, all his focus was on his date with Lily.

With Leilanna's help he'd set up braziers around a picnic area in the garden, producing enough heat that even in what would be early December for Collisa, with over two feet of snow on the ground all around them, the area was toasty. Then he'd set up a table with a fancy tablecloth, put out the plates and silverware the way he'd seen Marona's maids set her table for high society, and lit a few candles for mood lighting.

As a final touch, he strewed petals from some frostflowers that he'd found a few days ago across the ground around the table. He also put some in a vase for a centerpiece, the delicate blue flowers blushing pink at the edges in the heat.

Dare honestly didn't know what he'd do without his lovers. Not only did they help him get the setting ready, but they also helped him clean up and shave as well. And finally they helped him figure out the fancy suit Marona had gifted him, as part of his wardrobe for his trip to Redoubt to petition for knighthood.

At least he'd cooked the dinner on his own. He had it set on a fancy serving table at the edge of the picnic area, kept warm by a fire from another of Leilanna's spells.

Now, with everything in place, he stood by the table and waited for Lily to join him. He had to wipe his palms on his pants a few times, and not just from the warmth of the braziers around him.

He had six beautiful fiancees, multiple lovers, and had been with many more exceptional women. But this sort of formal wooing was outside his experience, either on Collisa or from his past life on Earth.

Dare hoped he didn't screw it up. He could handle embarrassment, but Lily had dreamed of a storybook romance all her life and he wanted nothing more than to give it to her.

It didn't help his nerves that even surrounded by beautiful girls, the sweet, innocent, slightly nerdy bunny girl was one of the most ethereally lovely women he'd ever seen. To the point that he sometimes felt like he'd wandered into a dream when he looked at her.

Like right now, as he saw her glide into the garden down the cleared path.

Lily had her silver hair down in a flowing waterfall to her waist, blending in seamlessly with the matching off the shoulder evening gown she wore. Her delicate, milky pale features were hauntingly beautiful in the light of the braziers and numerous candles, her figure lush and graceful and perfect all at once.

She'd elected to leave off her large wire-frame glasses, and her big gray eyes sparkled with wonder as she took in the dinner setting, albeit a bit fuzzily. Her white-furred bunny ears looked sleek and velvety, and the back of her dress was cut to free her adorable white cottontail.

"Wow," she breathed, stepping past the braziers. "You even put candles in the branches!"

Dare smiled and glanced up at the candles he'd fixed to the branches of the spreading sycamore overhead. "How could I not want to see your flawless beauty in the best lighting possible?"

Lily's pale skin showed a blush as he took her fur stole and guided her to her seat. "Wine?" he asked, pulling a bottle out of the snow where it had been chilling. She nodded, and he poured for them both.

She took a sip as she looked around, taking in the decorations. "So this is what a romantic dinner looks like. It's so much better than what I imagined from my books!"

That was generous of her to say, given how romantic stories tended to, well, romanticize things. He relaxed a bit as he rolled the food cart over to the table and lifted the covers off the trays.

"Oooh!" the bunny girl said as she offered her plate for him to fill. "There's barely any meat at all!"

Dare couldn't help but grin at that; between Zuri, Pella, Se'weir, Linia, and he could admit himself, their meals tended to be heavy on the meat. Especially since his hobgoblin fiancee was the one who did most of the cooking.

"I figured I'd try out some vegetable dishes I've been working on," he said as he filled her plate.

Lily took a bite almost as soon as he was done; her table manners had always included more enthusiasm than refinement, a reminder that in spite of her elegant beauty she'd been raised in a warren.

She made a noise of enjoyment as she chewed. "Wow, this is so good! The others told me you were a great cook but this is the first chance I've had to try anything you've made." She blushed a bit. "It makes me feel a bit embarrassed about the meals I cooked for you in Rosaceae's clearing."

"Are you kidding, they were some of the best meals I've had," he protested as he filled his own plate.

His date giggled. "Mother always used to say hunger is the best sauce, and you were pretty hungry for all those meals." She reached across the table and patted his hand. "No need to be too polite, I realize my concept of spice was limited to what nature provided in the food itself. When you mostly eat fresh fruits and vegetables, and maybe some grains, you don't have too many opportunities to improve your cooking."

"Well Se'weir says you've taken to the kitchen like a duck to water."

"When I have time between leveling." She focused on digging into her food, and for a few minutes they enjoyed the meal in relative silence.

"So I think I know what happened to Gurzan's Last Hold," Lily eventually said as she lifted a forkful of salad to her mouth.

Dare paused cutting his steak, leaning forward in interest. "Oh yeah? I wasn't sure that knowledge even still existed."

There'd been no filing system or organization to the sealed room full of dwarvish records they'd found, which made tracking the history a bit difficult. Although Ireni, bless her heart, was doing her best to organize it all.

It didn't help that they speculated that the books and scrolls they'd found, which had all rotted to dust over the ages even in the sealed records vault, were from the more recent periods of Gurzan's Last Hold's history.

She nodded eagerly. "I think it does! The dwarves kept a ceremonial set of plates where they recorded events of more religious significance. It was so important to them that they inscribed them on truesilver."

Dare whistled at that. Truesilver was prized by the dwarves, but also by everyone else since it was 100 times more valuable than gold. Which was actually pretty convenient because in the monetary system of precious metals with copper, silver, gold, truesilver, and godmetal, each coin was worth 100 of the previous one.

Although gold was by far the most commonly used, since its value was right about in the range where a majority of purchases larger than a meal or a room for the night were made.

"So those plates might be worth as much as the entire rest of the records combined?" he asked as he lifted a bite of steak to his mouth.

Lily laughed. "In terms of more than just monetary value . . . the dwarves will prize these records most of all due to not just their historical but their religious significance."

"So what happened to the city?"

She sobered. "Well the final entries in the truesilver plates don't say anything about it. But going back a few years, I found a mention that the dark elves they'd been warring with had fallen in league with an unknown dark power that was offensive to Thoronkir, dwarvish God of Delvers. With its aid the elves were able to bypass dwarvish defenses, appearing in what were thought to be safe tunnels to wreak havoc."

After taking another bite of salad and chewing, she continued thoughtfully. "Actually, it's pretty interesting. The dark elves seem to have unlocked or created an entirely new class, at least for that time. The Phasewarper."

Dare jumped slightly. He had perused all the possible classes and was at least superficially familiar with them. The Phasewarper was an odd class, with no offensive or defensive spells or abilities. It was almost entirely focused around teleportation and magical storage, as well as limited scrying. A bird's eye view of the world so the caster could have some small idea of where they were teleporting to.

Even so, it was considered a combat class in the same vein as support classes.

"So you think the dark elves had enough Phasewarpers to launch a surprise attack and send the dwarves fleeing, or wipe them out entirely?"

The bunny girl shrugged and adjusted her glasses as she took a sip of wine. "Like I said, the final entries don't mention trouble at all. Whatever happened must've happened quickly, but I still haven't found any direct reference to it."

She made a face. "It doesn't help that the translation stones can't do anything with like a third of the words . . . we really need to find a dwarvish scholar."

That was for sure. Although Dare didn't want to involve a dwarf until he figured out how he was going to gift the records to the dwarves, and thus reveal the existence of Gurzan's Last Hold, without the dwarves immediately laying claim to the underground city.

He didn't mind if they moved in, and even thought it would be beneficial to have a friendly neighbor to trade with and for mutual defense. But there was a Level 52+ dungeon in there he wanted to clear first if he could, and it would take a long time to even get to that level.

Although he couldn't put off giving the dwarves their prized history for too long; their gratitude could quickly turn to enmity if he handled this wrong.

"Speaking of which, how's the transcribing going?" They'd hired goblins from the Avenging Wolf village to copy the dwarvish runes down on blank books Zuri made using her ability to create one-use spell scrolls, with a few added steps.

The goblins were all literate, as most intelligent creatures on Collisa were since the class, ability, and information systems required reading. Even if they hadn't been, though, all that was required to copy runes was to make sure they'd made an exact copy.

The goblins they'd hired were surprisingly good at it, careful and patient and seemingly immune to boredom. Although it probably helped that Dare had given them a few translation stones to check their work, so they were no doubt also enjoying reading the dwarvish records as they worked.

Heck, they'd probably be experts on Gurzan's Last Hold before they were done.

He wished he had more time to read the records himself. As well as other books about Collisa's histories and stories. He still wanted to begin buying books and create an extensive library at Nirim Manor.

There seemed no end of things to do.

Lily spooned herself a portion of fried vegetables. "It's a slog, like we expected. Even doing their best the goblins can't make the runes anywhere near as small and closely spaced as they are on the plates and tablets, so it's taking a lot more paper. Each book takes days of steady work.

Not surprising. And most of the reason why books had been so expensive before the printing press and were valuable on Collisa . . . copying them was no small task.

Dare sort of doubted the gods would be pleased if he tried to introduce the printing press here. He was sure something that world-changing would immediately be banned, and he'd probably get Noticed 3 in the bargain.

Once his date pushed aside her plate he cleared them away and brought up the dessert tray, which included small cakes, fruit tarts, a trifle, and even ice cream; *that* had taken some work to figure out.

Although she seemed to have no complaints with any of the options, given how she enthusiastically took a generous helping of each.

Dessert was filled with light banter, and when they finally pushed away their plates Lily sighed contentedly and rubbed her tummy. "That was the best meal I've ever had, and I'm not just saying that."

Dare smiled as he cleared the table, pleased. Then he offered her his elbow and led her over to a new fixture of the picnic area he'd just made today, with quite a bit of tinkering and a bunch of aid from Irawn, whose secondary class was Blacksmith, and one of the goblin villagers whose main class was Woodcarver.

"What is it?" the bunny girl asked, squinting at the tarp-covered shape. Given how she absently reached up to adjust glasses that weren't there before remembering, her squinting might not've been all for dramatic effect.

He gave her a playful look. "Well I figure since we spend so much time out here looking at the stars and enjoying each other's company, we should do it in comfort. Besides, it'll be fun for the kids." He yanked the tarp away. "Ta-da!"

It was a bench swing, hanging on chains from an A-frame. An easy enough thing to make, but apparently it hadn't been thought of yet on Collisa. Although it represented another crafting pattern Dare had introduced to the system.

"What does ta-da mean?" she asked of the Earth phrase as she looked over the new piece of furniture.

He chuckled ruefully; Lily, and Linia for that matter, both didn't know that he'd died on another world and been reincarnated with his memories on Collisa, thanks to the intervention of his fiancee Sia.

Or as most knew her the goddess called the Outsider.

He had yet to tell Lily that incredible secret, and he wasn't sure whether he even would tell the catgirl, since she'd made it clear she wasn't interested in being anything more than a lover when it suited her.

Lily, though, deserved to know. And it was getting about time to tell her. Although he'd probably want to include the others in that conversation. Especially Ireni and Sia.

"It's a phrase from my home, what you say when you're showing off something you're excited about."

"Oh, fun!" The bunny girl ran her hand over the bench's polished armrest. "So what is this?"

"Let me show you." Dare helped her sit on the bench, grinning at her nervous squeak when it swung a bit beneath her. Then he sat beside her; she instinctively huddled close to his side, tucking her slippered feet beneath her, and held his arm.

He had to admit he enjoyed the closeness. Giving her hand a reassuring pat, he carefully pushed the bench back and then lifted his legs so they swung free.

"Oooh!" she squealed, clutching him tighter for a moment and then relaxing. "It's a swing! Mother had one in a tree outside the warren when I was growing up, although it was just two ropes and a board she bought from Lone Ox."

"I had one of these growing up," Dare admitted, swinging them a bit harder. "On our porch. I used to watch thunderstorms rolling across the plains on summer evenings."

He felt a sharp pang as he thought of those pleasant childhood memories, and of his parents. He'd visited them less often than he should've given he was only an hour away, and had way less contact than he could justify given all the different means of communication he'd had available.

Damnit, his mom used to call him faithfully every few days to check up on him. He'd always been impatient with her tendency to ramble, and had sometimes even failed to answer when it wasn't convenient.

He wished he could talk to her now. Tell her about his new life and let her know he was okay. She was probably just fine back on Earth, along with his dad and little sister, but it hurt to know he'd probably never see them again.

"Hey," Lily said, gently nudging his arm. "Where'd you go?"

Dare chuckled and rested his head against her long, velvety ears.

"Sorry, I got caught up in nostalgia. I think about home less often than I probably should, and there are a lot of things I won't miss. But some things I definitely do."

"I get it," she said, rubbing his arm. "I've found a wonderful new home here, but I still miss Mother and my sisters and brother sometimes. And all my friends back at the warren."

"I wouldn't mind going back to Lone Ox when there's an opportunity," he said. "It was the first place I lived when I came here."

"That would be wonderful." She gave him an impish look. "Although you'd be buried beneath a pile of eager bunny girls wanting me to share you."

Dare was startled for a moment, then laughed. Sweet and innocent as Lily was, not to mention a wholehearted romantic, he sometimes had to remind himself that most bunny girls were much more . . . well, horny than she was.

Or at least, openly horny. Lily had the same fertility stat as any other cunid, and she definitely had a healthy libido. She just kept it in check to fulfill her romantic dreams.

Although a part of him wondered just how wild she was going to be once they became intimate, given his last encounter with a bunny girl.

He was getting ahead of himself though, since he still had a lot of wooing to do to win the beautiful young woman's heart. They hadn't even shared their first kiss yet.

The talk turned to the night sky, as it often did. She was endlessly fascinated by the exotic and oftentimes physically impossible (at least according to his knowledge of science) stellar phenomena that dominated Collisa's starscape. Including such things as a black hole with a brilliant accretion disk, a binary star system, stunning nebulas, multiple arms of whatever galaxy this planet was in, and more.

Dare's love of science fiction as a kid had led him to take an astronomy class in college, and he'd watched a lot of interesting videos about future human space exploration and the universe. His interest paid off now as he was able to pass that knowledge on to Lily.

Little good as it would do them, but it was still fun to talk about.

Finally the fires in the braziers died, and Dare retrieved his date's fur stole and wrapped it around her shoulders, then offered her his elbow to escort her back to the manor.

With the beast folk refugees who'd come with Linia, mostly felids like her, Lily had moved into a guest room in the manor. It felt a bit odd to be walking the girl home to the same place he lived, but on the other hand the manor had plumbing and a central heating system and the guest houses didn't, and he wanted her to be as comfortable as possible.

At the front door Lily paused, big grey eyes looking up at him in quiet expectation. Her full lips glistened invitingly in the moonlight, and he noticed her breathing had quickened.

Then, as if to make sure he got the hint, she closed her eyes and puckered her lips slightly.

Okay then, this was happening. Heart pounding, Dare leaned down and gave her a soft, lingering kiss.

The beautiful bunny girl's lips were softer than rose petals, with a fresh, green taste of cucumber and melon. Her mouth opened eagerly against his, and it was obvious she was no stranger to kissing.

Although he noticed she didn't use her tongue, so he didn't either; that didn't seem like a romantic first kiss sort of thing.

After a sufficient time, she pulled back and looked up at him with shining eyes. "Thank you for the wonderful evening, Master Dare," she murmured with playful formality.

He smiled and opened the door for her, bowing. "I hope we can do this again soon, Miss Lily. I greatly enjoy the pleasure of your company."

With a delighted smile she leaned in to kiss him on the cheek, then bounded off down a side hallway to her room.

Dare headed up to the master bedroom on the second floor, grinning like an idiot.

Of course his fiancees and Linia were all waiting for him, eager to find out how the date had gone. They immediately dragged him to the big bed and undressed him, then gathered around him to pump him for details.

Dare found himself seated with Zuri in his lap, Pella cuddled up under one arm and Linia under the other, with Leilanna and Ireni hugging him from behind and Se'weir perched on his feet.

He looked around at all the expectant faces with a smile. "So tonight we talked about gas giants, the vacuums of the solar system that catch asteroids and comets before they can wipe out all life on-"

He was met with a chorus of groans from the girls around him, and Leilanna whopped him on the back with a pillow. "Come on, you know what we want to hear!" she snapped.

"Yeah!" Pella said eagerly, awkwardly leaning forward around her hugely pregnant belly. "Did you kiss her?"

Dare grinned mysteriously. "I never kiss and tell."

The girls all went nuts. "That means he did!" Zuri exclaimed.

"Your first kiss, that's so romantic!" Ireni said, nuzzling the back of his neck. "I remember our first kiss."

"Yeah, way to go!" Linia batted at his chest with a hand curled into a cutesy paw.

Se'weir bounced on his feet. "What else happened? Did she like the bench swing you made?"

Smiling, he settled back in the shared embrace of the women he loved to tell them about the evening. Although he was certain they'd all be pestering Lily for details in the morning too.

The sweet, beautiful bunny girl might be joining their family soon, and everyone was excited about that.

Chapter One
Fortune

Well, it looked as if the boosted luck Sia had given Dare when she brought him to Collisa was finally making an appearance again, after a bit of an unlucky streak the last week or so.

The last four days since his break day after the blizzard had been productive in terms of farming spawn points and exploring. Having the Home Ward had allowed him to plunge much deeper into the mountains than before, almost to the southern end where they descended into the Kovana region, with the knowledge that he could fast travel home.

As opposed to having to plan to circle back around at the tail end of each day's exploring to get there, taking time he couldn't spare on travel.

In those days he'd had a lot of success finding spawn points to hunt, as well as new and amazing things in the mountains. Including a beautiful mountain valley he wanted to bring his family to for an outing sometime, or even build some sort of hunting or skiing lodge.

Now that would be a fun sport to bring to Collisa. Not that he'd ever done it back on Earth, but his new life here seemed like a great opportunity to try.

He wondered if Fleetfoot and Cheetah's Dash would affect his speed on the slopes.

In any case, his stroke of good fortune came in the form of a hideous rodent the size of a pony, which he found dragging garbage to a hole in the mountainside that was obviously its den. It had patchy fur and skin covered in boils, its eyes were reddened and swimming in pus, and its narrow snout was crusted with snot and blood.

Given its repulsive appearance, he almost didn't need his

Adventurer's Eye to name the monster. "Dread Plague Rat. Monster, Party Rated. Level 26. Attacks: Flying Leap, Disease Cloud, Rabid Claw, Gnaw, Scramble, Sewer Spit."

Ugh. As if the giant rodent wasn't already hideous enough without the diseases. Dare wasn't sure he even wanted to loot this thing.

Oh, he was definitely going to kill it. In fact, this deep in the mountains and with the pressure to get his achievement before the first of the year, he decided he wouldn't even wait to invite others out to kill the Dread Plague Rat with him.

He could solo a party rated monster 10 levels lower than him. Hell, he'd soloed the Cursed Orc Warchief that was not only five levels higher than him, but intelligent.

Hopefully the others wouldn't mind him risking this; somehow, with all of them moving away from leveling, he had a feeling they wouldn't.

Dare activated Rapid Shot to put four arrows in his bow hand, waited for the cooldown to come back, then used Burst Arrow on his first shot with Nature damage, applying a 2 second snare. He was fairly confident he could kill this enemy before it even reached him, party rated or not.

At first things went well. He fired his next three arrows, used Rapid Shot again, and then things got tricky.

The giant rat used Flying Leap, closing the distance to him in a flash. He could've dodged it without abilities, but he wanted to put distance between them quickly so he used Roll and Shoot instead.

He came up firing an arrow, sure he'd only need another three or four to finish the monster off. Then found himself automatically dodging to the side with Prey's Vigilance as a disgusting green glob of Sewer Spit flew past his face.

The Plague Rat used Scramble to close the distance again, and Dare found himself swallowing back retches as a putrid smell rolled over him, coating his skin and clothes with foulness: Disease Cloud.

He activated Cheetah's Dash and bolted away a second too late, feeling a line of fire bloom across his arm as Savage Claw slashed into his tricep.

Damnit. He'd underestimated this thing just because it was 10 levels lower. He should've remembered how fast party rated monsters could be, and how effectively they used their abilities.

His defensive cooldowns used up, he threw himself into an all out sprint to put some distance between him and the giant rat. His status showed a disease effect on him that was slowly draining away his health and had reduced his stats, but it was nothing to worry about at the moment.

What was a bit more worrisome was the glob of foul spit that smacked the back of his head, smearing on the hood of his fur cloak. He instinctively yanked it off and threw it aside as he continued running, cursing.

He wasn't coming back for that.

Dare heard hisses and guttural squeaks from behind him, but from the sound of it the distance steadily grew as he outpaced the monster, even with its unexpectedly fast Scramble. Then he heard the giant rat falling behind much quicker and realized its ability must've fallen off.

He whirled, loosing an arrow at his enemy. Another glob of spit was headed his way and he dodged aside, then began running sideways as he loosed the rest of the arrows in his bow hand.

Burst Arrow came up just in time for the finishing blow, but he didn't need to waste the mana on it and just used a regular arrow.

As the hideous monster thrashed in its death throes text appeared in the corner of Dare's vision. "Party rated monster Dread Plague Rat defeated. 14,000 bonus experience awarded."

"Completed 8/10 towards Achievement Protector of Bastion: Slay 10 party rated monsters in the region of Bastion."

"Trophies gained: Plague Rat Tail, Malformed Rattus Head. Loot body to acquire."

Nope. Just nope. Fuck the trophies, fuck whatever loot was on that thing, even if it was probably worth hundreds of gold. Fuck retrieving his arrows, even. And if it had a hidden trove somewhere, like many beast-like party rated monsters he'd seen did, he wasn't touching that stuff either.

Dare checked his arm, then retrieved some bandages from his pack. It wouldn't stop the bleeding effect from a wound this serious, but would at least slow it. As for the disease status effect, it was doing the equivalent of about 1% of his health an hour, so he wasn't about to die of it anytime soon.

The effect might even fall off on its own before he had to worry about it, but if not Zuri got Remove Disease at 30 so she could help him. He didn't relish the thought of going the rest of the day with it on him, but it wasn't serious enough to warrant returning home early.

Spitting in the direction of the giant rat, he popped one of Zuri's Cleanse Target scrolls to clean the filth of Disease Cloud off him. Then he turned and set off at a swift run, searching for more spawn points that would give him experience. Even though at an ideal pace he should only be a few days from his next level, he was barely over 50% into 36.

He'd put a lot of focus into party rated monsters and exploring Gurzan's Last Hold, and of course the blizzard hadn't helped. Still, he had the potential to reach 39 before he had to go to Redoubt to petition for knighthood.

Although realistically, at this rate he'd be lucky to get 38. Especially if he wanted to get the Protector of Bastion achievement.

Still, he was more optimistic about his chances. Ireni was making arrangements to get a tank to fight the Level 39 Ancient Outpost Watcher, which was lurking just outside the elvish ruins they'd discovered, and after that he'd only need one more.

Should be possible to find it in a few weeks.

Dare got back to leveling, feeling grody about the disease ticking away at his life but not letting it stop him. He managed to clear several more spawn points before sundown, at which point he activated the Home Ward and was back at Nirim Manor in less than a half hour.

Lily had been waiting for him, although she recoiled when he warned her about his disease and asked her to fetch Zuri. His other fiancees and Linia gathered while the little goblin healed him and cured the minor disease, and from their expressions none of them were particularly happy about his decision making.

"So even though you were wounded and had bleed and disease status effects draining your health, you ignored them and kept going instead of coming home?" Pella asked, hands on hips.

"I managed to clear six more spawn points because of it," he protested.

"What if you'd been knocked unconscious?" Zuri fretted as she unwound the no longer needed bandage, then wiped off the blood from the faint scar where the wound had been. "What if another blizzard had blown in and you couldn't get to where I could help you?"

"Home Ward," he told her with a gentle smile, leaning down to kiss her head.

"They're called party rated monsters for a reason," Leilanna tried, arms crossed beneath her generous breasts. "As in, you shouldn't be fighting them alone even if you're 10 levels higher."

Dare shrugged. It was nice to know they worried for him, but he felt like they were making too big a deal of this. "All's well that ends well," he tried.

"Nuh uh," Ireni said, to his surprise also chiming in. "And this isn't the first time, either, after you scared us all half to death disappearing during the blizzard. If you're going to be out there leveling alone, we need you to promise us you'll be more careful. Don't get cocky and underestimate an enemy, don't take dangerous status effects lightly, don't ignore dangerous weather or risky environments like slippery cliff paths, and most of all don't be afraid to come home and get help."

He looked around at the anxious faces of the women he loved and relented. "All right, I promise. I'm sorry I made you worry, I'll do better next time."

"Good." Zuri hugged him, then took his hand and tugged him towards the door. "Come on, dinner's waiting. Then I think you owe us another game from your home to make up for scaring us."

"Deal." Dare couldn't help but grin. "And since you're all annoyed with me for taking risks, I think I have the perfect one."

* * * * *

Dare returned from a productive day of leveling the next evening to an unexpected but anticipated visitor.

His fiancees all seemed excited as they led him inside and directly to the parlor, where he found the Level 34 Fighter who'd been in Jurrin's raid with him when they fought the monster horde.

The man was in his early 30s, medium height and powerfully built with a blunt face and amiable features. He kept his brown hair cut short, likely more convenient in his helmet that way, and wore fine clothing, slightly worn but well mended.

The man had removed his chainmail and plate armor as well as its cloth padding, and was settled into one of the overstuffed chairs by the fire, sipping a glass of brandy and chatting with Ilin and Irawn.

"Ah, Master Dare," the man said, standing and stepping forward to offer his hand. "Thanks for the invitation."

"You're more than welcome, ah . . ." As Dare accepted the handshake, he was a bit embarrassed to realize that if he'd ever heard the name of the man, he hadn't retained it.

"Bradis," the Fighter said, laughing easily. "Don't worry, I wouldn't know your name either if you weren't a hero being celebrated in every tavern in Terana for taking out the monster horde's commander. Adventurers like us tend to think of each other in terms of our class until we become better acquainted."

"Well met then, Master Bradis." Dare motioned him back to his seat and found a spot on the couch with Ireni to one side, Zuri to the other cradling Gelaa, and Leilanna standing with her arms wrapped around his shoulders from behind.

"So," the Fighter said, taking a sip of his drink. "I came at the prospect of slaying a party rated monster. Perhaps you could tell me a bit more about it, and how you plan to kill it."

Fair enough. Dare leaned forward and described the Ancient Outpost Watcher, as well as the party he planned to kill it with.

Bradis listened gamely, although from his expression it seemed like even though he'd agreed to come out to hear their offer, he was now dubious. "You want me to act as defender against a Level 39 party rated monster?" he said, scratching his jaw.

Dare poured himself a glass of brandy, and topped off his guest's as well. "You've got the health and defensive abilities for it, and Ireni can buff you and provide barriers. Also, Zuri will use her Nature's Curse to slow its movement and attack."

The Fighter took a deep gulp and leaned back in the overstuffed chair. "Normally I'd say this is overambitious," he said with a dour laugh. "But then, you killed a Level 38 party rated monster all by yourself." He squinted. "And you've gained 3 levels since I saw you last . . . not even going to ask what demon lord you made a pact with to accomplish that."

The room filled with easy laughter, and Dare joined in. "This is very much doable," he assured him. "I wouldn't put anyone in danger, let alone my fiancees and best friend, if I wasn't confident."

The plan was to go with him, Ireni, Zuri, Leilanna, Ilin, and Bradis. A solid group.

Although the mercenary adventurer seemed to have his doubts. "How will we do damage? You're the only one even close to its level, and I can't see arrows doing much to a tree." He gestured to Zuri. "And I'd bet it's resistant to nature, even if she wasn't 9 levels lower than it. And same goes for the Mage when it comes to levels. The Priestess can't do damage at all, and my sword will only be so effective."

He nodded respectfully to Ilin. "And no offense, but can you damage wood with punches and kicks? Against an enemy 8 levels higher than you?"

The Monk regarded him blandly. "I can," he said with absolute confidence. Bradis started at that, but didn't challenge the claim.

"Ilin inspected the Ancient Outpost Watcher with his Third Eye a while back," Dare said. "It has a core of nature magic infused sap running up the trunk from roots to crown. Once we can drill through to that, we'll be able to do damage to it."

The Fighter opened his mouth, likely to ask how they were going to manage that, and Dare answered before he could. "Leilanna has Flame Needle, which has armor piercing. My Burst Arrow has an air element that does the same. Ilin's hands and feet are harder than wood and if he briefly opens his Fifth Lock, he believes he can punch through in a single burst of power, or at most a few second flurry."

"My Dazzling Thrust may also be able to help chip a hole towards the core," Bradis mused. "It's meant to pierce armor." He downed the rest of his drink and leaned forward, staring into the fire. "And you say I'll get a fourth share and one trophy? And first call on any plate or chain armor loot?"

Dare nodded and leaned forward to pour him another glass. "You'll have two healers looking after you, and multiple ways in which it'll be slowed. It may be a drawn out fight but in the end I'm confident we'll all see victory. What do you think?"

The man sipped slowly, eyes staring beyond the flames. Then he laughed. "For the man who downed a Cursed Orc Warchief in an epic duel? Done." He offered his hand. "We leave in the morning?"

"That's the plan." Dare returned his handshake firmly. "Welcome to the party."

The Fighter shook his head ruefully as he offered his hand to each of the others who'd be in the party in turn. "I feel hunting glory with Darren of Nirim Manor will be an adventure to tell my children." He let out a belly laugh. "When I finally settle down and have some."

Redoubt

That seemed to be that. They talked through strategy for a bit, exchanged a few stories of their adventures, and then Dare led Bradis to a room in one of the guest houses and bid him good night.

Tomorrow he'd be one monster closer to completing the achievement.

* * * * *

The party started early the next morning, heading out with the rising sun.

Dare had invited Bradis to the party and briefly inspected the pertinent information about him, mostly his stats and past conduct in parties. As far as he could see the man's reputation was clean enough aside from a few fistfights and brawls in his past.

The Fighter rode a powerful stallion, getting on in years but still a fine horse. Probably the best mount of the group, actually. He was fully kitted out in his chainmail and plate, which he obviously took good care of, and looked every inch an adventurer.

Although he seemed a bit dubious when they reached the first spawn point on their route, and Dare explained that they would be clearing them for extra experience and loot on their way to the Ancient Outpost Watcher. It took some demonstration to convince him that Dare was familiar with the monsters they fought, and his confidence that they'd be easy to farm was borne out.

After that their new tank became enthusiastic about how many spawn points they cleared, how much experience they earned, and how much loot they gathered. Which while a normal day for Dare and his companions was apparently explosive progress for the Fighter.

Although Bradis had yet another test of confidence when they reached the mountains and plunged right in, continuing to wind their way around some spawn points to go after the ones that would be ideal for them.

"How are you doing this?" he asked as they finished clearing a camp of Corrupted Harpies. "You can't have simply scouted this area out without committing suicide . . . everyone knows what mountains are like."

Dare shrugged. "I haven't met a monster yet that I couldn't identify." Which was truthful enough, if easy to take the way he wanted it taken.

Bradis shook his head. "Knowledgeable about the monster compendiums as well as powerful on the battlefield. I'm more and more glad I joined your party."

They reached the valley with the raid rated dungeon and its guardian a few hours before noon, lining up on the slope to look down at what they faced.

Their new tank whistled as he took in the steep-sided slopes hugged by ancient ruins shrouded in dense fog, overlooking a roaring river below with a powerful waterfall at the head of the valley. "That's a dungeon," he said.

"Raid rated," Dare agreed. "Early 40s." He arched an eyebrow at the man. "One day I'd like to clear it, if you're up for it."

Bradis laughed. "In five years when I reach an appropriate level? Certainly."

Dare just smiled; he'd reach that level much sooner than that at the rate he was going. Although then he'd have to find an entire raid party of similar level to go with him.

"If I promised you a spot in my raid to clear the dungeon, including helping you level if needed, will you promise to keep this place a secret?" he asked.

The man looked slightly offended. "I wouldn't dream of betraying your trust, even without offer of reward." He hesitated, then laughed a bit sheepishly. "Although I certainly wouldn't say no to a spot in your raid or help leveling. Whatever the secret of your swift jump in power, I'd be in your debt if you'd share it."

"No secret, I just know the monsters in the area. For a tank willing to be a longer term companion that's knowledge I'd be happy to share."

"Generous." Bradis glanced down at the huge, gnarled tree looming over the entrance to the ruins. "So what are we looking at?"

Just to be sure he could answer accurately, Dare again used his Adventurer's Eye on the monster: "Ancient Outpost Watcher. Monster, Party Rated. Level 39. Attacks: Ensnare, Root, Crush, Colossal Stomp, Leaf Blast, Infestation, Vine Whip, Regenerate, Dream Gaze, Stone Bark."

Fun. He quickly listed its stats and attacks, giving his guess about what each attack would do and how they could counter them. Bradis looked a bit intimidated, not only by the sight of the menacing ancient tree but by what it could do.

But as the group made their final preparations their new tank hefted his sword and shield and prepared to rush in; it took a special sort to face these sorts of monsters head on, taking whatever comes their way.

"Ready?" Dare called. He got nods all around, and he prepared his air type Burst Arrow. "Okay, go!"

His arrow hit almost the same spot as Leilanna's Flame Needle, the combined attack blasting a hole in the bark. He followed it up with a second arrow tied to a cord, and after it sunk in quivering he yanked it back out and began swiftly pulling it hand over hand.

Zuri stepped in to take the rope from him, leaving him to continue loosing arrows. He saw Bradis finish Charging in, but before the tank could begin hacking away at the weathered trunk a branch swooped in and caught him.

Ilin, rushing in right behind the Fighter, shouted, "Ha!" and in an incredible surge of power chopped the heel of his hand down on the branch, snapping clean through it in one blow. The Monk swayed slightly, likely having had to open some of his Locks for that, then kept going as Bradis tossed away the severed remnant of branch that had been looped around his chest and continued forward.

Dare's attention was briefly diverted as Zuri cursed, and he tossed her a quick glance as he loosed his next arrow. "There's no blood or sap or any residue to use for Nature's Curse," she said, scowling.

"Toss a Mana Thorn," he told her, grimacing as he watched Ilin and Bradis both snatched up by branches at the same time. "Or scratch that, switch to healing."

His goblin fiancee was already hard at work doing just that.

Leilanna was continuing to hammer the trunk with her Flame Needles, steadily tearing gouges in the bark. Dare's own arrows were having less effect in spite of his higher level, but they deepened the holes his dusk elf betrothed created.

Bradis hacked desperately at the branch clutching him, while other branches whipped in and lashed at his armor. Including a solid hit to his helmet that literally rang his bell. Although every second hit was turned aside by a flickering barrier as Ireni protected their tank.

Meanwhile Ilin flexed his perfectly honed muscles in a sudden surge of power, with a roar bursting free of the Ancient Outpost Watcher's grip and sending shattered fragments of wood flying in all directions. He dropped, landing on one knee, then wobbled to his feet and charged the trunk again.

But there was a marked difference to his motions now, his movements swifter and more focused; he'd obviously opened the Fifth Lock. With almost inhuman grace he dodged two more branches and finally reached the trunk, throwing himself into a kick with both feet as his entire body twisted like a corkscrew.

The collision struck right where Dare and Leilanna had been chipping away at the bark, struggling to beat the tree's Regenerate, and finished the job they'd started. The entire tree shuddered and gave a groan as if it had been caught in a high wind and was bending on the verge of breaking.

Bark and pulped wood flew away, and beneath the Monk's drilling feet they caught their first view of a brilliant green light shining forth from the deep crack in the wood.

"There!" Dare shouted. "Burn phase!"

Ilin dove away just in time as Dare shot a Holy Burst Arrow to slow the Ancient Outpost Watcher's Regenerate, at the same time as Leilanna's Fireball and Zuri's Mana Thorn struck. He used Rapid

Phoenix

Shot and quickly buried four more arrows into the glowing opening.

The monster made a creaking, cracking noise like a treeish shout of pain and the branches convulsed, tossing Bradis aside as they all dove in towards Ilin.

The Monk, staggering and clearly at his limit even with Zuri's and Ireni's healing, barely had enough left to leap twenty feet in a single bound before dropping and rolling. Ireni's barrier protected him as branches assailed him, but he was clearly in trouble.

Then the Fighter was there, using an ability similar to Pella's Intervene, except rather than giving him immunity to his next attack it seemed to taunt the Ancient Outpost Watcher. The branches moved their fury to the tank, who hunkered protectively over Ilin weathering the blows.

The burn phase had been doing work while all that had been going on, with Dare's and Leilanna's attacks tearing the tree out from within. Even Zuri's Mana Thorns were more effective against the core of nature magic, which didn't seem to have the same resistances as the rest of the tree.

They got it down to 70% health, then 60%, and were closing on 50% when the monster gave another groaning roar and changed tactics.

Dare had suspected Infestation meant a parasite type attack that would do damage over time or slow the target. He'd been dreading seeing it, not sure the healers had any way to deal with it and afraid his companions wouldn't be able to avoid it.

As it turned out though he was wrong. Alarmingly wrong.

With a deep woody creak the bark of the tree abruptly split near the crown and along several of the thickest branches. From the deep fissures black shapes began to pour in a chittering mass, only to suddenly be flung all across the battlefield as the Ancient Outpost Watcher lashed its branches wildly.

Almost as if it was hurling the creatures at them.

They were some sort of giant beetle or cockroach the size of Dare's hand, except with vicious pincers or mandibles that dripped with poison. While they were all between Level 30-33, and like most swarming monsters far weaker individually, they were still a serious problem in the midst of an already frantic fight.

"Leilanna!" he shouted.

His dusk elf fiancee grimaced, clearly repulsed, but began using her Gale spell to blow as many insects as possible into a pile. When she was satisfied with the number she rushed right next to the pile and began casting Ring of Fire repeatedly, burning the adds down while Ireni protected her with a barrier.

That accounted for half of them at least, but there were plenty more where that came from.

Dare switched targets to shoot a few of the roaches going after Ireni, Zuri, and Leilanna. At the same time he began moving around the battlefield to aggro and kite more of the revolting insects away from the casters, turning his focus back to the tree. His Burst Arrow came back, and he sent another Holy one in to keep its regeneration down.

They were getting closer. So close.

Ilin was back on his feet. He and Bradis working together had lopped off several branches, and the onslaught against them was faltering as the tree ran out of limbs to hurl their way.

At which point it decided to hurl something else.

The Ancient Outpost Guardian shook violently, and roots began flailing out of the ground and carrying it forward across the battlefield. As if it meant to trample right over their two melee fighters.

About that time the branches at the crown of the tree began to shiver, and its pine needles began to shake free in a rustling torrent.

Shit. "Down!" Dare yelled, Pouncing to Leilanna. "Leaf Blast!" His ability knocked her to the ground, and he threw himself over her and raised his hood to protect the back of his neck.

Moments later he felt a prickling agony as dozens, hundreds even, of pine needles speared the ground all around him and pelted his back. Some were stopped by his cloak and armor, but others

Phoenix

found their way through.

The barrage ended and his dusk elf betrothed rolled out from underneath him, coming back to her feet and not wasting a second resuming her attack on the monster's glowing core.

Dare rose to his feet as well, but he felt sluggish and odd. He turned, as if in a dream, and stared at the tree's waving upper branches, mesmerized.

Around him he heard shouts, cries of pain, the whoosh of Leilanna's spells and the warm prickling sensation of Zuri's healing.

Then his dusk elf fiancee grabbed his cloak, yanked it away with a furious shout, and began whacking at his back with her staff. Even that didn't shake him from his daze.

Until it did.

Dare jolted back to himself, realizing the needles piercing him must've hit him with some sort of enchantment. Dream Gaze?

Growling at his loss of control, involuntary or not, he looked around to take stock of his companions. Leilanna was fine because he'd covered her, Zuri's Sheltering Embrace had protected her, Ilin seemed to have avoided the spraying pine needles, and Bradis's armor had protected him.

That just left Ireni, who was staring at the tree slack-jawed.

Dare cursed; he'd hoped she would protect herself with a barrier, but either she'd been too slow to react or, more likely for the competent Priestess, too focused on protecting the others. Either way, he felt a surge of fear for her, even though the Leaf Blast hadn't really done much damage to him and the Dream Gaze was just a form of crowd control.

He threw himself towards his petite betrothed in a Roll and Shoot, loosing an arrow at the Ancient Outpost Watcher's core as he went. Between Cheetah's Dash and a full sprint he reached her in moments, and immediately tore off her cloak and began scraping away the needles buried in her soft skin with the haft of his spear.

She came to herself in time to toss a barrier around Ilin, protecting him from a lashing root as the tree tried to Colossal

Stomp the two melee fighters flat.

"Thanks," she said, hands glowing as she worked on another barrier for Bradis, who was wrestling with a root, trying to keep from being crushed.

Dare kicked a scuttling roach away from Ireni and used Rapid Shot again, comboing the fourth arrow with Burst Arrow as it came off cooldown. This time he used Fire, trying to eke out that extra bit of damage as the enemy's health dropped slowly towards a sliver.

"We're almost there!" he shouted. "Hit it with everything!"

His party responded with surprising smoothness. Ilin and Bradis charged the trunk together, Leilanna and Zuri wove a Fireball and Mana Thorn around them, and Dare loosed arrows over their heads.

The Fighter threw himself forward in a Dazzling Thrust, striking the core full on, while over his head Ilin slammed into the tree in a flying kick.

With a final creaking groan the Ancient Outpost Watcher convulsed, the glowing green core winked out, and the monster fell still with abrupt suddenness as it died.

Chapter Two
Spoils of Victory

Text appeared in the corner of Dare's vision. "Party rated monster Ancient Outpost Watcher defeated. 20,000 bonus experience awarded."

"Completed 9/10 towards Achievement Protector of Bastion: Slay 10 party rated monsters in the region of Bastion."

"Trophies gained: Living Core, Ancient Carved Face, Petrified Bark. Loot body to acquire."

He loosed arrows at the few final remaining roaches, then turned and swept Ireni into his arms. "Are you okay?" he asked her anxiously.

"I'm fine," she said, already casting a healing spell on herself. "Just need to patch up a few dozen small puncture wounds that are more painful than really damaging." She finished and brushed at her arm, smearing away a few droplets of blood to show smooth unbroken flesh beneath. "See? Not even any scars."

Dare kissed her tenderly. "Well from now on protect yourself first. A dead or incapacitated healer can't help anyone." Even saying the words sent a shudder of fear through him, and he hugged her close again. "Besides, you and Sia promised you'd stay out of danger."

Her eyes softened and she brushed at his forehead with soft fingers. "I will, my love. Thanks for breaking me out of the daze."

Together they went around to the rest of the party to make sure everyone was okay.

Zuri was unharmed. Leilanna had a minor poison from an insect bite that was due to fall off in a couple minutes that could easily be healed through. Ilin's body was beat to hell after how long he'd kept his Fifth Lock open, even after healing. He'd need days or even longer to recover, although the prospect of having Amalisa fussing over him seemed to be one he looked forward to. As for Bradis, he'd taken a beating and some of his armor pieces needed minor repairs, but after healing he was fine and dandy.

Dare had been mostly unharmed as well, aside from the needle punctures that Zuri had healed.

Together they gathered at the base of the dead monster, basking in their accomplishment. After a moment Bradis grunted in satisfaction. "That was some good experience there. Not just for the monster kill itself and the bonus for a party rated monster, but also from your quest."

Dare blinked. "I gave you a quest?"

"Yeah." His companion laughed. "An Audacious Venture: Assist Darren of Nirim Manor in killing a party rated monster five levels above yours. 20,000 bonus experience and apparently you like me better."

Dare and the others joined the laughter. "Well, the quest isn't wrong about that I guess." He wrapped an arm around Ireni, who grinned at him. "Actually, Ireni gave me a quest a while ago to kill 5 party rated monsters by the end of the year."

The Fighter stared at him incredulously. "Is that a joke? How the hell would you manage that?"

Dare's other companions laughed, and he smiled wider. "Actually, I just need one more now."

Bradis whistled, clearly impressed. "You're like Gorald the Legend, who performed the Five Great Feats."

Dare had no idea who that was. "Thanks, but I haven't managed it yet and time is running out."

His sturdy companion clapped him on the back. "Well if you need help with the last one, consider me." He clapped him on the back again, this time urging him forward. "In the meantime would you loot this thing already?"

Dare obligingly searched the dead monsters, then stared in amazement at what he found, which was better than he'd expected in even his most optimistic hopes.

First things first he dug through the pile of roaches Leilanna had roasted, which dropped scintillating carapaces at a rate of one every five or so. Probably not the most valuable, but pretty and likely to find buyers.

The Ancient Outpost Watcher itself dropped 5 Nature Essence Knots, which were apparently Enchanting materials. High level ones, too. But those weren't the only materials by a long shot.

He hadn't bothered to take note that the monster was a yew tree, but it also dropped bark, branch tips, and needles that could all be used by Apothecaries and Alchemists for medicinal purposes.

And best of all were the branches and roots.

The tree dropped three in total, two branches and a root, which just went to show how rare and valuable they were. All were classified "Ironstone Wood" and were materials for weapon crafters to make Level 40 items.

The root could be used to make a club, which Bradis quickly requested as part of his share; apparently it was nice enough that he'd happily switch from sword to club once he reached that level. As for the branches, they were both completely kickass and could've been specifically dropped as Dare's ultimate ideal loot.

Which, considering the great luck Sia had given him and the fact that she'd intervened to give him better loot before, probably wasn't a coincidence.

Nor was the fact that the Ironstone Wood branches could be used to make bows and spears, both of which he used and would want. Which just meant he needed to find a sufficient level Bowyer and Weaponsmith and he'd be set once he reached 40.

The party rated monster hadn't dropped any gold or other precious metals, or any gems or other valuables. But the items it had dropped would be worth more than whatever coin amount it might've dropped. And more importantly he had the crafting materials for two badass new weapons, which he would've *paid* extra for.

Now, assuming Lily was willing to level up high enough to be able to craft him an entire set of leather armor, he was basically set for gear for a while.

Dare walked over to Ireni and wrapped her in a hug, leaning down to whisper in her ear. "Thanks."

Sia looked up at him innocently. "Why, whatever are you talking about?"

"Oh, you know," he said with a laugh as he leaned down and kissed her.

The party finished looting the Ancient Outpost Watcher. While Bradis asked for the Ironstone Wood root for his club, he was more than happy to sell the rest of his share of the loot to them for a fair price.

Once they'd sorted out the few final details with the monsters they continued on the loop Dare had planned, moving on to the next monster spawn point.

"This is great," the Fighter said as they cleared it. "I just assumed we'd be heading right to the big tree and then heading back, but even split six ways this experience is nothing to complain about. And the loot's not bad either."

Actually, to Dare the experience felt agonizingly slow, even though he was happy about the progress his fiancees and Ilin were making. The fact that their new companion was so pleased about it served to show just how much trouble most adventurers had leveling up.

As the sun sank towards the horizon they left the mountains, clearing a few final spawn points between them and home. Including the firbolg camp not far from where Seris and Selis, the fox girl twins, had built their den.

At the insistence of Dare's fiancees, who wanted to meet his new lovers, they left Ilin and Bradis to continue on to Nirim Manor and made for the hidden den.

Dare had been doing his best to visit the midnight and arctic fox girl sisters when he could. Not just because they were sexy as hell, but also because they were carrying his babies and he wanted to check on them.

Although with Home Ward it was a bit awkward, since in the evenings he bypassed them and headed straight home. And given the way the fox girls practically hibernated in the winter they were always asleep in the early morning when he passed by their den.

At their insistence he'd come in anyway, stripping down and climbing into bed to snuggle between the drowsy twins, stroking their velvety ears and silky soft fluffy tails in greeting. A lot of the time he'd just lay there with them for fifteen or so minutes before kissing each of them goodbye, dressing, and continuing on his way.

Although in spite of their sleepiness the fox girls definitely wanted to have fun with him. Selis would often wake up enough to pull him on top of her, half dozing as he moved inside her until finally she climaxed. Most of the time she was startled fully awake by her own powerful orgasm, and clutched him tight while letting out delicious gasping moans as he finished inside her.

Seris, on the other hand, was by far the hornier of the two, but also the heavier sleeper. If he spooned her she would usually insistently push her shapely ass back against him, rubbing her sopping wet labia against his shaft until she finally found the right angle to push him inside her.

Then Dare would swear she just fell back into a deep sleep, although he wasn't sure that was possible given his size. But as he gently moved in and out of her tight warm tunnel, she'd lie there limp and peaceful with her mouth partly open, sometimes even letting out the most adorable little snores.

The first time she dozed off on him he stopped moving and tried to carefully extract himself, but if nothing else he did ever woke her up *that* did. The petite midnight fox girl made a disgruntled noise, pushed back against him demandingly until he was inside her again, then sighed and settled back down.

"Give it to me good," she mumbled before falling back asleep.

He couldn't deny there was something pretty hot about fucking the sleepy fox girls, and they definitely couldn't seem to get enough of it either. He always left them dozing more contentedly as he dressed and departed to begin the day's hunting.

Dare had gotten into the habit of just wandering in, again at their insistence. But with Zuri, Leilanna, and Ireni with him he took the time to knock, waiting until the petite, curvy midnight fox girl and taller, more athletic arctic fox girl answered.

The playful twins seemed a bit hesitant around the unfamiliar visitors, not quite suspicious but definitely unsure. Although when Dare introduced him as his betrothed they relaxed and became far friendlier.

In fact, it was obvious they reached the conclusion that since they were all his lovers, everyone could have fun together. As the fox girls generously shared stew with everyone they began subtly (or not so subtly) flirting with the goblin, dusk elf, and human women.

"Your hair is so pretty," Seris said, running her fingers through Ireni's auburn locks. They were both about the same height, and that seemed to have made the bookish Priestess more approachable. "My cousin Dalera has hair almost this exact same color, and white at the tips of her ears and tail."

Sia took the fore, obviously interested in the possibilities here, and boldly cuddled up to the midnight fox girl, whispering in her ear. Whatever she said seemed to startle Seris, but soon the fox girl was giggling and shooting Dare speculative looks.

Selis, on the other hand, seemed to find Zuri adorable. She'd wheedled the tiny goblin onto her lap and was contentedly braiding her hair while admiring her lotion-slick skin.

Leilanna, not one to be left out and fascinated by the fox girls' tails, especially Selis who had two, was seated between the sisters alternately stroking the fluffy fur on the white and sable tails.

Dare definitely liked where this was going, and was more than happy to hurry to finish his stew in anticipation of the fun to come.

Sia started it off, unsurprisingly. She began making out with

Seris, a small hand boldly slipping beneath the midnight fox girl's soft fur dress to rub her inner thigh. For her part Seris seemed fully into it, slipping her tongue into the petite redhead's mouth and practically sucking her face with eager slurping noises. After a while she impatiently grabbed the goddess's hand and pushed it the rest of the way between her legs, moaning softly as her new lover began rubbing her glistening petals.

That got Selis going to the point that as she watched her sister and their guest, she began kissing and sucking on Zuri's delicate neck. The tiny goblin moaned in enjoyment; when it came to sex she was unexpectedly bold for such a quiet, gentle woman.

Dare had a feeling the arctic fox girl was in for a surprise as Zuri grabbed her hands, moving them to her disproportionately large breasts.

Selis seemed delighted to play with the generous mounds, at least until her goblin lover got impatient, squirmed around, and got between the fox girl's legs, ducking beneath Selis's skirt. Whatever Zuri was doing down there soon had her lover moaning and twitching her hips.

Leilanna, seeing an opportunity, grabbed Dare while he was available.

She insistently dragged him farther up the bed, kissing him passionately the entire time, and only broke away to gracefully squirm out of her robes and toss them aside, then peel off her bra and panties.

Even as many times as he'd seen the beautiful dusk elf's luscious body in all her glory, he still found himself distracted from his own undressing to stare in wonder. She grinned at his reaction, pleased, and leaned in close to his ear. "I bet we could distract everyone from their own fun if we gave them a show."

Dare glanced over at the others. Sia and Seris had undressed and were writhing against each other as they made out, desperately doing their best to rub their pussies together as their arousal joined into a steady flow that wet the bed beneath them.

It would be one of the sexiest things he'd ever seen if Selis wasn't standing nearby, holding Zuri in the air by her hips with the sexy goblin's arms wrapped around her thighs for support. Zuri was happily eating the arctic fox girl out while suspended upside-down, while Selis bent far enough to bury her face in her goblin lover's pussy in turn.

"I don't think we're distracting them from that," he whispered with a grin.

Leilanna smirked up at him, dark pink eyes smoldering with lust. "You think so?" Her lips brushed his ear as her tone became low and sultry. "Fuck my ass."

Dare started in surprise. So far the only one of his lovers who'd expressed an interest in that had been Pella and Sia. The former only during baths to "clean" her insides, and the latter intent on seeking the most intense sexual experiences possible, even though they had to go slowly with her small body.

"I'm too big to just put it in without getting you ready first," he protested quietly.

The beautiful dusk elf grinned. "I'm ready. Pella's been helping me with toys." She paused. "And Se'weir's helped me with vegetables a few times."

Oh gods, his fiancees had been up to stuff like that? It made Dare regret being away from the manor so much.

Leilanna impatiently reached between her legs to slick up her hand with her copious arousal, then reached down and began jacking his rock hard cock, lubricating it. Finally she twisted around on all fours on the bed and raised her thick ass in the air, waving it teasingly in his face.

"Come on," she said with a giggle, looking at him over her shoulder, "let's see how you compare to an eggplant."

Holy shit, she'd managed that? In that case she should be just fine.

Reassured, Dare didn't need a second invitation. He knelt behind his curvy dusk elf fiancee, rubbed her pussy to relax her as well as gather more of her flowing nectar, and gently pushed a finger into her small pink rosebud.

Leilanna moaned and pushed back against him, and he was surprised by how easily he slipped inside. Looked as if she hadn't been kidding about getting ready for this.

He pushed in a second finger, then a third, and began sawing them in and out while his lover moaned louder.

Somewhere off to the side Selis gasped. "Sister, look!" she squealed.

"Oooh!" Seris said.

The next thing Dare knew the four other girls were clustered around them, watching in excitement. "You're going to put it in her butt?" the arctic fox girl asked eagerly.

"Me next, me next!" her petite sister shouted, leaning closer to watch his fingers spreading open the dusk elf's sphincter.

He paused, ignoring Leilanna's protests as he stared at the midnight fox girl. "You?"

She grinned. "Believe me, I can take it. Little sis might have the deep throat skills, but as long as she holds me and strokes my ears and tells me how adorable I look with my little butthole stretched wide around something big, I can fit anything in there."

As usual, the fox girls seemed to know just what to say to get him going.

Dare's twitching cock demanded action, and he had his beautiful betrothed waiting eagerly for him. So he withdrew his fingers and lined himself up with her delicate rosebud, his erection looking massive in comparison.

But as he pushed his tip against the dusk elf's sphincter it opened easily, and she moaned in encouragement while he kept going. Until finally her tight ring popped closed around the base of his glans, his head buried in her bowels.

"Yes!" she said. "This is easy compared to some of the stuff we tried." She wiggled her hips. "Go ahead, I'm ready. Take it slow but keep going."

Dare gently thrust in deeper, encouraged by her sounds of pleasure. Around him the other women were rubbing themselves or each other as they watched, also moaning in passion.

Sia, grinning wickedly, pursed her lips and let saliva trickle down to coat the last inch of his cock as he pushed it in. Then she slapped the curvy dusk elf on the ass, making her jump and squeal, her sphincter snapping closed around the base of his cock.

"That's it, sweetie!" the goddess said with a giggle. "He's balls deep in you!"

"I know," Leilanna moaned with a blissful smile, forehead glistening with perspiration. "I feel so stretched and full. This is incredible."

"Well don't stop there," Seris protested, leaning in close. "I want to watch it go in and out."

Dare began moving in slow, deep thrusts, luxuriating in the feel of being buried in the depths of the beautiful dusk elf's bowels, feeling her sphincter massage his length with every motion. The sight of his girth spreading her straining ring as it disappeared inside her was sexy as hell, and he knew he wasn't going to hold out long.

The other girls obviously knew it too, because they began cheering him on, obviously impatient for their turns. Although in spite of their cheerleading he managed to hold out for almost five minutes, giving Leilanna at least one orgasm as she tensed and he felt her sphincter wink around him.

It wasn't until Zuri reached between his legs to fondle his balls that he finally tensed up, groaned, and with a final thrust spurted deep into Leilanna's warm insides.

She pulled off him with a soft *plop*, pink rosebud gaping obscenely and a trickle of his seed dripping out, and flopped onto her side to look back at him with a dreamy smile.

Dare had no time to savor his post-orgasmic bliss before Seris scrambled into the spot the dusk elf had vacated, lifting her smaller but just as curvy ass upwards at him as her fluffy sable tail waved eagerly. Her asshole already glistened, coated in her own arousal or someone else's, and was puckered open slightly as if she'd been fingered to open her up.

His cock was still hard, and he had a feeling it would be even after coming a few times with how erotic this evening was turning out to be. His lovers were urging him on to the point that Selis was insistently pushing on his butt, so with a laugh he positioned himself at the petite midnight fox girl's glistening rosebud and started to push inside.

There was more resistance than with Leilanna, and he could feel Seris tense with only a bit of his tip stretching her sphincter. He paused, giving her time to adjust, as Sia and Zuri both leaned in to drip saliva through pursed lips onto where his cock met the small fox girl.

It took a few minutes of patience and slow movements before his head popped through her ring, which clamped down around his shaft as she squealed, "Nature's bounty, I've never had anything this big inside me."

"Good girl, sister," Selis crooned, moving around to stroke her velvety ears. "He's enjoying it so much, I can see it on his face. You're making him feel so good with your soft little bum. Just imagine how amazing he's going to feel when he's all the way inside you."

It was an effort not to spurt at her sexy words. And apparently they had Seris worked up too. "Keep going!" she moaned. "Stretch my little butt with your giant bovid cock."

Sia collapsed next to Leilanna with a whimper, shuddering through an intense orgasm as she furiously mauled her clit. Zuri lay down next to her and hugged the petite redhead tight, kissing and sucking on her small breasts and nipples.

Dare kept going, gently and patiently, as the midnight fox girl relaxed and adjusted to his size. Although in spite of his best efforts he bottomed out with a few finger widths of his nine inch cock still outside. He waited for a minute to make sure his lover was ready, then at her insistent urging slowly withdrew.

Redoubt

"Wow," Seris gasped, squirming. "It stretches just as much going out. This is incredible."

He thrust in again as she arched her back and pushed against him. Then again, and again, a bit faster and harder each time. He was able to keep a bottle on his orgasm in spite of her tight sphincter and the inviting warmth of her insides, but the moment his petite lover collapsed in an orgasm with a wail of pleasure he lost it.

With a groan he grabbed her hips to hold himself still, not even having the time to push in and bottom out inside her before he exploded into her bowels with jet after jet of his seed.

The midnight fox girl's fluffy tail batted at his face as she quivered her way through her climax, and he grabbed it and stroked her silky fur as his cock pulsed a few final times before gradually softening and slipping free of her well used asshole.

At which point Sia pounced on him.

Not content to take the lead, the petite redhead pushed him onto his back and positioned herself over him, arching her back to get the right angle to push his tip against her delicate rosebud. Her arousal dripped freely down his length, lubricating him as she impaled herself on him with a needy whimper.

She was just as tight as Seris, but far more daring in her movement; the goddess's relentless pursuit of intense sensations meant she had a high threshold for discomfort.

And she made full use of that as she bounced up and down on his cock, her tight ring sliding up and down his length as he plunged deep into her bowels again and again. Whether because she was more used to his size or because she was a bit bigger, she could take his full length up her ass, if barely.

After two subsequent orgasms Dare's tip was hyper sensitive, and he grit his teeth at the surging sensations as Sia rode him, his own intense pleasure bordering on discomfort.

Thankfully he had a distraction as Zuri, either coming to his rescue or out of her own mounting lust, straddled his face and pushed her small pussy against his mouth. As she insistently grinded against him he kissed and licked her delicate folds, savoring the rich pheromones of her arousal.

His refractory period warred with his pleasure, teetering on the point of orgasm as Sia moved faster and faster, gasping and crying out in ecstasy. Her warm insides massaged his length, her sphincter seemed determined to wring his seed out of him, and finally with a groan against Zuri's dripping pussy he gave in.

His back arched against his petite redheaded fiancee's slight weight, and with a groan he shot his seed up into her bowels as her tight ring milked him for every drop. The goddess seemed to know exactly how to bring him the most intense pleasure, and he felt lightheaded as his orgasm stretched on longer than usual before he was finally spent.

Dare lay there panting as Sia and Zuri both lifted themselves off him, basking in the afterglow of three consecutive orgasms in quick succession. That had been something else.

Selis and Zuri cuddled him on either side, trading deep openmouthed kisses with him and with each other. He felt soft hands clean him with warm soapy cloths, and then more soft bodies pressed close as the other women cuddled in around him.

After giving him time to recover Zuri and Selis did earth water air fire (a variation of rock paper scissors) to see who got to go next. Neither were interested in anal, the tiny goblin mostly because she didn't want to stretch her equally small rosebud that much, and the arctic fox girl because it just wasn't to her taste.

But they definitely wanted to fuck him.

Selis won and eagerly dropped to all fours, fluffy twin tails lovingly wrapping around him and caressing his chest and butt as he positioned himself at her dripping pussy. Thanks to his previous orgasms he lasted almost ten minutes thrusting into her, taking her through several intense climaxes before finally pushing into her core and releasing with a groan of pleasure.

Zuri didn't seem to mind going last, and at her and the fox girls' insistence he showed them his standing fuck with his little goblin fiancee. He held her by her hips with her back facing him and lowered her onto his cock while she whimpered, finally bottoming out with almost half his cock still outside.

Then, as the other women all watched and rubbed themselves or kissed and groped each other, he lifted Zuri up and down at the pace she loved. She squirmed on his cock, whimpering with pleasure as her nectar flowed down his length and across his thighs.

He kept going until she climaxed once, twice, three times, and finally squirted all over Seris's upturned face, who'd moved close to watch from practically beneath their joined bodies.

Even though Zuri was last and Dare should've been able to go for the longest with her, he could never hold out long inside her vise-tight pussy. He was able to keep his orgasm at bay until she finally went limp in a final orgasm, arms and legs hanging as she flopped and her soft walls milked him urgently.

He erupted inside her with a gasp, swaying slightly from the intensity of it as they came together as they had so many times before. When he finished he lifted his little fiancee up so he could kiss her tenderly and hold her close.

The other women crowded around for their own kisses, then they all cuddled together for a few minutes to rest.

A few of his fiancees talked about staying the night with their new lovers, but Dare didn't want to leave Pella, Se'weir, Linia, and Lily wondering where they were.

Besides, he wasn't sure when Bradis would head back to Terana, and he wanted to give the man a warm sendoff and also have a talk with him about future plans.

So they retrieved their horses and continued for home, the fox girl twins waving after them from the entrance to their den.

Chapter Three
New Arrivals

The next morning after breakfast Dare, Ireni, and Bradis settled the last of the business with distributing loot into equal shares and buying the Fighter's portion.

Then, not wasting any time, the man said his goodbyes to everyone and headed out to the stables to saddle his horse. Dare went with him to keep him company, as well as discuss future plans.

"Well, that's me off," Bradis finally said, offering his hand to Dare. "Thanks for the invitation, Master Dare. I daresay that's the smoothest hunt I've ever had the pleasure of being on. Let me know if you ever need a tank again and I'll be happy to step in."

Dare was amused that the man had adopted his term for defender after just a day or so, at least around them. "Thanks for the help," he replied, firmly returning the handshake. "I most likely will." He paused. "Although if you want something more formal than that . . ." He motioned towards the gate. "Let me walk you out."

The Fighter perked up, interested as he fell into step beside Dare, leading his horse behind him. "What did you have in mind?"

Dare inspected the man thoughtfully, hoping this was the right call. Bradis had proved to be competent, quick to learn, good tempered, and a good companion. "First, just how intent are you on leveling? It's something I intend to do for the rest of my life, and I plan to get as high level as possible before the end."

The tank rubbed his jaw, considering him shrewdly. "Well, I can't say for sure what the future will bring, but that's certainly been my goal for as long as I can remember. I want to join the heroes of Haraldar and make my mark on the world."

He looked around the walled grounds and grinned. "And as my success grows, have a setup like this with a luxurious mansion and a harem of beautiful women."

Dare chuckled. "Finding a tank has been difficult, and you're every bit as competent as those I saw in Lord Zor's raid." He bit back a grimace, thinking of Ollivan. "Better, even. So if you're interested in leveling and maybe slaying more party rated monsters and clearing dungeons in the future, I'd be pleased to have you in the party."

The Fighter mulled that over. "I'll admit, seeing you shoot up in level since I saw you last, and how smoothly we not only defeated a powerful monster yesterday but cleared over a dozen spawn points, has me interested in riding your coattails to glory."

He laughed. "Give me time to think about it, my good man. And certainly, consider me for future adventures." He paused significantly and motioned towards the mountains. "Particularly that raid rated dungeon, assuming we don't settle on anything before then."

"Fair enough." Dare led the way through the tunnel between the front gates, then with a final handshake watched Bradis mount up and ride off.

Although the man had only gone a few hundreds yards before a goblin came pelting down the road past him, expression frantic. "Master Dare!" the scout shouted as soon as he was in earshot, piping voice frantic. "High level riders approach along the path!"

Almost as soon as the warning was given three riders, two men and a woman, appeared in the distance, approaching at a gallop. The fine mounts the three new arrivals rode, as well as their expensive gear and fancy clothes, marked them as people of note.

Seeing it, Bradis urged his own mount off the path and saluted with fist to shoulder as they passed him, then continued on his way with more haste than before.

Discretion was the better part of valor, apparently.

A glance showed the levels of the three wealthy travelers were 48, 44, and 42, which was alarmingly powerful for an unannounced visit. Dare was immediately on edge, fearing this might have something to do with the trouble with Ollivan that he'd hoped was over and done with.

He activated his Adventurer's Eye to get more information, mind racing to figure out what he was going to do if these three heroes happened to be enemies.

The Level 48 man was an Archer, tall and long-limbed with a sort of rangy power. The Level 44 was a Priestess, tall and gaunt with severe features. The Level 42 was a Soldier, big and bearded with a no nonsense demeanor. All three looked to be in their late 40s or early 50s in age, with graying or fully silver hair and a solemn dignity about them.

Any one of them could probably lay waste to Nirim Manor by themselves, aside from the healer maybe, and it was no wonder Rek's sentry had looked in such a panic.

Before starting forward to meet them alone, Dare caught the panting messenger by the shoulders and leaned close. "Tell Miss Ireni to prepare the gate."

Hopefully he could stall these visitors until his fiancee made sure the legendary chest was in its place in the roof of the gate tunnel. And he also hoped the previous nerf to the item, which made it so it couldn't grow in the case of imminent collision, didn't apply to if it was just sitting there and triggered a structure to collapse beneath it.

It would be the last line of defense for his family if these adventurers proved to be enemies.

Although hopefully that wasn't what they were here for. As they got closer he recognized the sigil on the chest of the Priestess's robes and on the two men's surcoats: the crossed silver bow and pike on a gold field of the Marshal's Irregulars. The mercenary company Linia, Felicia, and Irawn were part of.

The three notables reined in at his approach, and the Archer nudged his mount forward a few steps. "Dare, Master of Nirim Manor?" he called.

Dare bowed low. "I am he. How can I assist you?"

Redoubt

The Archer glanced past him at the walls of the manor, as if searching for something. "I am Marshal Jind Alor," he said with a curt bow from his saddle. "My companions, Evram and Malia."

Dare whistled under his breath. He'd suspected that such a high level man was the leader of the Irregulars. "Welcome to Nirim Manor, Marshal," he said respectfully. "Please, I would be honored if you and your companions would be my guests. Allow me to offer you the hospitality of my home."

"Thank you, most kind," Jind said tersely, eyes still roving the walls. "I received a report from my subordinates that you'd taken in the refugees from Melarawn village. I'm here to see to their welfare and check in on my lover."

Dare hadn't realized the village was named after Linia's and Felicia's family. The Melarawns must've been among the founders, or prominent in the community. Although what bothered him more was the man's declaration; he felt a stirring unease that he did his best to hide.

"Your lover?" he asked politely.

"Linia Melarawn!" the Priestess, Malia, snapped with the tone of a stern school headmistress. "The one carrying his child?"

Fuck. If that was the case then no wonder Linia had been so familiar with the Marshal's bedding habits when he first met her, beyond any rumors that might've circulated through his mercenary company.

Also she'd mentioned she had friends in high places within her mercenary company, which had apparently been an understatement.

Dare took a careful breath, realizing he was treading on potentially delicate ground here. "Your pardon, Marshal. I am of the impression the child is mine."

Jind's eyes narrowed. "Who the good blazes are you?"

Since the man already knew his name Dare went with the obvious point of the question. "I met Linia in Jarn's Holdout at about the time when the child would've been conceived, and have strong reason to believe I'm the father."

At that the Marshal and his Soldier companion both guffawed in genuine amusement, and even Malia gave a thin-lipped smile.

"Lad," Jind said with a patient smile, "knowing Linia, I daresay half a dozen men could make that claim. Although I believe my own claim is the strongest, since I was taking that adventurous little pussy to my bed three or four times a week for months before and after she fell pregnant and begged leave to return to her village."

Damnit, Linia, you couldn't have warned me there might be a paternity dispute? Also what the hell, half a dozen men during that time?

The leader of the mercenary company must've guessed at his alarm, because he laughed again. "Be at ease, lad. I'm not interested in staking a claim to the child and certainly not in fighting about it. I know how felids are, and however Linia wants to raise her baby is fine with me. I'll assist her if I may, as is my duty, and might like to see the little rascal from time to time if I can get away."

Dare breathed a bit easier as he bowed again. "Of course, my Lord. Please, come in and let us care for your horses. We can have a guest house prepared for you, or the room set aside for honored guests in the manor as you prefer."

"Your guest house would be fine, lad," Jind said as he nudged his horse towards the gate, his companions following. "Linia tends to make a lot of noise, as only a catgirl enjoying a good fucking can, and I wouldn't want to disturb your household with our reunion."

Dare froze in leading the way. "What?"

The Marshal gave him a surprised look. "She's my lover and the potential mother of my child, lad. I came all the way to see her. Of course we're going to have an eventful reunion."

The asshole seriously intended to lure Linia out of Dare's own bed and screw her within these walls?

"She's currently my lover," he said as evenly as he could. It was probably a stupid idea to pick a fight with a party that could wipe the floor with everyone in Nirim territory combined, but he couldn't just let the man waltz in and take Linia away like that.

Jind looked startled and a bit confused. "Lad, you're talking as if you think you've made a catgirl part of your harem."

Dare frowned. "Well no." Linia had made it perfectly clear she wouldn't be part of his harem, and that she'd have other lovers besides him if she wanted.

But knowing that not only had she been Jind's lover for months, but that he intended to bed her right here and now, set Dare's teeth on edge.

The older man looked almost sympathetic. "Lad, catgirls will find a different bed every night. But I'm obviously not going to force Linia to do anything . . . isn't it best to leave it up to her?"

Fuck, that was a reasonable compromise Dare hated. Because part of him was afraid Linia would happily jump into Jind's bed while he was visiting, then want to come back as if nothing had happened.

He turned without a word and led the three riders through the gate, noting that most of the residents of Nirim Manor had assembled near the stables.

His fears became a sinking sensation when he saw his catgirl lover running ahead to greet the Marshal, face lit up with pleased surprise.

"Jind!" she cried happily, making what should've been a pretty much impossible leap up into the saddle to land on the older man's lap, particularly in her gravid condition. She immediately began peppering the mercenary leader's face with kisses.

Dare didn't like what was happening. At all. He cleared his throat. "Linia."

She gave him a startled look. "What?"

You're kissing another man in front of me, that's what. "What are your plans here?"

Linia bristled slightly. "To spend time with Jind while he's here. I've been his lover longer than yours, Dare."

The words hit him like a punch in the gut. "Spend time as in?"

"Do you really need me to tell you?" she asked slowly.

Jind looked between them, frowning sympathetically. "Ah, lad, you really did expect to bring a catgirl into your harem?"

"No he didn't!" Linia snapped. "I made that very clear. We can have fun, but it's nothing more than that and I'd take other lovers if I wished."

Dare grit his teeth; she wasn't wrong, but that didn't make this any easier. He hadn't fully appreciated her words when he invited her into his bed. "You're free to do whatever you want," he said curtly. "But be aware you're making a choice."

She simply sniffed and cuddled closer to Jind, and a leaden weight sunk in Dare's gut.

The Marshal frowned, and his companions shifted uncomfortably. "I think we'll stay in the refugee village after all, lad. Thank you for your offer of hospitality. I hope I can still count on your kindness to the refugees from her village?"

Dare wasn't petty enough to refuse people in need over this. "They're all welcome to stay and make a home here, if they wish. I'll give them what aid I can and offer them generous rates on rent for land to found a new village."

"My gratitude again, then." Jind nodded curtly to his Priestess companion. "Malia will check on them, and provide you with coin for their first year of rent." He looked over to where Felicia and Irawn stood with the other felids. "Leave is over, mercenaries. Pack up and report to Evram . . . you'll be returning to Redoubt with us."

The teenager and older man both saluted crisply before hurrying towards their rooms.

Ireni stepped forward smoothly. "I hope you'll at least join us for dinner, Marshal. I'd like your stay to be amicable."

Fat fucking chance.

Jind hesitated, then inclined his head in agreement and began to turn his horse. He was holding Linia protectively, running anxious hands over her slender body and round tummy as if afraid she'd been hurt. "Are you all right?" he asked as he started for the gate. "You

Phoenix

and the baby? When I learned you'd been forced to march across all of Bastion in your condition I nearly killed Hovan for not stepping in to help you."

"Oh don't be mad at him," the catgirl said anxiously, resting a hand on his chest. "He couldn't help all of us, and I wasn't about to leave the others no matter what he insisted."

The Archer chuckled and stroked her soft ears. "Yes, you do go your own way, don't you? I know your kind are independent and aren't bound by attachments."

He tenderly brushed her delicate face with calloused fingers, his other hand resting protectively on her round belly. "But even if our relationship is casual, that doesn't mean I'm not interested in your wellbeing . . . when I learned your village had been razed I was more worried than I expected, for both you and the child."

He chuckled. "I guess you left more of an impression on me than I thought. I want you to continue to be in my life, as much as you're inclined to and I'm able to get away. You and the child both."

Linia kissed him tenderly. "I didn't realize you felt that way, sir. I thought I was just one more of the recruits warming your bed until you moved on to the next."

"Perhaps I'm finally learning some wisdom with age. Or maybe fatherhood has put things into perspective. Both, most likely."

Dare watched the display as the two rode across the yard, feeling sick as they passed out the gate and out of earshot. He was so lost in the turmoil of Linia leaving him without a second look that he was only distantly aware of Ireni gathering him into her arms.

"I'm sorry, my love," she murmured gently into his chest.

"She left me," he said, unable to keep his voice completely neutral. "Went to him right in front of me."

Zuri joined the embrace, big yellow eyes sad. "She did. She's a catgirl, my love, it's not surprising."

It certainly had been for him. "You all warned me," he said bitterly. "I'm the idiot who didn't listen."

Redoubt

"What will you do?" Ireni asked, rubbing his back.

He sighed. "I don't know. In my head I know the situation, but I don't think I can accept it."

"We understand," Pella said as she and his other fiancees joined the group hug. "I'm sorry, Dare. I was afraid of this."

Dare pulled himself together with effort and turned to the mercenary lieutenants Jind had left behind, who were doing their best to look anywhere but at him. "Shall we get back to business?"

Ireni smoothly took over, having Johar care for the mercenaries' horses and speaking to Malia about the refugee village, while Evram waited for Felicia and Irawn.

The stern Priestess insisted on an inspection of all the refugees, listing their names and circumstances in Melarawn village. Then she wanted to go out and see the new village they were constructing, wanting Dare to go with her.

Looked as if he wasn't getting any leveling done today.

"Would you be agreeable to us sending more refugees your way?" she asked as they rode northeast to the new village. "Family and friends of members of our company, who got displaced in the chaos up north. Of course we'd see to their temporary needs and pay the first year of rent on any land you lease them. And should they prove unable or unwilling to support themselves or turn out to be troublesome, you're well within your rights to evict them."

Dare had wanted more people living on his land, but the plan had been to free slaves and offer them a new life. He wasn't sure he wanted to be tied so closely to the Irregulars, especially if they were going to just waltz in and make themselves at home.

And screw the mother of his child, damnit.

But beastkin would find few options even in Bastion, especially not refugees. He couldn't just leave them to the wolves. "I think that would be possible," he agreed stiffly. "It'll be a long way for them to travel from the border."

"But all the more safe for it," the severe Priestess said. "And of course we'd make the arrangements for their travel."

"You're good to your people," he couldn't help but observe a bit grudgingly.

"The Marshal insists on it. He practically treats everyone under his command like family." She sniffed. "Which I suppose isn't far off, since he seems to go out of his way to screw half the women in the company. I guess he had it coming finally messing up on Prevent Conception or the spell failing, so he knocked one of his lovers up."

She winced and looked his way as if realizing what she'd just said, but didn't apologize.

Dare resolved not to get on this woman's bad side; if she had such a sharp tongue for a man she obviously respected and was fond of, he shuddered to think how she'd react to someone she didn't like.

He was afraid he'd encounter Jind and Linia in the village, but thankfully the man's horse was nowhere to be seen. He remained wary, though, as Malia inspected the longhall and various cabins under construction with a critical eye. Then she did some pacing out beyond the village, measuring out more structures.

Finally she turned to him. "A decent beginning, clearly halted by the snows." She folded her arms sternly. "But winter or not you'll need to pick up the pace. Hire more workers, if necessary. More arrivals could be coming as soon as within the next few weeks, upwards of two hundred to begin with. You need more space for them."

This was exactly the sort of thing Dare had been worrying about, them just flooding his land and taking it over by sheer assumption they'd get their way. "I'm happy to offer reasonable aid to those in need . . ." he began carefully, trying to keep his tone neutral.

The Priestess sniffed. "You will of course be reimbursed for materials, labor, necessities for the new arrivals, and of course the rent paid. And a modest stipend for your household's efforts in organizing affairs. Any charity you offer on top of that is appreciated."

She paused, then gave him a close look. "We realize this is an imposition, particularly at this time of year and especially given your . . . complications with mercenary Linia. But the need is great, and your assistance is much appreciated. Know that you'll have the friendship of the Marshal and his Irregulars for your kindness."

Dare found it hard to give a shit about the man's friendship. "Would you like to look at other prospective village spots while we're out here, in case the number of refugees grows beyond what this plot of land can sustain?"

Malia shook her head and started towards her horse at a brisk walk. "I trust you'll manage such arrangements. Now, let's return to your manor and sort out the fine details. If you're not the one in charge of your household's finances and other affairs then we should fetch whoever is as well."

By her tone she assumed he wasn't, which irked him a bit. He could certainly handle the manor's affairs if need be. Ireni was just better at it, especially with Leilanna to help her.

And anyway he was busy with leveling and farming gold.

The rest of what had promised to be a productive day got dragged down into paperwork, negotiations, and playing host to the Priestess. The very fair and reasonable agreement they reached resulted in a few thousand gold changing hands. An amount Dare could make in less than a month of determined farming depending on drops.

Even better, most of that coin was devoted to construction costs and wouldn't actually go into his pocket, unless he wanted to pick up tools and earn a laborer's wage.

At dinnertime he wanted nothing more than to excuse himself claiming a headache and retreat to his room. But Ireni gently but firmly insisted he attend.

"I know this is eating you up inside, my love," she said as she helped him clean up and get ready. "But whatever the relationship fallout with Linia, would you be willing to at least give Jind a fair chance? He's a decent and honorable man, and we can never have too many of those as friends. Especially with your upcoming petition for knighthood."

Phoenix

Dare grunted noncommittally.

To Jind's credit, although he sat next to Linia he tried to gently but firmly curtail her public affection during the meal, doing his best to spare Dare that uncomfortable sight.

Unfortunately, keeping with the customs of polite society neither of them could be spared the next discomfort, when the men retreated to Dare's study for cigars and brandy while the women played games.

He supposed it was good practice for when he petitioned for knighthood and had to run in these circles. Although he'd rather battle a party rated monster with his bare hands than make small talk with the Marshal.

Jind seemed well aware of that, because as soon as they'd settled into their seats by the fire he cleared his throat. "Listen, lad, I never meant for there to be bad blood between us over Linia. I've had plenty of opportunity to resign myself to catgirl nature and keep it strictly fun, doing my best to shrug off the knowledge they'd take other lovers. I realize now you haven't had that same experience, and I was thoughtlessly cruel."

The man actually rose from his seat to bow. "Please pardon me, Master Dare. I didn't mean to insult you in your own home."

Dare could honestly admit he hadn't expected the overture. "I can't say I like any of this," he admitted. "But all things considered that's between me and Linia."

"I expect so." Jind gave him a thoughtful look, full of regret. "I know the last thing you want is my advice, but pardon an old rogue for speaking out of turn. Given how far your relationship with her has already progressed, if you can't accept her nature as a catgirl it might be less painful to break it off now."

Dare tensed and bit off a sharp reply.

The man continued quietly. "I've seen a few, men and women both, who gave their hearts to a felid hoping they would change. A rare few were pleasantly surprised, but the vast majority were bitterly disappointed." He hesitated. "And fond as I am of Linia, I fear she's the type who won't change."

Dare just nodded curtly, quickly changing the subject.

To knighthood, as it turned out; the Marshal had been hosted by Marona while passing through Terana, and she'd mentioned Dare's intent to join the nobility.

"I have a seat with the Lord Judges for the Order of the Northern Wall," the older man said. "I help evaluate the year's new prospects, so I daresay we'll be seeing each other again."

In spite of his dour mood Dare perked up at that. "Any advice?"

Jind laughed. "Be born noble." At Dare's crestfallen look he laughed again; spending the day shacked up with Linia certainly seemed to have put the man in a good mood. "Having noble sponsors is a good alternative, and Baroness Arral is well liked and respected. You should fare well enough with her patronage."

He gave Dare a shrewd look. "I imagine you're hoping I'll vote in your favor, lad, but I'll do you one better . . . I'll give you a fair judging. Which is more than I can say for some of the others on the Council." He downed his brandy with a gulp and a faint hiss through his teeth. "Backbiting weasels, half of them."

"A fair judging is all I hope to need, my Lord," Dare said as he sipped his own brandy.

"Yes, we all certainly hope that," the Marshal said with a faint smile. "But the wise might plan in case that hope doesn't pan out."

Soon after that the man excused himself to Melarawn village, Linia insisting on going along. Specifically by once again jumping into his arms, nuzzling his face with a purring noise.

Dare looked away, gut churning as he made his way up to his room. Where his fiancees all soon joined him, wrapping him in their love and support.

"Linia made her choice," Leilanna told him gently. "We support you."

"And you can be sure none of us would *ever* leave you for another man," Pella said fiercely, hugging him tight. "We're yours

Phoenix

and only yours in this life and whatever comes next, my love."

His other fiancees all voiced their fierce agreement to that, and their dedication to him and the family they'd built together.

Dare gratefully held them all tight, wondering how he'd ever gotten so lucky as to have all of these wonderful women in his life.

He felt a bit better as he settled down to sleep with them in a cuddly pile around him. Although it took him a while to drift off, his heart remaining troubled.

* * * * *

The Marshal and his companions left just after breakfast, waiting impatiently for Johar to saddle their horses while Jind soundly kissed Linia goodbye where he thought nobody could see.

Dare pointedly looked away, focusing on the goodbyes he and his family were giving to Felicia and Irawn, who'd be heading to the border to fight monsters and invading savage tribes. The older felid merely exchanged nods and clasped a few hands, but the young teenager took the time to give each of them a big hug.

"You're welcome back any time," Ireni told her. "Consider this your home."

"I will," Felicia said with a grin. "I'll be wanting to visit my niece or nephew, after all."

With a final flurry of activity the group mounted up. "Farewell, Darren of Nirim Manor!" Jind called, waving. "You have my gratitude for offering your home to my lover, and your willingness to raise the babe as your own. Know you have a friend in the Irregulars . . . I'll look forward to seeing you soon in Redoubt."

Dare bowed politely, and with a sharp cry the Archer nudged his horse's flanks and cantered out of the yard, ducking through the tunnel with his companions close behind.

Once the man was away Dare turned to his family and friends, doing his best not to look at Linia, who still looked tousled and sleepy, dressed in nothing but a man's undertunic. And not his.

"Well, back to the routine," he said. "I'm heading out to get

Level 37 and find that last party rated monster." He gave all his fiancees and Lily a quick kiss, went in to fetch his gear, and headed out.

In spite of his determination to make up for the wasted day, he felt like he didn't accomplish much. He'd been avoiding the area of mountains he explored that day because the rough terrain made moving around difficult, and because there were so many steep slopes and cliffs that few spawn points had formed. But he harbored the faint hope that a party rated monster might be lurking in such a forsaken spot.

He hoped in vain.

There were no party rated monsters to be found. No other secrets either, aside from a deep shaft that led into the ground that he thought might connect down to the dwarvish ruins below for ventilation or as a chimney. Although he wasn't about to try that entrance when he could just go through the front door.

Or more likely a side door, given its size and location.

The monster spawn points were few and far between, and most of them in the high 40s and low 50s, nothing he wanted to tangle with. It seemed nobody wanted to travel here any more than he did, and the monsters had begun to roam. Although their path of meandering seemed to take them east, into Elaivar; it had likely been going on for a while now, and hopefully the elves of that kingdom had the sporadic incursions well in hand.

Still, Dare needed to come back here once he was high enough level and clear these spawn points, before they became fully open ones that produced nothing but roamers. He was surprised they weren't already, unless the elves ventured across the border to here every now and then to do it themselves.

All in all, though, it was a mostly fruitless day, and he was more than happy to use Home Ward Bound to turn ethereal, floating above or through all the nasty terrain he'd spent the day crossing for an easy trip back to Nirim Manor.

When he got back he found that Ireni had been busy. She'd

organized the felid refugees and hired many of Rek's goblins to construct the refugee village the Irregulars had commissioned, as well as sending into town for craftsmen for the more complicated work.

They talked over the details during dinner, and Dare briefly explained what he'd found in the rough terrain. Amalisa wanted to talk over details for her wedding, so they all retired the the parlor where Dare and Ilin settled down in the overstuffed chairs by the fire for a few drinks while the women gathered on the couches and discussed food preparation, decorations, and other things.

It seemed even in a more medieval setting, weddings could get pretty elaborate.

"You seem a bit pensive this evening, my friend," Ilin said.

Dare carefully didn't look over at where Linia was nestled up to Amalisa, passionately trying to convince her that she should have felid acrobats and contortionists at the wedding for entertainment. "Just tired," he said with a tight smile. "I had to do a lot of climbing and scaling steep slopes today."

"Fair enough." His friend looked casually over at the orange catgirl. "A wise man once told me that a man may tarry at the base of a cliff all he likes, but eventually he's going to have to either turn back or start climbing."

Dare snorted. "Is that your way of telling me to get over it?"

The Monk blandly took a sip of his brandy; he was drinking more often these days, although always in moderation. "Or walk away. I know what I would do. But whatever the problem, face it."

Dare supposed he'd probably have to, and soon. But as it turned out the issue forced itself when they all turned in for the night.

He and his fiancees were all in the master bedroom undressing for bed when Linia sauntered into the room, yawning and stretching in one sinuous, full body motion, before starting to undress herself.

He froze in pulling his shirt over his head, giving her an incredulous look. "What are you doing, Linia?"

The catgirl looked at him, surprised, then at the other women who'd also paused their preparations. "Oh. Are you still mad?"

"You just jumped into another man's arms in front of me," he said as evenly as he could. "You were in his bed all day and night."

"I told you I wasn't part of your harem!" she snapped back, defensively folding her arms. "I also told you I'd have other lovers."

"You did," Dare said, more sharply than he'd intended. "And mentally I believed you and thought I was ready for it." He hesitated, heart aching; he wished Jind had never come to Nirim. Although he suspected this would've come up anyway when Linia found another lover.

With a sigh he continued as gently as he could. "But emotionally I'm not. Not when you were in my bed every night acting like part of the harem. Not when you were all over him in front of me. I'm not going to be just another lover."

Linia looked away, biting her lip miserably. "I'll never understand humans and other races who settle down," she muttered in a small voice. "I'm sorry, Dare. I didn't mean to hurt you. I like being your lover . . . you know I *do* care for you, right?"

Dare believed she did, in her own way. "I want you and the baby to still be welcome here, and I'd still like to raise it when you return to the Irregulars. But . . ."

He took a shuddering breath. "It's best if we found another room for you. Maybe in a guest house."

She nodded, a tear trickling down her cheek, and quietly gave the other girls hugs. A few were sniffling as well, although they all stood with him.

When she moved to hug him he stiffened and stepped back, and she nodded sadly and turned away.

As Ireni and Se'weir led her off to help her get settled in a new room, he slumped down on the end of the bed while his other fiancees wrapped their arms around him, murmuring comfortingly.

Pella had warned him when they first met the catgirl that Linia might end up hurting him, if he let himself forget how felids were. And that was exactly what had happened.

Chapter Four
Eagerly Awaited

Eight days later Dare had done his best to put the situation with Linia out of his mind and focus on leveling.

He'd long since reached Level 37 and was making steady progress towards 38. In spite of that he was feeling like he was running out of time.

There were only 11 days left until the first of the year, and realistically probably only a week before he needed to set out for Redoubt, even if he went on his own and traveled as fast as possible using Cheetah's Dash.

Which meant a week left to find another party rated monster, then gather up a party to kill it if it was too high level to solo. He'd already spent longer than that searching with no results.

Even more than that, he was frustrated to be out here looking when Pella was due to give birth any day now, and most likely today. Which they could be very confident in.

Apparently for most races besides humans pregnancies took a fairly consistent amount of time, with a normal variation of only days instead of potentially weeks. And usually in rounded numbers by the month, like six months for canids.

Maybe the gods preferred orderly patterns.

Dare wanted to be with his beloved at this time, giving her his strength and support however he could. Not out here running around mountains he'd already mostly explored, searching for a party rated monster that wasn't there.

Whatever happened with his hunt, Leilanna, Ireni, and Lily would be heading to Terana the day after Pella gave birth, whenever that was. He'd wanted to go with them, but it was looking like he'd have to stick around to keep looking.

Redoubt

The family had already discussed it and agreed that if Dare didn't find a party rated monster before the others left, he should set out and search farther west along the mountains he hadn't explored yet. Not returning home each evening but instead camping so he could make the most out of each remaining day.

He'd only return if he needed help killing a party rated monster, bringing Zuri and Ilin to give him a hand with it. Otherwise when his time ran out he'd head straight for Redoubt.

Today's searching ended with frustration, when he explored a small side valley surrounded by places he'd already searched. He'd already eyeballed the spot but was hoping that a closer look would reveal a Stealthed monster, or one that hibernated in a cave or something like that. When it didn't, he looked at the sun, still hours away from setting, and decided to call it a day anyway.

Thirty minutes later, when the Home Ward deposited him in the stable yard, he was glad he had.

Ilin, who was meditating on the front doorstep for some reason, leapt to his feet the moment Dare appeared. "It's time," he said tersely. "Pella's asked for you."

Dare blinked. "In the birthing room?"

He would be more than happy to be there with her when the time came, holding her hand and offering her his full support. But that wasn't how things were done on Collisa, and his fiancees had made it very clear that childbirth was women's business. At best they thought it was sweet that he wanted to be there for them, even if his place was out in the parlor waiting for news.

But Pella thought differently, apparently. "Yes," Ilin said, looking a bit baffled. "We didn't think you'd be back in time, but if so she wants to see you."

Dare wasted no time rushing inside, tearing off his armor and gear and hastily washing his hands and face. Then he gingerly approached the master bedroom, where he could hear a susurration of women's voices inside, and after a brief hesitation knocked.

"Dare!" Pella called through the door, voice excited but strained.

Phoenix

"Get him in here!"

"I don't think that's-" Leilanna started.

"It is! Dare, come in!"

He cracked open the door and hesitantly stepped inside. All the women of his household were there, including Amalisa, Lily, and even Linia, who looked a bit uncomfortable but was clearly doing her best to be supportive.

They crowded even the large room, filling it with bustle as they fetched clean towels and sheets, heated water, or just gathered around the bed in silent encouragement.

Pella was reclined back against several pillows, a sheet over her lower half. Her face was drawn with effort, skin flushed and sweaty, but her radiant smile when she saw him was nothing short of angelic.

"I'm glad you're here," she said eagerly. "It's time, the babies are c-ah!"

Her face twisted with discomfort and she gripped the sheets in her fists.

"Breathe," Zuri said, stroking her forehead. "Come on, you're doing great. Big breath in, big breath out." Her hands glowed with healing magic, and Pella's features relaxed.

Dare stepped up to the bed, freed one of his dog girl fiancee's hands from its death grip on the sheet, and let her grip his hand instead. He wasn't sure what to say, what to do, but he did his best to show his deep love and support for her with every fiber of his being.

Pella smiled up at him, eyes bright. "The others all think I'm crazy, but I wanted you here with me. At least for a bit."

He leaned forward and tenderly kissed her forehead. "I'm here," he murmured. "And you're doing great."

The next twenty minutes or so were a blur as women bustled around, Pella did her best to breathe as the contractions came closer and closer together, and he held her hand through it all, offering encouragement.

Redoubt

Finally, though, Ireni looked beneath the sheet to check Pella's progress. "It's time!" she said excitedly. "Just a few more pushes for the first baby, Pella. You're so close!"

"Finally!" The new mother made a happy sound around panting breaths. "Thank you, Dare, but you can wait outside now."

He would've been willing to keep her company through it all, but part of him was a bit relieved to head out into the hall. He waited there anxiously until Pella gave a last cry and then there was expectant silence.

Then the most beautiful sound ever: a baby's cry.

Dare's heart soared. His child was here.

He wanted to go in, but he remembered that there was another baby coming. Moments later the door cracked open and Leilanna slipped out, smiling. "Congratulations, daddy," she said, kissing him softly. "You have a beautiful, healthy canid boy."

A son. He stared at the door in wonder.

His dusk elf fiancee gently took his hand and led him down the hallway. "Just a few more minutes. Zuri was wondering if you'd check on Gelaa and keep her company for a while, until the other baby's born and you can meet them."

As it turned out his daughter was sleeping peacefully in her crib. Leilanna left him to return to the birthing room while Dare settled into a chair, staring down at his baby girl.

"You have a little brother, sweetie," he whispered. "And soon you'll have another little brother or sister. That's pretty amazing, isn't it?"

Gelaa slept peacefully on.

After what felt like an eternity he heard footsteps in the hall. The door cracked open and Se'weir, eyes shining, motioned to him. He joined her in the hall, and she whispered, "You have a son and daughter, my mate. Would you like to meet them?"

A daughter too. Heart full, Dare followed her back down the hall and into the master bedroom, where the women were all gathered around the bed cooing in wonder. Pella lay propped up against the pillows covered with a sheet, limp and exhausted but practically glowing with joy.

Against her chest she held two babies as they quietly nursed, making soft little noises. His son had a fluffy golden tail and ears like his mother, while his daughter's ears and tail were raven, like Dare's own hair.

He approached in a daze of wonder, and Pella looked up at him with tears of happiness in her eyes. "Meet our son and daughter, my love," she whispered.

"They're beautiful," he murmured. "They're perfect." He gently stroked their soft cheeks. "Nic and Rellia?" Those were the names they'd discussed if they had a boy and a girl.

She nodded, tenderly stroking Nic's soft floppy ears, then Rellia's. "Nic and Rellia." She closed her eyes for a moment, a tear slipping down her cheek. "Our babies. Our precious babies."

He smoothed a strand of limp hair from her forehead. "How are you doing?"

"Exhausted. Overjoyed. I can't describe just how wonderful I feel right now." She looked up at him with her soft brown eyes. "I never could've believed I would have this six months ago, before I met you and Zuri."

Her eyes were drooping wearily, and Zuri gently but firmly took Dare's hand and led him out of the room.

That seemed to be that. He made his way to the parlor, where Ilin poured him a drink.

"This is becoming a tradition," Dare said with a laugh as he accepted it and settled down in a chair to stare into the fire.

"For a time," Ilin agreed, a reminder that he and Amalisa would eventually be moving to Terana to start their own life.

Dare lifted his glass in salute. "I hope to be able to offer you the same congratulations and companionship as your children are born."

"My children." His friend let out his breath in a whoosh. "That's an incredible thing to think of. I spent most of my life assuming I wouldn't have any."

Dare laughed ruefully. "Hard to believe it now, but so did I." He clapped his friend on the knee as he stood. "I need to go tell Eloise."

He bundled up in his coat and cloak and stepped out into the chilly late afternoon air, making his way down to where his plant girl daughter's seed waited beneath the ground for spring. "Great news, Eloise," he said, kneeling to place a hand on the snow-covered mound. "You have a new baby brother and sister. Nic and Rellia. They're both healthy, and Pella's doing great."

He paused for a moment, looking around at his estate yard, the garden, all the buildings, feeling a deep sense of contentment. His home, where his family was growing by the day.

"I'll leave you to sleep," he said, patting the mound. "I love you, Eloise. I can't wait to meet you when you're ready to grow big and strong."

* * * * *

After having a chance to hold his new son and daughter, marveling in how small and perfect they were, Dare wanted nothing more than to change all his plans the next morning and stay with Pella and the babies.

But his fiancees all insisted, and the new mother most of all. "We'll be fine here," she said firmly as she cuddled Nic while Rellia slept in a crib nearby. She was still in bed recovering, even with Zuri's healing, but she looked up at him with a bright smile. "The babies aren't going to be doing much besides eating, sleeping, and pooping for a while, so you won't be missing much."

"That's not really the point," he protested, looking down at his daughter's peaceful face. "I'll be missing them. And you."

"And you'll go anyway," Pella said peacefully. "So that our children will have the brightest future we can give them, including a noble heritage."

Dare wasn't sure he was convinced, but he reluctantly kissed her and the babies goodbye before making his final preparations to leave.

Ireni, Leilanna, and Lily were also preparing to leave, making for Terana to join Marona's entourage heading for the region's capitol. There were some concerns about that since Leilanna's magic provided heating for the manor. And also because everyone unanimously agreed that without Ireni there keeping an eye on things, everything would fall apart.

But the bookish redhead just laughed and assured them they could handle it with all the help they had. As for the heating, one of the Melarawn refugees and a goblin from Rek's village both had fire spells, and were high enough level to mostly pick up the slack in the dusk elf Mage's absence.

Mostly, although they would need to use the trick of sleeping for four hours, emptying their mana pools, and then sleeping another four hours to refill them before emptying them again later in the day. And the water and heating stone wouldn't be quite as warm as Leilanna could make them.

That wasn't the only inconvenience Dare was leaving his loved ones with, though. His fiancees and friends had all unanimously agreed that he should take the legendary chest with him. "We can work the pumps by hand," Se'weir insisted stubbornly, "but if the chest could save your life again, like it did against the Cursed Orc Warchief, then you need to take it."

She spoke for everyone, it seemed, so he grudgingly put the peanut-sized item with its load of lead bars into its special carrying pocket on his belt. He'd designed it to all but guarantee the precious item wouldn't fall out, but also to be easily retrievable at need.

Although he felt bad about leaving his family without that convenience to automate the plumbing and heating systems.

Marona had offered Ireni, Leilanna, and Lily the use of her carriage for the trip to Redoubt, which they'd graciously accepted. Even so, they'd decided to also bring mounts just in case.

Although only two, since Lily was a poor rider at best and

preferred to run anyway. Not to mention she could run much faster and farther than any horse.

They also brought a train of several packhorses, the accumulated results of weeks of planning.

It turned out that preparing for a trip to Redoubt to petition for knighthood was a bit more involved than just tossing some clothes in a bag and taking off across the countryside. Marona had given them very detailed advice on what the Lord Judges of the Order of the Northern Wall, who would select the new inductees from among the prospective knights, would expect from those petitioning.

As well as ways to improve their chances.

First and foremost were the pragmatic considerations. Of course Dare should dress in the finest clothes of the most current fashion, and equally importantly be equipped with the highest quality gear of his level he was able to find. It helped that Amalisa was able to enchant it; such improvements were usually costly.

Along the same vein, the Lord Judges would also want a list of his personal and estate assets and a logbook of the estate's finances, to ensure he was in good financial standing. He wouldn't even be considered if he boasted less than 50,000 gold in wealth and assets, although thankfully that included the value of his land and projected yearly income.

Even so, the baroness had been obliged to "invest" in Nirim Manor to the tune of nearly 16,000 gold for him to be eligible. A shuffling of wealth from sponsors that she claimed was common among prospective knights, and he could pay back after he gained knighthood.

Dare also needed to be above Level 30, which was no surprise. Any level above that only counted more strongly in his favor, although oddly enough the Lord Judges preferred people with levels in the multiples of five. Maybe a quirk shared by all humans and most other thinking beings, who preferred rounded numbers and orderly patterns. Failing that, for the same reason even levels were also preferred.

Phoenix

Sadly, Level 37 wasn't a nice rounded number *or* an even number. Although Marona had assured him that the extra level would weigh stronger than an even number. For most.

It certainly would help if he had the Protector of Bastion achievement, as well as the fact that he could claim participation in Lord Zor's raid to defeat the Magma Tunneler. Even more to his credit would be his aid in defeating the monster horde and killing its commander.

And the list went on.

Ireni had again proved to be a literal godsend as she arranged the details, far more competently and efficiently than he could've. Dare was again struck by just how fortunate he was to have her in his life. Her and Marona, since on top of providing advice his noble lover provided a great deal of aid in making all the arrangements.

Especially in securing more endorsements and support from the nobles and the rich and renowned of Bastion, which would've been hard for him to manage since he didn't know many people in those circles.

Their tireless efforts reassured him that all the arrangements were in place, which freed him to go out and search for the final party rated monster he needed. Which was going to be a lonely ten days as he ran around by himself.

On the plus side, forking out money for top tier gear and the best enchanting materials Amalisa could use at her level made a huge difference in his gear. Probably eventually enough to pay for itself as he farmed money.

And he could pass the gear down to one of the other leather wearers, ideally Lily with her Archer subclass, if they ever got to this level.

Speaking of the bunny girl, she'd apparently decided to change her plans at the last minute.

After Dare, those headed for Terana, and those staying home all said their final goodbyes, Lily made her way over to him. She was all kitted out in her adventuring gear with with her bow and short sword, one of the few melee weapons Archers were capable of using, as well as her pack and warm weather gear.

"Traveling on foot?" he asked her with a grin. "I thought you were all going to be riding in comfort in Marona's carriage."

She grinned back. "That's going to be a bit hard to do when I'm up in the mountains with you."

He blinked. "You want to come with me?"

The gorgeous bunny girl nodded, fiddling with her glasses. "I love Leilanna and Ireni, of course, and Marona's been such a dear. But if it's a choice between slogging along with them at an agonizing pace for days or running around with you, it's not really much of a choice."

Dare was oddly pleased by that. "We're probably not going to be doing much leveling," he said. "I'd like to get to 38 if I can, but finding the party rated monster is my top priority."

"I know." She hooked her arm through his with a playful grin. "I mostly just want to spend time with you. We all hated the thought of you being out on your own for so long, and since I'm the only one who can keep up with you this is perfect."

He couldn't argue with any of that logic, and he certainly had no desire to. Having Lily with him changed the prospect of the next 10 days from a lonely slog to a delight.

Although he had to admit that spending several days out in the mountains exploring new terrain was something he'd been looking forward to in a lot of days, in spite of the prospect of cold winter camps and loneliness.

Maybe he'd find more dungeons, or another ancient ruin. Or meet some tribe hidden away in a secret valley to befriend and possibly get quests from.

An idea struck him and he grinned. "Stay here," he blurted as he ran back inside, ignoring the confused and curious looks of the others.

Maybe it was silly, but he'd gotten Lily a big gift and during this trip would be the perfect time to give it to her. He grabbed it, and also his new invention, and shoved them both to the bottom of his pack.

Back outside he just grinned at the questions his fiancees and friends peppered him with. "Tell you when we get back," he said, then bowed to his unexpected companion. "Ready to go?"

They accompanied Leilanna and Ireni as far as the beginning of the path to Terana, then with a grin and a laugh Lily took off across the snowy plains to the southwest. "Catch me if you can!" she called, voice drifting back to them on the wind.

Dare shared a grin with his fiancees, then with a laugh activated Cheetah's Dash and bolted after her.

Like always, trying to catch the bunny girl was an exercise in futility unless she held back for him. Not only was she faster in outright speed, even when he was going nearly 40 miles an hour, but she was also much more agile and could change directions in ways that seemed impossible.

Although he always knew he was at least giving her a challenge when she went from running to a bunny-like bound that increased her speed like she'd lit up afterburners.

In the nearly knee deep snow neither of them were reaching max speed. In fact, Dare kept to a reasonable speed to avoid hidden obstacles that might cause them to injure themselves at higher speeds.

Cheetah's Dash increased his agility when it came to movement and helped him avoid those sorts of disasters, but only to about the same level as if he was sprinting at his fastest usual speed. And there was no way he'd sprint at top speed in these conditions

Still, playing tag with Lily made the trip to the mountains pass in an enjoyable flash.

Although at his insistence they stopped at any spawn point they found that was closer to Lily's Level 24. Time notwithstanding, he wanted to make sure she could enjoy her gift as soon as possible.

Beyond that, Dare wanted to see what his companion was able to do in a fight. They'd be together in the wilds for a week and half and he wanted to help her get some experience in that time, and also in an emergency he needed to know she could take care of herself.

It just showed how focused he'd been on his own leveling and finding monsters; the bunny girl had been with them for over a month an a half now, including a ton of leveling with the others, and he hadn't seen her in action yet.

Also, he wanted to see how different combat subclasses were from main classes. From what he'd heard they missed out on a few key abilities over the levels, and also only had 75% of the usual hit points for that class and took a stat loss across the board. Although the main hit was that they only did two-thirds to three-quarters of the base damage of a main class.

But he had a feeling those damage estimates were made by people without Adventurer's Eye, and he liked to get his own information anyway so he could crunch the numbers himself.

He had Lily pull a single Level 26 monster first, kiting it while she damaged it down. She had the highest quality bow that was reasonable for her level, enchanted by Amalisa for extra damage, so even with the subclass damage reduction she did pretty well.

And soon she'd be doing even better.

Dare only had his own memories of doing damage to similar level monsters at Level 24 as a Hunter. But all the bow classes did about the same damage to unarmored single targets, so he should be able to draw a pretty good comparison.

Next, for fun, he had his companion pull three targets at once. With her main Archer ability she was able to hit up to three targets with every shot, with a damage reduction of 50%. Or in other words potentially 150% damage compared to single target. The ability could be activated or deactivated whenever she wanted with no cooldown, which was incredibly powerful and one of the reasons Archer was such a popular class.

It certainly helped with leveling faster.

With her subclass damage loss combined with doing less to each individual target, Dare had to kite the monsters more before she managed to kill them all. But overall there was no reason why she shouldn't be killing three enemies at a time whenever possible for best efficiency.

He could handle much lower level monsters with no problem.

They cleared the rest of the spawn point, and by the end of it Dare had determined that combat subclasses did 75% of the damage of a main class. Which was definitely a huge hit, but not terrible.

It was within the margin where skill, gear, and effort could make the difference.

They continued on, but while he was actually happy with the results of their hunting Lily looked unexpectedly glum. "What's wrong?" he asked, veering a bit closer to be heard over the wind of their speed.

She looked away quickly. "Oh, nothing really. I was just thinking how fun it is to finally be able to level with you." She fiddled with her glasses, eyes downcast. "But I realized that I won't be able to adventure with you like a real companion, because I won't be able to contribute."

Dare hesitated, feeling a bit bad because he'd had similar thoughts. Although now he felt differently. "That's not true," he said firmly. "I'd rather have you doing 75% of a main class's damage than some random idiot barely competent enough to put an arrow to the string."

The bunny girl glanced at him hopefully, then her face fell and she looked away again. "You're just saying that."

He chuckled. "I'm not. When I was Level 30 I joined a raid of mostly people in their mid-30s, fighting a raid rated monster around that level too, and I topped the damage boards."

"Well that's just because you have Fleetfoot," she argued. "You have more of an advantage compared to other people your level than I have a disadvantage." Her long white ears drooped. "That just widens the gap between us that much more."

Dare was silent for a while, carefully choosing his words as the landscape flashed by. "I'm not going to say that the damage and abilities don't matter," he finally said. "But ultimately what matters most is time doing damage to the target. And there you can shine."

Lily slowed to a stop, looking at him intently. "How?"

He grinned. "Party and raid rated monsters have area of effect attacks. Even regular monsters have ranged attacks they often hit random targets with. In all my raiding and dungeon experience, I've seen plenty of cases where people with the best gear and most powerful classes ran around like chickens with their heads cut off trying to avoid damage, and lost out to more competent people."

He tapped her collar bone for emphasis. "But you're one of the smartest people I've met, and also by far the fastest. As long as you keep alert you shouldn't have to fear incoming attacks. While everyone else is scrambling to avoid taking damage while still doing damage, especially against multiple targets, you'll be loosing one arrow after another and ultimately coming out on top."

"Aside from you," she said, smiling tentatively. But she looked heartened by his words. "So if I caught up to you, you'd take me with you to the elvish ruins and the underground dwarvish city? You'd let me come with you on adventures, leveling and exploring the world?"

Dare's heart caught at that, then soared. With all his fiancees dropping away to have children and raise them at home, even Leilanna and Ireni eventually, and with Ilin and Amalisa leaving to start their life together, he'd felt more lonely than he'd expected.

His happiest days had been spent with Zuri, then Pella joining them, then Leilanna, adventuring together and conquering a dungeon as a team. And he wanted that again.

Or, well, it wasn't fair to say his *happiest* times. Nothing could compare to his children's births, and the life his family was building together at Nirim Manor. But after spending so long going out alone to level and scout, he hadn't realized how much he longed for that companionship again.

He met Lily's gaze solemnly. "If you want to share that life with me, it would make me very happy to have you by my side."

Phoenix

Her eyes lit up, and her sudden excitement exploded into motion as she darted ahead with a giddy laugh. "Yaaaaaaay!" she yelled as she bounded across the plains.

Dare laughed and rushed to catch up.

* * * * *

The rest of the day was productive enough, although party rated monsters continued to be elusive.

Dare supposed he shouldn't be too surprised by that, since even after all his searching over the last month and a half since accepting Ireni's challenge, he'd only found four. And he'd scoured the Gadris Mountains within a day's run of Nirim Manor.

Still, they found plenty of spawn points for Lily to clear, and even several for him. They also found a lot of places where there *weren't* party rated monsters, meaning he could cross them off the map and keep searching westwards.

It was kind of nice to watch the sun sink towards the horizon and not have to worry about heading home. At sundown they found a nice secluded gully sheltered from the bitter winter winds blowing down from the north, with a good flat spot for their tents, and set up camp.

They'd brought enough provisions for a few days, since they'd planned to travel fast and it wasn't certain they'd always be able to find food. But Lily was an expert at foraging greens, small surprise, and Dare had brought down a vicious piglike animal with tough but flavorful meat.

Honestly, neither of them had to worry about ever going hungry under any but the most extreme circumstances. As a bunny girl Lily could eat plants humans couldn't, and digested them far more efficiently, so even in winter she could eat pine needles and sapling bark and grass. Not to mention digging up roots to eat raw or cook up.

And with his bow and plentiful animals everywhere, especially predators, he'd always be able to get meat. Not to mention his own Forage ability.

So they were able to work together to cook a delicious and satisfying dinner of salad and a stew of root vegetables and meat.

As Lily pulled out her collapsible hair to sit down, Dare stopped her. "You can throw that away," he said with a grin.

She gave him a hurt look and clutched it protectively to her chest. "But it's one of the first leatherworking patterns I ever made, and besides that it's your design so it reminds me of you!"

He felt his cheeks flush in embarrassment. "Sorry, I just meant I have something better." He reached into his pack for one of his inventions he'd regrettably not been able to use very often.

It was his collapsible chair, but extended to fit a couple with minimal supports between them to allow for snuggling. An improved version of the one he'd brought on his date into the mountains with Ireni, when they'd shared their first time together.

He'd been eager to perfect the design, looking forward to being able to cuddle with his fiancees when they camped while out adventuring. Only to realize that the women he loved all wanted to stay at home and raise their children, so his new chair would go unused as he ventured out to level alone.

Until now.

Lily laughed and clapped her hands when she realized what it was. "A collapsible chair for two people!"

He grinned as he finished setting it up and settled into one of the seats, patting the other one in invitation. "Yep. I figured when most of my companions are women I love, why am I making individual chairs?"

"Because this was probably ten times as hard to make work?" she teased as she settled down with a contented sigh. "It's no bench swing, but it's still amazing. Do you spend all your time inventing things to make our lives more comfortable?"

"Absolutely." Dare stretched out his legs towards the fire. "I've got plenty of time to think while I run around, and how to make you and the others happy is my favorite topic."

"Ah, that's so romantic!" Lily scooted over to snuggle up to his side, resting her head on his shoulder.

Even with them both bundled up for the cold, that felt nice. Especially when he pulled out a blanket to cover them both as they waited for their food to cook.

"I'm glad I came with you," she said with a happy sigh after a few minutes. "Being able to spend so much time with you like this is wonderful."

Dare put an arm around her shoulders and pulled her closer. "I was thinking the same thing."

After dinner they settled back in the chair to look up at the stars, as they so often did. The night sky on Collisa was always breathtaking, since there was barely any light pollution and the view was always clear.

"It hasn't changed, has it?" the beautiful bunny girl said after a while, absently playing with one of her long silver pigtails as she stared up at the brilliant vista. "Not since as far back as I can remember as a child. Sure, maybe the moons and planets move around, but they do it in predictable ways. Nothing big or permanent changes."

"Probably not," Dare agreed. "Things move much differently up there. Down on Collisa we scramble around, packing so much activity into each day, each hour, each minute." He chuckled. "Just think about how much our lives have changed just in the last few months."

She gave him a soft smile as she kissed his shoulder before staring up at the sky again. "So much, and in such wonderful ways."

"The most wonderful ways." He motioned up at the starry expanse. "But the things we see up there take millions or even billions of years to change. They've probably been the same since the beginning of the world, with only rare major events to break up the pattern."

"Billions?" she asked in awe. "I can't even imagine such a number."

Dare nodded. "It's too big to really imagine, except as an

abstract. Our lives are blinks in the stellar timetable. We'll look up at this same sky next month, next year, in a decade. And when we're old and gray, the sky we sit together under will be the same as it always has."

Lily turned to look at him, eyes wide. "Together?" she whispered, voice trembling slightly.

He felt his cheeks heat at that bold prediction. "It's what I dream of," he said honestly.

Her eyes shone behind her glasses, and when she turned her gaze back to the sky she wore a quietly happy expression. "Old and gray together, looking up at the stars. That does sound like a dream come true."

She cuddled closer and rested her head on his shoulder, velvety ears brushing gently against his cheek. They sat contentedly together, looking up at the brilliant nighttime display as the fire in front of them popped and crackled.

After a minute or so Dare became aware of a pleasant scent permeating the air, gradually growing strong enough to overpower the smell of woodsmoke and the sharp bite of snow and ice.

It was . . . intoxicating. Warm and welcoming, wild and heady, rousing yet intimate. He'd never smelled anything like it, and he was certain without a doubt that it was coming from the beautiful bunny girl in his arms.

For a moment he thought it was like the scent Linia had given off when she was in heat, where her sweat was laden with pheromones meant to entice a mate. But while this scent was certainly enticing and made him desire Lily, like just about everything about her did, it was far more than that.

Dare wanted to hold her. Wanted to feel her in his arms forever. Wanted to listen to her breathing as she slept next to him. Wanted to run with her for hours, tickle her and play tag and other silly games. He wanted to be with her every second of every day, basking in the wonder of her.

It was as if all the growing feelings of love he felt for her, all the desire, all the friendship and camaraderie, had taken form and filled his mind in a fog. It was wonderful.

Almost without realizing it he found himself nuzzling her soft white ears, running his hand through her silky silver hair, breathing in deeply to catch more of her intoxicating scent.

Lily giggled, turning to give him a quizzical look. "You're more cuddly than usual," she said, a question in her voice.

"Mmm," Dare murmured, kissing the tip of her ear as he hugged her closer. "You smell so good right now." He abruptly froze, his own words taking him out of the pleasant haze as he realized that usually wasn't considered a romantic thing to say.

She stiffened as well, already big eyes becoming huge. "Oh. Goddess damn it."

Wow. He didn't think he'd ever heard her curse before . . . she'd consider it too unromantic and unladylike. He backed away slightly, feeling embarrassed. "I'm sorry. I don't know what came over me."

The beautiful bunny girl sighed. "I do." She dropped her face into her hands, heedless of her glasses. "Curse it, we don't even have children yet or anything! I'm still a virgin, for the Goddess's sake!"

This really wasn't like her. "Lily?" he asked worriedly.

Her shoulders slumped as she kept hiding her face. "You're going to think I'm a lovesick girl and laugh at me."

Dare couldn't help but smile. "All these times you think I'm going to laugh at you, when really all I'm doing is marveling at what a wonder you are." He took her hand and gently squeezed it. "What is it?"

Lily sighed and peeked up at him through her fingers. "You know cunids have seven girls born for every boy, right?" He nodded. "And we've got ridiculously high fertility?" He nodded again. "Well as you can guess, that makes bunny girls super horny. Like, when we can't find a mate even satisfying ourselves isn't enough after a while. So we seek out each other, plant girls, or go find travelers and present ourselves to them naked and seemingly helpless hoping they'll mount us."

Redoubt

He coughed, feeling his cheeks heat again, and had to do his best not to picture finding Lily the same way he'd found Clover soon after coming to Collisa.

With her scent growing stronger and stronger, pushing aside the mental image was more difficult than he'd expected.

"Well most people only know bunny girls for those fun encounters in the wilds," she continued. "We keep to ourselves in our warrens and don't really have much contact with the outside world, aside from mating with random travelers. So what people don't know is that with so many women for few men, bunny girls have developed extra measures to bind themselves to their lifelong mate when they find one."

Lily covered her face again, squirming in embarrassment. "Basically, it's a scent we naturally develop for a man we've come to have strong and lasting feelings for. Tailored specifically to him, and often only noticeable by him. It, um, I guess you could say it's like all our feelings for him are broadcasted in that scent we give off. To let him know we want to be with him for the rest of our lives."

Wow. That was . . . incredible to hear. "So you're basically shooting "I love you" rays at me right now?"

She nodded, blushing so deeply it was visible even in the flickering firelight. "Along with "Please mount me right this second and hammer me into the ground like a nail" rays."

Dare sucked in a sharp breath, surprised at her unusually blunt admission given her determined efforts to be romantic.

With a mortified cry the bunny girl leapt up. "Gah, please excuse me, I'm all out of my head right now!" she wailed, starting to flee to her tent.

He caught her hand, gently turning her back. "I love you too, Lily," he said quietly, "and I want to spend my life with you. And while this may not be classically romantic, like in a story, what you just confessed to me was one of the most romantic things I've ever heard."

Lily looked at her feet, blushing furiously. "I'm sorry, Dare. You've been so wonderful courting me, and it's been so romantic. But with my high fertility and constant horniness, sometimes I get so I just want to tear your clothes off and rub myself against your abs like a cheese grater."

She bit her lip, peeking up at him. "So whenever I ran off for no apparent reason when we were together, that's been the reason why. So we can keep our relationship romantic until it's time for, you know, the other stuff." Her expression became longing. "All the other stuff."

Dare lifted her hand and kissed it gently. "If waiting is too difficult for you we can always speed up the timetable. The romance doesn't have to end when we get together."

The beautiful bunny girl giggled. "That's the most romantic way I've ever heard someone say, "Want to breed?" She sobered and shook her head, smiling. "If you're willing to keep it cool about the love scent I can't help but waft whenever I'm having particularly strong feelings for you, I'm willing to keep my desire to ravish you in check."

She hesitated, then leaned close to his ear. "At least until, say, you give me a grand marriage proposal, all right?" she whispered. "I know in all the stories the couple waits for the super romantic marriage night, but I figure if you're sleeping with your other betrothed then it's okay if we sleep together too." She bit her lip again. "I won't mind if it's sometime soon, either."

He felt his heart pound as that sank in. "It'll be a wedding proposal for the ages," he promised.

Lily beamed. "I can't wait." She looked longingly at the chair, obviously wanting to cuddle with him some more, then reluctantly turned towards her tent. "Good night, my love."

"Good night, dearest heart," Dare said. This had certainly been a conversation, that was for sure. He was still wrapping his head around it.

She'd just told him that she loved him so deeply she wanted to spend her life with him, and would be showing the proof of her love with her scent when they were together from now on. That was more than he ever could've dreamed of with her.

It went beyond the simple fact that she was ethereally beautiful, although that would've made him the luckiest man alive all on its own. But she was also so gentle and affectionate. So smart and curious about the world, so funny and overall fun to be with. Had such a good and genuine heart that he couldn't help but love her.

Not to mention her passionate quest for the perfect romance was sweet and endearing.

He couldn't help but grin like an idiot as he tidied up around the camp and climbed into his own tent, burrowing under the covers. Then, feeling his cheeks heat, he pulled his blankets up to cover his ears so he wouldn't hear the soft but insistent noises coming from Lily's tent.

His bunny girl sweetheart was innocent, adorable, and lovably romantic. And she was also incredibly sexy.

Those weren't mutually exclusive.

Chapter Five
Timely Gift

Two days later they were well west of Nirim Manor, past the goblin ravine and getting close to Jarn's Holdout.

Passing through the goblin ravine made Dare think of Se'weir, and he felt a pang, missing his beautiful hobgoblin fiancee. He hoped she and the others were doing well back home. Especially Pella and the babies, and Zuri and Gelaa.

They'd still seen no sign of a party rated monster in spite of their careful searching. But the day was still a great one because Lily reached Level 25.

She initially seemed downcast about it, because where most Archers would get a choice of two abilities for that level, her combat subclass meant she only got offered one. It was a bland one in comparison to an active ability, a passive boost called "Quiver Optimization" that increased her speed retrieving arrows from a quiver by 10%.

Taking the arrow from the quiver was only one part of shooting the bow, along with fitting it to the string, drawing, aiming, and loosing. Still, it was one of the more time consuming steps, and anyway a speed increase with one increased the speed of the whole, letting her shoot faster than before.

Dare could understand the bunny girl's disappointment, though, because the other choice was "Heavy Draw" which increased damage for an arrow by 100%, with a 1 minute cooldown. Comparing the cooldown and other factors, the passive damage boost from Quiver Optimization was actually more than Heavy Draw, but front loaded damage was always better.

And abilities were fun.

Thankfully, he had just the thing to excite her about her new level. So as she somewhat unenthusiastically practiced pulling arrows from the quiver and them putting them back to check the speed increase, he shrugged off his pack so he could dig into it.

"Congratulations on your level," he said, grinning at her. "I got something for you."

The bunny girl perked up. "For my 25th level? That's so sweet of you."

"Well it's something I loved at that level, and it helped me a ton. I was actually excited that you'd have the chance to use it too."

She jumped up and down eagerly. "An item?"

"*The* item," he said solemnly, reaching into his pack. "The only thing a ranged class with quick feet and quicker wits really needs." He withdrew the hunting bow and held it out to her. "Entangler."

Twice the damage of Lily's current bow, with better range, speed, accuracy, and vastly improved durability. But where it shone were special item attributes: it had a 10% chance to apply a snare effect and a 5% chance to apply a root effect. It also did bonus nature damage, although on top of that Dare had gotten Amalisa to enchant it with extra electricity damage as well, so it was doubly lethal.

Best of all, at least as far as he was concerned, it had a use on cooldown ability. "Vine Lash: Spawn a vine from the bow that can be aimed at a target up to 20 yards away, then retract the vine on command. 5 minute cooldown."

Dare had sold it to the Terana Counting House for a very satisfactory price when he out-leveled it. But anticipating Lily could use it when she finally reached Level 25, he'd approached them to see if it was still available.

As it turned out it was. Better yet Norril, owner and proprietor, had seen an opportunity to ingratiate himself to the swiftly rising star of the Master of Nirim Manor, and had offered to sell it back at the price his establishment had bought it for.

And it was worth every gold of the 1,350 to see the way Lily's face lit up in wonder.

Phoenix

"It's Master quality," she breathed, reverently accepting the item. "It must be worth a fortune."

"If it keeps you safe and helps ease your way to Level 30, it's worth every copper."

Dare was suddenly awash in the warm scent of Lily's deeply felt love as she threw her arms around him and kissed his cheek. "Thank you," she whispered, eyes shining. "It's wonderful."

He did his best to focus through the blissful haze of her broadcast feelings and grinned. "If you think it's great now, wait until you try out Vine Lash. It's a blast."

She blinked and pulled back, a bit wary. "It explodes?"

He laughed. "I mean it's really, really fun. And I have a feeling you're going to love it just as much as I did."

Dare quickly showed his companion how the ability worked, helping her avoid the pitfalls (sometimes literally) that he'd encountered when testing it. Then he watched with a huge grin as she sent the vine whipping out to wrap around a tree up the slope, and with a gleeful whoop shot away towards it.

She managed the entire thing with much more grace than he had his first time, and he doubted his advice was fully responsible for that.

For the next few minutes the bunny girl ran around, testing out her new bow by shooting arrows at various targets. She was obviously having a blast, but although she kept saying she couldn't wait to get back to hunting monsters she didn't seem in a hurry to get going.

"Almost done having fun?" he finally called with a laugh. "Why don't you test Entangler out on the rest of the monsters in this spawn point?"

"Oh, but I still want to have fun." Giggling, Lily pointed the bow at him.

The next thing Dare knew he was wrapped in a vine, binding his arms to his sides. He found himself simultaneously flying towards her as she flew even faster towards him, and only Vine Lash's effect that slowed the user before collision kept them from slamming into each other.

Then he was held there, panting a bit from the exhilarating and terrifying trip, as she leaned in and softly but firmly pressed her lips to his. Engulfed in the thrill of the kiss her loving scent suffused him, and he lamented the vines pinning his arms when all he wanted was to hold her close forever.

The beautiful bunny girl stepped back, chest rising and falling quickly from more than just the exertion of running around. "You need to propose to me soon," she whispered playfully as she finally retracted the vine, freeing him.

He did. He really did.

Dare shook out of his daze and led the way back to the spawn point they'd been clearing. "Okay, let's see how fast you kill three of these things at the same time."

The answer to that was ridiculously fast; she was going to catch up to him in no time at this rate.

* * * * *

Another day of exploring and farming spawn points, not finding any party rated monsters.

Although they *did* find something pretty amazing, a giant broken statue filling a valley that was so weathered its features were unrecognizable. Pacing out the size of it, Dare determined it would've stood at least fifty feet tall, and the giant obsidian block that formed its pedestal was covered with the remnants of carvings too faded to make out.

What civilization had called for such a wonder, out in the middle of nowhere in these mountains? Was it connected to Gurzan's Last Hold? The elvish ruins? Some other race of people who had risen to power to the point they could carve such a wonder, then faded away until all that remained was this broken monument?

He felt a bit wistful as they left the statue behind and moved on, having a feeling he'd probably never know.

The weather turned bitterly cold that evening. To the point that Dare piled extra furs on his tent for insulation, and he and Lily agreed they should share it for warmth.

Rather than sitting out watching the stars in the frigid wind, which tore through even their thick winter clothes to chill them, they each piled under their own blankets in the tent. Then they spent a while talking while listening to the wind howl and the fur walls thump and shift.

"Storm's blowing in," the bunny girl murmured. Even under their individual blankets she still did her best to cuddle close, and her love scent was filling the confined space and making Dare want to hold her and run his hands through her silvery hair.

He did his best to push back the pleasant haze and nodded. "We're almost to Jarn's Holdout. If the weather stays bad tomorrow we can spend the day there, even rent a couple rooms for the night."

"What about finding the party rated monster?" she asked, and he could hear the concern in her voice.

Dare shook his head in resignation. "I learned my lesson trying to travel through a blizzard. Better to sit it out." He sighed. "Besides, we're close enough to a town that even in the mountains the spawn points are getting so low level that if we found one, I wouldn't get credit for it. Although we could kill to progress your achievement."

"Oh." The bunny girl was quiet for a moment. "So what are we going to do?"

"Strike north for Redoubt," he said; he'd been thinking this over ever since the spawn points got too weak for him to get experience. "We can stick to the wilds between towns and hope to get lucky."

She was slow to answer; she didn't need to mention that even the wilds between towns were traveled regularly enough that party rated monsters would've been found and killed. Especially if they were roamers and forced adventurers to put them down.

But there wasn't much choice. They only had a week left to get to Redoubt, and if the weather was foul it would slow them down, forcing them to spend more time traveling.

After quietly talking for an hour or so Lily fell quiet, and Dare heard her breathing deepen in sleep. He drifted off as well, suffused in the warmth of her love scent that carried him into pleasant dreams. Playing tag with her in sunny meadows, and having playful tickle fights, and finally just holding her in his arms for a pleasant eternity.

He would've been happy to never wake up, but when he did the next morning he felt like he was still dreaming.

Unsurprisingly for a bunny girl, he supposed, Lily was good at burrowing. In spite of them both being practically rolled up in blankets she'd somehow managed to wiggle her way into his while they slept, and he felt her warm, soft body pressed to his side. She was giving off a gentle love scent that, broadcasting her emotions, spoke to the deep contentment of being close to the person she loved.

Dare could've luxuriated in the feel of cuddling with her all morning. But he wasn't sure he could maintain his discipline when she stirred and began to wake, sleepily throwing an arm and leg around him and pressing closer with a soft moan.

He gently extricated himself, piling the blankets back around the sleeping bunny girl to ward off the chill that had seeped into the tent in spite of their combined body heat. He quickly pulled on his coat, gloves, thick socks, boots, armor, and finally his fur-lined cloak, pulling the hood low as he ducked outside.

Only to find that in the night the tent had accumulated a few inches of snow, and thick flakes swirled around him. Not quite a storm, but definitely snowing and it didn't look as if it was going to stop anytime soon.

In spite of the heavy cloud cover he judged it was around sunrise, and he got to work cooking a hearty stew of root vegetables with a generous dollop of honey to warm them.

A while later Lily emerged from the tent, bundled up for the cold. As a bunny girl she was a lot more able to tolerate the cold than he was, as proven by how her kind often ran around in the buff during warmer months, even when it got chilly. So rather than shivering like he was she looked around at the falling snow with bright eyes, obviously enjoying the beauty of the morning snowfall.

"That smells incredible," she murmured, coming over and hugging him from behind.

Dare could've said the same about her, with the gentle love scent she was giving off. He turned and wrapped his arms around her, kissing her softly. "Good morning," he said. "We can probably reach Jarn's Holdout in an hour or so, and it looks like this snow is going to be falling for a while. Want to make a day of it in town?"

"Okay!" Lily said, smiling. "I haven't visited any towns other than Terana with you, and we were kind of in a hurry then. It'll be fun to just take our time and enjoy what Jarn's Holdout has to offer."

Given her previous unease with being around people, he felt like she was really blossoming. He resolved to make sure her trip to town was the best experience possible.

There had been less pleasant encounters with people when he'd been with his other fiancees of different races, especially Zuri as a goblin. Although he'd noticed that the higher level they all got, the less people were openly rude.

Although even at this level, some still gave them the stink eye. Bastion was better than Kovana had been when it came to how people treated other races, but it still wasn't perfect.

They ate breakfast cuddled on the two person seat, packed up the camp, and then with a laugh Lily bolted off in the direction of Jarn's Holdout, wanting to make a race of it.

Dare was more than happy to accept the challenge, and it turned out that in spite of the storm they reached the town in less than an hour, panting but exhilarated after the early morning run through the mountains.

They took a few minutes to compose themselves, then strolled up to the gates.

The guards on duty, looking surly at having to be out in the cold

Redoubt

and snow, curtly saluted them and asked a few routine questions. If they were curious about the stunningly beautiful bunny girl who'd strolled up to their gate, they were too miserable to show it.

Or too professional; Bastion was surprisingly reasonable when it came to travelers, the guards throughout the region encouraged to be helpful and friendly. Dare and Lily didn't even have to pay a tax before being waved through the gate.

He was used to drawing attention thanks to his height and looks, but add to that his high level and the fact that his companion was an otherworldly beautiful bunny girl, not usually seen around other people, and people were actually stopping in the street to stare.

Doing their best to ignore the attention they made for the market, where Dare got to enjoy the pleasure of haggling to sell the loot they'd accumulated over the last few days. Something that Ireni, Leilanna, and Pella had previously taken over so he could focus on farming.

But what could he say, he liked the challenge.

"67 gold," the Trash loot merchant they visited to sell the majority of the goods said after an irritatingly lengthy perusal.

Dare chuckled at the insultingly low offer. "Thanks for your time, much of it as you took." He started to pack the items away.

The vendor seemed to realize he'd pushed too hard, and with someone whose level meant he had more important things to do than have his time wasted. "130," he corrected hastily. "If you also throw in the reagents."

Dare glanced at Lily; she'd told him she wanted to learn how to barter, something she'd never really had to do in her life, and he wanted to teach her by including her.

At his silent question she frowned. "Didn't you tell me that if one of the parties in a negotiation feels insulted, they're more likely to push for a less reasonable deal with the insulting party?"

He bit back a laugh at the vendor's chagrined expression. Usually Dare didn't specifically call vendors out for insultingly low offers, since he tended to be aggressive enough in his haggling without being that confrontative. But it was definitely a valid bartering tactic.

"134 gold and 50 silver," the vendor grumbled.

Dare looked to Lily again, and she nodded. "All right, you have a deal," he told the man.

Lily grinned and clapped her hands.

The vendor grunted, gathered up the loot, and counted out their payment. Dare had paid attention to the distribution of loot from the monsters each of them had killed, and he insisted the vendor pay the bunny girl her smaller but certainly reasonable share directly.

His companion seemed a bit reluctant about accepting her share, but when Dare finally convinced her he wouldn't take it himself she got excited about having money in her hands for the first time.

Apparently Ireni had been handling her finances for her from all their days leveling together, since Lily wasn't too interested in the wealth. She kept trying to give it to the the bookish redhead to help with Nirim Manor's upkeep, and they'd eventually settled on Ireni holding the money for her in case she had need of it at some point.

Now, though, Lily had money and wanted to buy things.

At her insistence they stopped by a soap merchant so she could browse the scented soaps, bath salts, and perfumes and scented oils; it was obvious she was hoping for the luxury of a bath while they were in town.

Dare left her to haggle on her own, promising he'd come back and see how she'd done, then went in search of a book merchant to see what was on offer.

He found some romantic stories for his companion, as well as a book of more well known Haraldar stories and another about the history of the kingdom. He also tossed in a travel account from a lord who'd visited other continents, and even passed as close as was safe to Nil, the Lost Continent. Dare wanted to learn more about the larger world, so he was eager to read it through.

Last of all he bought a cheap packet of war reports from the north, to get a better idea of just how things were going along the border.

Lily found him while he was still bartering down the book prices, excited to tell him about the deal she'd gotten from the soap merchant. As it turned out, at least to Dare's judgment based on her description and his knowledge of soap prices, the vendor had used a common bartering trick of offering a significant sale from an inflated initial price. But only for a limited time, to make the buyer feel urgency to quickly accept before it was too late.

He hated to burst her bubble, but he walked her through the tactic while she listened, a bit crestfallen. "It was a good first attempt, though," he said with a grin. "Some tricks you can be forewarned about, others you learn through experiencing them yourself."

"I assure you I use no such tricks," the book merchant chimed in helpfully. Dare smiled, not quite accepting that claim, and finished his negotiation with the man.

Before taking too long in the market Dare led the way to the Sally Fourth, the inn he'd stayed in on his last visit here. Where he'd enjoyed an incredible night with Linia.

The reminder of his former lover made him grimace, and he quickly put her out of his mind, not wanting to spoil the mood.

He left Lily to take a long, luxurious bath with her new soaps and salts, then spend a while relaxing and reading in the room she rented.

Then he went out to plan a romantic evening in lieu of the perfect proposal.

Where with the previous merchants Dare had enjoyed pushing for the best price possible, now he spared no expense. He found a flower merchant who grew them in a greenhouse with the help of a fire mage, and paid an absolutely stupid amount for a dozen roses to be delivered to the Sally Fourth that evening.

Then he found a tailor and got fitted for a fancy suit that could be done that evening for the right price. Which he was more than willing to pay. At the same shop he was also lucky enough to find an absolutely beautiful cream silk and satin dress, getting the tailor's agreement to come to the inn and have a fitting with Lily in a few hours.

Then he returned to the Sally Fourth and rented a private dining room, arranging for the fanciest wine they had. It took some talking to iron out a menu with a salad of fresh greens (from the same greenhouse as the flower merchant, actually) and a few of the bunny girl's favorite vegetable dishes.

All elevated by the inn's cook to be as fancy as possible.

Dare checked in with Lily and found her in her room, scrubbed pink and super relaxed after her bath and snuggled under the covers reading a book. He let her know the tailor was coming for a fitting, although he playfully left her mystified as to why.

Not that she'd have trouble guessing.

Then he set out again and made a few final preparations, including finding a barber to neaten his hair and shave his beard, before heading back to the inn for his own bath.

To his amusement the serving girl who drew his bath offered to scrub his back. She was a cute brunette with a very bold smile that promised more than just a back scrub, but he grinned and turned down the tempting offer, pressing a silver into her hand as a tip for her efforts before heading in alone and sinking into the tub.

Lily didn't mind him sleeping with other women any more than his fiancees did, and even seemed to enjoy discussing details with them, much to his chagrin. But he wasn't about to get laid with a random woman the day he proposed to his bunny girl sweetheart.

Assuming things went as perfectly as he hoped.

He relaxed into the water, all arrangements made, and focused on scrubbing himself squeaky clean while he waited for the tailor to bring his suit around.

※ ※ ※ ※ ※

That evening Dare approached Lily's door, dressed in his new suit and holding the bouquet of roses in the crook of his arm.

Redoubt

He heard a floorboard creak on the other side of the door and had a feeling she knew he was there. No surprise given her sensitive hearing, which put even Pella's to shame. But as was proper she waited for him to knock, then delayed for a few more seconds so it didn't seem like she'd rushed right to the door.

Although her excitement was obvious as she demurely opened the door, hands clasped in front of her. Her big eyes widened behind her glasses at the sight of him. "Wow, you look really handsome!" she blurted.

Dare was too busy staring in wonder to respond, momentarily driven speechless by the picture of perfection she made.

The bunny girl's new cream dress elegantly molded to her lush figure, the color a perfect contrast to her milky skin and white ears and tail. She'd done something to her normally straight silver hair so now her pigtails hung in ringlets, draped over her shoulders and flowing down her back to her waist.

He was fairly certain she'd put on makeup, although with such a light touch that it was hard to be sure, other than that her already flawless features were even more accentuated. Her ears stood straight up in a clear sign of her eagerness, and a brilliant smile lit up her face.

Her love scent radiated from her in quiet, warm ripples, tender as a lingering hug.

Dare finally picked his jaw up off the floor and offered her the roses. "I wish I had the words to describe your beauty, but I don't think they've been invented since they were never needed until you graced the world." He would've liked to say that he'd thought of that off the cuff, but it was a sentiment he thought often when he looked at her.

Lily's eyes softened. "Oh, that's wonderful." She almost reverently accepted the roses, breathing deeply of their delicate fragrance. "Mmm, these smell delicious." At his startled look she laughed. "Don't worry, I'll save them for later, after I've had time to admire them."

He supposed that was better than letting them wilt and eventually die. And if she liked the taste then it was kind of like a combination of flowers and chocolates, right?

Dare offered his best bow and extended his arm. "Shall we go to dinner, Miss Lily?"

She beamed and stepped up beside him, soft arm slipping through his and holding tight. "Yes, let's-" She abruptly gave a start. "Oh, my glasses! I was just reading and forgot them."

Hurrying back into the room, she took them off and set them on the nightstand. "Wait!" he blurted. At her uncertain look he felt his cheeks heat. "Keep them on. Unless you really don't want to, that is."

She looked at him with wide eyes. "You want me to wear them on our formal date? My sisters always told me mates would think they look silly, and I should try to avoid wearing them around any man I want to entice."

He grinned. "Are you kidding? I love your adorable glasses. And your pigtails . . . they're my favorite things about your look."

The beautiful bunny girl smiled and blushed a bit, obviously pleased. "I didn't realize." She retrieved her glasses and put them back on, then smiled tentatively as she returned to slip her arm through his. "Thank you . . . I want to see everything tonight."

Dare led her to the private dining room and opened the door, bowing. "After you, miss."

"Why thank you," she said with a small smile as she stepped inside. "Oh, this looks wonderful!"

He followed her in, and was pleased to see how elaborately the serving maids had set the table. They'd brought out the fine silverware and plates, and in the abundant light of the candles everything sparkled welcomingly.

He pulled out Lily's chair for her, then poured the wine before taking his own seat. "Cheers," he said, holding out his glass in toast.

"I do kind of feel like cheering," she said with a silvery laugh as she clinked glasses, then took a sip. "Mmm, I love this. It reminds me of the strawberry wine we make in the warren."

That was a lucky coincidence, since Dare hadn't known that. He took a sip, appreciating the fruity flavor. "I'll have to see about getting some bottles of it for the manor."

Dinner was pleasant. After some initial nervousness from both of them about the formality of the occasion, and the feeling that this was an important event, they relaxed and remembered that they were already close and had spent a lot of enjoyable time together.

Lily surprised him by mentioning that for the book she'd occupied herself with that afternoon, she'd passed over the romance stories to read from the book about the history of Haraldar. "I guess now that I've had a chance to see more of the kingdom, and I'm living as more of a citizen of it than I was back in the warren, I wanted to know more about it."

She grinned. "Also, reading the ancient dwarvish histories about when this area was first settled made me curious about how far back Haraldar's history goes."

"Not as far back as Gurzan's Last Hold?" he guessed.

"Nope, not nearly." She absently pulled a petal off one of the roses, which she'd deposited in a vase Dare had made sure was prepared for them, and nibbled on it as she continued. "Before Haraldar's first king ventured into the area, it had been wild and unclaimed for centuries."

"I guess as kingdoms fall they tend to vanish as monster spawn points pop back into existence to reclaim the area."

The bunny girl nodded. "It makes for a lot of lost cities and civilizations waiting to be rediscovered."

Dare took a bite of grilled carrots. "Are there any places that have been settled enough that spawn points were completely eliminated?"

She laughed. "You're asking me? I grew up in a hole in the ground outside Lone Ox." He returned her smile with a sheepish shrug, and she sobered. "Actually, a lot of popular romances come out of Elysin, the most civilized continent. The kingdoms there have grown so much in population that spawn points only exist in the inhospitable places people didn't want to settle, like deserts and mountain peaks, and those spawn points are kept farmed and weak."

"So an interesting place to visit for culture, and a terrible place to visit for adventure?" he asked.

Lily sighed dreamily and nibbled on another rose petal. "Maybe, but some of the cities there are terribly romantic. They have things like promenades where eligible bachelors and unattached young ladies walk in the evenings, socializing and finding love."

Dare reached across the table and took her hand. "Maybe we'll find a reason to visit there in the future."

"That would be nice," she said, squeezing his hand.

They finished eating, and Lily grabbed the roses to take with her as Dare again offered her his arm. He retrieved a stole for her as well as his coat, and they headed down through the Sally Fourth's bustling common room.

The large space took up the entire first floor of the building, as well as a wraparound balcony on the second floor to make a very high ceiling. It was a warm and inviting place, which Dare had fully enjoyed on his last visit here.

But he could tell the crowds and noise made Lily a bit uncomfortable, especially given the attention the two of the drew in their fancy formal clothes, and she was obviously relieved as he led the way outside.

The cold hit like a hammer after the warmth of the inn, but thankfully they didn't have far to go.

Dare led the way to a room he'd rented in a nearby building. As soon as they stepped inside the musician he'd hired began playing her lute, and his date stopped in amazement. "It's beautiful," she breathed. "Did you do this?"

His money had, at least.

It was a small, private dance floor that he'd decorated with the help of an Illusionist from the Adventurer's Guild. For a modest fee the man had agreed to cast a glamor on the ceiling, walls, and floor that made it look as if they were dancing among the stars and other stellar phenomena of the Collisan night sky.

He held out his hand. "Shall we dance, Miss Lily?"

Lily gave him a shy smile and lightly rested her fingers on his palm. "I'd be honored, Master Dare."

In the corner he thought he heard a wistful sigh from the musician, although when he glanced her way she seemed focused on her music.

Ireni and Leilanna had been teaching them to dance in preparation for their trip to Redoubt. Dare hadn't had many opportunities to learn back on Earth, or at least hadn't *taken* any opportunities. So the closest he'd come was those awkward school dances where the music pounded deafeningly and everyone just sort of stood there like idiots and maybe swayed a bit.

As for Lily, she apparently loved dancing in meadows, but her moves had little to do with the formal dancing of Haraldar's nobility. So they'd both had an opportunity to learn together.

Thankfully natural athleticism went a long way, and Dare felt like something close to a proper gentleman as he took the beautiful bunny girl in his arms and they moved together through the steps they'd learned.

"Do you think we could really dance among the stars one day?" she asked dreamily, looking around at the glamour.

He chuckled. "If we could get up there, and we had airtight suits that provided us with air, and protected us from radiation. And also jets so we could move around, since otherwise we'd float forever in whatever direction we were going, unless something else changed our direction."

Lily frowned at him. "How do you know all this? I know you learned it in your old home, and I've accepted it at face value since you're not the type to just make all this up. But how?"

Dare tensed, realizing that he'd put this off for too long. If he really planned to marry Lily, he couldn't keep something like his true origins a secret from her. It wouldn't be fair to ask her to bind

Phoenix

her life to him unless she knew who she was with.

So he took a deep breath and motioned to the musician, who showed admirable professionalism as she packed up her lute and retreated to a different room. He led his confused date to some chairs in the corner, around a table with a few refreshments, and sat down with their knees touching, looking into her wide eyes.

"You know Sia is the Outsider," he murmured.

Lily nodded hesitantly; Sia and Ireni hadn't even tried to keep that secret from her. Which was fair since a Priest of the Outsider had in many ways given the romantic bunny girl the prod she needed to leave her warren, when the man visited to check on Petro, Dare's son with Clover.

If Lily thought living in a home with a goddess, who might one day be a fellow lover in a harem, was in any way incredible or daunting or even just odd, she'd never shown any sign of it. Maybe because the rest of them were so natural around Sia, who definitely didn't act like the Outsider with them, that it was just a simple fact.

"But what does that have to do with where you came from?" she asked.

Dare took a deep breath. "Because in a way I'm an outsider too. The reason I know so much about what's in the sky is because I'm from a different world than Collisa, and on my world we've studied it with powerful telescopes for centuries. We've even sent people up into space to visit our one moon. The world I came from is called Earth."

She stared at him blankly. "Um, what? Your world's name is Dirt?"

He couldn't help but grin, charmed by the fact that with everything he'd told her, *that* was the point she'd settled on. His adorable bunny girl sweetheart really was a bit of a nerd, and he loved the way she thought.

Although his grin disappeared quick when she gave him a hurt look. "Why are you smiling? Are you laughing at me? Is this all some mean joke?"

"Of course not, I'm sorry," Dare said hastily, taking her hand. "I was just thinking about how wonderful you are."

Lily gave him a narrow look through her big wire-frame glasses. "Thanks, but maybe focus on the craziness about being from another world?"

"Right, sorry."

He told her all of it then. Dying on Earth, or at least suddenly finding himself in a gray void and having a disembodied voice tell him how he'd died. About how he'd been given the choice to go on to whatever afterlife awaited him, or come to Collisa and live a second life.

Of the gifts he'd been given, Adventurer's Eye and Fleetfoot, and being sent down to the forest near Lone Ox where he suddenly found himself forced to pick a class and learn as he went.

Everything. Saving Zuri and falling in love with her. Befriending Ilin and eventually parting ways for a time. Being approached by Pella and coming to love her as well. Traveling up to Bastion and saving Leilanna, then eventually falling in love with her in spite of their tumultuous start.

Saving the goblins of the Avenging Wolf tribe from slavers, and offering them a home at Nirim Manor. The arranged marriage with Se'weir to bind him to the goblin tribe and then eventually falling in love with her. Ireni approaching him in Terana and learning she was sharing her body with Sia. Falling in love with the goddess and with Ireni.

And everything that had happened from then until now.

A lot of it Lily knew, of course. She'd lived with them and they hadn't exactly kept anything secret. But now she was hearing it from the context of him being from another world, knowing nothing of Collisa and discovering it all as he lived there.

When Dare finally fell silent Lily said nothing for what felt like ages, and he was afraid about how she was going to take this all. Even more worrying, the gentle love scent that had permeated the air around her the entire night had faded.

Phoenix

He gently rested a hand on her knee. "Lily?"

She let out a shaky laugh. "Well, I can see why you'd be hesitant to share that. I can't even be hurt that you waited so long to tell me."

"So you believe me?" he asked.

The beautiful bunny girl shook her head slowly. "We live with a goddess. And you don't seem to be insane." She looked at the ground. "Does everyone else know?"

"My close friends and family." Dare gently squeezed her knee. "I took even longer to tell them. Sia wanted to make sure they were ready to hear it."

She bit her lip thoughtfully. "And she told you to tell me now?"

He shook his head with a smile. "I wanted you to know. But I think she'll approve."

Lily abruptly stood. "Let's dance some more. Don't worry about the musician, we don't need music." She paused. "Actually, can you tip her and send her home?"

Dare wasn't sure what to make of that, but he went and pressed a gold into the woman's hands, quietly thanking her as she curtsied and disappeared out the door.

Then he returned to his date, who stood in the middle of the floor waiting, achingly beautiful surrounded by stars and nebulae. She silently stepped into his arms, resting her head on his shoulder as they moved to unheard music.

Finally she murmured, "I've read stories where the handsome stranger has come from a distant land for mysterious reasons. But never another world." She looked up at him, expression impossible to read. "Were you a lord on this Earth?"

He chuckled wryly. "Far from it. I was a common nobody working a dead end job and spending my free time playing video games."

Lily didn't ask him what those were. "But you're so smart and educated, and speak so well and with such confidence. You know how to make so many things, like the collapsible chairs and the

Redoubt

running water and flushing toilets and all the other improvements for the manor. And even if Adventurer's Eye is a huge help, you seem to figure out the best way to hunt monsters and earn experience."

Dare shrugged, not sure how to answer that, and she poked him. "Are even the common nobodies of your world like the kings of ours?" she asked.

"No. Although we're fortunate to have lots of luxuries and opportunities most on Collisa don't, and have learned a lot of things that people here haven't."

"Like how to go up into the sky." The beautiful bunny girl sighed and rested her head on his shoulder again. "It's hard to believe the man I love is from another world."

He felt a weight lifting off his chest. "Then you still love me?"

"The man who died and was reincarnated a few miles from me, only to disappear until we could meet again later and fall in love?" She laughed softly. "Our lives really are like a romantic story, aren't they?"

"If they are, I want to keep reading. Page after page, chapter after chapter, throughout all our wonderful adventures together." On impulse Dare pulled back from her and went to one knee, reaching into his pocket for the small velvet box there.

As he withdrew it he looked up into Lily's wide eyes, staring down at him with her breath quickening as she realized what he was doing. Her love scent suffused him in gentle waves, and he felt like he was in a wondrous dream.

"I love you, Lily," he said solemnly. "From the moment I first saw you I saw you I felt drawn to you, and that bond between us has grown into something special and precious beyond words. Every moment I'm with you is a joy, and every moment I'm away from you I think only of when I'll be able to be with you again."

He opened the box and held it forth, revealing the truesilver ring set with a large diamond that Se'weir had crafted for him. "Lily of Brighthill Warren, will you marry me?"

"Yes, Dare," she said, eyes bright and smile like the rising sun. She reverently took the ring and slipped it on her finger, then dropped down to her knees as well to kiss him fiercely. "With all my heart, yes!"

Dare wrapped his arms around her and held her close, love scent swirling around him and lifting his already soaring heart to new heights as he felt her joy.

Chapter Six
Haze

Dare wasn't sure how long he held Lily for, treasuring the feel of her in his arms, exulting in her acceptance of his proposal.

She'd agreed to marry him.

Sure, she'd all but told him she would beforehand. But even so that thought filled him with wonder. That such a beautiful, elegant, intelligent, and loving woman could so freely give him her heart.

About the time he became aware of his knees aching from kneeling on the floor for so long, Lily stirred with a happy sigh and brushed his ear with her soft lips. "The hour grows late, my love. Should we retire?"

The blissful fog of her warm love scent combined with his joy quickened to a nervous anticipation as that sank in, and he realized what she meant. He swallowed around a sudden lump in his throat. "Yes, my love," he said, rising to his feet and gently raising her up with him. He offered his arm, and she took it with a beaming smile.

His heart was pounding in his chest as they made their way back to the Sally Fourth, through the bustling common room, and up to Lily's room. As she unlocked the door she smiled back at him. "I hope you didn't rent a room for yourself."

He sheepishly scratched at his jaw. "I did. I didn't want to presume."

She giggled. "Oh, my sweet betrothed, the perfect gentleman. You've been so wonderfully romantic." As she opened the door she leaned up and kissed his cheek, then whispered in his ear. "It's romantic to show how much you desire me, too. Especially now that we can finally be together."

Dare's heart pounded in his chest as he followed her into the room. Taking her words to heart, he pushed the door shut and pulled her into his arms, leaning down to press his lips to hers.

His beautiful bunny girl fiancee melted against him, body wondrously soft and yielding. Where before their kisses had been chaste, now the wire frame of her glasses pressed urgently against his cheek as her mouth opened against his, her tongue slipping into his mouth and seeking his out.

He ran his hands through her ringleted pigtails, luxuriating in the silky feel of her beautiful hair. In the taste of cucumber and wild greens on her tongue as he teased it. At her perfect body feeling so right against him.

Dare barely noticed she was subtly maneuvering them until the backs of his knees hit the bed, and she abruptly pushed him down to sit on the edge of it. He began to pull her down into his lap, but with a playful giggle she twisted away and danced back.

Lily's eyes were bright behind her glasses, face flushed. "My love, I want to show myself to you. All of myself."

He swallowed, feeling his manhood begin to stiffen as her love scent filled the room, drawing him to her. "I would like that," he said quietly. He could admit he'd longed to see her flawless body in all its glory.

She smiled knowingly. "If you want to see me as much as I want to be seen by you, you've been a true gentleman to not tear my clothes off already." She shrugged off her fur stole, kicked aside her soft slippers, and slipped the straps of her cream gown off her shoulders.

In spite of the beautiful bunny girl's bold words a fierce blush spread over her milky pale skin, and she almost shyly held his gaze as her lovely dress slid down her body to puddle at her feet. Revealing an unexpectedly innocent white bra and matching panties, with a bit of lace around the edges.

That just made her all the more sexy.

Dare looked wonderingly over her smooth flawless skin. Her flat tummy, her long graceful legs, her slender shoulders and delicate collarbone. The perfect mounds of her breasts beneath the bra, her curvy ass and adorable fluffy cottontail.

Biting her lip, Lily unfastened the clasps to her bra and let it fall away, revealing globes that found a pristine balance between firm and soft. Her pale pink nipples were small, and whether from the cold or arousal already poking out proudly, just begging to be played with.

He could've happily stared at them all day, but tore his gaze away eagerly when she hooked her thumbs in the waistband of her cute little panties and slid them over her hips, revealing a hairless mound and surprisingly plump lips, already flushed and glistening with her nectar.

Dare's cock throbbed insistently at the sight, and he had a fierce longing to touch her.

His fiancee seemed to sense it because she glided forward, every movement a wonderful blend of innocent and seductive, and took his hand. "I want you, my love," she whispered as she gently pressed his fingers to her sex.

He'd been with enough women since coming to Collisa that he'd genuinely need to sit back and think to count them all. He'd made love to beautiful women countless times. His control was only exceeded by his stamina.

But at the feel of her warm, silky petals it took a heroic effort not to explode right then and there.

Chalk it up to almost a week without relief, and almost two months of eagerly anticipating this moment with Lily. Or the simple fact that she was unbelievably sexy and felt incredible.

It seemed like he wasn't the only one who reacted strongly, either. As she insistently pushed his middle finger between her plump labia, over her throbbing bud, and against the warm entrance to her love tunnel, he felt a fresh surge of wetness flow from her depths.

"Goddess," the gorgeous bunny girl moaned, squirming against his hand. "I've wanted this for so long."

Phoenix

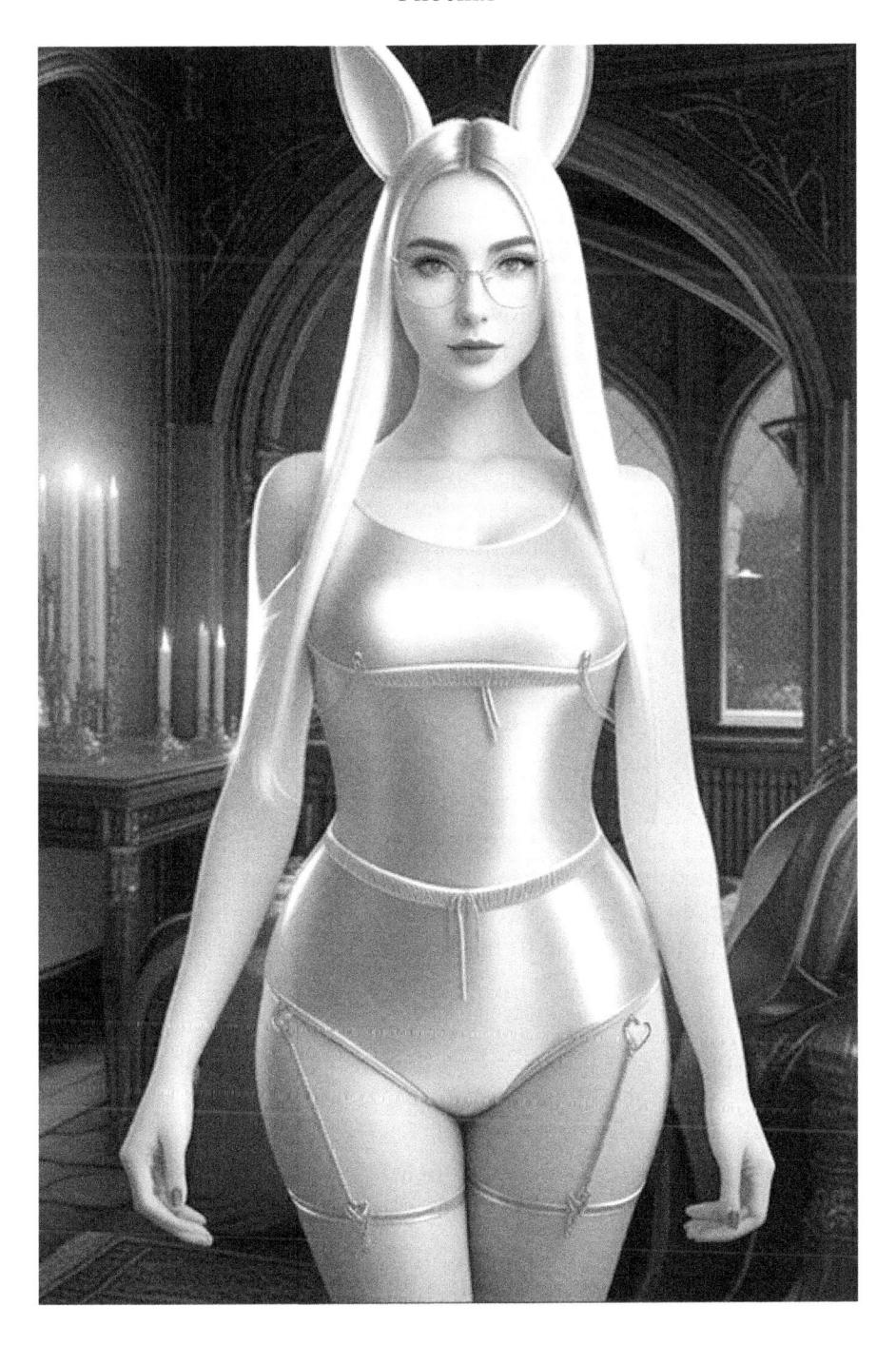

Redoubt

Dare pulled her down onto his lap and kissed her fiercely, running his hands over her soft back, sides, hips. Down to her flawless ass to squeeze her glorious buns before playfully stroking her little white cottontail.

Lily moaned, looking almost wistful as she ground urgently against his thigh, soaking his suit pants with her arousal. "I don't think it's going to happen," she panted, running her hands over his chest and back before grabbing his ass and squeezing hard.

He paused in sliding his hands up her tummy to her glorious breasts, uncertain. "What isn't?"

She whimpered and pressed her sex even harder against him. "I wanted our first time to be the romantic lovemaking I've read about. Where the lovers tenderly kiss and caress and give each other pleasure with their hands and mouths, before finally the man pushes inside her while looking deep into her eyes, showing his deep love in his heartfelt gaze. Like what you always share with Ireni."

His bunny girl fiancee gripped his ass tighter, fingernails lightly digging into his taut muscles through the cloth, and she made a plaintive sound. "But I guess it's going to have to wait for our second time, because this time it's going to be a lot more . . . primal."

Dare's cock lurched at the suggestion, but in spite of his urgent need he wanted to give the woman he loved what she wanted. He tenderly stroked her long, velvety white ears, leaning down to kiss her softly. "It doesn't have to be. I can hold back and make our first time every bit as loving as an innocent, blushing maiden like you could hope for."

"Are you sure you can?" Lily looked up at him, her heaving chest doing very nice things to her perfect breasts, eyes glazed. "Are you feeling it, Dare?" she panted.

"I'm definitely feeling it," he murmured with a smile, running his hands up and down her sides and reveling in her silky skin.

She shook her head urgently. "My love scent." At his blank look she nodded slowly. "It takes a second to kick in, I guess." She bit her lip with her adorable bunny teeth. "I should probably warn you before it hits. My love scent broadcasts the feelings I'm having for you, right? When I'm feeing playful, or cuddly, or tender and deeply connected, or . . ."

She took his hand and pressed it between her legs again, where her nectar was flowing freely from within her delicate folds. "When I'm feeling very, very horny."

"Oh." Dare's erection throbbed urgently as he tenderly stroked her perfectly shaped petals. "Okay."

His sexy fiancee was breathing harder, eyes glassy. "I mean it. My oldest sister moved to another warren and became lifelong mates with a man there. She told me that her love scent hit him like a boulder dropped off a cliff the first time. Even though they'd already been together a bunch of times and she had a baby with him, he told her it was some of the most intense sex he'd ever had. All of her arousal plus his building into something incredible."

"Oh," he said again, gulping.

He wondered how it would compare to his dream sex with Sia, when she'd been the alabaster mannequin. Where the scent of her arousal had pulled him into a fog of lust where he fucked her relentlessly for what felt like hours, coming inside her repeatedly but never getting soft.

It looked like he was about to find out.

Lily grabbed his fingers and shoved them inside her, urgently fucking herself on them. "It's not exactly romantic," she gasped, practically drooling. "But just remember that everything you're feeling is what I'm feeling. How much I want you. How much I *need* you, my love. My betrothed."

With an almost plaintive whimper she scampered to the center of the bed and positioned herself on her hands and knees, cottontail twitching as she raised her gorgeous ass in invitation, presenting her glistening petals.

Dare wasn't sure he'd ever seen a more glorious sight.

His bunny girl fiancee looked back at him over shoulder,

adorably big wire-frame glasses slipping down to the edge of her nose as she met his gaze with eager anticipation. "Don't hold back. Give me what I've been waiting for since I first met you. And now we can finally share, when our love is as deep as our lust is towering."

Oh gods, she was sexy. Dare's cock throbbed urgently at the invitation and he scrambled to shed his formal suit, finally tossing his underwear aside to free his desperate manhood.

But he hesitated a moment before climbing onto the bed with her. "Are you going to be okay? You've seen my size, and you're a virgin."

Lily moaned and waved her ass hypnotically. "We might be thinking of different things when it comes to that, my love. I've been saving myself for you so I've never been with a *man*. But you know I've been with other bunny girls and plant girls and slime girls and any other girls I can find."

She giggled. "And then there's toys . . . what bunny girl doesn't love a good carrot? And since I've been saving myself for a storybook romance I've had to relieve my needs with some *very* large carrots."

He groaned at the mental image. He'd been wanting to give her the romantic first time she was asking for. To kiss her tenderly, caress her, get her excited. Taste her sweet sex and bring her to climax with his lips and tongue, then climb on top of her and push into her while looking lovingly into her eyes.

Everything he could to do make it perfect for her.

But as he stared at his bunny girl fiancee's perfect, glistening sex, arousal dripping down her thighs, her love scent's shift to overpowering arousal and desire for him finally hit.

And like she'd warned, it hit him like a boulder falling off a cliff.

With a growl Dare surged forward, pinning her to the bed while she gasped in pleased surprise. He lined himself up with her entrance and pushed inside in one urgent thrust, making her squeal with pleasure. The sheer delight of her tight walls stretching to welcome him in made him groan in relief and mounting need.

He was drowned out by Lily. "Oh goddess yeeesssss!" she cried, jerking her hips back at him as he bottomed out in her tight channel. "Finally! This is everything I ever hoped for with you!"

Dare was sunk deep in the haze of her scent as he withdrew and plunged in again, hard enough to slide her along the covers and make the headboard thump against the wall.

If her love scent accurately represented how horny bunny girls got then it was incredible she'd managed to hold back from jumping him before now. And the fact that with the overwhelming lust in her scent came a complete and unreserved love and trust just made it all the more amazing.

The feelings were incredible, all of his own desire combined with hers. Added to that the pleasure of his ethereally beautiful fiancee's furnace hot, silky tight walls urgently gripping his shaft as he moved inside her was indescribable.

Then her scent spiked again, and he felt not only Lily's lust but also her own pleasure. At that point he was lost.

He grabbed her elbows and pulled her against him so he could drive into her with his full body, her back arching with every wild thrust. Their desperate movements pushed her along the bed until finally she ended up pinned against the wall above the headboard as he slammed into her.

His bunny girl fiancee squealed and squirted on his cock as they both sated the lusts they'd been holding back for so long, while they'd focused on falling in love with each other.

And Dare was glad they had, because sharing an intense experience like this with the woman he loved only made it all the more wondrous.

Even though his wild lover had already come half a dozen times at least, he didn't think it took long for him to feel the first rush of pleasure as he gave one last thrust to pin her against the wall, pressed hard against her cervix, and released inside her welcoming sex as her crushing walls urgently milked him.

Redoubt

The sheer intensity of his orgasm made him dizzy, and he sank fully into the sensations as he emptied his balls in his sexy fiancee.

"Goddeeesssss!" she moaned, trembling as her own climax surged through her. "You don't know how much I want to cancel the Prevent Conception scroll and get pregnant. You realize bunny girls love having babies almost as much as the sex? We want lots of children, as many as we can. Especially with a lifelong mate we love with all our heart."

"Let's make a baby, then," Dare growled, spurting cock pulsing even harder at the thought of his seed taking root in this sex goddess. "Cancel it."

Lily giggled. "And miss out on years of adventures with you? I'm young, I can wait on a large family . . . bunny girls stay fertile practically until we drop dead of old age, so we can have as many babies as we want."

She squirmed against him desperately as she felt him spurt a final time. "You're not done already." It wasn't a question.

And he definitely wasn't. He didn't even pause after just coming, pulling out of her only long enough to toss her onto her back on the bed before climbing atop her again and shoving back into her gushing sex as her long legs wrapped eagerly around him.

She fit him like a glove. She fit him perfectly, and he never wanted to leave her welcoming warmth.

Lily pulled herself up against him with surprising strength, mashing her breasts against his chest and burying her face in his neck, velvety ears tickling his cheek. She was barely even touching the bed as she rolled her hips in time with his thrusts, all of her athletic speed and grace coming into play to make them sync up perfectly.

The entire time she moaned in his ear in a way that seemed intended to drive him wild, especially because her love scent confirmed he was driving *her* wild.

Dare lost himself in the haze of her scent and the passion of their wild lovemaking, lasting longer the second time. Minutes passed as they moved urgently against each other, his cock slamming into her needy pussy again and again while she squealed and squirted on him in rolling orgasms.

Finally he tensed and released in her again, the pleasure every bit as intense as the first time. And even then he stayed hard as she urgently pushed him onto his back, mounted him, and impaled herself on his sensitive cock with a throaty moan that pierced right to his primal brain, further inflaming him.

It was safe to say they fucked like bunnies for hours. Their crazy high libidos and stamina combined with the better part of two months of waiting had left them insatiable, and they definitely went wild sating themselves and each other.

Dare would've thought that with him basically feeling double the urgency, his own need combined with the feelings Lily was sending through her scent, she would be the first to run out of steam. But she kept going as long as he did, if anything getting even more adventurous as she got used to his size, until finally they both collapsed in mutual exhaustion and satisfaction.

After that they could finally hold each other tenderly, caressing sweaty bodies and murmuring loving words.

Lily adjusted her glasses, which had been askew for most of the last few hours, and sighed contentedly as she nuzzled his neck. "That was everything I was hoping my first time would be."

"Oh?" Dare asked, surprised. "What about your storybook romantic first?"

She just smiled blissfully. "Maybe I got some clarity around the twentieth mind shattering climax you gave me. But I realized that those stories are written about human women. They tend to be way less horny than human men, who are way less horny than cunids. So while the romance is all wonderful, I have to accept that as a bunny girl some things are going to be different."

Giggling, she playfully rubbed her velvety white ears over his face. "What about you, my love? Can you accept that your hopeless romantic of a fiancee is also relentlessly horny, and wants nothing more than to have wild sex just like this as often as possible, and also have lots of babies with you?"

He laughed and lovingly ran his hand through the sweaty ringlets of her long, silvery pigtails. "Sounds pretty romantic to me."

"It does, doesn't it?" Lily looked up at him, gray eyes shining. "We found something even more wonderful than a storybook romance." She playfully kissed his neck, then nipped it. "And now I can look forward to playing games where you find me helpless in the forest, and chase me down and pin me and mount me as you sate the wild lust I inspire in you."

Oh hell yes. Dare reached down and played with her fluffy cottontail, voice teasing. "I thought you weren't interested in that sort of thing."

"With strange men, of course not," she said with a laugh. "But I *am* a bunny girl, and you know a part of us enjoys that thrill of feeling like prey to be captured and taken." She nipped his neck again. "As long as it's by the man I love."

He groaned, feeling his limp cock start to swell. "Careful, you might get me going again."

"Is that a promise?" With a carefree laugh his bunny girl fiancee kissed her way down his chest and abs, then finally took him into her mouth and began inexpertly but very enthusiastically trying to get him hard.

Looked as if they weren't done after all.

Whatever she said about being happy to have a bunny girl style romance, Dare still did his best that final time to be as romantic as possible as he made love to her. Everything he'd learned from his other lovers, especially Ireni who always wanted to make love in the purest sense, he used to show his deep feelings for Lily in the tenderest of ways.

When his gentle ministrations finally brought his new fiancee to a more peaceful climax, her soft walls rippling over his lovingly moving shaft, he came inside her a final time and then gathered her into his arms and held her close.

She sighed happily. "Maybe there is something to romantic sex too," she admitted, kissing his shoulder. "We'll have to do lots more practicing to help me decide which is better."

"I'm at your service, my love," Dare said, kissing her ears.

Lily made a contented sound and rested her head on his chest, sounding sleepy. "I'm so glad we'll be able to do this as often as we want. We can finally hold each other without having to worry about getting too horny and acting in haste. We can finally sleep in each other's arms."

She gave a giddy little giggle. "And now I can finally share your bed with all the other wonderful women in our harem. Can finally be with them the way I've longed to, as well. A part of the family with all of you. Our family."

He stroked her back as her breathing deepened and she finally fell asleep in his arms, basking in the wonder of being with this incredible woman.

"Our family," he murmured as he drifted off himself, sinking into heavenly dreams of Lily, suffused in her scent.

* * * * *

The next morning Dare woke to the glorious sensation of his new fiancee's warm mouth wrapped around his cock, sucking him gently.

That blew away the last of his fog of sleep, and with a rush the urgent need of her love scent filled him. Not as powerfully as last night, thankfully; he wasn't sure he could handle that sort of intensity all the time.

But she was definitely ready for more.

For the next hour they coupled with just as much passion as they had the night before. Then they headed to the bath room to clean up, and at Lily's insistence he showed her how he gave Pella baths. He was more than happy to run soapy hands over his new fiancee's perfect body while she moaned in enjoyment, and enjoyed it just as much when she returned the favor.

Redoubt

They ended up fucking again. Twice.

Finally, though, closer to midmorning than dawn, they gathered up their things, returned the room keys, and headed down to the common room for breakfast, walking with their arms around each other as if they couldn't bear to be apart for a second.

Dare was ravenous, tearing through two full plates of bacon, eggs, ham, hash browns, and buttered toast. Meanwhile Lily eagerly cleared four plates of salad with more than her usual enthusiasm.

The plan had been to turn north when they reached Jarn's Holdout, finally making for Redoubt. But he was feeling more optimistic about his chances of finding a party rated monster after the amazing night and morning he'd just had, and wanted to take every opportunity.

"What would you say about exploring the mountains west of Jarn's Holdout today?" he asked.

She blinked. "I thought we were going to head north, search for party rated monsters in the wilds between here and Redoubt. Going farther west will add that much longer to our trip, and we might not get there in time if there are more winter storms."

He looked around and leaned closer, lowering his voice. "We can set the Home Ward here, just outside of town. As long as we set a quicker pace for the next few days."

Lily beamed. "Okay, let's do it! Maybe we'll find another dungeon too, or more ruins. Or a clearing with an ancient and benevolent being like Lady Rosaceae."

Dare loved that she shared his sense of adventure. That she wanted to experience the wonders of Collisa with him. He loved her, everything about her.

Standing, he moved around to her side of the table and dropped to his knees, kissing her tenderly. "I love you," he murmured, ignoring the stares and whispers from the light morning crowd and serving girls.

His bunny girl fiancee blushed. "What brought that on?"

"Just being struck again by how incredible you are." He grinned.

"So you should expect lots more kisses from now on."

She giggled. "I'll hold you to that."

They set out, running as fast as was seemly on the narrow streets of Jarn's Holdout. A minute or so west of town Dare bound the Home Ward, then with a giggle Lily took off, shouting back at him to try to catch up.

The snow was a few inches deeper after yesterday's storm, the landscape breathtakingly pristine and the air clean and cold. Running across undisturbed snow after his fiancee, it was easy to believe they were the only people in the world.

Lily seemed determined to test that assertion, because after a half hour or so of playing tag in the foothills she tackled him into the snow, then boldly freed his cock. He shivered as the cold hit it, but before it could shrink in response she determinedly jacked him to hardness with her soft, warm hands.

"My pussy's been greedy," she said, grinning at him. "I want to taste you this time."

She dove onto his shaft, taking him in far enough his tip pushed against the back of her throat, making her gag. But she kept on determinedly, trying to get him into her throat and then when she achieved it making a triumphant noise and struggling to push him even deeper.

The sexy bunny girl was inexperienced, but her eager enthusiasm soon had him pumping his seed down her throat, then into her mouth as she pulled back. She eagerly swallowed it all, and when she finally pulled her mouth off his softening cock she gave him a satisfied smile.

"I really like that," she said. "I hope you won't mind if I taste you lots more times."

Dare groaned in bliss as he put his damp cock away before the frigid air could freeze it. "We won't get very far at this rate."

Lily giggled. "But we'll definitely enjoy the journey."

In spite of their joking they got down to business after that, clearing a few ideal spawn points and running up valleys and along ridges. The mountains grew less steep and more rolling the farther west they went, towards where they finally dropped into hills and then disappeared entirely at Bastion's western border.

They didn't find any party rated monsters, to his disappointment. But they did find a beautiful little valley, growing green in the midst of the snow, with a little spring trickling out of the mountainside and forming a babbling brook that flowed through the midst of it.

"Oh!" his fiancee exclaimed. "This valley is blessed by Geresa, Spring Maiden. Lady Rosaceae's mother." She caught his hand and tugged it. "Let's rest and eat lunch here! It'll be safe and the air will rejuvenate us. And I'm certain the spring is blessed."

Even if Dare had been inclined to disagree, one deep breath taking in the sweet, fresh, unaccountably warm air of the valley decided it. He took her hand, and they made their way to a patch of soft moss near the spring that seemed made to be a picnicking area.

To his amusement Lily dug the remaining rose petals out of a piece of oilcloth and began contentedly munching on them. He pulled out some dried meat for himself and got to chewing, washing it down with water from the stream.

Her words about the blessed water seemed true, because with each sip he felt more refreshed and energized. Almost to the point he could feel his hair growing faster, there was just that sense of vitality flowing through him.

He didn't see any status effects from it, like some food he could cook that gave short term buffs. But damn did it taste good.

His bunny girl fiancee seemed to have realized the same, because she kept going back for more. Then he had to laugh when she dunked her head directly into the water pooling beneath the spring and just drank deep, cute little butt waving back and forth and fluffy cottontail twitching in enjoyment.

If it had been later in the day Dare would've been tempted to set up camp in this peaceful valley, where their rest would've surely been safe and blissful. But it was too early in the day, and lounging in soft moss drinking enchanted water wasn't going to find them a party rated monster.

So when Lily finally came up for air she found him up and ready to go. "Ready to move on?" he asked.

She looked disappointed at that, but was too energized and in a good mood to protest. She happily shrugged back into her pack, and as they left the valley behind practically skipped at his side.

At least until she took off like an arrow, calling playfully for him to catch up.

He wasn't sure how she could run like that after filling her belly with spring water; she had to be sloshing like a water skin. He knew he sure felt heavy from just having eaten and drank his fill as he struggled to keep up.

Although eventually the bunny girl fell back to rejoin him as they approached a spawn point. A quick look at the monsters inside showed they were Level 12, too low for either of them, so they ran on, scaling a slope.

About an hour after leaving the valley Dare became aware of Lily squirming in discomfort, and couldn't help but grin as he drew the obvious conclusion. "Drank too much blessed water?"

She blushed. "I need to pee," she admitted. Then, eyes lighting up with sudden mischief, she began shimmying her leather leggings and pants down around her knees right there. "Want to watch?" As she made the offer her milky pale cheeks blushed pink.

He stared, entranced by her shapely thighs and plump labia, and nodded like an idiot.

Giggling, the sexy bunny girl eagerly squatted, positioning herself to give him a good view. She gave him a sultry look, bit her lip, and reached down to part her petals with one hand, revealing her glistening pink interior.

Then with a moan of relief she let loose, a thick stream of urine gushing forth to dig into the snow between her feet. The view was soon partially obscured by steam, and Dare stepped closer, feeling his cock stiffen eagerly at the naughty sight.

Most of his other fiancees weren't shy around him, especially

Pella, but Lily was the first one who'd outright invited him to watch. It was more erotic than he'd expected, probably because she was doing her best to get that response from him.

And it was obvious the bunny girl was just as turned on by him watching as he was by seeing the thick stream flowing from between her plump lips. Her blush deepened to a flush of arousal, her breaths quickened, and her eyes watched him hungrily.

When the stream finally slowed to a trickle, joining her arousal to form dewy droplets on her petals, she shook a couple times. But instead of pulling up her pants she scurried a few feet to one side of the yellow snow and twisted around onto her hands and knees, presenting her shapely ass with her adorable little white cottontail twitching eagerly.

"Take me, my love," Lily panted, craning her neck to peer back at him over her shoulder with bedroom eyes. "When I see you looking at me like that I need you inside me."

Dare wasted no time freeing his cock to the cold air. He dropped to his knees behind her, plunging into her steaming depths with a groan of pleasure.

In spite of the cold he was sweating within minutes as he slammed into her tight pussy, grabbing her lush hips to pull her back into him. She squealed and moved against him eagerly, rising and lowering on her arms to change his angle of penetration so he could hit the spots she wanted.

At that point the bunny girl's love scent shifted to show her raw desire, and as it washed over Dare he moved with new intensity. He also let go of her hips and grabbed her long pigtails instead, pulling her up and back against him as he jackhammered into her.

She went nuts, throwing herself back on his plunging shaft in pure delight as her arousal dripped onto the snow, melting it between her knees. It didn't take long before she squealed and squirted in a series of shuddering climaxes once, twice, then three times.

With the third one she reached a new peak of pleasure, soft walls clamping down urgently as her arousal flooded him yet again.

That was it for Dare. He groaned and pushed in to press against her core, releasing inside her in powerful surges of pleasure as her pussy eagerly milked him.

They knelt joined together in the snow for a minute or two as they came down from their shared orgasm, panting as the cold air cooled the sweat on their exposed skin. Then with a giggle Lily pulled herself off his cock, with effort tugged her pants up her sweaty thighs and tied them again, and bounced to her feet.

"Okay, let's keep going."

Dare put away his well satisfied cock and followed, grinning; he was going to have his hands full with this little sexpot.

And she was going to have a ton of fun with their other fiancees.

In spite of the day's fun, the most they accomplished was finding some good spawn points to clear. They found no party rated monsters, no dungeons or ruins or ancient wonders. Although the Spring Maiden's valley had been wonderful and he'd like to return some day.

As the sun sank below the horizon they reluctantly agreed to call it a day. Dare dropped crosslegged on the ground, Lily settling into his lap, and they cuddled as he activated Home Ward Bound.

At least they'd be able to spend the night at the Sally Fourth in Jarn's Holdout again, which was definitely a more welcome thought than camping in the cold. And he anticipated an exciting time with his new fiancee as they made the most of having a comfortable bed.

Still his heart was a bit heavy as he and his fiancee went ethereal and zoomed away, whipping through mountains at times and flying over valleys at others.

They were out of time. Their path would have to be north, and at a hard pace, to reach Redoubt in time.

In spite of Dare's best efforts it looked as if he'd be petitioning for knighthood without the Protector of Bastion achievement.

Chapter Seven
Arrival

Two days later they finished circling Lake Amsvartnir in the center of Bastion and started directly for Redoubt.

They'd gone the other way around than the road leading from Jarn's Holdout to the region's capitol, which took them deep into an area that remained untamed in spite of the rush of settlers Bastion had enjoyed. The spawn points here had originally been super high level, and only with towns springing up all around the area and adventurers persistently farming them down had they slowly dropped.

Even so, some of them were as high as Level 40.

This was where Ollivan had been farming when Dare and Thorn had gotten him killed to monsters. A well known place where high level adventurers from the capitol, especially nobility who jealously guarded information about monster levels and abilities, came to farm.

While Dare and Lily had gotten the chance to clear some good spawn points as they passed through the area, he had little hope that they'd find a party rated monster here that hadn't already been hunted down. And from here the land would just get more and more settled.

It had been a scant hope that they'd find what they were looking for going through the center of Bastion, and he was becoming more and more resigned to the fact that in spite of his best efforts, he'd failed.

They stopped for lunch at the top of a tall hill, which commanded an excellent view of the majestic landscape around them. The lake to the south, plains to the north, a forest to the east that might connect to Lady Rosaceae's woods, and rolling hills to the west. All blanketed in snow.

Such sights never failed to fill Dare with awe, but even this view couldn't lift his heavy spirits as he munched on dried meat and trail rations, Lily cuddled up to his side nuzzling him in between bites of her foraged greens.

"Three days left," he murmured, staring into the distance.

She nodded, kissing his neck. Her love scent had a urgent spike to it, as she had most of the times they stopped. Which made for exciting nights, adventurous mornings, and amorous lunch breaks. Not to mention more than a few sudden bouts of passion during the day; honeymoon periods with bunny girls were intense.

"Still time," she said as she chomped a mouthful of tender pine needles.

Dare shook his head with a sigh. "We're only a day or so away from Redoubt if we push. And the closer we get to the city the more certain we won't find any party rated monsters. Or even spawn points high enough level for you to farm, let alone me."

She kissed his neck again, love scent shifting to tenderness and commiseration. "It feels like a waste of time, if we can't find it."

"It is." He grit his teeth, looking out at the breathtaking beauty around them. "I could possibly be Level 40 by now if I hadn't spent so much of my time running around searching. At least 39. Instead I probably won't even get 38 by the time we reach Redoubt." He rubbed her shoulder. "And if we hadn't been running around everywhere we could've gotten you to Level 26 by now, easy. Probably even 27."

His bunny girl fiancee pulled a pigtail out of the way and slipped into his lap, also staring out at the landscape. "This is one of the wildest spots in Central Bastion," she said. "We could search more here."

"We could, but if I'm not going to find the last monster here then I might as well spend that time in Redoubt, preparing to petition for knighthood."

She gave him a stubborn look. "The Outsider wouldn't have

given you a challenge to kill those monsters and turn your efforts away from leveling if it was just going to be a waste of time."

Dare chuckled. "It was Ireni, bless her heart, who issued the challenge. And I don't regret trying . . . we found a lot of neat things because of my search, like the dwarven ruins. And it made the last couple months fun."

Lily looked out at the landscape again, then pointed almost due westward. "That hill, way in the distance. Let's split up and both search on our own as we make for it. When we meet up we can find a new landmark and split up again."

That was a good idea. Not the sort of tactic he would've wanted to do the entire time, since it meant she wouldn't have been able to identify spawn points she could clear for experience, and he wouldn't have been able to keep the monsters away from her as she fought them. Not to mention that in the mountains, with so many roaming monsters and animal predators of wildly random levels, splitting up to search separately could've gotten her killed.

"All right," he said, taking his own turn to kiss her neck and savoring the clean scent of sweat on her skin, subtly layered with her ever-present love scent. "We'll hold onto hope for a bit longer."

Her love scent spiked with arousal again. Not nearly as urgent and overwhelming as their first time, but enough to make his heart beat faster and his cock begin to stir. "I think I know a way you can thank me for the idea," she murmured teasingly, shifting to straddle him so her sex was pressed against his erection.

Dare checked the pocket on his pack where he kept the scrolls Zuri made for him, chuckling at what he found. He'd laughed when his goblin fiancee insisted on giving him plenty of Prevent Conception scrolls, joking he'd be too busy scouting to get busy.

He'd been proven the fool there, since they only had four left. Hopefully Ireni had thought to bring more with her, otherwise his honeymoon period with Lily was going to get a lot less exciting.

After some intense fucking surrounded by the beauty of Bastion all around them, they exchanged a fierce kiss before splitting up for their individual searches. He didn't have much hope of success, but the thought of his determined fiancee out there, searching with all her heart to help him achieve his goal, spurred him to keep up his own efforts.

He didn't find anything, of course. But not for lack of trying.

Dare reached the hill first and got to work clearing a Level 30 spawn point to pass the time. He was a bit surprised his bunny girl fiancee hadn't made it here before him with her greater speed, and felt a bit guilty at the thought she had put in more effort than he had searching for his sake.

He also felt a faint concern that something had happened to her. He knew she could handle herself and was more than fast enough to escape any threat, but things could always go wrong and he worried even so.

To his relief Lily bounded into view going crazy speeds for the snowy environment, easily 40 miles an hour, at around the time he finished looting the last monster from the spawn point he'd cleared. Her expression was excited, but his faint stirring of hope didn't blossom into full blown excitement until she skidded to a graceful stop in a spray of snow and shouted, "I think I found one!"

Dare laughed and pulled her into a fierce kiss, heart soaring. "You're a lifesaver," he said.

Her love sent lapped over him warmly as she beamed at him, pulling back to tug insistently on his hand. "Come on, I'll show you."

She sped off again, and with a laugh he activated Cheetah's Dash and did his best to keep up. At one point he tripped and rolled crazily across the snow, losing his bow and a few things from his pack, but he only laughed again as he gathered it all up and kept going.

It only took a few minutes to reach a muddy hollow where a stream had made a deep cut through a hill. Within that cut shambled a hideous, bulbous figure that was over eight feet tall and probably nearly that wide. A nightmarish monstrosity of rotting gray flesh and dried parchment skin sewn together in ragged patches.

Lily bounced up and down eagerly, although he noticed her face twisted in revulsion whenever she looked at the monster. "It's party rated, right? It's too hideous to be a normal monster, even a roamer."

Dare checked it with his Adventurer's Eye and let out a whoop of victory. "Flesh Golem. Monster, Party Rated. Level 28. Attacks: Blade Punch, Toxic Miasma, Horrifying Presence, No Vitals, Unstoppable, Gore Spray, Etheric Eruption."

The details were as hideous as the rest of the Flesh Golem, but that didn't dampen his excitement at all. He was sure he could take this thing, since it was slow. But it also seemed to be an arrow sink that would take time to kill, and had some worrying ranged abilities.

"What does it look like?" Lily asked eagerly. "Can we kill it?"

He blinked, looking at her. He realized he'd done her a disservice by not even considering asking for her help, especially after everything he'd told her about being his adventuring companion.

She was only a few levels lower than the Flesh Golem, she knew what she was doing, and she was quick enough, both physically and mentally, to stay out of trouble. Also she had Entangler.

"We can kill it," he said, wrapping an arm around her shoulders.

He quickly described its abilities, then spent more than a little time planning their strategy and giving advice on the fight. Even though his bunny girl fiancee had been with him for killing two other party rated monsters, he'd had her stay out of the fight due to her low level and relative inexperience.

And, he could admit, the simple fact that he hadn't known what she was able to do and didn't want to put her in a situation over her head.

But now Dare had a better idea of her capabilities, and she'd impressed him over the week. He had full confidence in her.

Although that didn't mean he didn't worry. Especially with her combat subclass's 75% health pool and reduced stats. So before he pulled the Flesh Golem he reached into his belt pouch and withdrew one of his more valuable items.

"Here," he said, pressing the healing potion into her hands. "In case of an emergency." That was word for word what Zuri, Pella, and Leilanna had told him when they insisted he take it with him, back when they convinced him to start leveling by himself.

Lily's eyes widened. "This is a drop!" she exclaimed. "Comparable to a potion made by a Level 50 Alchemist."

Dare nodded. "We got it from the Glittering Caves dungeon."

"It's worth hundreds of gold," she said quietly. "Healing effects outside of healing classes are rare."

He grinned and trailed his fingers through one of her silvery pigtails, then leaned in and kissed her forehead. "Right, so be extra careful in this fight so you don't have to use it. Remember you can use Vine Lash to get away, and it's better to run and come back than to take a hit or get caught by this thing."

Sobering, he rested his hands on her shoulders and looked deep into her eyes. "I trust you, my love. If one of us has to take a hit, let it be the higher level one."

His beautiful fiancee's love scent spiked sharply, a powerful wave of fondness followed quickly by intense desire. He had to focus to push aside the urge to pull her down to the ground and make love to her right then.

Instead he invited her to his party, waiting for her to accept, then activated Rapid Shot to put four arrows into his bow hand and nocked another to the string. "Ready?"

She nodded, ethereally lovely features set in determination, and fitted an arrow to Entangler's bowstring. She moved to her position a safe distance away, so they wouldn't both be hit by area of effect attacks, and nodded again.

Dare flooded fire mana into a Burst Arrow. He assumed the Flesh Golem's Unstoppable ability meant it was immune to crowd control, so trying to snare or stun it would be a waste. Likewise, its No Vitals likely meant that he wouldn't get any critical hits, so he aimed for center mass on the very, very slight chance he might miss a target that large.

Redoubt

With a last glance at his betrothed, he took a breath. "Draw. Loose." He followed his words and shot a unstably burning fire arrow at the Flesh Golem, Lily's hitting only inches from his a moment later, and the battle began.

The arrow impacts caused puffs of foul gasses to erupt from the undead monstrosity, permeating the area for several feet in all directions. Harmless for them as they backed away from their lumbering foe, loosing arrow after arrow.

Although melee would definitely have trouble getting close to this thing. Yet another time Dare was glad he'd chosen a ranged class.

The Flesh Golem opened its misshapen mouth several times wider than any normal mouth should be able to gape, revealing rows of hideous rotted teeth that had to have come from several larger predator animals. It contorted, and then a spray of filth so deep red it was almost black shot towards Lily.

She was already gone, flying twenty feet to the side in a single effortless bound with a flick of her white cottontail. Even more impressively, she only took a moment to make sure the danger was past before continuing to loose arrows.

The monster kept up its Gore Spray as it continued lumbering towards them, shifting the firehose flow to target Dare instead.

He activated Cheetah's Dash and stayed ahead of it, using Rapid Shot as it came off cooldown to shoot four more arrows in quick succession. The Flesh Golem's health was chunking down rapidly, as expected giving his withering onslaught.

Although he was impressed by how much damage Lily was managing; she hadn't wasted even a fraction of a second since the battle began.

For all the monster's hideous appearance and awful attacks, the fight was one of the smoothest Dare had ever experienced as they continued to pepper it with arrows. Until finally it froze in place, shuddering violently as its flesh bulged and roiled from inner pressure, making alarming rumbling noises.

Etheric Eruption. Fuck.

"Take cover!" Dare shouted. He looked around and desperately used Roll and Shoot to cover the distance to a small dip in the ground, flattening himself inside it and pulling his cloak around to cover him.

Moments later the ground beneath him quaked violently, throwing him up a couple inches. He heard the disgusting sound of liquid splattering, as well as the dull thuds of fragments of bone shrapnel peppering everything.

But he didn't feel any pain from impacts, or even the sensation of gore splashing on him. A few seconds later everything went quiet, and he risked standing to view the nightmarish blood-soaked terrain around him.

Text appeared in the corner of Dare's vision. "Party rated monster Flesh Golem defeated. 18,000 bonus experience awarded."

"Trophies gained: Rusted Blade Hand x2, Reanimation Philter Fragments. Loot body to acquire."

"Completed 10/10 towards Achievement Protector of Bastion: Slay 10 party rated monsters in the region of Bastion."

"Quest objective completed: Playful Challenge. Kill 5 party rated monsters before the end of the year. High Priestess Ireni of the Outsider will be pleased to hear of your success."

Then much bolder text, accompanied by the triumphant sound similar to the victory cry of an army that he heard when he leveled up. "**Congratulations, Protector of Bastion! Title added to the list of public accolades you may claim. 100,000 bonus experience awarded. All who view you will know your selfless service and sacrifice to keep the frontier safe for settlers.**"

Then beneath it came the less in his face text of a normal notification. "Completed 10/100 towards Achievement Champion of Bastion: Slay 100 party rated monsters in the region of Bastion."

Dare couldn't help but chuckle ruefully at that; there was always a higher honor to achieve. Or, if this had been a game, another goal to keep him pushing to greater heights.

Then again, he supposed that applied to real life as well.

He was nearly tackled as Lily threw herself at him, wrapping her arms and legs around him and peppering his face with kisses. He was relieved to see she looked unharmed by the monster's final revenge.

"You're a Protector of Bastion!" she squealed. "I can see it on your information screen now!"

That information screen was usually blank of anything but a person's level, so this achievement was a big deal.

Dare couldn't help but grin like an idiot as he wrapped an arm around her back and another under her ass to support her, returning her fierce kiss. "All thanks to you. You not only encouraged me to keep going and found the monster but also kicked its ass."

The bunny girl giggled, rubbing her nose against his. "You're just saying that. You did all the damage."

He shook his head solemnly. "You handled that fight perfectly. Not a single moment wasted from doing damage, using all your abilities the moment they were off cooldown, and when you had to dodge an attack you got right back into the fight."

He kissed her softly and smiled. "You know how many people have been that good in the parties and raids I've been in? A fraction. You've not only got the heart of an adventurer but the mind and the nerves of one."

Lily's cheeks flushed in a furious blush, and she bit her lip as she shifted position until her crotch was pressed against his, undulating her hips urgently. "If you're going to say things like that, I'm going to need you to pin me down and channel this victory into a wild celebratory fuck."

She giggled as she felt him swiftly harden against her, lifting herself to press her leather-clad breasts against his face. "To the victor goes the spoils."

Dare looked around at their macabre surroundings and picked his way to where the snow was clean, well out of view of the dead monster and the charnel field it had created. They could come back to loot it later.

The entire time he looked for a more suitable spot his gorgeous bunny girl companion insistently showered him with kisses, grinding her luscious body against him while whimpering with need. Not to mention her love scent spiking wildly, driving him into a fog of desire.

He eagerly shrugged out of his cloak, laying it flat on the ground before lowering her onto it and tearing at her clothes.

* * * * *

Looting the Flesh Golem was disgusting but fairly straightforward, since the loot was just sitting there on the bloody field.

Along with the trophies the monster dropped a hundred or so gold, go figure, and some disgusting reagents that he hoped weren't intended to be used for anything meant to be consumed or applied topically. There were also a few enchanting materials, although he wondered what sort of enchantments they'd provide.

Needless to say, they made liberal use of Zuri's Cleanse Target scrolls to wash everything, and themselves.

Once that was done Dare was eager to get back to work. Completing his months long goal energized him more than he'd believed possible, and with Redoubt just a good run away at the fastest pace he decided to achieve other goals.

Lily was close to Level 26, and the flood of experience he'd just gotten from killing the Flesh Golem, and especially the Protector of Bastion achievement, had pushed him tantalizingly close to Level 38. So he suggested they stick around for the rest of the day, and maybe the next one as well, and try to get those levels.

Getting her Level 26 was easy enough, since most of the monsters were higher level and gave more experience when she killed them. At which point she firmly insisted he stop worrying about helping her and focus on his own experience.

It was a good thing he did.

Redoubt

That last chunk of experience he needed stretched on interminably as he rushed from spawn point to spawn point, massacring monsters by the dozens. Even with his efforts speeded by his bunny girl fiancee insisting on serving as squire, staying back to gather the loot so he could continue on, he realized he was looking at days.

They kept farming right until full dark, then he used Snap and Strobe Arrow to see by so he could finish off the final few monsters in the spawn point they were clearing.

After that they lit a fire and set up their tent, eating from their few remaining provisions before collapsing together beneath the blankets. Even as tired as Lily was, though, she insistently mounted him and rode his cock to a few eager climaxes before he spurted inside her and they fell asleep cuddling contentedly.

The next day they hit all the previous spawn points, then Lily went scouting for more while Dare finished up the final one. She led him with few pauses from one to the next, sprinting full speed in short bursts, and the frenzy of experience farming continued.

Even so, the sun had sunk below the horizon before he finally got the glorious notification that he'd reached Level 38.

The level had a few humble gains. He could put another point into Bows, and also into Snap to slightly increase the brightness and duration. Although the pleasant surprise was that Roll and Shoot got a new rank he could put a point into, increasing the distance he could move with it from 10 feet to 12.

Unsurprisingly at this point, his bunny girl fiancee wanted to celebrate his level. Which they ended up doing for over three hours into the night, then a few more hours the next morning.

Then, out of provisions and eager for the trip to be over, they ran at a hard pace for Redoubt.

Dare was eager to see Marona, Ireni, and Leilanna. He wanted to share the good news of his engagement to Lily, and she was equally excited to share the news, and finally be fully included in the family and their shared intimacy.

Phoenix

She'd also spent the last night further inflaming his desire by talking about all the things she wanted to do with her fellow fiancees, and the mature baroness, too.

Between the snow and the cold they couldn't manage the highest speeds they were capable of, but he was still proud of the fact that they came in view of the walls of Redoubt in the early afternoon.

It was the 29th of Pol, which meant he'd managed to get the achievement and reach the city with over a day to spare.

Lily looked awed as she took in the high walls rising proudly out of the plains in the distance, straddling a gleaming silver ribbon of water. "You were on your way here when I met you," she said. "What's Redoubt like?"

Dare grimaced. "It's a cramped warren of streets for the most part. The market's pretty nice, definitely worth visiting. The nobles district is about as fancy as you'd expect, but I didn't spend much time there." He shook his head grimly. "I'll admit, my last visit here I spent most of my time in the slums and the red light district."

"Red light district?" she asked with adorable innocence.

He grinned at her. "Where you can go to buy sex. Or sell it I guess. Also there was a tavern I visited where women got tossed coins to dance on a stage and take off their clothes."

"Ohhhhh." His fiancee adjusted her glasses, blushing a bit. "I've read about that a bit in romances. Sometimes the handsome lord is a bit of a rascal who needs to be civilized by the chaste young woman, although usually she looks down her nose at him before getting to know him."

She raised an eyebrow at him, smiling. "Are you a rascal who needs to be civilized?"

Dare laughed. "I guess you could ask the women I've fucked in pretty much every village, town, and city I've visited. And out in the wilds."

The bunny girl giggled. "Can we visit that tavern? Now you've got me curious."

He slipped an arm around her waist. "As long as you don't hop up on the crate yourself," he teased.

She gave him a look of mock outrage. "Of course not. I only want the man I love to see me. And all the women I share him with, of course." She hesitated. "Or if I'm in the woods by myself, or go back home to my warren."

After a few moments she waggled her eyebrows at him. "Although if there's a place where I could watch *you* dance and take off your clothes . . ."

"Hey if that's what you want, when we get a room tonight I'll give it a shot and do my best not to look ridiculous," Dare said, leaning in to kiss her velvety ears.

Lily playfully slapped his ass. "I'll hold you to that."

As they approached the south gate he recognized one of the guards from his night in the Crate gathering information about Ollivan, the grizzled veteran. The man obviously didn't recognize him in turn, which was no surprise considering Dare had been in disguise.

Also he'd been 5 levels lower. Which meant even if he looked exactly the same, some people might assume he was a twin or doppelganger of the person they'd met.

"Here for the festivities?" the guard asked with a polite salute. He paused, then blinked and bowed with more genuine respect. "Protector."

Looked as if the new title from Dare's achievement wasn't just window dressing. "I am," he said, offering his hand. "I imagine the city's been bursting at the seams the last few weeks, eh Macor?"

The veteran jumped slightly in surprise as he awkwardly returned the handshake. "It has, aye. Your pardon, I didn't realize we'd met before."

"We shared drinks at one point. I've a good head for names and faces." Dare motioned through the gate. "Tell me, do you know if Baroness Marona Arral of Terana has arrived yet?"

"Not that I'm aware, Protector."

Phoenix

Dare frowned; her entourage could've made it here by now at the pace they were going, although the storm probably slowed them. Or it could be Macor just didn't know.

Luckily he'd been privy to Marona's plans and knew the inn she planned to stay at. He withdrew a gold and pressed it into the older man's hand. "If she happens to arrive during your shift, could you let her know Darren of Nirim Manor and his fiancee Lily have arrived and are waiting at the Gilded Chalice?"

"Of course, Protector," the man said, making the coin disappear with commendable alacrity.

"Good man." Dare clapped him on the shoulder. "We'll have to share a drink again soon."

"Of course." Macor said, stepping aside with a polite bow. "Welcome to Redoubt."

Lily slipped her arm through his as they entered the city, although once they were out of earshot of the guards she shivered in obvious delight. "Fiancee," she repeated. "I really like the sound of that."

"I like saying it," Dare admitted with a grin.

She reached up to grip the ring he'd given her, which she'd been wearing around her neck on a chain for safekeeping while they were out in the wilds. Then she slipped it free of the chain and slid it onto her finger, admiring it.

He immediately began watching the people around them far more closely for thieves and pickpockets; much as he loved seeing his engagement ring on his beautiful betrothed's elegant finger, it was a truesilver band set with a huge honking diamond.

It was going to draw the wrong sort of attention.

Maybe it did, but even though the streets were packed with people who must've come for the festivities, apparently nobody wanted to risk such a bold grab on the hand of a Level 26, right next to a Level 38. They were able to walk the bustling streets undisturbed, aside from hails from streetside vendors and beggars.

Their path took them through the market district, and Lily

looked around in eager excitement. While Dare wanted to get to the Gilded Chalice to see if the others had arrived, he took the time to stop by one of the Trash Loot vendors and sell the loot they'd gathered on the trip north.

Especially the stuff from the Flesh Golem; he was glad to get it out of his pack.

He left the bartering up to his fiancee, and was pleased by how well she did. Although her efforts were probably helped by the fact that the man seemed stunned to be talking to a real life bunny girl, and clearly flustered by her otherworldly beauty.

After shaking hands on the deal they continued on to the rich part of the city, where rows of high end shops offered only the best goods, then beyond it to an inn set up just a stone's throw from the governor's palace.

Marona's group hadn't arrived yet so they headed into the common room, which looked more like a fancy restaurant complete with sound dampened booths. In spite of the opulence the place was bustling with customers, likely people who'd come for the Council of Lords and trials for knighthood.

The serving girl who greeted them looked a bit surprised to see customers in their adventuring gear, when all the other patrons were wearing expensive and fashionable clothes. But she curtsied and led them to a booth with a good view of the door, where she served them attentively.

Dare was in the mood to splurge, especially after living on provisions for the last few days, so he ordered a bottle of the wine Lily had liked from back at the Sally Fourth, as well as enough gourmet food to fill them both up.

After the meal they lingered in the booth, finishing off the bottle. After about an hour Dare gave up. "Want to visit the market again and do some shopping?" he asked. "We can come back and check if they've arrived later."

"Mmm." His bunny girl fiancee's cheeks were flushed with a buzz from the wine, and she was affectionately pressed up against his side, rubbing him beneath the table. "Or we could enjoy a long, relaxing bath, then rent a room and take a nap after our tiring run this morning."

That sounded like an even better idea. Dare was about to flag down the serving girl and ask if any rooms were available when there was a commotion at the door, and he saw a matronly woman who seemed to be the Gilded Chalice's proprietor hurrying in that direction to greet new arrivals.

Maids in familiar black and white frilly uniforms were stepping in out of the cold, lugging saddlebags and baggage up the stairs towards the second floor. Dare spotted Belinda and Marigold among them, and Miss Garena coordinating efforts while speaking with the proprietor.

He and Lily were out of the booth and halfway to the door when three women followed the maids in, and his heart soared at the sight of them.

He rushed the remaining distance and threw his arms around Ireni and Leilanna, kissing them both fiercely.

Ireni gave him her million watt smile. "You did it!" she said, hugging him tight. "Protector of Bastion!"

Text appeared in the corner of Dare's vision. "Quest Completed: Playful Challenge. 60,000 experience awarded."

"Thanks to Lily. I couldn't have done it without her." He hugged his fiancees tight again. "I missed you."

Dare was equal parts amused and bemused when, at the mention of the bunny girl, Ireni and Leilanna immediately pounced on her. When they saw his ring on her finger they went nuts, hugging and kissing her and practically spinning her around in circles.

They wasted no time dragging Lily back to the booth, where they put their heads together and whispered fiercely, with frequent giggles and glances in his direction.

Marona, at least, took her time giving him a warm hug and kissing his cheeks. "Congratulations on your engagement," she said, smiling at his glowing new fiancee. "You make a stunning couple."

She paused with a chuckle. "Couples. Family."

"He did *what*?" Leilanna exclaimed excitedly from the booth. The other two girls quickly shushed her, ducking their heads and giggling when he glanced their way.

Dare shook his head with a grin and offered the baroness his elbow. "How was the trip, Marona?"

She grimaced as she accepted it and they started for the booth to join the others. "Long. Uncomfortable. Intolerably delayed by snow. It gets harder on my old bones with every passing year. And the morning sickness has been no picnic."

In spite of that last complaint she smiled happily as she rested a hand on her belly.

He gently rested his hand on hers. "Difficult journey or not, you look beautiful. Motherhood suits you."

Marona smiled contentedly. "Yes, I believe it does."

They joined the others in the booth, and Ireni and Leilanna immediately moved around to either side of him, showering him with the affection they'd skimped on earlier. "Congratulations!" Ireni said, sliding onto his lap so Lily could take her place cuddled against his side. "It sounds like you had a really romantic week."

"Yeah, Lily says you romanced the shit out of each other," Leilanna said with a grin, snuggling up to his other side. "I'm a bit jealous."

Dare felt his cheeks heat and quickly looked around to see if anyone had overheard that. He didn't think anyone had, but surrounded by three gorgeous women he was definitely getting jealous looks.

His redheaded fiancee kissed his neck, then leaned in close to his ear. "By the way, Zuri gave me plenty more scrolls to bring, just in case." Her big green eyes twinkled. "We had a feeling you might need them."

"Yeah," Sia said practically on top of Ireni, a startling shift as she took the fore. "We had a "feeling." Her knowing grin suggested she'd enjoyed the last week too.

Phoenix

He laughed and leaned down to kiss the goddess. "Thanks."

Marona watched it all from her seat beside Lily, a warm smile fighting to escape her stately facade. She cleared her throat gently. "To get to business, after I freshen up I'm going to call in at the Governor's palace and pay my respects to Duke Valiant. There'll likely be some business to handle with the Council of Lords."

She rested a hand on his on the table. "But I'll formally present your petition as well, and sometime tomorrow or the next day you'll be summoned to report to the Lord Judges. They'll want to look over your petition and ask you questions."

Dare felt a surprising bout of nerves, like he did before being called to do public speaking or go in for a job interview. "All right. Any questions I should prepare for?"

The baroness gave him an amused smile. "I couldn't say . . . I'm not a knight." She laughed at his expression. "It'll be all the things we've prepared for, about your finances and history and accomplishment and lineage. Perhaps some probing questions to get a feel for you as a person."

Her expression turned weary. "Honestly I'd rather spend the day sleeping off this awful trip, but the beginning of year festivities are always a flurry of activity. I've been informed that this evening Duke Valiant is hosting guests at his palace for a formal ball, same as he does every year. As members of my entourage, particularly a prospective knight and his consorts, it would be a good idea for all of us to attend. I'll return in time to help us dress and prepare for the event."

She scooted towards the edge of the booth and stood with a soft groan of effort, knuckling her back. "Now I'm going to go get a bath. The bath room here has a proper sunken tub large enough to fit a dozen, and you're all welcome to join me."

After spending most of the last ten days running around and hunting monsters, not to mention how Lily had done her best to wear him out, a bath sounded heavenly. His fiancees all agreed, because they couldn't scramble out of the booth fast enough to follow the baroness.

Chapter Eight
New Position

Large tub or not, only a small portion of the space was used as Dare found himself swarmed as soon as he dipped into the hot water. Soft bodies rubbed against him from all sides, warm and soapy and affectionate.

In spite of her weariness Marona wanted intimacy with him just as much as the others, claiming the spot on his lap. She reclined back against his chest with her head on his shoulder, cheeks flushed from the heat and breathing slow and peaceful.

He did his best to massage her sore muscles from that position, and she moaned in appreciation.

It wasn't just his fiancees and Marona, either. Belinda and Marigold were there to "attend" them, the beautiful draconid and adorable gnome stripping down and climbing into the huge tub to properly do the job. Although if he had any doubt about the women's plans, the fact that Belinda cheerfully insisted he use a scroll of Prevent Conception before getting into the tub was a big clue.

Underneath the sudsy surface of the water he wasn't sure who was touching what, but he was definitely sure that before long his erection was sticking up between the baroness's legs, and there were no shortage of hands exploring it. Marona just giggled softly as those hands found her as well, moaning contentedly as they teased her folds.

Although it wouldn't be completely accurate to say that he was the center of attention. Now that he and Lily were engaged all the women seemed fascinated by the beautiful bunny girl's gorgeous body. And if they had any doubts about Lily's horniness being enough for all of them, she proved them wrong as she pounced on Leilanna and pushed her tongue into her mouth in a fierce kiss, grinding against the beautiful dusk elf while playing with her glorious breasts.

At least until Sia took the fore; the petite redhead aggressively claimed the beautiful bunny girl, who was only too happy to return her affections in full. The two women were soon writhing against each other, moaning into each other's mouths as their fingers worked furiously beneath the sudsy water.

That was enough to get everyone else going. Marona was happy to get out and recline on a waterproofed padded bench to rest and watch, while Marigold gave her an expert massage.

That left Leilanna and Belinda to descend on Dare with hungry purpose. The beautiful draconid's green scales shone even more bright and brilliant when they were wet, and were particularly striking as they shimmered with her version of an aroused flush.

Her thick reptilian tail lashed eagerly, frothing the water behind her as she climbed into his lap, grinding her soft pussy against his throbbing shaft while kissing him fiercely.

Then she leaned in close to his ear, slender forked tongue tickling him as she whispered, "I turn 26 today. Ireni tells me where you're from birthdays are celebrated, so you can give me the present of a toe-curling orgasm."

Dare grinned and nuzzled her neck, running his hands over the soft slick scales covering her small breasts and teasing her erect little nipples. "Happy Birthday. Let's make it a special one."

"Oh, I plan to." The sexy dragon girl rose up and impaled herself on his shaft with a husky moan, soft pink walls clamping down on him.

Meanwhile Leilanna hugged Belinda from behind, running her hands over the dragon girl's beautiful scales while passionately kissing her neck. Once the dusk elf got hold of the other woman's clit the maid didn't last long, and with a moan began climaxing hard on his cock, sinking into his embrace.

Lily had been taking *very* good care of him ever since their engagement, taking the edge off his horniness. But in his excitement

Redoubt

at watching the beautiful women all around him playing with each other, and his eagerness to join in, he didn't hold back as he felt his balls churn.

He grabbed her round ass with both hands, pulled her down on his shaft until his tip pressed hard against her core, and with a groan powerfully released inside her.

The maid sighed in satisfaction, kissed his neck, and brushed her lips against his ear, again tickling him with her tongue. "Dragons are covetous," she murmured, grinding her hips against his spurting cock. "On my next birthday I claim you again, lover."

That was a tradition Dare could definitely get behind.

Birthday or no, Leilanna barely gave him time to finish inside Belinda before impatiently pulling her off him and taking her place. His dusk elf fiancee buried his face between her large breasts as she lowered herself onto his shaft with a whimper, tight walls clamping down on him with unexpected urgency.

"Finally," she moaned. "I've been missing this."

Dare ran his hands over her curvy body, luxuriating in her silky soft, ash gray skin as he sank into the heavenly valley between her boobs. Her soft tunnel welcomed him eagerly, and he was soon thrusting his hips back up into her as they shared their pleasure.

Lily gave a familiar cry of rapture as she orgasmed to Sia's fingers, and a moment later the goddess also cried out in pleasure. Dare started to free his face from Leilanna's breasts to look, but she stubbornly grabbed his head and pushed him back in.

"Uh uh, my betrothed," she panted. "Lily had you for a week and a half. You're mine right now."

"All right then," Dare growled. He pulled her down to bottom out in her rippling tunnel, and held her tight against him as he stood and turned, setting her on the edge of the tub. The beautiful dusk elf reclined back, pulling him with her as he began driving powerfully into the bliss of her pussy.

"Yessss," she moaned. "Take me, Dare. Show me how you railed our new bunny girl lover!"

Phoenix

He moved faster, giving in to the pleasure. When Leilanna finally clamped her thick legs around him with a squeal, squirting on his cock as her tight walls massaged him, he blissfully released inside her.

When he came up for air, so to speak, Marona was leaning over him to kiss him softly. "I need to go, my paramour," she murmured. "Belinda, attend me."

The draconid maid climbed out of the tub, green scales glistening brilliantly, and helped the baroness dry off and dress. Dare glanced over at Sia and Lily, ready to join in their fun, but to his surprise Marigold stepped up to the edge of the tub and quietly wrapped her arms and legs around him, hugging her plump little naked body against his chest.

He thought she was ready for her turn, but she looked up at him with a solemn expression that was uncharacteristic for the normally playful gnome. "I need to talk to you," she murmured quietly.

He blinked. "Oh, okay." He suddenly realized that the other women had gathered around to listen, even Marona pausing her preparations to leave. Lily looked as confused as he was, but everyone else seemed to know what was going on.

Uh oh.

The tiny gnome held his gaze. "I have good news and bad news," she said. "Which do you want to hear first?"

There was only one logical assumption Dare could leap to here. He bit back a sigh. "Bad news?"

Relying on him to hold her, she took one of his hands and pressed it to her soft tummy, still holding his gaze. "I'm pregnant."

There it was. Lily gave a surprised squeak, and he looked over to see that she seemed excited by the news but unsure how she was supposed to act. The other women were grinning expectantly, obviously waiting for his reaction.

He fought to keep the conflicting expressions off his face; whatever he might feel about this news, he knew Marigold had shown little desire for a more serious relationship with him and had outright stated she wasn't ready for children.

"And the good news?" he asked carefully.

"That it's yours, duh." She glared up at him with her big blue eyes. "Maybe we messed up with a Prevent Conception scroll when we were together, but I think it's thanks to your stupidly fertile cock, so just rubbing my pussy against the tip that one time was enough."

"Sorry," he said with a wince.

Marigold sighed. "Meh, you tried to stop me as quick as you could. I'm the idiot who got so horny I ignored your fertility and started riding you anyway."

Dare gave her a wary smile. "Well, I'm glad you consider that it's mine good news."

"If I'm going to have a baby, I definitely want it to be with you." The other women sighed at that, and he felt a bit awkward about having this conversation with an audience. Although he supposed they were all part of this too in one way or another.

The tiny gnome absently lifted his hand to kiss his knuckles. "When I missed my maiden's flow I went to the Baroness, and she had the healer who's tending her with her pregnancy confirm my condition."

Marona nodded in confirmation of that.

The pink-haired maid looked at her, got another nod from the noblewoman, then looked back at Dare solemnly. "Our Lady gave me two options. Stay employed with her and work as well as I'm able while tending the baby, and she'd give me what assistance she could, or talk to you about moving to your manor."

Lily squealed excitedly at that, while he saw Sia and Leilanna both grinning; they obviously weren't opposed to the idea.

Still, he was surprised given Marigold's previous stance. "You want to be with me?"

She grinned. "Every day. I want you to hire me as your Head Maid." Her smile became her more usual naughty expression. "And of course, in my new position it'll be my duty to serve you in whatever way you wish, and make sure *all* your needs are met."

"So when you say Head Maid, you mean a maid who gives head?" Leilanna asked, prompting a storm of giggles.

"Oh hell yes," Marigold replied, smirking at the dusk elf. "And not just to the master of the house . . . I need to attend to the needs of my mistresses as well."

Dare could definitely see the benefits of that sort of arrangement. Although it didn't seem fair to her. "You don't need to work for me. You know I'll take care of you and the baby whatever you choose to do, and I'll be happy to have you with us. So will the others."

Leilanna, Ireni, and Lily all made noises of agreement.

Marigold giggled. "I'm not sure I'm ready for any more serious commitment just yet. I guess you can consider me part of your harem if you want, and I certainly want to have fun with you, as long as I get to serve as your maid. It's what *I* want."

He wasn't sure he understood that, but if it made her happy then he saw no reason not to agree. Marona's maids were the most well trained and professional to be found, and Nirim Manor could certainly use a more formal structure for the servants.

Especially now that they had Johar's family serving them. And the girls had been talking about bringing in a few women from the Avenging Wolves or the new Melarawn village, to help with chores and babysitting as needed.

"All right," Dare said with a smile, tenderly stroking her cheek. "I'd be honored to hire you as Head Maid for Nirim Manor."

"Goody!" the tiny gnome squealed, hugging him tighter and beaming up at him in delight. She shot a triumphant look at Belinda. "How do you like that? I not only get to be his Head Maid but also have his baby."

The draconid girl sniffed. "You realize any of us who got knocked up by him could've done the same. And I bet he'd rather have a beautiful dragonkin baby and a Head Maid who's actually competent."

"Girls," Marona chided firmly.

Redoubt

Dare had to agree that their exchange wasn't exactly romantic. But then again he knew the maids were competitive; even about sleeping with him, according to Marona.

As he was still processing all this news his new Head Maid reached down to play with his cock until it was hard, then wiggled her hips until his tip was pushing between her plump little lips. With a whimper she started to slide down it, her arousal dripping down to provide lubrication for the most crushingly tight pussy he'd ever felt. Even though thanks to the world system that let races of different sizes breed, he slid in easily.

"Speaking of being together," she panted, "now that I'm knocked up you can bury your shaft in me whenever you want. No need to worry about the hassle of Prevent Conception."

Hard to refuse an invitation like that. Grinning, Dare let go so she could control her own movements on him. "How long do gnome pregnancies last, anyway?" he asked as he reached down to where they were joined and rubbed her swollen pearl.

"If it's a-ah!-a gnome, about eleven months." His little lover moaned and squirmed against his fingers as he bottomed out inside her. "Goddess, keep doing that. I've been missing this for months now. I can't wait to move to Nirim Manor, where you can bend me over any surface whenever you want and take me as master of the house."

Oh gods, that was sexy.

The pink-haired gnome tried to lift herself up on him and her soapy legs slipped, making her slide back down with a little squeak. She tried to lift herself up with her arms and slipped again, making a needy plaintive sound. "Can you help your new Head Maid in her duties, Master Dare?"

Marona shook her head wryly, blew him a kiss, and headed out to attend her own duties. Belinda followed her mistress, blowing him a kiss as well and shooting Marigold a jealous look before disappearing through the door.

The other women all gathered around, giggling at the little

Phoenix

maid's plight.

Dare grinned playfully as Marigold continued to squirm, trying to fuck herself on him as she slipped and slid around, stimulating them both but not able to get any sort of rhythm. He had a sudden urge to tease the bold maid. "Are you saying you're not up to serving the master of the house like a good servant?"

She giggled, giving him a seductive look. "You're right, Master. I've been a very naughty maid and failed to do my duty. You should punish me."

"Oh, like this?" He gave her round ass a good firm smack, making her squeal and jerk up his shaft a few inches, then slide back down with a moan. "See, you almost got it." He spanked her again, urging her to higher heights.

Marigold managed to get just enough of a hold that with every good smack she moved all the way up his shaft before losing her slippery grip and sliding back down. He timed his spanks to get a good rhythm going, and her round face flushed with effort as she squirmed on his cock.

"Fuck, this is incredible," she panted. "I wish you were putting a baby in me right now." She giggled giddily. "I can't believe I'm having your child. I just know it's going to be the most adorable baby ever."

Like with Zuri, Dare could never hold out long against the pleasure of such a crushingly tight pussy. Especially when she was talking like that.

With heroic effort he managed to last until with a squeak the pink-haired gnome abruptly slid down his shaft to bottom out again, trembling against his chest in a powerful climax. Her soft walls squeezed so tight they actually pushed her partly up his cock just from the force of it.

There was no way he could stop his rushing orgasm after that, so with a groan he grabbed her pillowy ass to hold her still and spurted powerfully inside her.

As they both collapsed into the bath, spent, the other girls gathered around to congratulate Marigold on her baby. His fiancees also welcomed her to Nirim Manor, taking turns hugging the little gnome.

After they finished bathing and dressed in fine new clothes they set out to explore the capitol, their new Head Maid insisting on coming along to attend them. A duty she took seriously, as whenever anyone made a purchase she insisted on carrying it, until she was buried beneath a stack of boxes and bags, stubbornly refusing any help.

The girls all wanted to pamper themselves with luxury items from the fancy shops around the inn, and Dare was only too happy to spoil him, gold flowing out of his pouch in a steady stream as the purchases mounted. Even Ireni, usually the sensible one, apparently had a list of expensive comfort items to ensure the family lived up to their station at Nirim Manor.

Meanwhile Marigold looked so longingly at what was on offer that Dare finally pulled her aside, and told her that as Head Maid of Nirim Manor she needed a standard of comfort fitting her station. So anything she needed she should get now.

His tiny lover hugged him happily around the waist, then rushed away to join the other women in picking out her own items.

By the time they finished their high end shopping spree, even the maid's most valiant efforts couldn't hold all their purchases. Dare took most of the items to carry without giving her a chance to protest, and she pouted adorably all the way back to the inn.

At that point they discovered that Miss Garena had been impatiently waiting for their return. Apparently the formal reception tonight required more preparation than just a quick comb through the hair and throwing on some nice clothes.

A swarm of maids descended on Leilanna, Ireni, and Lily, leading them away as the Head Maid gave Marigold a stern look. "Are you adequate to prepare Master Dare for tonight's formalities?"

The gnome looked indignant. "Of course I am, Hea-that is, Miss Garena."

Phoenix

The stern older woman didn't look convinced. "We shall see. In any case I'd best spend what little time you have left in the Baroness's service training you properly for your new duties. Whatever standards Master Dare may be content with in his home, I will not allow you to tarnish the reputation of Lady Marona's maids by being anything less than perfect in any new position you take."

Marigold swallowed visibly. "Yes, Head Maid." She turned to Dare. "Come, Master Dare. Your things should already be laid out in your room."

He hadn't even had a chance to get a room, but with her customary efficiency Miss Garena had made those arrangements for him. Sure enough, his suit and other necessary items were waiting, and his new Head Maid determinedly got to work dressing him.

Although once she had him naked she seemed to feel that part of her duties involved walking face first into his cock. She took him in her mouth and sucked enthusiastically while jerking his shaft firmly with her plump little hands, making pleased little sounds.

Dare stroked her silky pink hair, deciding he could get used to such an attentive maid. Finally with a gasp of pleasure he emptied his balls down her throat, while she swallowed contentedly with an extended moan of enjoyment.

"Mmm," she said as she pulled away, licking her lips with a satisfied smile. "I believe I should perform this service regularly, Master. To ensure your needs are met, of course."

"Of course." He chuckled and leaned down to kiss her forehead. "But now shouldn't you help me dress?"

* * * * *

As the sun set Dare found himself in Marona's carriage with her and his three fiancees, seated between Marona and Lily with Ireni and Leilanna across from them.

Whatever the vehicle's normal speed, at the moment it was crawling through the crowded streets while the driver shouted irritably. And audibly; even from within the padded interior the man could be clearly heard.

Redoubt

"Come on, you louts! This is the broad street to the Governor's palace, not the slums! Make way for nobility!"

At first Lily stared out the carriage's leaded window, eagerly taking in the sights. But at the pace they were going she finally sighed and curled up on the seat, shifting to rest her head in his lap. He had to admit that looking down and seeing her lovely features looking so peaceful and contented was nice.

Maybe riding in the bumpy carriage going at a snail's pace wasn't so bad after all.

Dare began idly stroking her long, velvety white ears, gently scratching around the base, and she made a quiet sound of enjoyment. "Mmm, that's nice. Keep doing that."

"I wish that was me," Leilanna said, pouting.

Sia took the fore and snickered as she jostled the dusk elf's elbow. "Having your ears rubbed by Dare, or rubbing Lily's ears?"

Leilanna grinned. "Yes."

After what felt like an eternity the carriage driver thumped the roof. "We've entered the palace grounds, my lady."

Lily popped back upright and eagerly crowded the window, craning her neck to look at everything they passed. Although with a bit of a squint, since she was carrying her big wire-frame glasses in her clutch rather than wearing them.

Dare had tried to insist she should wear them regardless of what other people thought, and his fiancees and Marona had all stared at him as if he'd suggested running through the streets in a clown suit. Even Lily insisted that she'd rather have everything be blurry than wear such a gawkish contraption to a formal event.

Which was why his four companions had also all done their hair up in elaborate styles that he knew for a fact had taken over an hour to arrange. Although even if the precarious towers of hair and pins weren't to his taste, he had to admit his consorts all looked incredible.

In fact, he felt a bit like an ugly duckling seated with his four beautiful companions in their formal gowns, his three fiancees wearing their engagement rings and bedecked with the elegant jewelry Se'weir had made for them.

Lily, innocent and sweet and absolutely breathtaking in silver. Ireni, petite and stunning in rich emerald. Leilanna, lush and gorgeous in gray and white like a winter queen. And Marona, regal in a subtle gown that started light red near the collar and deepened to dark crimson at the hem, with an ermine stole.

Dare was fairly confident that no woman at the reception would come close to matching their beauty, and that wasn't just love speaking. He wasn't sure how he'd ever gotten so lucky as to have such remarkable women at his side.

None of his pregnant lovers were showing yet, aside from perhaps a subtle swell to Ireni's tummy with her a bit more than three months along. Although Marona's ruffled skirt that started above the waist likely hid an even more noticeable swell, with her about four months along.

Lily leaned over, fussing with the ties to his leather armor. While they'd been out shopping the maids had thoroughly gone over his gear, mending and polishing and oiling until everything looked better than new.

Still, it was adventuring gear, going to a formal event. Hard not to feel like a fish out of water.

"I still don't understand why you didn't dress in your new clothes," his bunny girl betrothed said. "You look so dashing in them."

Marona opened her mouth to answer at the same time as Dare, and with a smile she nodded for him to go ahead. "I'm trying to break into the nobility, and the nobility doesn't like being broken into," he said. "I wasn't raised to their lifestyle or etiquette, and I certainly wasn't born into it. Trying to pretend I was by dressing the part, no matter how finely, would just make me look contemptible to them."

The baroness nodded, looking impressed. "Adventurers can gain knighthood through merit, but even if some are able to inveigle themselves into polite society, it does not happen quickly. And they usually have to be very rich, very high level, and very heroic to achieve it."

Leilanna laughed easily and nudged Dare's leg. "Luckily the dress code for men allows formal guard and military uniforms, as well as adventuring gear. As long as it's of high enough quality and they're of high enough rank or level."

"Oh." Lily shrank in on herself a bit. "If you're so out of place here, and you're a dashing hero, then I probably shouldn't come at all."

"Nonsense," Marona said briskly. "Consorts are an exception to most rules, as long as they keep to the background and don't embarrass their escort." She smiled warmly and leaned across Dare to rest a hand on the bunny girl's knee. "And as my mother used to tell me, a beautiful woman is welcome anywhere. You are unquestionably that, my dear."

"Besides, you'll probably be the only bunny girl there," Leilanna said cheerfully. "You'll be the center of attention."

If anything, that seemed to distress Lily even more; she'd actually looked relieved at the prospect of staying in the background. Dare couldn't blame her, given she'd been raised in a small warren of close family and friends and had never really been around other people before she left in search of him.

Hell, Dare was feeling nervous about being in polite society himself. The noble class wasn't a thing where he was from back on Earth, where if anything the rich and famous seemed to behave even more juvenilely and shamefully than everyone else.

He may have a better education than most if not all of the people here, and come from a place where technology allowed a lifestyle they couldn't even dream of. But he definitely didn't belong among nobility.

Thankfully Marona, Leilanna, and Ireni would be there to help him fit in. And he and Lily could be awkward together.

"How do you know so much about the nobility if you've never

really been around them?" Leilanna asked him. "You made it sound like things are different on E-" she broke off and glanced at Marona, then hastily amended, "where you came from."

Dare realized at some point he'd need to tell his noble lover the truth about himself too. But at the moment she remained ignorant of not just him being reincarnated from another world, but also the fact that Ireni shared her body with the Outsider.

For now he just fielded the question with a wry smile. "No matter where you live, people are interested in the rich and the famous. We had plenty of entertainment about the nobles of previous times and the sort of lives they lived."

"Well, let's hope your knowledge serves you in good stead tonight," Marona said as the carriage rattled to a stop at the apex of a grand circular drive, the front doors to the palace open and streaming bright light out into the fading dusk just to their right. "The men and women in there will be elegant of dress and refined of speech, but never forget for a moment that the upper class is sharks eating sharks to remain in their position of wealth and power."

A footman approached the door, waiting politely, and she looked around. "Is everyone ready?" The women all checked themselves and each other one last time, Leilanna fussing with Lily's long silver hair for a moment.

Satisfied, the baroness rapped on the door with her ringed fingers, and the footman opened it with a bow and offered her his hand to help her descend. She took it, resting two fingers on his palm as she gracefully moved out onto the carriage's step, then down to the ground.

Dare followed, taking the footman's place in offering his hand to Ireni, Leilanna, and Lily in turn. The three women took their places behind him, which Marona had insisted on even though he would've preferred to walk with them.

The baroness gave him an expectant look, and he offered her his elbow. She lightly rested her hand on it, and together they made their way up the dozen steps to the palace doors.

Servants waited there to take their coats and stoles, and after a moment a grandly dressed man hurried out. "Ah, the Baroness Marona and her retinue," he said briskly. "Welcome. I have the honor of being the herald for this event. Duke Valiant is not in attendance as yet, although he may step in later. He bids me invite you to enjoy the full hospitality he's able to offer in his absence. Are you ready to enter?"

Marona nodded. "I'm not accustomed to standing on the doorstep in the bitter cold."

"Of course, my Lady. Your indulgence for just a moment." The herald looked them over. "It's best to be introduced in smaller groups. Baroness, you'll descend on Master Dare's arm, if you please. His consorts will be introduced shortly thereafter."

The baroness inclined her head graciously. "Very well."

"You girls don't mind?" Dare worriedly asked his fiancees.

"We'll be fine." Leilanna grinned and nudged his elbow. "Actually, the three of us will look much better descending the entry steps without a big leather-clad lug walking with us."

The herald looked a bit impatient at the banter. "I'll go in and announce you now. Follow exactly five seconds later, if you please."

The man disappeared, and the palace servants ushered Dare and Marona to a spot just inside the doors, in a brilliantly lit antechamber that opened out into stairs leading down into a lavishly decorated great hall.

Chapter Nine
Mingling

The herald's voice drifted back to them through the antechamber. "The Baroness Marona Arral of Terana Province. Her escort and sponsoree for entry into the Order of the Northern Wall, Prospective Darren, Protector of Bastion and Master of Nirim Manor."

Marona subtly nudged him, and he started forward across the antechamber. She nudged him again, and he slowed down a touch.

They emerged into the great hall at the top of the stairs, glittering in the light of dozens of crystal chandeliers hanging at least fifty feet overhead. A grand purple carpet led down to a floor the size of a football field, divided into sections: one with small tables and chairs, one for socializing, and finally a dance floor.

The room was filled with enough guests to make its size seem less cavernous, all dressed in their finery and comfortable as ducks in a pond. A legion of servants moved among them, offering drinks and delicacies.

Dare moved down the steps at a steady pace with Marona stepping gracefully at his side, aware of hundreds of eyes on him. He could see a few other people in adventuring gear in the crowd, but most were in elaborately ornamented plate and chainmail that looked grand and heroic.

His armor was Journeyman quality with a few Exceptional pieces, dull black and well fitting with all the pieces complementing each other. Beneath it he wore silver velvet to offset the grim color, and his consorts all agreed he looked like a hero out of a story.

He felt like a rustic ass. But better than a fraud, trying to fit in wearing finery he wasn't comfortable in and that they wouldn't consider him worthy of.

At the base of the steps Marona gestured to a spot just off the carpet, and they made their way over to wait for the others.

Moments later the herald, standing to one side of the doors, called out, "Lady Leilanna Aleneladris, of the ancient and esteemed Aleneladris lineage. Ireni, High Priestess of the Outsider. And Miss Lily of Brighthill Warren."

The three women appeared, gracefully moving arm in arm, and descended the stairs as if they did this every day. Even Lily, whose nervousness was overshadowed by the wonder of the romantic setting she'd entered.

As Dare admired his fiancees, he couldn't help but overhear the whispered comments of the people around him.

"Wow, they're beautiful."

"Diamonds dug out of a shit heap, you ask me. I didn't even know dusk elf tramps had nobility among them. And where even is Brighthill Warren? Is that an actual cunid settlement?"

"I've never seen a bunny girl! I half thought they were fantasies made up by horny boys."

"Look at that hair. I could check my makeup with it . . . you think it's natural?"

"I should check the pleasure slave markets and see if I can find one of those."

Wow. Good to know that beneath all their finery, some of these people were the same sort of gilded shit as Ollivan and not even trying to hide it.

His fiancees stepped off the carpet to join him and Marona, and the baroness subtly directed Dare as they set off across the great hall.

"Ah, well met my friend!"

Dare jumped and turned to see a small, homely gnome in the classical dress of a court jester standing practically on his toes. "Oh. Well met."

The man clapped him on the elbow with undue familiarity. "Always good to meet a fellow practitioner of the art of ridicule."

"What?" Dare asked with a frown. At his side Marona sighed.

"But don't you know?" the jester asked, large eyes widening comically. "Surely you must've heard you're the laughingstock of Redoubt." He thumbed his chest. "And you know you're in trouble when it's the Court Fool telling you that."

Well shit. Dare hoped this was just a bit, although he feared it was true. "Well, if nothing else I can be content that I gave everyone a good laugh," he said lightly.

Marona sighed again.

"Ah, but is it good laughter?" the little gnome murmured, stepping closer. "It can't have escaped your notice that you're the upstart here. You come from nowhere, no one's heard of you and you have almost no deeds to your name. And yet you have the temerity to seek to join this "esteemed" company?" He injected a subtle hint of irony into those last words.

"Then I keep trying until I prove their laughter foolish in its own right," Dare said. "Nobody climbed a mountain without setting foot on the slope."

"Yes, but most don't choose face first into a cliff as their first step." The jester laughed easily. "It's not too late to change your mind and switch professions. I bet you'd be good at juggling . . . we're already fools together, might as well practice our routine."

"The only fool here is you," Leilanna snapped, ash gray skin darkening to charcoal in her pique. "A good jester should know when he's taken his japes too far and is in danger of being punted across the room."

Marona sighed yet again.

"Mercy!" the fool squeaked mockingly, dancing back a few steps. "Once the dusk elf tinker finishes mending pots she means to lay hands on my diminutive person!"

Dare rested a hand on Leilanna's arm, and her flush turned into a blush of embarrassment; smart and refined as she was, she also had a bit of a temper. And not so long ago when he'd first met her she'd been more than a little spoiled, immature, and foul mouthed.

Redoubt

He loved his fiery dusk elf fiancee, but now wasn't the time to lose her cool.

The gnome started to walk away, but Dare called him back. "Tell me." The man gave him a curious look. "A fool's job is to prick the bloated egos at court, isn't it?"

"Among other things we have the opportunity to prick," the jester said, pulling a comical face as he lewdly thrust his small hips.

Dare leaned closer and lowered his voice. "From one fool to another, anyone in court whose ego you'd hesitate to poke?"

The gnome gave him an appraising look. "Perhaps you're not completely hopeless, my friend." He clapped him on the arm again. "There's a delightful place in the red light district called the Rose. A simple place for simple folk such as myself. If you happen to be in the area some night after sundown, perhaps you can buy me a drink and some companionship and we'll talk further."

Without waiting for a response the jester threw himself into a series of back handsprings, tucked into a final roll, and came to his feet strolling away through the crowd.

"Fuck that guy," Leilanna muttered under her breath.

Dare was inclined to agree; he doubted he'd take the jester up on his offer. No doubt the man had plenty of gossip he could sell, but Marona already had her ear on the pulse of the nobility, and now that she was in Redoubt she'd be able to speak to all her contacts and learn even more. Not to mention begin exerting what influence she had on their behalf.

The baroness shook her head wearily at the exchange with the court fool and nodded to their left. "There's Lord Zor," she murmured. "We should pay our respects."

Dare tensed slightly, and on his arm felt Ireni tense as well. "Is that a good idea, given how we left things with him?"

The baroness's lips tightened. "He's one of the Lord Judges who'll be deciding the fate of those petitioning for knighthood. Good idea or not, I fear it's necessary."

Fantastic. Dare led her over to where the older Paladin stood with a small group of well dressed men and women of similar level, obviously noble adventurers. "My Lord," he said as the man looked his way, bowing as the baroness gracefully curtsied.

"Ah, I thought I recognized . . ." As Lord Zor had been speaking his eyes briefly took on the vague, unfocused look of someone checking a person's level. Then he cut off with a choking noise, expression briefly displaying shock. "How the f-" He cut off into splutters.

Dare had trouble holding back his smile. When the Paladin had last seen him he'd been Level 30 to Zor's Level 36, and now Dare was two levels higher than him. And also had the achievement Protector of Bastion.

Considering how long it took most people to reach these levels, and the fact that the older man remained 36, Dare's rapid rise in level was understandably shocking for those who didn't know he had Fleetfoot and Adventurer's Eye.

"Lord Zor," Marona said smoothly into the awkward silence, offering her hand. "How nice to see you again. I trust Lady Melina is well?"

The Paladin gratefully accepted the opportunity to recover from his surprise as he took her hand with a bow, brushing his lips across the back of it. "My Lady. She's very well, thank you. Eager for the birth of our third child."

"Ah, I hadn't heard she was expecting. Do congratulate her for me, and of course my heartfelt congratulations to you as well."

"My thanks. I'm sure she'd be pleased to have you visit sometime." Zor managed to completely ignore Dare even though he was standing right next to the baroness. And in the man's tone it was clear Dare wasn't included in his invitations, either. He similarly ignored Ireni, as well as Leilanna and Lily. "Please, my Lady, join us."

Marona gracefully refused to acknowledge the clear snub to her escort. "Thank you, but I believe I'll seek out the dance floor. It's been far too long since I've taken the opportunity."

Redoubt

"In that case let me escort you, my Lady," the Paladin said, offering his arm while steadfastly not seeing Dare standing in front of him.

Even the baroness's flawless poise faltered as her lips momentarily tightened. "Thank you, but that is not necessary. My escort is a peerless dancer."

Actually they'd only practiced for a few nights in preparation for this, at Marona's insistence. Although a combination of Dare's elite athlete's body, Fleetfoot, and Power Up stat boosts had made him preternaturally graceful and a quick study, so he learned the dances after only a few tries.

He only hoped that had ingrained them well enough in his mind that he wouldn't embarrass himself here. And more importantly wouldn't embarrass Marona or his fiancees.

They excused themselves from Lord Zor's group and Dare led the way to a table, where servants were quick to provide food and drink. Then he escorted his noble lover out onto the dance floor.

"I'm not just imagining that the introduction with Zor didn't go well?" he murmured as he took her in his arms and they began moving in step with the dancers around them.

Marona's lips thinned. "I'm afraid we probably can't count him an ally."

"Not sure I mind," he said, remembering the bitter confrontation after Ollivan had attacked Ireni. "With allies like that, I'd have no need of enemies."

She stepped closer and rested her head on his shoulder, still elegantly keeping to the moves. "I fear we're already facing an uphill battle, my paramour. We can't afford to spurn aid from any source."

The music reached a natural break a short time later, and the mature baroness patted his arm. "Thank you for the dance. I think I'm ready to sit for a while."

Dare bowed and offered his arm again, leading her to back to the table. Where to his immediate concern he saw Leilanna sitting by herself, delicately eating a small fruit tart. "Where are the others?" he asked.

She huffed. "Dancing. I've yet to be approached."

He turned back to the floor, and sure enough spotted Lily in the arms of an elderly gentleman, while Ireni danced with a man in some sort of fancy cleric's robes.

They seemed okay, even to be having a good time. But Lily was shy and out of her element, and he knew Ireni was wary of close contact with anyone but him and the other fiancees.

"Is that okay?" he asked, worried for them.

Marona and Leilanna both gave him quizzical looks. "It's part of the fun," the baroness said with a smile. "A way to socialize and make valuable political connections. All very civilized, of course." Her smile widened as she took in the two dancing young women, then Leilanna. "And I daresay none of your consorts will need to worry about her dance card remaining empty."

"Yeah, I can feel lots of admiring eyes on me," his dusk elf fiancee said sarcastically. "I've had to beat back dance partners with the pans I'm supposed to be mending."

The jester's words were obviously still rankling.

Dare offered her his hand with a smile. "More fools they, then, when you're one of the most beautiful women in the room. And undoubtedly the most graceful."

She humphed, but looked in a bit better spirits as he led her out onto the floor and they joined the circling couples seamlessly moving around each other there. By the time they returned to the table she was smiling and even laughing.

Ireni and Lily had rejoined Marona, although gentlemen were crowding around to take time slots on their dance cards. The two young women looked politely pleased.

The men reluctantly scattered at Dare's arrival, although from the way they hovered they likely hoped to swoop in again. "I see you're the belles of the ball," he joked as he accepted a champagne flute from a servant and sipped.

Redoubt

Lily's characteristic blush made its appearance, suffusing her milky pale skin. "It's very romantic," she admitted, taking a gulp from her own champagne flute. "But also a bit embarrassing to be the center of attention . . . I'm used to being surrounded by women with only one or two men about, not the other way around."

"Well if we're getting a lot of attention from gentlemen, it's nothing to the attention Dare's getting from the ladies," Ireni said with a quiet laugh.

Dare blinked and looked around, realizing that several women ranging from around his age to older than Marona had subtly gathered around. They were casually holding their dance cards to be highly visible to him, and when he looked their way smiled invitingly.

"Well yeah, but that's just Dare," Leilanna said, playfully nudging his elbow. "I'm not sure he even realizes vaginas exist in any state besides sopping wet."

He felt his cheeks heat and Marona cleared her throat sternly, giving the hobnobs around them a pointed look. The dusk elf blushed and hastily snatched up her cup of fruit juice, taking a drink to hide her embarrassment.

Ireni patted his arm. "You should probably go ask each of them for a dance. Have fun."

"Oh," Dare said, a bit disappointed. "I wanted to dance with you."

"Plenty of time for that, but remember what we're here for." She looked at their companions. "We should all be acting as his champions on the battlefield of the dance floor, supporting his cause."

Her words warmed him, but he hesitated. "Are you sure?"

The petite redhead smiled and put a hand on his arm. "It's dancing, Dare. Fun and socializing. Didn't you have dances back home?"

She had to know the answer to that was yes, sure, if you counted standing in a dark room with deafening music while people crowded

Phoenix

in a dense clump and swayed awkwardly. Or if they were feeling adventurous grinded against each other.

Aside from actual venues for dancing, which had never been his thing.

"I think it'll be fun!" Lily agreed, blushing slightly. "You always read about balls in romantic stories."

"What kind of romances are you reading?" Leilanna teased, then laughed lightly when the gorgeous bunny girl blushed harder.

"You know I didn't mean it like that," Lily protested, taking a gulp of her wine.

The curvy dusk elf turned her smile to Dare. "We'll be fine. Dancing is fun, and a great way to break the ice with people who'd otherwise be wary of condescending to speak directly to us off the dance floor." She pouted. "Assuming anyone ever asks me."

Well, it was decided, then. Dare made his way over to an pleasant looking little old lady and bowed. "My Lady, have I been fortunate enough to ask you for a dance before your time slots have all been filled?"

She grinned at him, wordlessly calling him on his BS. "In fact, I believe I have a slot open right now."

"In that case may I have this dance?" He offered her his arm.

As it turned out she was Dowager Viscountess Lynessa, grandmother of the current Lord of the Southeastern Marches, which included Terana Province. She was a friend of Marona, and mostly dancing with him as a courtesy to her and to support his bid for knighthood.

"Although you were pleasant enough company," she said as he led her back to her table.

"Well I for one found your company delightful." Dare bowed in farewell. "Thank you for this dance, Viscountess."

"Of course, young man. If you happen to be passing near Angrad Manor please stop in. Particularly if you succeed in your bid for knighthood."

Redoubt

Dare paused at the table, which was empty, to take a drink and cool down. The room was warmer than he'd like given he was wearing thick leather armor, and he was glad Marona had advised him to bring a few handkerchiefs.

As he dabbed at his forehead he searched for his consorts on the dance floor, picking them out fairly easily as some of the most beautiful women there. As well as the most graceful, in his opinion.

All of them were excellent dancers, of course, although each in their own way. Marona was stately and flawless in her technique, as could only come from a lifetime of perfecting the moves. Leilanna had her elvish grace, as well as her own experience with formal dancing as a child.

Ireni was so light on her feet she almost seemed like a feather in her partner's arms, covering for any missteps with sheer airy poise. And Lily, who had as little experience with dancing as Dare, or formal dancing at least, was able to get by through sheer athleticism.

The bunny girl looked like she was having a good time, eyes bright and face radiant as if she was in a dream.

If his consorts had no shortage of men offering a dance, Dare soon found himself equally inundated as ladies gathered around his table. Although since he was expected to ask for the dance, it took the form of hopeful women engaging him in lingering conversations, with plenty of pauses to give him a chance to invite them out onto the dance floor.

Older women especially seemed to flock to him, maybe because word had gotten out that he was Marona's paramour and his first dance partner had been Lynessa.

Dare took them out to the dance floor one after the other, doing his best to not only dance well but engage each woman in pleasant conversation. He hoped he was doing a good enough job, based on their pleased smiles.

One exception to the various dowagers gathered about him was a strikingly lovely young woman who looked to be a few years older than him. She was tall and willowy, wearing a black gown and black

Phoenix

half-veil attached to her elaborate black hat, with blood red roses tastefully sewn into hems and seams and sashes across the whole ensemble for accents.

The coloring only served to highlight her shockingly pale skin. Not pale like Lily, whose complexion was closer to the color of milk, but more like the palest redhead. Far more so than even Ireni. Her bold, aristocratic features were framed by raven hair so dark and sleek that it shone with blue highlights beneath the chandeliers, and her full lips were the same blood red as the roses on her outfit.

Her eyes, on the other hand, were a dull silver that under some lighting might be called gray. Or that is to say eye, because her left eye was covered by a black satin eyepatch with a tiny red rose embroidered in the center like a pupil.

She boldly stepped up to him and curtsied with a practiced poise rivaling Marona's. "Veressa," she said, offering her hand.

Dare took it with a low bow and kissed the back; her skin was cool and dry but very soft. "Dare of Nirim Manor."

"Well met, Master Dare." She held out her dance card. "My next dance is open, if you would be so kind." She had a precise way of speaking, enunciating every word with care. Very aristocratic, although she'd offered no title.

Ironically, bold as she'd been she wasn't the most forward woman he'd met tonight. And on top of her obvious beauty, it was refreshing to have a break from women old enough to be his mother. At the least.

So he took the card and carefully scribbled his name in the open slot. "It would be my pleasure, Miss Veressa."

"Very good." The tall, pale woman tucked the card into her sleeve, and he offered his arm and led her out onto the floor.

She was an excellent dancer, as experienced and skilled as Marona, as graceful as Leilanna, and with a hint of Lily's athleticism. Dare actually found that he was enjoying himself, almost as much as when he'd danced with Marona and Leilanna at the beginning.

Redoubt

Phoenix

"So what do you do, Miss Veressa?" he asked as they floated across the floor.

The young woman arched an eyebrow. "Please excuse me, I'm quite sure you said "How do you do", as would be a perfectly proper question to ask a woman of refinement in this situation."

Dare felt his cheeks heating. "Of course, forgive me for speaking unclearly."

"That is quite all right. And in answer I am faring quite well, and enjoying myself immensely at this esteemed gathering." She smiled. "And now that we've dispensed with the formalities, if you wish to know more about me I believe I'm in the same profession you are."

"So you're an adventurer?" he asked, perking up.

"Oh, I do leveling here and there," Veressa said airily. "But I steer clear of the Adventurer's Guild . . . on top of being stuffy and elitist, they seem to take a greater share than what they offer in return. As often seems to be the case with guilds, I must say."

She seemed awfully knowledgeable about that given her age, and out of curiosity he looked at her with his Eye.

And, good gods, she was a . . . "Vampire, adult female. Humanoid, intelligent. Class: Lifetangler Level 36. Attacks: Sprout, Animate Growth, Vine Whip, Thorn Grasp, Creeper Choke, Wild Maze."

To her credit, the vampire noticed how he suddenly stiffened and her lips twisted wryly. "And I've seen that face before. You've somehow discovered the truth about my nature."

Dare looked at her warily. "And that is?"

Veressa smoothly danced her way towards the edge of the floor, looking around. "Somewhere out of earshot, if you please."

He gave her a polite smile, more than a bit uneasy. "As long as it's not out of sight," he joked feebly.

She laughed. "No fear, young man, you out-level me. Although I am no threat to you even so."

Perhaps, but there was no telling what a vampire could do. Lily could outrun just about anything just by virtue of being a bunny girl, Pella had super acute senses and also ran faster than humans, Linia was incredibly flexible and dextrous, Enellia could fly, and the list went on.

Actually, humans kind of got the short end of the stick it seemed like.

Dare followed the pale woman into a more secluded corner of the room, trying to act casual about the fact that his guard was up. Not just from potential physical attacks but from mental attacks as well.

He knew what vampires were capable of on Earth, in all their various representations. No telling what they were like on Collisa, although he'd noticed that in most cases the similarities of races here to their counterparts from stories back in his old life were too close to be a coincidence.

Veressa stood with her back to the rest of the hall, which considering how worried she'd been about eavesdroppers seemed surprisingly unguarded. "All right then," she said. "Tell me."

He shifted uncomfortably. "Well, let's just say I imagine you have trouble putting on makeup."

She looked startled for a moment, then laughed richly. "I haven't heard it put like that, but you have the right idea. Although generally I have no need of makeup." She fiddled with her eyepatch, expression pensive. "I imagine my nature concerns you."

Dare didn't want to be rude, but hell yes it did. Veressa seemed very nice, but then vampires in stories usually put on a cultured and charismatic face in public. "There are numerous legends."

"Yes, there are." She sighed and offered him a patient smile. "Tell me, Master Dare. I imagine a tall, muscular man such as you enjoys his meat."

He half wondered if that was an innuendo, although her expression showed no hint of it. "I eat plenty of meat, yes," he admitted.

"So I imagine you've been tempted on occasion to eat, say, cunid meat?"

Dare jerked back in revulsion. "What the f-no! Why would you even ask that?"

Veressa chuckled a bit sadly. "And yet you think a civilized woman such as myself would have different moral views on the matter of where my blood comes from?"

That was an interesting point. One he hadn't considered before. "So you only drink the blood of animals?"

"That's right. I keep livestock that I bleed humanely, small quantities over reasonable amounts of time so they can recover. In many ways I'd say it's kinder than slaughtering animals for their meat. And where possible I also catch animals in the wild to feed on in the same gradual, humane manner. I even picked a class which would aid me in that."

That seemed reasonable enough. The Lifetangler class seemed to be mostly crowd control, with spells that used plants to hold targets. Ideal for catching animals in the wild to feed on. "I hesitate to ask, but does that include monsters?"

The vampire grimaced. "Some are . . . palatable. At need. The ones that closely resemble animals are more tolerable, anyway. Although my tastes are far more refined than that." She waved that aside. "In any case, I assure you I do not pose any threat to anyone, and I would take it as a kindness if you would be good enough to keep my secret in confidence."

"Of course," Dare said with a polite bow. "If you mean no harm to anyone, I could hardly do other than protect the privacy of a lovely young woman such as yourself."

"Young?" She laughed richly and pointed. "See the Level 41 over there?" He followed her gaze to a gentleman who looked to be around 60. "He was my escort to these festivities, and I'm old enough to be his mother." Her smile widened. "Although I've allowed him to believe I'm young enough to be his granddaughter."

That was a genuine surprise. Although she wouldn't be the first woman he'd met who seemed far younger than her years. "Are vam-

Redoubt

your kind long lived, then?"

Veressa looked pleased. "I thought you'd ask if we were immortal, as the legends say. Although of course only the gods and demigods have that gift." She patted his shoulder. "It is easy to see how people would make that mistake, though, since we *are* longer lived than most. And like cunids we never show our age until we drop dead of natural causes, so those who see us endure the years unchanged may draw incorrect conclusions."

She glanced over at her date again and sighed when she saw him frowning their way. "Speaking of the good Lord Dorvin, I'd best get back to him."

"Of course." Dare bowed. "Thank you for the dance and the diverting conversation, Miss Veressa. It's been a pleasure."

"Yes it has." The vampire gave him a speculative look. "Speaking of the pleasure of each other's company, perhaps we could make an arrangement."

He blinked at that bold proposition. "Oh, I, um . . ."

She laughed richly. "Which is to say, Master Dare, that should your adventuring party ever need the services of a crowd control and ranged damage specialist, I hope you'll think of me. I'm feeling the wanderlust again, and something about you draws my Notice."

Noticed again. Fantastic.

Veressa stepped away, preparing to return to her date. "Should you wish to find me, I am at the Crate in the red light district most evenings."

Dare blinked. "You are?" He somehow had trouble seeing this poised, refined woman at the combination of strip club and brothel he'd visited on his last trip to Redoubt.

She smiled widely, showing upper canines that were perhaps a touch overlong. "It's a favorite spot for adventurers not affiliated with the guild. And, to be frank, I can sometimes make as much for fifteen minutes on the stage as in a day of adventuring. And for no more danger than a roomful of lascivious eyes. Which can often be fun."

That was even more unexpected. "All right, I'll know to find you there."

"You're surprised." The vampire winked with her single eye. "Perhaps I was hasty in saying I don't fit most people's view of my kind . . . I can be as driven by passions as the next vampire."

She turned and glided away, and he couldn't help but admire her firm backside.

Well, that conversation had given him a lot to think about. Shaking his head, he started back for his table.

It was a long way to go, and while weaving through the area of the hall where groups were socializing he was intercepted by a gentleman who smoothly stepped away from a conversation with several other worthies.

The man was short, slim, impeccably dressed, and not a hair on his head was out of place. "Master Dare," he said amiably, offering a gloved hand with long, clever fingers. "Bero Milane."

"Master Bero," Dare replied, accepting the handshake in the light, brief manner of Bastion's nobles. "Pleasure to meet you."

"Ah." The man's nondescript face remained neutral, but his eyes glimmered with amusement. "Not something I'm used to hearing." He cocked his head. "Let me make a guess, Dare, if I may be so informal?"

Not sure what was going on here, Dare nodded.

"Dare, then. I would guess you clean your dishes with a scouring pad."

What? "I, um . . . my fiancee is a Healer, and she usually uses a spell."

"Sensible." Bero gave him a keen look. "But on the occasion you do clean the dishes, you use a scouring pad."

Dare thought back to his old life on Earth, where true enough he kept a scouring pad by the sink for dishes. "Good guess."

"There is no guessing involved, my good man," the slim man said. "It's the common habit for most to use the easiest and most

Redoubt

effective means to get a job done. It saves time and energy." He tsked. "But it tends to leave the dishes scratched, yes?"

"I suppose," Dare said cautiously.

Bero's lips quirked as he reached into his jacket and produced an embossed card. "Well, should you ever need your delicate dishes handled properly with a sponge or polishing cloth, do remember me."

With a slight bow the man walked away, hands clasped at the small of his back.

Dare stared down at the card, on which "Bero Milane, 23 Founder's Way" was written in simple lettering.

Perplexed at the encounter, he turned away. Then jumped at the sight of Marona standing a polite distance away rather than coming to join him. She waited until Bero was well away before approaching.

"Do you know him?" Dare murmured.

His noble lover grimaced. "By reputation. He carries a certain . . . odor about him in polite society. A necessary evil, you might say. One who's proved useful enough to enough people to be invited to functions like this."

He looked at the card again, then tucked it away. "What uses?"

Her grimace became an uncomfortable frown. "Information only he seems to know. Problems only he seems able to make go away."

Ah, that sort. Dare inspected the man with his Eye, then lowered his voice. "He's a Stealth class." And as they could both see, Level 46 in spite of his indeterminate age.

Marona didn't seem surprised. "As is well known. And he's influential enough he doesn't care." She lowered her voice. "Best steer clear of him. He'll untangle whatever knot you're caught in, perhaps, but not without looping a strand around you first."

Dare fully agreed with that. Especially since a scouring pad had been enough to clean up his previous mess with Ollivan.

He hoped.

As they made their way back to the table his noble lover sighed. "He's watching us. Now I think of it, we may not be able to steer clear of him."

Well that was ominous. "What do you mean?"

She looked up at him, dark eyes worried, and lowered her voice. "He's a Knight of the Northern Wall, although many aren't happy about it. And senior enough that he could claim a spot as one of the Lord Judges if he wished. Although normally he doesn't."

"You think he's interested enough in me to do so this year?" Dare asked grimly.

"Perhaps. As a rule he doesn't approach others, they approach him. You've drawn his attention in some way."

Shit. Maybe he'd been Noticed again. Or maybe, since the man was a Stealth class, he had some ties to the Assassin's Guild and had identified Dare as the one who'd been sniffing around their headquarters.

He sighed. "Well, we'll have to keep our eyes open."

"As is wise at any time." Marona nodded towards the dance floor. "Let's get back to hobnobbing. You'll need a lot of support for our petition and we don't have much time."

Chapter Ten
Petition

The rest of the night was uneventful.

Dare made a special point to dance with Lily, Leilanna, and Ireni at least a few times each. He would've shown the same attention to Marona, but she spent most of the time seated at the table or on one of the couches in a corner, speaking to friends and allies.

As for dancing with his fiancees, finding opportunities proved to be a challenge since they had no shortage of gentleman asking for a dance. Even Leilanna, once people grew used to her dusk elf heritage and were able to focus on her beauty instead.

All of them had fun, with Leilanna wanting to show off and pushing him to more complicated steps. Ireni, on the other hand, just wanted to hold him close with her head against his shoulder while they spun lazily at the periphery of the dance floor.

But of them all, Lily had the most fun by far.

For the entire evening she wore an expression of delighted wonder as she fully enjoyed the ball, as if she was in a dream or transported to one of her beloved stories. And her starry eyed eagerness and clear enjoyment of the event drew dance partners to her every bit as much as her otherworldly beauty or the novelty of a cunid.

On the few occasions she was available for a dance she floated in Dare's arms with a dreamy expression, filling his mind with a love scent of such deep fondness and contentment that he just wanted to find a couch and cuddle with her all night. And damn what anyone had to say about it.

It was always with great regret that he let her go at the end of a dance, both of them returning to dancing with new partners so they could get a foothold among Bastion's elite.

Phoenix

When he wasn't dancing with his fiancees he schmoozed with the wealthy and powerful of the region, told stories of his adventures to politely interested listeners, and tried to figure out whether the people around him were simply curious or had ulterior motives. Because the entire vibe of the nobility in the great hall screamed ulterior motives.

Marona, bless her heart, fought off weariness to help him as much as she could. She seemed well liked in the capitol, in spite of her rather humble station. Dare got the sense people had greatly respected her husband, Orin, and in her younger years she'd been the darling of Bastion.

Age had only lent dignity to her great beauty, and she was still held in high regard.

But finally he saw her visibly wilting in spite of her best efforts, and firmly insisted it was time to retire. The party was winding down anyway; it had mostly settled into men playing cards around a few of the larger tables, and women gathered on couches exchanging gossip. A few who'd overindulged dozed in chairs or sprawled over tables, drawing the derision of all.

On the carriage ride home Marona slept with her head in Dare's lap, while he gently ran his fingers through her silver streaked dark hair and rubbed her back. "Thank you," he murmured quietly. His fiancees, cuddled up beneath a blanket on the other bench yawning sleepily, all gave him soft smiles, and tender looks for the worn out baroness.

They loved her as much as he did.

Marona had rented the Gilded Chalice's largest room for herself, and sleepily insisted they stay with her. The bed was maybe big enough for four, but somehow they managed to squeeze all of them onto it.

Also Marigold, since in the middle of the night the little maid snuck in to drape herself on top of him, snoring softly and adorably drooling all over his chest.

The next morning they all woke up early when Miss Garena

roused Marona for meetings. They shared a hasty breakfast, then the baroness gave Dare a brief but heartfelt goodbye kiss.

"You'll likely be called before the Lord Judges sometime today to present your petition," she warned. "Don't stray far from the inn, or make sure Miss Garena knows where to find you quickly. I'll try to be there with you, but if I can't be Ireni knows what you'll need."

"Best of luck with your meetings," he said.

The baroness grimaced. "Bah. A bunch of idiots who can't be bothered to tear their attention away from hunting, drinking, bedding their mistresses, or leveling up long enough to actually figure out what's happening on their own land, let alone Bastion in general. Yet every year they cloister for a week to determine the policy of the region for the next year."

"Good thing they have you to offer sage advice," Dare said lightly.

She laughed, expression rueful. "I'll be lucky if I'm included in the roll call." She sighed. "I won't fault them for ignoring me, I don't have the clout or political presence in Redoubt to get anything done. But it would be nice if they at least listened to my suggestion to invite their personal clerks and secretaries to the proceedings, as well as the mayors and captains of the guards of various large villages and towns of Bastion. People who might actually be able to paint a clear picture of what's happening, if they have the balls to do it."

"And have commoners telling the great lords of Bastion what to do?" he scoffed.

Her laugh became more genuine. "It's almost like you've been to a Council of Lords."

The Head Maid cleared her throat in polite reminder, and Marona grudgingly bid them farewell and hurried out.

Since they needed to stay close to the inn Dare suggested they tour the wealthy part of the city. Miss Garena had been here often enough to know some nice parks, gardens, a museum, and other places of interest, and with her recommendations they set out.

Phoenix

It was a pleasant morning. A chance for them all to catch up on the last ten days, and for Ireni and Leilanna to get closer to Lily as a fellow fiancee. Also for Marigold, who'd insisted on attending them as Head Maid, to get better acquainted with the three other women.

They were just talking about heading back for lunch when another of Marona's maids, the stunningly beautiful blonde woman who always seemed to be in the background but whose duties Dare had never quite been able to pin down, rushed up the street to catch them and inform him that the Lord Judges had called him to the palace.

"When?" he asked, wondering if he'd have time to grab a quick bite.

"At your earliest convenience," the maid said between ragged breaths as she bent over with her hands on her knees. "Which is formal speak for right fookin' now. You can please the lords by arriving before the summons was given, and not a second sooner."

Fantastic. "Ireni?" Dare said, holding out his arms. She nodded and he picked her up. "Thank you," he told the blonde maid. Celissa? Elyssa?

"If you want to thank me you could consider that the Baroness has more maids than just Belinda and Marigold," the beautiful blonde said, looking a bit petulant. Marigold cleared her throat sternly, but the other maid just glared back with a stubborn set to her lovely features.

Dare didn't have time to sort out that particular issue, so with a polite nod he dashed down the street, carrying his petite betrothed. He couldn't benefit from Cheetah's Dash's speed, not with these crowds, but he activated it anyway to give him extra agility as he darted through openings and around obstacles at the best possible pace.

Ireni was talking a mile a minute, listing what he needed. He was glad he'd put on his armor and formal clothes beneath it before heading out this morning, since that was the preparation that would take the longest.

Redoubt

They stopped at the inn, gathered the required documents as well as his weapons, and then he picked up the bookish redhead again and bolted for the palace.

"If they ask about your childhood the kingdom you hail from is Gradin on the Elysin continent," she reminded him. "A portal accident deposited you in the forest outside of Lone Ox, where you eventually made your way up here." She grinned. "Best to gloss over the speed of your leveling, and if it's brought up say that on Elysin you had access to numerous monster compendiums."

Dare slowed down at the gates of the palace and identified himself and Ireni to the guards. They directed him on to a different door into the palace, where a servant greeted them. "Your consort will be escorted to a waiting area," the woman said briskly. "In the meantime follow me, please."

Ireni pressed the packet of documents into his hands, then grabbed his head and pulled him down for a warm kiss. "Good luck," she murmured. "You're going to do great."

He gave her a confident grin he didn't entirely feel and followed the impatient servant.

After winding through a series of fancy corridors the servant left him outside a set of ornate double doors. "One moment for me to announce you, Protector," she said with a curtsy. She rapped on the door, then disappeared inside.

A moment later she popped out. "The Lord Judges bid you wait their convenience." Without waiting for a response she hurried away to resume her duties.

True to form: Insist Dare rush, then when he got there waste his time to show their superiority. Or just because they were inconsiderate assholes.

He moved to the wall of the hallway and stood at his best estimation of military rest, feeling like an idiot as servants and courtiers passed, shooting him curious looks. He probably stood there for fifteen interminable minutes, wondering if he'd been forgotten or if he was supposed to follow up somehow.

Phoenix

Then a servant passing him abruptly squeaked in surprise and dropped into such a low curtsy her skirt brushed the floor, holding it like a statue. He turned to follow her gaze, then stiffened and dipped into a low bow himself.

The man's resemblance to Ollivan was clear, powerfully built with dark hair and a strong jaw, his clothing ornate and rich in a manner that elevated it even above the wealthy and powerful Dare had seen at the soiree last night. It didn't take much to put two and two together with the servant's response and conclude this was Valiant Harling, Duke of Bastion.

The duke wasn't just powerful physically, politically, or militarily, he was also a Level 43 Mystic. And while he wore no gear, holstered at his belt was a Master quality wand.

Dare felt more than a little trepidation about how Ollivan's uncle was going to greet him; if Valiant wanted he could simply order his guards to arrest Dare and toss him in a dungeon. Or denounce him outright and torpedo his hopes of gaining knighthood.

"Your Grace," he said in his most courtly tone.

Duke Valiant looked him over coldly, then curtly waved away the servant and waited until she scurried out of earshot before speaking. "So this is the man my nephew ruined himself feuding with. Such a joke."

Dare grit his teeth around a surge of anger; it certainly hadn't been a joke to him and his family. Hopefully his lowered head hid any emotions he failed to hold back. "A regrettable misunderstanding, Your Grace. My condolences on his death."

"Shut your godsdamn mouth!" the duke snarled. He circled Dare, regal features dark with rage. "Make no mistake, the boy caused me embarrassment on numerous occasions, giving my detractors more excuses to speak against me. But my nephew he remained, son of my beloved sister."

He stopped in front of Dare again, looming over him in spite of being a few inches shorter. "I have no cause to denounce you or punish you under the law, and ultimately the fool boy died trying to fight monsters alone in the wilds. But I despise you all the same, and that will never change."

Dare wisely kept his mouth shut, as instructed.

After a few moments Valiant clamped down on his anger, becoming cold once more. "For political reasons I will not openly oppose your petition to knighthood. My enemies would be happy to use you against me if they could, and I have no need to give them any more arrows for their quiver."

He pressed a finger into Dare's chest, voice lowering to a growl. "But make no mistake, any other nobles I have in my pocket will be openly against you. Perhaps you will achieve knighthood in spite of that, my current position is more tenuous than I'd like. But you had best content yourself with that title and disappear back to your shitty little house on the border. It is as far as you will rise in Bastion."

The man whirled away, speaking over his shoulder. "Do not approach me for the rest of your stay in Redoubt. Do not speak to me. And by the gods you'd better not even show your face to my sister and her grieving family."

The duke swept through the ornate double doors and slammed them behind him, leaving Dare alone in the hall.

Well, that had sucked.

It was another fifteen minutes before the doors opened and a courtier poked his head out. "Darren of Nirim Manor, you are summoned."

Dare wasn't sure whether to be relieved or full of trepidation as he followed the man into the chamber. It turned out to be a circular room, austere save for the rich purple carpet on the floor, a crescent table at one end set with eight occupied seats.

The Lord Judges.

He recognized four of the men there. There was Valiant, of course, and next to him Lord Zor. And Marshal Jind had told him he'd be a Lord Judge, so it was no surprise to see him seated on the duke's other side.

The last familiar face, and perhaps not a welcome one, was Bero

Milane. He sat at one end of the crescent table, lounging in his seat with an expression of mild amusement.

The courtier motioned for Dare to stand in the center of the room, and he moved to the indicated spot and bowed low to the assembled lords.

"Darren of Nirim Manor, Protector of Bastion, here to petition for entry into the Order of the Northern Wall," the courtier intoned. "Sponsored by Viscount Timeor Angrad of the Southeastern Marches and Baroness Marona Arral of Terana Province."

That came as a pleasant surprise; apparently he'd made a good impression on the dowager viscountess. Or she was that good of a friend to Marona.

"Your credentials," Valiant grunted curtly. The courtier approached Dare, and he hastily handed over the packet Ireni and Marona had prepared. The paperwork inside had been copied eight times for each of the Lord Judges, and the man wasted no time passing them out to each man at the table.

The duke accepted his sheaf of papers and began perusing it, looking bored and irritable. Although he read intently, likely searching for something he could use as an excuse to dismiss Dare out of hand.

Finally the man raised his eyes, staring down at him coldly. "Your age is listed as 27. That can't possibly be true."

"It is, your Grace," Dare said, bowing low. "I've been told I have youthful features." There were a few snorts at that, and he couldn't help but hold his breath as he waited to see if the claim would be accepted.

He'd been fearing for a while now that his level combined with his age would draw the wrong kind of attention. But now, at Level 38, it had gotten to the point where most flat out wouldn't believe an eighteen year old could have attained it, not even through dishonest means.

So even though in other circumstances they would've laughed at him claiming to be almost a decade older, it was an easier idea for them to sink their teeth into than that he was almost Level 40 as a teenager. Even at 27 years old his level would've drawn remarks, as most around this level were in their 30s, 40s, or even older. And those were the adventurers who'd put serious time into leveling.

Besides, that was technically his actual age, since he'd been 27 on Earth when he died and came here. Although by this point a birthday would've come and gone back home.

Jind chuckled. "With respect, your Grace, could you be suggesting he's *younger* than that at his level?"

Valiant scowled. "He looks like exactly what he is, a baroness's plaything. Not an adventurer."

"His credentials say otherwise," Bero said mildly. "As does his title of Protector of Bastion. You may argue he was handed everything he has, but he wouldn't be the first. I find no fault with his paperwork."

That seemed to be the general consensus. From everyone save Valiant, however, who stubbornly didn't look up from perusing his finances for anything he could find fault with. "I trust you are aware that part of the information we require from you is your stats. To be worthy of entering the nobility you must have something that sets you apart from the common rabble."

The duke motioned to an elderly man in robes embroidered across the chest with a set of silver scales standing to one side of the chamber. "For the sake of your privacy we'll ask you to accept a party invite from a Cleric of Henor, God of Fair Dealings. He'll read off your stats with the assurance of keeping your other information in confidence. Is that agreeable?"

Dare had been warned about this. "It is, your Grace."

Valiant gestured curtly. "Then proceed."

The cleric stepped forward, and Dare got the blaring notification of a party invite. He accepted, and the elderly man bowed slightly and his eyes went unfocused.

"Of the inborn, level affected, and ability affected attributes of Master Darren of Nirim Manor," he intoned. "Strength, 47."

A surprised murmur rose among the assembled lords and their attendants. Dare had compared stats with a few people and knew his were high, which was unsurprising considering Sia had given him a body comparable to an elite athlete and a mind equal to a top scientist or other thinker from Earth.

"A wiry strength, Master Darren," Jind said, looking amused; true, Dare did have the physique of a decathlete as opposed to a bodybuilder, so high strength might not be readily apparent.

The cleric cleared his throat. "Stamina, 63." Again exclamations of surprise, although if they knew how much time Dare spent running around everywhere they might not have been. "Agility, 61. Constitution, 43." The exclamations were dying down to intent focus as people got over their surprise and listened in shock.

Having one or two unusually high stats, especially which fit his class, were to be expected. But high stats across the board would stand out.

"Dexterity, 57. Intellect, 69."

"Nice," Bero said, to a few chuckles from the lords.

The cleric cleared his throat apologetically and continued. "Speed, 73."

Finally, the room reacted again with an uproar of incredulity. "73?" Zor demanded. "That's faster than a canid. Hell, *cunids* reach the high 90s on average, and you might as well chase the wind!"

"I'm more interested in his intellect," Bero said. "That's uncharacteristically noteworthy."

"Fertility," the cleric concluded, "56."

That drew the greatest uproar at all. "Not just the speed of a cunid but the fertility of one," Bero said with a laugh. "You must have the devil of a time getting high enough level Prevent Conception."

"Is this man actually human?" a lord near the other end of the crescent asked.

The question was likely rhetorical, but the Cleric of Henor

fielded the question, unruffled. "He is, my Lord."

"In that case I find no fault with his stats, either," Jind said. "If we're looking for exceptional specimens, he unquestionably qualifies."

Valiant looked pissed, although he tried to hide it. "Thank you," he told the cleric curtly. "You may drop party."

The elderly man nodded, and Dare got a notification that his party had been disbanded.

"Where do you hail from, lad?" the doubting lord at the end of the table asked.

"The Kingdom of Gradin, Elysin continent, my Lord."

That drew a surprised stir. "That's over on the other side of the world, through waters infested by naga pirates, merfolk Seaguard Punishers, orcish longships, and all manner of other perils," Bero said, leaning forward intently. "How did you manage to find yourself here? That must've been an adventure in and of itself."

"It was, my Lord," Dare said with a self-deprecating smile. "Although not in the manner you might think. As I was running an errand for my family's patron I was obliged to hire a Phasewarper to make a portal to a location on the other side of the kingdom. I can only assume something went wrong with the spell, because next thing I knew I was waking up in the woods a few miles from Lone Ox in southern Kovana."

A surprised murmur spread through the Lord Judges.

"That must've been quite the portal failure," an elderly man with long, snowy white hair and beard, who turned out to be a Level 56 Phasewarper himself, said. "I've never heard the like."

"Nor have I, my Lord." Dare shook his head regretfully. "For the dangers of traveling the seas that you mentioned, and also because Haraldar is landlocked, I determined that I might have difficulty returning home. Particularly without funds."

He smiled, letting some genuine emotion show. "However, in the course of raising those funds I found enough opportunities in Bastion, and was so struck by its wild beauty, that I decided to make it my home. I purchased land in southeast Terana and intend to live there to the end of my days."

"Well said," Jind murmured, nodding his approval. "No land compares to Bastion."

Zor cleared his throat impatiently. "Very sentimental, but I'm more interested in your identification of the Magma Tunneler my raid fought." He leaned forward with his chin on his fist. "In spite of your young age and the fact that you referenced no books or other materials, you recognized a rare monster two expert monster lore Scholars with a wagonload of books failed to."

Damnit. He'd hoped they wouldn't think to bring this up. "I was fortunate to have access to the Grand Royal Library of Gradin. My mother and father were both Scholars who worked as librarians there."

"So you learned enough about monsters, of which there are tens of thousands at the least thus far recorded, to recognize this particular one?" the Paladin pressed. "Without falling back on books or other materials?"

"Party and raid rated monsters are more memorable than others," Dare said with a polite bow.

"But they aren't the only ones you've recognized," Bero abruptly said. "There are numerous instances in which you have shown knowledge of monsters of all types and levels. Most notably when you scouted the Terana Monster Horde for Lady Marona Arral."

Fuck. "I committed a vast number of monsters and their information to memory," Dare said with as much confidence as he could muster.

"Indeed?" Zor pounced on that. "What is the name of the monster that appears to be a hybrid of a cat, bird, and orc and wields in its ability arsenal a swooping attack, a talon claw attack, and high evasion?"

Double fuck. Dare didn't want to go too far down this rabbit hole, since every evasion would make it that much more likely he was caught out. But he and Ireni had gone over all of this and he had a lot of very convincing answers to give.

He took a breath and bowed again. "With respect, my Lord, I'm afraid my memory doesn't work that way. I am hesitant to give away the secrets of the Gradin Royal Scholars, but I can at least reference the name of a technique and its vaguest details, as they're widely known among some circles."

Bero leaned forward abruptly at that, very intent. "Please, do go on."

"It is called the Memory Palace. With it I was able to commit an unimaginably vast number of monsters and their details to memory. However, the mind is not normally able to hold that much information, and it is impossible to simply recall any of that information on a whim."

"How convenient for you," Valiant said snidely.

Dare bowed to the man. "Pardon, Your Grace, but it can be very inconvenient. Unless I spend a great deal of time wandering my Memory Palace to find a specific fact, the information only comes to mind when I see a monster out in the wilds. Or in some cases if I see a picture of one, if the artist was detailed enough."

"Fascinating," Bero said.

"That's not the word I'd use for it," the duke snapped. "I'm calling your bullshit, Hunter. If it's a likeness you require we'll get you one." He motioned curtly to a courtier, who ran off.

Fantastic. Dare could always claim the drawing was too poor, but he wasn't sure that was going to fly. Certainly not with Valiant, and probably not with Zor either.

Although it wasn't time to panic just yet. Dare had seen hundreds of monsters in his time on Collisa, and recorded the information of most in his leveling journals. Even more, part of the new body Sia had given him *did* actually seem to include the ability to think more quickly as well as an enhanced memory. He'd been proud of his ability to recall events back on Earth, but even more than that here, he could pull small details at need.

Like the name of the veteran guard he'd met at the gates

Phoenix

yesterday.

The most commonly known monsters were logically going to be the lowest level ones, because they were the ones found closest to where people lived. And Dare had seen lots of those.

Of course, he doubted Valiant and his cronies would give him an easy one.

The courtier returned, panting, with a few sheets of parchment clutched carefully to his chest. Dare watched with quiet dread as the man passed them to the duke, who looked them over with a frown before picking one.

"This," he said, flipping the drawing around to display it.

Dare nearly gasped with relief, silently thanking the fact that the mountains had such a random variety of monsters of all levels.

Valiant's courtier, that weasel, had given his lord at least one high level monster to choose from. One Dare probably wouldn't have encountered before while leveling.

Except he'd seen this monster before, in that hard to reach valley on the eastern end of the mountains, with the overflowing spawn points sending their roamers towards Elaivar across the Tangle.

"Your Grace, while the picture lacks some of the finer identifying details, a common variant of that monster is the Swooping Egari. Monster. Level 51-53. Attacks include: Dive Bomb, Rake, Wing Whirlwind, Deafening Screech, Eviscerating Snap, and Deadly Glide."

The Lord Judges, who'd gathered around to read the information on the picture, murmured in surprise and grudging admiration. All save Bero, who'd remained lounged in his seat watching Dare closely.

"Our adventurer has a keen eye," the slight lord said lightly.

Fuck, had that been a convenient choice of words or did the man guess something? Dare cursed that while he'd thought of everything else, he'd failed to consider that describing the monster in the same way his Adventurer's Eye did might hint at where he was getting his information.

Redoubt

Except that was the logical way monster compendiums would list the information as well, since that was also where *they* were most often getting their information. From high level adventurers in the past who had the ability.

Zor settled back in his seat. "So if I'm hearing you correctly, you're from a distant and very civilized land. You're the son of Scholars who worked at a royal library, and by indulgence or corruption you were also given access to the reading materials there. At which point you decided to choose one of the most commonly ridiculed classes, widely believed by all to be primarily populated by uneducated yokels, and set out to adventure. At least until you came to be involved in an accident involving a failed portal that sent you to southern Kovana."

"That is accurate," Dare said. "Aside from the opinion held about Hunters in Gradin."

"You claim no noble lineage," Valiant said harshly, "yet you have benefited from opportunities many princes would envy."

"I cannot speak to the opportunities of princes, Your Grace. Only my own life. But yes, I have been given many great opportunities. Not least of which have come in Bastion since my arrival."

The lords peppered him with more questions for maybe fifteen minutes. Then, after briefly conferring with each other, Valiant rapped his knuckles on the table with a grimace of displeasure. "The Lord Judges approve your petition for knighthood. You will take part in the trials." He motioned curtly. "Dismissed."

"Thank you, my Lords," Dare said, doing his best to hide his relieved grin as he bowed low and turned towards the double doors.

Just outside of them he was intercepted by Jind. "Master Darren," the man said, clapping him on the back. "How are Linia and m-" he cut off with a cough, "the child?"

Dare decided not to comment on the man's claim. "She's well. Resting in comfort with my family and eagerly waiting the birth."

The Marshal eyed him warily. "Then did you manage to find

some, ah, accommodation you were comfortable with?"

Dare grit his teeth; that wasn't any of the man's business. But then again Jind had been more decent than he needed to be about the entire painful situation.

"In a way," he said as neutrally as he could. "I still intend to raise my child, but our romantic relationship is over."

"Ah, lad." The older man rested a sympathetic hand on his shoulder. "I'm sorry I had to be the one to kick off that whole mess, and again for how I handled matters that could've been treated more delicately. I hope it doesn't impact our friendship."

"Thank you, Lord Jind. You've been decent about this, which I appreciate. For my part I'm sorry you got caught up in it as well."

The Marshal sighed. "We can't control our heart, much as we try."

Dare nodded, then hesitated. "Linia wanted me to give you this," he said, withdrawing a small letter and handing it over.

Jind quickly opened it and read, smiling fondly. Then he shook his head with a sigh. "Your pardon, Master Dare, but Linia's asked if I'll come visit her again. Am I still welcome at your lovely home?" He hesitated, then added hastily. "Or at least at Melarawn village."

Dare fought down a surge of conflicting emotions. "Linia's free to see who she wants." He paused, then added grudgingly. "And I'd like you to feel welcome at Nirim Manor as well."

"Then with your permission, I'll have to see if I can make time to visit in the next few months." The older man clapped his back again. "In the meantime, thank you for caring for her, and for your generosity to the refugees from her village. Malia tells me your contract was very reasonable."

"They've proven good tenants, and Linia's glad for their company."

"No doubt. I also appreciate that you've been so accommodating on the matter of more people taking refuge on your land. The chaos on the border continues, barely kept in check by the efforts of my Irregulars and those few others who could be bothered to help, and refugees are flooding south. I imagine the friends and family of my people you've agreed to take in are already arriving at Nirim Manor in numbers."

Dare couldn't say he was overjoyed by that news. Especially happening while he and more importantly Ireni were gone. "Then I hope to get back there as soon as my business in Redoubt is finished, so I can make sure their needs are being met."

Jind laughed and clapped his back a third time. "I need to get back in there, but I just wanted to thank you in person again, and wish you the best of luck in your trials. Congratulations on your petition being accepted."

"Thank you, my Lord." Dare paused. "If I could briefly ask, how are Felicia and Irawn faring?"

Jind grimaced. "Good, I'm sure. They've been sent on to the border with most of the rest of the company. Where I should be myself, if I didn't have to deal with this politicking and farcical show of providing government to the region."

Brow furrowed distractedly, the Marshal gave him a last nod before disappearing back into the chamber. Leaving Dare to find Ireni and tell her the good news.

Close as the matter had seemed in there, his petition had been accepted. Now on to the trials.

Chapter Eleven
Proving Grounds

When a servant led Dare to where Ireni had been kept waiting, he was pleasantly surprised to find Marona there as well. She hadn't been in time to stand at his side and speak in his favor, but was there to hear the good news.

He looked at their anxious upturned faces, doing his best to keep his expression impassive to let the tension build. Then he grinned. "My petition has been approved."

Ireni shouted for joy and threw her arms around him, peppering his face with kisses. Marona was more reserved, keeping her serene public facade, but she did kiss his cheeks and her eyes shone as she congratulated him.

Dare suggested they head back to the inn to celebrate over lunch, and the baroness regretfully announced she had to get back to meetings. "Every year the big merchant houses require new renegotiations for trade to the province," she said with a sigh. "Always pushing for better deals. Add to that the Governor's stipulation about low taxes and it can be hard to raise funds."

She must be feeling the squeeze more than she let on, because usually she was in favor of the low taxes fostering growth and prosperity in the region. "Anything I can do to help?"

Marona gave him a warm smile. "Become a knight and serve as Terana's resident champion."

He laughed. "That I can do." He bowed and Ireni curtsied as the baroness departed.

With another laugh he offered his beautiful betrothed his arm. "I suppose there's not so much of a rush to get back, so I don't need to pick you up and sprint."

She favored him with her million watt smile. "I don't know, if

Redoubt

we didn't have to be careful of our image at the moment I don't think I'd ever complain about a chance to be held by you."

Dare made a contented sound and leaned down to kiss her softly, ignoring the stare of a passing servant. "I don't think we have any other engagements today. What do you say we spend the afternoon doing just that?"

"Mmm." Ireni leaned contentedly against his side. "You do owe me, since we haven't had a chance to be together yet after reuniting here." She pouted adorably. "Not to mention Sia had all the fun in the bath yesterday, so I didn't get a chance to make love with Lily in the most romantic way possible."

He grinned. "Would it spoil the romantic atmosphere if I watched that?"

Her big green eyes danced. "Watched, my love? I was hoping you'd join us."

The stroll back to the Gilded Chalice was pleasant. Dare had missed Ireni, and in all the bustle yesterday he hadn't had a chance to just be with her. She'd obviously missed him too based on how cuddly she was; she even climbed under his cloak with him, insisting she was cold.

Their talk was mostly about the upcoming trials, as well as wondering how things were going back at Nirim Manor. But when Dare spotted a secluded garden he pulled his betrothed in out of view of the street and stole a few kisses with her, luxuriating in her soft warmth as she melted against him.

"I love you," he murmured as he buried his face in her auburn hair, hugging her close.

She sighed contentedly, nuzzling his neck. "I'll never get tired of hearing that."

They stayed there for a few minutes, shutting out the world around them to just be together. Then his stomach rumbled hard enough that Ireni laughed. "I could feel that," she said, patting his abs. "Come on, we better get some food in you. The servants gave me some snacks, but you haven't eaten since breakfast."

Hand in hand, they returned to the inn to share the good news with Lily, Leilanna, and Marigold. Over a lavish lunch Dare spared no expense for.

True to his word, they retired to the room Miss Garena had rented for him and cuddled on the bed as their meal settled. Before long Marigold and Leilanna began kissing and groping each other, shedding their clothing to press soft lush bodies together.

That left him, Ireni, and Lily to do as planned and make sweet tender love.

The afternoon passed in blissful enjoyment of each other, with Ireni and Leilanna becoming more familiar with Lily and Marigold. And of course the bunny girl and gnome enthusiastically doing the same with each other. After a dinner of delicacies and snacks ordered up to the room Sia made an appearance as well, injecting some excitement into the fun as she did her best to wear the rest of them out.

Which resulted in the goddess becoming the tiredest of all, so Ireni quickly curled up and fell into a contented sleep when she finally returned to the fore.

Dare and the others gently kissed her goodnight, then headed down to the common room. "I'd like to make a trip down to the Crate in the red light district," he told them as he and Lily drank cups of her favorite wine while the others sipped chilled fruit juice. "I was going to meet someone there about possibly moving to the Terana area to adventure with me, when I need a full party or raid."

The others excitedly pressed for details. Especially Lily, since she planned to be his permanent adventuring companion. Dare told them about his dance with Veressa, although he kept her secret about being a vampire.

"I wanted to see the Crate anyway," Lily said. "And I'd like to meet anyone who's going to be adventuring with us."

Marigold grinned. "You had me at "girls dancing and stripping."

Leilanna hesitated; while she could be surprisingly naughty, her dusk elf honor sometimes made her prim at unexpected times.

Redoubt

Especially if she wasn't sure how she was supposed to be acting. "Somebody should chaperone you so you don't get into trouble," she finally said.

"There's my naughty Mistress," Marigold said with a laugh.

Fetching their coats, they set out through the crowded streets towards the red light district. There was a festival mood in the air, which he supposed was to be expected because this was Collisa's version of New Year's Eve, and the city pulsed with excitement even with the sun sinking towards the horizon.

Dare kept an extra eye out for pickpockets and muggers, although as it turned out in the crowd the greatest threat was drunken assholes wanting to grope the girls. Dare stopped the first few, none too gently. Although when Leilanna wreathed her hands in flames and glowered around at the drunken revelers, they seemed to get the hint and backed off.

The Crate was practically bursting at the seams, with a line to get in that stretched past several other establishments. All of which happily took advantage of the opportunity to sell to bored people in the queue.

Going under the reasoning that nightclub rules might apply, Dare tried approaching the door directly. The bouncers took one look at their fine clothes and the three beautiful women and decided they were just the right sort of clientele, stepping aside with polite nods.

To his surprise, even though it was standing room only along the walls, with harried serving girls rushing about with trays of drinks, the booths and tables right next to the stage weren't all occupied. Dare flagged down one of the serving girls and flashed a gold. "What's the story on that booth there?"

Even holding a tray loaded with mugs, the pretty dog girl managed to make the coin disappear as if by magic. "Tables are 50 gold for the evening, ending at midnight."

"Fuck," Leilanna muttered. "We could just find a brothel and buy every girl there for the night."

Phoenix

Lily giggled. "Why are all the people who're throwing silver making such a big deal about that harpy taking off all her clothes? Harpies are usually naked anyway, at least the ones I've played with . . . haven't they seen a naked girl before?"

Dare filed that under items he wanted to ask about later . . . he'd never been with a harpy before.

And judging by the girl up on stage, he wanted to. She was only a bit bigger than Zuri or Marigold, but had the sort of delicate frame you'd expect from a creature that needed to be light enough to fly. Not a spare ounce of fat on her, like an elite gymnast, and the way she drifted over the stage made him wonder if she had hollow bones.

She was the first humanoid he'd seen who didn't have arms, instead showing off large wings with brilliant red and gold plumage. As was the plumage that made up her hair, trailing halfway down her back and swaying with her graceful movements, which joined the plumage of her long tail that dragged on the ground behind her. To compensate for not having hands her legs were long and slender and seemed to be double joined, with feet that were almost hands so she could grasp things.

It all should've combined to make her look odd, but instead she was distinctly feminine, with an undeniable and surprisingly compelling beauty.

Dare looked at her small breasts with pepperoni sized dark pink nipples, and at the panties she was teasingly lowering with one double jointed foot to reveal a delicate slit, and couldn't help but want to see if she'd be interested in renting a room with him upstairs.

It'd be a better investment than spending a king's ransom on a booth.

Speaking of which . . . "So that's a no on the booth?" the canid serving girl said impatiently, shifting her tray.

"Thanks, no," he replied. She gave him a strained smile and bustled off.

Marigold tugged on his sleeve. "Master, your Head Maid needs to be able to see so she best knows how to serve you."

Redoubt

Dare couldn't help but grin as he hefted the plump gnome up onto his shoulders. Which normally would've drawn some curious looks but was just one of many oddities in the crowded tavern.

"Ooh, she's so cute and little, Master," the maid whispered, leaning forward in a way that made her ankle-length pink hair trail down to cover his eyes. "Maybe she wants to join your harem too. As your Head Maid it's my duty to help you find consorts."

"Yeah, no," he said. "You're going to run into a brick wall with my fiancees if you try going around them like that."

"Of course I'd consult the Mistresses," Marigold said patiently. "Mistress Lily, Mistress Leilanna, should we try to see if the harpy wants to have fun with us tonight?"

"Yeah!" Lily said eagerly.

"Hate to bust your bubble, but the harpy just picked up her coins and flew the coop," Leilanna said.

She wasn't wrong; with a last shake of her pert little backside, ruffling tail feathers all the way down to her feet in a shimmering red and gold wave, the harpy gripped a coin bag in one foot and her clothes in the other and flapped up into the air. Moments later she disappeared behind the curtain where the dancers got dressed and settled up with the Crate's management.

The crowd shifted as another woman climbed up onto the stage, beginning a less than graceful dance that soon had the crowd booing. She eventually climbed back down, disappointed, and the crowd cheered as one of the serving girls climbed onto the crate to take her place.

Leilanna's hands abruptly whooshed alight with blue flames. "Want to keep reaching for my ass, dipshit?" she snarled at a surprised looking man who suddenly found himself looking at a flaming fist shaking in front of his nose.

The crowd backed away from them, and Dare noticed bouncers approaching. With a sigh he reached for his fiancees' hands. "Time to go, I think."

"That's okay," Lily said, pressing close to his side with a slightly anxious look on her face. "This place is way too crowded. Let's come back when it calms down."

He couldn't disagree; he'd never been a fan of crowds like this.

They made their way outside and spent a while wandering down the streets of the red light district, watching the various performers on each corner. There were even more of those than when Dare had last come here, acrobats and contortionists and street magicians and illusionists, to name a few. As well as musicians ranging from single pipers to bands with over a dozen players.

And then of course there were the expected hucksters doing the ball under the three cups scam, back alley card games, and more than a few fortune tellers and soothsayers.

They explored the various attractions, nibbling on hot honey cakes and skewers of roasted meat (vegetables for Lily). In spite of the crowds it was fun, and Dare was almost surprised when all at once bells began to ring and a growing murmur spread through the crowd.

Then brilliant spells lit up the sky, vast multicolored fireballs and illusory monsters and showers of sparks. With a roar people began waving their hats or scarves in the air, clapping each other on the back, hugging, kissing, and celebrating.

It was the new year; apparently some things were celebrated the same on Collisa.

Dare kissed Lily, Leilanna, and Marigold in turn, and then they hugged each other as they watched the continuing light show in the sky.

He would've thought that nothing could compare to fireworks back home, but magic trumped them. While Redoubt's festivities were smaller in scale than many he'd seen, no firework could replicate the splendor of vast detailed illusory dragons, giants assaulting castles, small armies battling huge gryphons and wyverns and other beasts, and fanciful fairy gardens.

"What year is it, anyway?" he asked.

The girls all looked at each other blankly. "954, maybe?"

Leilanna said. "Most people don't pay much attention to the year aside from historians."

Well that was a bit different from home. "What does the year mean?"

"How should I know?" she said. "I'm originally from Elaivar."

Marigold cleared her throat uncertainly. "I think it was when the Harald Foundership and Bristil banded together against encroaching dwarvish settlers, forming Haraldar."

Wow, so the different kingdoms didn't even use the same years in their dating systems? That had to make things hugely inconvenient for international commerce and diplomacy. "I thought Haraldar was pretty friendly with dwarves. Almost as much as with elves."

Leilanna snorted to show what she thought of the kingdom's "friendliness", considering only Bastion really treated other races well. "Well it *was* almost a thousand years ago. Do people back where you're from hold grudges that long?"

"Sadly, some do," Dare said with a wry shake of his head.

"And dwarves do," Marigold supplied. "They're usually pretty good about accepting formal apologies if they're given sincerely, and you make some grand display of contrition like reparations or trade concessions or generous gifts. But if you piss them off and don't make things right they'll never let it go, down to their last descendant."

Lily nudged him with a furrowed brow, and he found himself thinking the same thing she obviously was; they needed to finish transcribing the dwarvish records and deliver them to the dwarves already.

The light show in the sky finally ended, and he noticed Marigold yawning hugely and leaning heavily against his leg. He picked her up and she gratefully rested her head on his shoulder and began to snore.

"Come on, let's head back to the inn," he said to his fiancees.

Phoenix

* * * * *

Bright and early the next morning Dare stood on a large field on the plains just outside of Bastion, surrounded by a few dozen other prospective knights. The field had been converted into a proving grounds complete with all sorts of odd and obscure obstacles, roped off around the perimeter with city guards standing at intervals along it to make sure no one intruded.

Although the event was obviously intended for entertainment because a crowd of thousands had formed on the other side of the rope, with food and novelty vendors moving among them hawking their wares. As well as numerous temporary stalls where merchants enjoyed a bustling trade.

There were also a few necessary fixtures like a large latrine ditch, and makeshift fountain where an earth Mage and water Mage were working together, making sure everyone had water free of charge with their wages undoubtedly paid by Duke Valiant or the city of Redoubt.

Somewhere in that bustling crowd Dare knew his loved ones were watching. He wished he could see them or at least have some sign they were there, to help boost his confidence.

Because he was definitely feeling nerves; he'd played a few sports growing up, but never anything like a formal league or on a school team. His competitive spirit had always been channeled into gaming.

He'd been in some big tournaments before, even ones where there'd been far more than a few thousand spectators. But there was a huge difference between having all those spectators be a number on some screen and maybe a chat bar, as opposed to actually being there in person.

As it turned out, a few thousand people crowding around even a large field was a ton. A vast sea of faces turned his way, all waiting for him to make an ass of himself.

Sure, in some ways Dare had been preparing for this since the moment Sia set him down in the woods outside Lone Ox. But in other ways he was woefully unprepared even with all of Marona's and Ireni's help.

Nothing could prepare him for being the center of attention for thousands of eyes, feeling that pressure to perform, other than actually experiencing it. And he never had before.

Unlike the other competitors, who'd probably been getting ready for this moment all their lives.

The prospective knights on the field around him were varied when it came to size, appearance, and certainly choice of class. But what stood out most to him was that they were all human, almost all men, and from the looks of it either nobility, wealthy merchants, or land owners.

And adventurers, he supposed. He had to remind himself that level and achievements were a consideration here, on top of the things that tended to lend prestige back on Earth.

The young and middle aged men all formed their own groups based mostly on social status or friends and acquaintances. The snippets of conversation Dare heard confirmed another thing Marona told him, that most of these people benefited from having influential families, famous and renowned relatives, and/or a parent who'd been a knight before them.

All things that weighed heavily in their favor for joining the Order of the Northern Wall, and things Dare didn't have himself. Which meant he'd just have to shine all the more brilliantly to compete.

The audience abruptly roared in excitement, and he turned to see what had drawn their attention in time to watch the crowd part, making way for the approach of a grand parade. The eight Lord Judges, flanked by a dozen high level guards as dozens more clerks and attendants followed behind.

The judges made their solemn, majestic way to an elevated platform in the center of the field, only them and a handful of other people climbing up to look out over the proving grounds and the surrounding crowd. Then, with a sudden pop and hiss, an air Mage amplified Duke Valiant's voice, while an Illusionist created a fifty foot tall image of his smiling face over the platform.

Neat trick; easier and probably way cheaper than a giant screen or projector.

"Welcome, citizens of Redoubt and of greater Bastion, to the Great Trials!" Valiant announced with a broad smile. A roar swept over the crowd, and with the patience of a skilled orator he waited for the noise to quiet somewhat before continuing. "Here we will test the prospective knights wishing to join the ancient and sacred Order of the Northern Wall!"

Another roar, lasting longer this time, until finally the air Mage shifted the image back to the duke's whole body so he could pat the air for silence. "And now, as you've waited eagerly for long enough, let us delay no more to begin the proceedings!"

The crowd went nuts, and it was several minutes before they quieted. During that time the illusion shifted to Lord Zor, who apparently was officiating the first trial.

The Paladin raised his arms and an expectant hush settled. "Our first trial, as always, will be the Trial of Body!"

As the crowd shouted their approval again Zor turned to the prospective knights. "Let me be very clear!" he said sternly. "These trials are designed to test the mettle of a man, not their class choice or level! Therefore class abilities are not allowed, nor will you benefit from passive bonuses in any of these tests. We will be watching to see if you have quick wits, quick feet, steady hands, and a stout heart."

Good to know. Any high level idiot with points in the right ability trees could take their bow and hit a bullseye in most cases. Dare would've been disappointed if these contests were as simple as that.

Jind stepped forward to join the Paladin. "Therefore, unsurprisingly, the first trial is a foot race. You'll combine speed, agility, and quick thinking as you navigate obstacles, pass through a gauntlet, and go all out on a straight stretch."

Redoubt

Phoenix

His voice became stern. "No physical contact with other prospectives! No abilities! No outside interference or sabotage! You are being watched, and the first infraction disqualifies you, not only from this year's trials but forevermore."

Zor cut in. "Passively triggering abilities are exempted . . . we know you can't control those."

Dare sure couldn't; he would've been pissed if Prey's Vigilance got him disqualified after already nearly getting him killed.

Finely dressed attendants led the prospectives to a clear starting line, where they were deliberately lined up by, as far as Dare could see, how much the judges liked them. It was probably a bad sign that he ended up at the very back of the group.

"Ready!" Zor shouted. "Steady! And go!"

For all the buildup of the race, it was almost disappointing.

The prospectives burst forward, at first moving awkwardly to avoid touching anyone else. Aside from Dare, that is, thanks to Fleetfoot's speed and improved reaction time. He wove through the other racers with ease and soon burst ahead of the pack, sprinting towards the first obstacle.

It was surprisingly familiar, a prone crawl through a two foot tall tunnel that ran for about forty feet. It reminded him of military training back on Earth. With Fleetfoot he could practically fly through the confined space even crawling prone, coming out the other side in an explosion of movement sprinting for the next obstacle.

He tensed as he heard an outraged cry from the judges' stand. "He's using Cheetah's Dash!" an unfamiliar lord shouted, his words carried by the air Mage's spell and immediately drawing a boo from the crowd. "Or should I say Cheater's Dash!"

"Don't be ridiculous, Herren," Jind snapped, silencing the crowd's jeers. "That's the boy with the cunid speed. No surprise he'll breeze through this trial, unless he screws up."

"Lord Jind is correct, my Lord. He is using no ability." That seemed to shift the crowd's mood on a dime, and Dare was pleasantly surprised to hear them cheering for him.

The banter from the platform continued, but he let it fade to the background and focused on the next obstacle, which was a sort of bamboo forest type thing. Except the closely spaced poles were covered in wicked thorns, and if you stayed close to one for too long it began to twist towards you.

Ironically, his passive Forest Perception activated inside it, not only increasing his movement speed but also making him more surefooted around obstacles. Between that, Fleetfoot, and his natural athleticism he was able to twist and swerve his way between the poles, so quickly that most didn't even have time to quiver before he was past.

Again he heard complaints from the onlooking lords, although from the crowd he only heard admiring cheers and applause.

The third obstacle was a succession of hurdles, but set up so that the highest and most closely spaced ones were the straightest shot forward, while as the hurdles got easier the path got longer and more twisty. Until finally the most roundabout route had no hurdles at all.

Logically Dare knew he could make the best time on the longest path with no hurdles, because he could sprint full out at over 30 miles an hour even without Cheetah's Dash.

But something about it felt off. He knew he was being judged on more than just speed here, and even if he blazed through this obstacle by the easiest path he might not impress the judges or the crowd.

Besides, he could run all out whenever he wanted out in the wilds. It wasn't every day he got to test himself against hurdles higher than his waist, and closely enough spaced he'd only be able to get a running start on the first jump.

Thankfully Fleetfoot also affected his jumping ability. He could vault these standing if he needed to, and didn't need a running start for a good jump. So, thinking of Lily as he vaulted the first hurdle, he bit back a smile as he bounded over each.

There were no rules other than the ones Zor and Jind had told

Phoenix

them, so he assumed he could touch the hurdles or even scramble over them if he wanted. But he took pride in making sure he cleared each one without so much as brushing them.

There was even wilder cheering as he left the hurdles behind. Where the path passed close to the rope separating the crowd from the proving field spectators pressed against the rope and waved wildly in encouragement. A dozen or so women even tossed colored bits of cloth onto the path ahead of him, blowing kisses.

One even shamelessly pulled down her bodice to reveal a very nice pair of breasts.

Dare didn't spare the time to look, though, because at his speed he was past her in moments and on to the gauntlet.

The name wasn't an exaggeration; he remembered a movie that had had something like this, but it had been tame in comparison.

Logs embedded with spikes on all sides swung back and forth across a narrow balance beam. Beyond them swords attached to a swiftly spinning column slashed the air above a narrow path circling it. And past that was a straightaway where several men with blunted spears and rocks waited, presumably to hurl them at those passing by.

Falling off the path landed you in a pit of viscous mud. Presumably you were expected to slog back to the start and begin again as the crowd jeered, muddy, embarrassed, and likely injured as well. Which offered some incentive to slow down to face each challenge in the gauntlet.

Dare, feeling the exhilaration of overcoming the previous obstacles, sped up.

He vaulted the first log between two of its tall, wicked spikes, leapt forward just ahead of the second, and on instinct threw himself into a twisting flip that took him over the spikes of the third.

At the sword column he slid beneath two of the higher up blades, right through to the other side just before a lower blade swung in where he'd been, and came up at a full sprint down the last straightaway.

Redoubt

Prey's Vigilance activated to get him around the first hurled spear. He took a rock to the shoulder because of it, nearly knocking him off balance, but grit his teeth and and kept going.

Getting through was the best way to avoid further pain.

He managed to dodge a couple rocks and spears, took a spear right to the stomach and staggered for a few paces, wheezing painfully, as a couple more rocks hit his back. Then he sped up again in a bound, avoiding a few more thrown rocks, and took a glancing blow to the top of his head from a spear haft as he burst out onto the last straight stretch of the race course.

Screw the assholes throwing that shit and screw that gauntlet. The judges obviously seemed to intend that their knight prospectives would need healing at the end of this race. He grit his teeth and ran full out, eyes on the finish line ahead.

And fell right into a hidden pitfall, slamming hard into its dirt wall.

Dare was moving fast enough that he was able to grab the top of the pit, clutching and scrambling desperately until he pulled himself out. As he rolled on the ground he finally felt the pain blooming in his chest from the hard collision, along with the sick feeling of having the wind knocked out of him.

Go all out on a straight stretch, his ass. These judges really were assholes.

Still, he refused to pause so close to the finish line. So, sucking in ragged breaths and feeling his ribs creak painfully, he did a clumsy kip up and stumbled forward, eyes on the ground.

Now that he was paying attention he could see the disturbed sod of the pitfalls. There were fewer than he'd thought, but enough that anyone running full out was guaranteed to fall into one. He wove through them, gradually speeding up as he caught his breath and the initial blinding surge of pain from his injuries faded to a dull throb.

As Dare approached the finish line, flanked by cheering crowds on either side, he half wondered if the judges had some other surprise to spring on him. Maybe they'd hurl poisonous snakes?

Phoenix

Fireballs?

He was so pessimistic that it was almost a surprise when he crossed the line without mishap. He wanted to drop to the ground and curl up into a ball, but that didn't seem like a very chivalrous thing to do.

To his vast relief he felt healing magic wash over him, and then Ireni was there to half support him, half lift his arms in victory. The cheering crowd roared their approval and threw flowers and scraps of colored cloth.

In spite of the BS Dare had just been through, and the fact that he was still a bit pissed, the absence of pain plus the celebrating crowd did a lot to improve his mood. He couldn't help but grin and turn in a circle with his arms still raised, accepting the adulation.

Leilanna and Lily joined them, and together they stepped off to the side and watched as the other prospectives stumbled their way across the field, exhausted and bleeding. The crowd roared laughter every time one fell into a pitfall, although Dare didn't think it was particularly funny having been there himself.

In any case the later runners saw the pits and most were able to avoid them.

As far as he could tell he'd beaten the course in less than half the time of the next fastest man. Meanwhile the slowest runner took almost a half hour, and some didn't finish at all and needed to be healed due to injuries.

Dare had a feeling his winning threw a wrench in the plans of the judges. Or not just winning but completely overshadowing everyone else. There seemed to be a lot of pomp and ceremony around the trials, but with his win they almost seemed to hurry the victory proceedings for the foot race, just to get him out of the spotlight.

He could almost hear a herald intoning, "Yea, verily yea" as the judges rushed through the usual accolades to get to the next portion of the Trial of Body.

This one was strength based, lifting and hurling weights as well as wrestling. Strength was one of his lowest stats, but still high enough above average to be noteworthy, especially for his build.

Even so, he wasn't the strongest person there. He led the middle of the pack in weight lifting and throwing, since he hadn't really done much of that since coming to Collisa. Plenty of running and shooting bows, and even carrying heavy packs, but not so much bench pressing.

His speed let him eke out wins in wrestling, but in a few straight up grapples with men twice his size he got fairly quickly overpowered.

On the plus side, he got to see what the victory ceremony was supposed to look like. With all the winners paraded before the lords, showered with praise, and presented to the crowd for cheers. It looked nice, if a bit overdone.

The next part of the trial was several displays of equestrianship, which was by far Dare's weakest competitions. He had a good horse, but he would by no means say it was the finest on the field. But more importantly he'd never done more than pet a horse in his old life on Earth, and even since coming to Collisa he'd preferred running to riding.

Meanwhile most of the other prospective knights had been born in the saddle, riding from a young age.

The race, which put horse and rider through their paces on a twisting course with lots of ups and downs and obstacles to avoid, was simply a poor performance; he came in second to last ahead of a massive man whose horse simply couldn't handle his weight at a hard pace in spite of its own size and obvious strength.

But the next challenge, meant to test pure riding skill and the horse's quality of training, was downright embarrassing. He came in dead last and even drew ridicule from the Lord Judges and the spectators.

As Valiant put it, "Stick to skulking about the forest setting snares and leave horsemanship to those who aren't a sack of potatoes in the saddle."

Phoenix

It was a relief when the equestrianship challenges were over and they moved on to the next portion of the trial.

Those challenges turned out to be similar to the drills and training Dare had done in Zor's raid. Things like avoiding a monster's ranged and area of effect attacks, staying on target while moving. Even straight up tests of the prospectives' effectiveness at their role, whether it was tank, DPS, or healing and support.

In those trials he blew everyone away again. His speed made all the difference in avoiding damage and staying on target while moving. And his extensive raid experience on Earth, albeit in video games, allowed him to perfectly execute his role.

Honestly, he thought it would've been fun to try out the tank and healing challenges too, if he was able. And the melee DPS. He'd always been much more proficient at tanking or DPS in MMOs, maybe a matter of preference and focus, but with practice he'd done well enough at healing as well.

These trials were varied enough that even though he dominated in everything he competed in, there were plenty of winners to parade around. So Dare finally got to be celebrated along with the others.

It was okay. The best part of it was definitely seeing Marona with the nobles clapping her approval, and Lily, Ireni, and Leilanna in the crowd cheering for him.

After the Trial of Body came the Trial of Cunning, which tested the prospectives on their proficiency at planning raids, leading parties, and even testing unknown spawn points to determine the level of the monsters inside.

His gaming experience in his past life helped him with those trials. Although leadership quality was a big factor, and apparently the judges thought he lacked that based on his common heritage and relative lack of fame or achievements.

Which, while not entirely fair, wasn't entirely unfair either; people would be more willing to follow him if he had a well known and respected reputation.

He didn't win any of those portions of the Trial of Cunning.

While his tactics and ideas gained some approval from the sympathetic judges, ultimately he barely squeaked by passing them. From, as far as he could determine, matters that were entirely out of his control.

Or at least deficiencies in his social standing that he hadn't had time to address, which again wasn't entirely unfair since he'd decided to petition for knighthood this year when he could've waited and been better prepared.

The worst part was Bero, looking amused, commenting that Dare's dazzling intelligence should've served him better here, and it had been a disappointing display.

Those trials took up the full day. As the crowd dispersed, talking about the day's events, the Lord Judges led a procession with the prospective knights to a feast Valiant was hosting in the great hall of his palace.

It was another grand event for the rich and influential, with the added twist that the prospective knights had a table of honor and had lavish praise heaped upon them by the judges, to the applause of the crowd. Some men were singled out for particular achievements of note, although in spite of Dare's commanding performances he was overlooked.

Small surprise, he supposed.

But even though the Lord Judges had much praise to give to those who'd done well, they weren't giving any hints about who was favored to gain knighthood. Which fueled a lot of speculation from the partygoers.

After the meal Marona led them in once again glad-handing their way through the influential of Bastion. Dare was gratified to find that even if the judges hadn't acknowledged his achievements, the world wasn't completely insane and he *had* been seen. He got a lot of praise, particularly from wealthy merchants and landowners who weren't nobles themselves.

Although he also got a lot of deliberate snubbing. In part most likely because he was seen as an upstart and looked down on by the nobility, so anyone who wanted to curry their favor would also look down on him.

And he had no doubt Valiant had also quietly been pressuring his supporters to give him the cold shoulder.

After a few hours of mingling, the crowd around Dare abruptly thinned and he saw Bero ambling towards him with his hands clasped at the small of his back. "A moment, Dare?"

Dare glanced at Marona and his fiancees, then bowed. "Of course, Lord Bero."

The slight man led him to an edge of the room, which while already clear of people became even more so as Bero casually looked around at the nearest clumps of partygoers. When he was finally satisfied of his privacy he briskly turned to Dare. "Let's get down to the final coppers in the chest, shall we?"

"I wasn't aware we had any coppers to get down to," Dare said cautiously. "But I'm all for straightforward discussion."

"Good." Bero looked him over carefully, idly scratching his jaw. "There are things that interest me in Redoubt and greater Bastion. Which privileged assholes glad-hand their way into knighthood is not one of them. So would you care to guess why I insisted on being a Lord Judge this year?"

"I've drawn your Notice?" Dare asked dryly.

The slight man gave him a thin smile. "When someone appears out of nowhere, and no one seems to know where they came from or how they have achieved what they have in such a short time, the wise are well served to look more closely at that individual. Especially when they start making big plays."

"Is knighthood such a big play?"

The lord smirked. "In the grand scheme of things? Nobility always gives clout, and a title is a title. But no, it certainly won't be shaking the foundations of Bastion."

His dark eyes inspected Dare keenly. "But I have learned to follow patterns, and numerous small plays can combine to a suggest a big play is forthcoming. Appearing out of nowhere to buy land, seducing the baroness of that province-"

"I didn't seduce her," Dare protested. "Our feelings for each other are genuine."

"And?" Bero smiled tightly and continued in a firm voice. "Then there's rushing to gain knighthood, rushing levels to a frankly ungodly extent, pulling the Protector of Bastion achievement out of your ass. Charming the Dowager Viscountess of the Southeastern Marches. Ingratiating yourself with the Marshal by taking in the displaced family and friends of his mercenaries, who he in turn views as family. It all hints to you pushing for more and more. To get a foothold in Bastion's political scene in pursuit of larger plans."

Put like that, it sort of did. "I assure you that's not the case at all. I'm seeking knighthood to protect my family and secure the future of my children."

"Is that so?" Hands still clasped behind his back, the Lord Judge boldly circled Dare, continuing his keen inspection. "I'm a firm believer in the idea of not fucking with those who don't fuck with me, Dare. I'm already beset by enough fools who can't seem to resist taking their shot, even when it never turns out well for them."

"What a coincidence," Dare said, resisting the urge to crane his neck or turn when the man went behind him. "You could be speaking for me as well."

"Excellent." Bero clapped him on the shoulder, making him jump, and returned to his former spot. The man began idly repeating a fidget where he snapped the fingers of both hands in quick succession and smacked his fist into his palm, creating an surprisingly even rhythm that almost sounded like a galloping horse.

He kept it up as he continued. "I anticipate no trouble, but let's be clear. Do you have any interest in Redoubt, political or business, or in greater Bastion as a whole?"

Dare gave the question the consideration it deserved. "Unless the situation in the region becomes so corrupt or unstable it affects my family, not anytime soon and probably not at all," he finally said. "I'm not interested in politics or governing, only adventuring and

Phoenix

looking after the interests of my family and those on my land."

"Very admirable, Master Dare. Let's hope your simple goals aren't frustrated by those who can't seem to resist taking their shot." The slight man gave him a somewhat sad smile, as if he didn't believe it possible. "Although something tells me it wouldn't turn out well for them with you, either."

He abruptly stopped his snapping, which was a relief since it had been getting irritating, and his tone became brisk. "One last thing. Bribing a Lord Judge is terms for immediate disqualification, this year and thereafter. The penalty for a Lord Judge taking a bribe is similarly harsh. However, if you were to donate 25,000 gold, preferably anonymously in the form of two godmetal and fifty truesilver, to the charitable cause "Widows and Orphans of the Border Collapse", you might find an extra vote in your favor when the time comes."

Before Dare could be surprised, outraged, or even consider the offer the man held up his hands with a grin. "Donations are strictly voluntary. Merely a means of improving your chances, if you don't believe you can manage to succeed on merit. The Lord Judge in question will of course view your case fairly even should you not donate."

"In the interest of not fucking with people who don't fuck with you?" Dare asked wryly.

"Exactly so." Bero smiled. "If I may say, Dare, I believe I rather like you. I find myself sincerely hoping we have no cause to do business in the future."

That was an unexpected twist on the usual sentiment. Although considering the man's line of work, probably understandable. "You'll probably call me a fool for saying so, Lord Bero, but I find myself liking you as well. This has been a very interesting conversation."

The man laughed. "Not a fool, lad. Just charmingly naive." With the slightest of bows he turned and strode away.

Dare found himself wondering if that little chat had been as amiable as it seemed on the surface. And how close he'd been to trouble he would've rather avoided.

Chapter Twelve
Lifetangled

It was late by the time the party wound down and they returned to the Gilded Chalice.

The girls were all asleep on their feet as they piled into Marona's bed, but Dare was feeling oddly restless. The physical exertions of the day had been enough to get him in an adventurous mood without tiring him out, especially after an evening of mingling with the notables of Bastion.

So he tucked his lovers in and kissed them goodnight, then headed back out in his finery and made for the red light district.

To his relief the Crate wasn't jam packed tonight. Still busier than the first time he'd come, sure, but he had no trouble finding a table by the stage. And he didn't have to pay for it, either.

A somewhat mousy woman was swaying to the song the musicians in the corner were playing, blushing furiously as she lowered thick woolen leggings to reveal white panties embroidered with pink hearts. The crowd seemed to be charmed by her shyness and perception of innocence, because several tossed silver hoping to encourage her to keep going.

But maybe the girl really was innocent, because with a final bashful giggle she gathered up her coins and clothes, waved, and darted for the curtain.

Dare ordered a drink and settled back as one of the serving girls, the strikingly beautiful high elf he'd seen on his first visit, took the stage and began to dance.

He was resigned to waiting for Veressa, possibly without her showing up at all given the late hour. But he was pleasantly surprised.

After a sultry dance that earned a shower of silver and a few gold, the elf gracefully departed the stage. Again after stripping down only to her underwear before the show was cut short by a wealthy patron pointing at the ceiling, wanting to continue things in one of the private rooms upstairs.

The woman who took her place was Veressa.

Winter must be good for the women who took the stage in the Crate, because they had an excuse to dress up in heavy cold weather clothing. More articles of clothing to shed for coins.

Following this trend, the vampire was clad in full adventuring gear, a heavy knee-length coat and cloak over caster robes, and an under tunic and leggings beneath that.

The patrons seemed to approve of the adventuring gear as a style, and many apparently recognized her. Copper immediately began to fly, as if hoping she'd hurry losing the bulky clothing to get to the good parts. But she took her time, waiting until silver made an appearance before losing her under tunic, leaving her in only a thin camisole and her leggings.

Veressa was a striking beauty, nearly six feet tall and slender, with an aristocratic face and figure to make any supermodel jealous. Her pale skin contrasted sharply to the black with red accents clothing she wore, enticing you to wonder what was underneath.

Dare had refrained from throwing a coin, not wanting to muddy a potential adventuring relationship, but even so she definitely knew he was there. Her eye constantly strayed to him, and her small smile seemed intended only for him as more silver flowed onto the stage and she gracefully stripped off her leggings, then her camisole, leaving her in a dark red silk bra and panties.

A man on the other side of the stage threw a gold, and with a grin the vampire lowered her panties enough to reveal her pouting pink slit, then bent over to give the donator a good show. That allowed her to also lock gazes with Dare the entire time, her small smile widening slightly.

A few more gold appeared, and she gracefully cast off her underwear and dropped to her knees, arching her back until her shoulders pressed against the floor. Which thrust out her breasts and pussy as she quivered with the strain of holding the position.

Dare felt himself getting hard as the beautiful adventurer undulated her hips, humping the air as more gold clattered across the coins already on the stage. Continuing the display, she spread her knees apart as much as she could, causing her lower lips to part to reveal her glistening pink interior.

Pointed directly at him. Damn.

To his surprise, the show didn't end there. A man in the crowd tossed a handful of silver and shouted, "Lose the patch!"

To Dare's further surprise, the cry was taken up by other patrons, accompanied by a shower of silver and copper. Was it some sort of weird kink to see what sort of disfigurement the woman hid beneath her eyepatch?

Veressa beckoned to the crowd, egging them on to toss more coins, until finally with a tinkling laugh she reached for her patch, lifted it, and twirled so they could all see her dull silver eye, identical to the other and apparently working just as well.

He also caught a flash of reflected light from the inside of the patch, but only for a moment before she dropped it over her eye again, bowed gracefully, and began to gather up her clothes and the coins she'd earned.

Dare admired her shapely ass as she walked to the curtain, wondering if he had a shot with her. He had to sternly remind himself that that wasn't what he'd come for.

Or not come for, so to speak.

He was still hard when Veressa, fully dressed in her adventuring gear again, reappeared and made directly for his booth, sliding in across from him. He'd been hoping she'd approach him so he already had a glass of pricey wine waiting for her.

"I wasn't sure if you drank," he said by way of greeting.

"I do, thank you," she said, taking a sip. "Enjoy the show?"

Dare felt his cheeks heat. "I'm not sure it would be possible not to."

"Mmm." The vampire smiled just wide enough to show her slightly larger fangs before taking another sip. "But that's not what we're here for, is it?"

"Not just for that," he replied with a grin. "But yes, your offer to be an adventuring companion interested me. Crowd control classes seem rare from what I've seen, as if people don't fully appreciate their value."

She shrugged carelessly. "In most fights a good defender and healer serve the same purpose, just absorbing the attacks from extra monsters with a little added pain. For fights difficult enough to require one or two monsters to be controlled in some way, or a monster powerful enough that slowing and weakening it in some way is required to keep the defender alive, most adventurers will just avoid them entirely." She smiled slightly. "I've already told you why I chose my class, and it wasn't for utility."

"But the utility is there. And if groups and raids made better use of crowd control then deaths might be less common." Dare sipped his ale. "You can do damage as well?"

Veressa nodded. "Of course. Less than a pure damage dealing or defender class, but better than what healers and support with damage capabilities can put out. And I can also grow fruits and vegetables for a party at need, although it's very mana intensive."

She drained her glass and leaned forward sharply. "But now it's my turn to ask questions. I saw your mastery at functioning in your role during the Trials today. As well as your competence and obvious experience at leading a party and even a raid. And no doubt your ability to do damage is considerable, if the rumors I've heard about Lord Zor's raid a few months back are true, where you topped the charts as by far the lowest level damage dealer there."

"But?" he asked as he waved for a serving girl to get her another drink.

"But one Hunter, no matter how good, and one support caster do not a party make. What do you have in terms of healers, defenders, and other damage dealers?"

That was a good question, and largely depended on who among his friends and family would be able and willing to join him at this point. Ireni and Leilanna seemed the only ones, but before long they'd be progressed enough in their pregnancies to make going out adventuring unreasonable.

And they had to be extra careful to ensure they stayed safe, which could make difficult fights even trickier.

"Long term, I have a Fighter to tank for us, as well as an Archer for damage once she levels up a bit," Dare replied. "I'm going to be visiting the Adventurer's Guild here to see about others, but there's also the Adventurer's Guild in Terana. I've fought beside the adventurers our level there and could probably convince more to join us."

He leaned forward, enthusiastically getting into the topic. "But most of our fights will be clearing spawn points, and we don't need a full and well balanced party for that. In fact, it might be more efficient to split up into smaller teams."

"Really?" Veressa said, leaning forward as well in sudden interest. "Most party leaders are just going for a specific goal, a quest or party or raid rated monster or a dungeon. You want companions for leveling as well?"

"Like I said, I want long term companions. Ones who'd be willing to join me for adventures into the high levels. I've already found a couple dungeons, and I mean to find more. As well as more powerful monsters to tackle."

The serving girl arrived with another glass of wine, and the vampire took a long sip as she stared at him over the rim. "Hmm. You wouldn't be the first to gather a full time party as more than acquaintances, but also friends and often permanent guests in their home. Although usually people who make such groups don't recruit relative strangers."

She set her glass down with a sharp clink. "I can't say I'm entirely opposed. I find myself liking you, and your consorts are charming. But what do you have to offer to make me willing to make such a commitment?"

That was the question. "First off yes, if you wish of course I would offer the comforts of Nirim Manor. Which you might be surprised by. Secondly, I know all the spawn points in that area. Farming monsters for levels and loot will be easy and safe with the information I have. Also among the opportunities I'm offering is a raid rated dungeon in the low 40s I intend to clear, as well as a party rated dungeon in the low 50s. The mountains are also a great location to find other party rated monsters we can hunt."

"I see," Veressa mused. "You may be daring to the point of insanity to explore the mountains and experiment with spawn points learning the secrets of their monsters. Unless of course you've spent an exorbitant amount to purchase a more detailed monster compendium and have studied it diligently."

She paused, giving him an appraising look. "Or is there some other secret to how knowledge so readily comes to you? Perhaps an unparalleled intellect able to spot the most subtle clues?"

Dare was proud of his ability to solve problems and think of clever workarounds, but he wouldn't say he was any sort of genius. He shrugged. "As I told the Lord Judges just yesterday, I've memorized numerous monster compendiums. I know most common monsters, as well as rarer and more powerful ones. Rest assured I should be able to identify any we come across."

The vampire arched an eyebrow. "Memorized? And had access to *numerous* rare, precious, and jealously guarded monster compendiums. That's quite the claim."

He smiled. "Believe me or not. My claim is easy enough to prove."

She smiled back. "All right, keep your secrets. But as to your offer I believe I'm intrigued. Perhaps a move to Terana is in order, and perhaps even taking you up on your offer to stay at your manor."

Before he could celebrate managing to convince her she wagged

Redoubt

her finger playfully. "Although I should probably make one thing clear right from the start, given how much you obviously enjoyed the show I put on. As a young man like you certainly would."

He felt a moment of regret. "Not interested in me that way?"

"Oh, I wouldn't say that." The Lifetangler frankly appraised him. "At my age I'm robbing the cradle with just about any man I find, and you're certainly an admirable specimen by any measure." She shook her head with a sigh. "But I have a longstanding policy of no romantic entanglements with party members or adventuring companions. It rarely leads to anything lasting, and when it ends it tends to tear parties apart from within."

"Hard to argue that," Dare said. "Although I'll admit I'm curious to know what it's like to be with a vampire."

She gave that toothy grin again. "No need to be too disappointed. My kind is rare but there are more of us out there. I'm sure you'll get your chance at some point." She gave him a narrow look with her single eye. "I believe I can trust you to abide by my policy? Judging by the radiantly beautiful consorts you came to the party with, you have no shortage of other romantic options."

"That's certainly true." He returned a crooked grin. "I'll respect your wishes."

"Good." Veressa looked him up and down again and sensuously licked her lips with a small, pale tongue. "Because as long as I can trust you to accept this is a one time thing, we're not companions *yet*, are we?"

Dare immediately perked up, pulse quickening. "No, no we are not," he agreed, trying not to sound too eager.

She laughed and drained her glass in a few elegant gulps. "Good, then I suggest we retire to my room in an inn a short walk away." She pointed upwards. "The rooms here cater to wealthy clients and are very nice, as well as kept clean by a Healer with Cleanse Target. I've enjoyed myself well enough the few times I've been up. But I think we'd both prefer a different venue."

Yeah, no reason to bed his new companion (or soon to be) in a whorehouse neither of them even had any connection to. He stood and offered the elegant woman his arm. "Lead the way, Miss Veressa."

The vampire gracefully slipped her arm through his and they started for the door. "I daresay we make a striking couple, Master Dare. Just look at all the admiring gazes. And the jealous ones."

Dare supposed that was true, although his attention was all for the beauty on his arm. "You would make any couple striking by your presence."

She smirked at him as they stepped out onto the busy street. "I appreciate the sentiment, but no need to lay it on too thick. You already have me in the sack, so to speak. And just remember that after tonight we're going to be professional and wholly platonic adventuring companions."

"I remember."

Veressa led the way to a nice inn in the market district, then up to a small but well furnished room. She was all over him almost the moment he shut the door behind them, pressing her slender body to him as her lips hungrily pressed against his. She tasted of plums with a hint of iron, a pleasant flavor he enjoyed. And while her skin and lips were slightly cool, the sensation was pleasant given the heat of her passion.

Her tongue soon slipped into his mouth, also cool but soft and nimble, and he eagerly played with it with his own tongue as they both shed their coats and cloaks.

Before she could get too hot and heavy he reached into his belt pouch and pulled out a Prevent Conception scroll. At the sight of it she chuckled throatily. "No need. I anticipated the possibility of some excitement tonight and purchased the spell from a Healer in the red light district."

Dare grinned and kept unrolling the scroll. "It's probably not high enough rank, so better safe than sorry."

Now the vampire laughed outright, a rich, pleasant sound, as she pressed against him again and ran her tongue along his jaw. "Any

Healer worth their salt has the rank that'll work even with cunids."

It was his turn to laugh, playfully kissing her elegant swanlike neck as he stepped back to cast the scroll. "Like I said, it's not high enough rank."

She just shrugged, a bit baffled but also amused, and teasingly began dancing and stripping for him. "If you don't trust me that's fine. I've certainly used Prevent Conception even when my lover insisted it was already active on him."

"I trust you," Dare assured as he watched her robes slip off her slender shoulders and slide down her body, revealing her under tunic and leggings. "I have a fertility of 56. Believe me, it's caused complications before."

Veressa just smiled indulgently. "You don't need to impress me with your potency, my dear young man. You already have enough to recommend you."

Dare gave up and just enjoyed himself as she repeated her performance from the stage, showing off her supermodel body to him with every sensuous sway while her clothes found their way onto the floor. Until finally she was revealed in all her glory, sexy and clearly ready for him.

Last of all, as if she was even more reluctant to remove it than her red silk panties, she carefully removed her eyepatch and set it on the bedside table.

To his confusion, he saw that there was a mirror on the inside of it. Which would be useless since it would be in the dark, and why would she just want to stare at a reflection of her own eye all the time anyway?

His vampire lover saw where he was looking and laughed. "Ah, curious? I suppose since you know my secret already there's no reason not to explain that. Although given your earlier comment about makeup, I would've thought you could put two and two together."

Dare was embarrassed that no answer was coming to mind. "I guess not," he said with a sheepish laugh.

Phoenix

Redoubt

"Well let me put it this way . . . you think I've been half blind this whole time?" She smirked. "Actually, I have twice the vision anyone else does."

He stared at her blankly. "Is that some sort of scrying mirror?"

"Nope. Just an ordinary mirror." She laughed and tapped the eyepatch. "Come on, you're almost there."

That was generous to say when clearly he wasn't. He still couldn't figure out what use covering a perfectly functioning eye would be, just to have a completely dark mirror that would only reflect your own eye even if some light did leak in around the edges. And why the hell would she even want it, when she was a vampire and mirrors didn't work-

His eyes widened as realization finally dawned. "Vampires don't have reflections."

The pale woman winked her previously hidden eye at him. "So I can look right through my own head and see backwards," she agreed with a vulpine grin. "No one ever sneaks up on me."

Dare swore in admiration. "Does it work?"

"Perfectly, now." She grimaced. "Although it took longer than you'd think to get used to simultaneously looking in front of and behind me. Luckily your brain can adjust to pretty much anything, and now I have nearly 360-degree vision."

"So you can see the guy's expression when he's fucking you from behind?"

Veressa collapsed back on the bed laughing, thumping the mattress with one fist in pure mirth. "Darkness below, *that's* the first thing that popped into your head?"

Dare couldn't help but laugh too. Blame years of browsing the internet and seeing some of the most bizarre thinking imaginable.

Her mirth gradually faded, leaving her lying languidly on the bed with on leg bent and the other flopped out to the side, giving him an unapologetic view of her hairless pink pussy. "We're going to have fun," she purred at him. "Are you ready?"

He grinned and started to remove his remaining clothes. "I'm ready."

"Really, really ready?" The vampire's hands began to glow green, and her expression was almost predatory.

He hesitated. "Um, ready for what?"

"It'll be a surprise," she said in a low, throaty voice, deep red lips pulled up in a lascivious smile. Then she began to cast a spell.

Dare leapt backwards as vines thrashed their way free of the floorboards, new growth from dead, carved wood. But his alarm turned to bafflement as he realized he wasn't the target.

The four vines whipped towards Veressa and caught her around the wrists and ankles hard enough to make her lurch several inches across the bed. Then, with one violent heave, they yanked her limbs out spread eagle, straining as the enchanted growth continued to pull her hands and feet each towards a different corner of the bed.

"Oh," he said as realization dawned. "Fuck."

"I should hope so." The vampire grinned at him down the length of her bound and helpless body, showing her fangs. "Come now, lover, do whatever you want to me."

His cock, already hard at the sight of this beautiful woman fully revealed to him, now throbbed urgently in his pants with her literally spread out for him. Her modest chest strained upwards, small pink nipples diamond hard, and her pussy gaped open to reveal her pink interior, arousal beginning to flow from her depths.

Still, he hesitated at the unexpectedness of it. "Is this a vampire thing?" he asked. "Something to make me feel more at ease? You don't need to, I trust you."

Veressa laughed merrily. "No, silly boy, it's a kink thing. I would've thought that with a harem of beautiful women, at least one of them would have a naughty streak."

Dare could admit he'd done naughtier things than this. Although not with a near stranger. Well, aside from Ashkalla the Succubus, but she'd been a very odd exception. "It just, um, seems like a huge jump when we barely know each other."

"Maybe, but if this is going to be our only time, hopefully because we'll have a long and lasting friendship as adventuring companions, then I want to make the most of it." She licked her red lips. "I did tell you I have a vampire's lusts."

His gorgeous lover urgently undulated her hips. "Now quit standing there gawking as if you've never seen a nude female vampire bound hand and foot on a bed, ready and eager to be used for your pleasure."

"If you insist." Grinning, Dare resumed shedding his clothes.

Veressa watched him hungrily, moaning and quivering with pure lust at the sight of his bare chest, washboard abs, and muscular legs. "Darkest night, you're beautiful," she panted. "I can't wait for you to ravish me."

He couldn't help but look forward to her reaction as he pulled off his underwear. His cock made a more than impressive tent, but once freed the full nine inches bounced with a heavy gravity.

Sure enough, the vampire's eyes got huge. "It seems the gods blessed you with more than great talent and ridiculous good looks. You're literally the complete package."

She was closer to the truth than she realized, since Sia had given him the body of her ideal lover.

And hopefully he'd learned a few things, too. He moved to the foot of the bed and rested a hand on her ankle, caressing her cool, silky soft skin. She shivered, breath quickening. He leaned down and gently blew on her skin, making her shiver again, then began kissing his way towards the prize, alternating between each leg as he continued to run his hands higher and higher up her thighs.

"You don't need to titillate me," Veressa gasped. "You don't need to worry about making me feel good. I know that's exactly what you should be doing most of the time as a skilled and considerate lover. But sometimes you should take a woman's word for it, and believe that what makes her feel good is you doing what makes you feel good."

Dare looked up at her, saw the impatient need in her eyes, and mentally shrugged. Okay then.

He climbed up between her legs, running his hands over her silky inner thighs, around her pussy and across her hairless mound. Then he leaned in and kissed her glistening petals, tasting the familiar plums and faint iron combined with a sensual musk.

"Ah! That's nice," she said. "But is it *really* what you want to be doing right now?"

He grinned up at her, licking his lips. "You think I don't like tasting a beautiful woman? If what makes me feel good makes you feel good then you should be over the moon right now."

The vampire laughed, undulating her hips. "Don't play that circular logic with me. We could go on forever like that." She playfully licked her lips. "If you want me to just shut up and let you work, maybe you should fill my mouth up with something." She parted her lips expectantly.

Dare finally figured out that she wanted to top from the bottom. Which he was more than fine with.

He climbed over her body, playfully brushing his throbbing cock across her glistening pussy, over her mound and flat, well toned tummy, against each of her small hard nipples, and up her swanlike neck. Finally he moved around so he was above her head, massive erection hanging right over her delicate face.

At which point the vines holding Veressa tight lifted her enough she could drop her head back, giving him a straight shot through her mouth into her throat.

"I can take it," she said with an eager smile. "Give it to me. You're not the only one who enjoys tasting your lover."

He slid his tip over her luscious red lips, coating them with precum as he savored their softness, then gently pushed inside her mouth. He encountered no resistance, and she moaned encouragingly as he reached her throat and began to push inside.

Dare would declare Zuri the queen of deep throating, although Rosie had definitely been good. And he couldn't complain about Ulma the dwarf maiden, who didn't seem to have a gag reflex.

Redoubt

But Veressa seemed determined to vie for the crown. Even though she didn't have use of her hands, she somehow managed to provide incredible sensations with her lips, tongue, and esophagus, which she seemed to be able to control in minute detail as it rippled over his shaft.

Not to mention that the obscene sight of his bulge pushing down her long, slender throat was incredibly erotic. And thanks to her swanlike neck he was able to fully push inside her, so his balls brushed against her nose.

The vampire's contented humming became a bit deeper and more throaty, and she made a few insistent sounds and jerked her head against his cock.

Taking the hint, Dare began to fuck her beautiful face, gently holding her head with both hands as he penetrated her throat again and again. She quivered with delight, swallowing and gagging as tears streamed from her eyes and saliva and mucus began streaming from her mouth and up her cheeks.

He watched carefully for a sign of her tapping out, but she must've sensed his concern because she locked eyes with him, as if to silently tell him he'd sure as hell better not stop.

Or at least he hoped that was the message she was laying down, because this felt so incredible he wasn't about to stop without some clearer signal. He thrust faster, making her squirm and moan louder, until finally with a satisfied groan he went balls deep down her esophagus and began shooting powerful jets into her throat while she eagerly swallowed.

When he finally pulled out, panting, Veressa choked, coughed, and beamed up at him delightedly as she squirmed in her leafy bonds. "More!" she begged. "You can't stop now."

Dare couldn't help but laugh. "Don't worry," he said, teasingly trailing his fingers down her graceful neck, luxuriating in her cool, soft skin, "I'm not even close to done."

He started to wipe her face with the covers, but she did her best to jerk her head away. "Leave it," she said, grinning. "I need you to ravage my pussy."

He climbed his way back down the vampire's sexy body, again teasing her with the tip of his cock and luxuriating in running his hands over her beautiful curves. Then he positioned himself between her legs, watching as she squirmed frantically against her bonds to get him inside her, spread eagled and helpless.

"Gods, you're sexy," he murmured.

"Then fuck me already," she whined, panting.

Grinning, Dare rubbed his tip between her silky folds, adding her arousal to the saliva coating his cock, then found her entrance and gently pushed inside her.

Veressa's back arched and her head pressed back against the mattress. "Yessssss!" she squealed. "Stretch me open with that monster! Rip me in two! Darkest night, I need this."

He slowly pushed deeper, her tight walls opening welcomingly as her arousal flowed around his invading length. In spite of her pleas his girth was obviously stretching her to her limits, so instead of moving faster he kept up his pace to give her time to adjust, while reaching down to press his thumb against her clit, rubbing gently but firmly.

His vampire lover's back arched again and her hips bucked wildly, her pussy clamping down on him as she came hard. "Yesssss," she moaned. "Yessssss, yessssss! Give me more!"

Unfortunately Dare couldn't, because he bottomed out with an inch to spare. He began to pull out, still rubbing her quivering bud, timing his movements and his attention to her clit to her responses to try to give her the most pleasure possible.

Although honestly, it seemed like the only thing he could do wrong was slow down or ease up. As he thrust faster, savoring the feel of her delicate walls clutching at his invading girth as if reluctant to let him go, and rubbed harder on her throbbing pearl, she just seemed to go more and more wild.

He thought she climaxed a few times, but it was when her pussy clamped down on his cock hard enough that movement was difficult, and at the same time she squirted all over his crotch with a squeal of delight, he finally groaned and pumped his seed inside her in intense surges of pleasure.

"More," Veressa whimpered as he began to pull out. "I need more."

Dare couldn't help but laugh, because he was fairly certain he'd given her multiple orgasms there. "I can fuck through a few orgasms if I have to, but a rest would be nice."

"No, more!" The vampire struggled plaintively as he pulled away, then with a determined squeak lurched up into the air as her vines thrashed.

They held her helpless like a fly caught in a web, spinning her around as more offshoots of the vines sprang out to further bind her across her legs, stomach, ass, and around her swanlike neck and her small breasts. Until finally she was fully bound, curled up on herself in a fetal position with her ass sticking up in the air, her glistening sex pressed tight between her closed legs.

Veressa craned her neck to look back at him, shimmering raven hair hanging below her to puddle on the bed below, partially hiding silver eyes glazed with lust. "More," she moaned.

Gods, she was insatiable. And ridiculously sexy. Dare got behind her, playfully pushing her a few times in her improvised swing so she swayed forwards and backwards, then lined himself up with her entrance and pushed between her pouting lips into her soft, tight tunnel.

"Yeessssss," she sighed, walls rippling around him. "Fill me up. Stretch me out. Use me for your pleasure."

With the vampire not only bound but now swinging free, it made for some interesting motions. He could either grab her by the hips and hold her steady as he pounded into her, while she squealed and strained against her bonds in delight, or he could let her go and time his thrusts to her swinging.

That novelty carried its own unique pleasure, but it was harder to get a good fast pace going like that since she could only swing so

Phoenix

quickly. And he gave up on trying to swing her out farther so she slid off his cock, then thrust back in, when he missed and just ended up mashing his tip against her clit as her helpless body pressed against him.

She loved it, of course, but it threw off the rhythm.

Even after coming inside her twice, he was still so turned on that when he felt his orgasm building deep inside him to finally erupt in a torrent, spraying her soft walls with his seed, he remained hard and kept fucking right through his refractory period.

Then Veressa got really wild. "More!" she begged. "Plow my ass. Start slow, but once I adjust really give it to me. I *need* this."

Dare wasn't one to refuse such a convincing plea. He pulled out, gathered some of their combined juices to coat her puckered rosebud, and positioned himself at her entrance.

Then, mindful of his girth, he began very slowly pushing inside, giving her a chance to relax and ease into it.

His vampire lover took it like a champ, easier than anyone he'd been with besides Rosie and slime girls, who could accommodate any size. He didn't need to stop as his length slid slowly inside her inch by inch, the ring of her sphincter pale and stretched obscenely, until he was pleasantly surprised to find he was balls deep inside her.

The entire time she moaned in pure ecstasy, drool leaking from her mouth to drip onto the soiled sheets, joining the huge damp patch from her continuously flowing arousal.

"I. Love. Your. Cock," she panted, clenching her asshole down on his shaft in a surge of pleasure before relaxing again. "I need you to ruin me with it. Break me until I'm a mindless drooling heap of pure pleasure. No man is ever going to compare after this, so make it the most indescribable experience ever since it'll be our last."

That was a lot to live up to, but it was also incredibly sexy. Even the fox girl twins' dirty talk couldn't compare to her sheer wanton need.

Dare pushed Veressa's hips forward, making her swing slightly.

She was so tightly wrapped around him that she didn't swing back, even when he pushed harder so she almost slid free of his length. So he pulled her back against him gently but firmly, groaning at the pleasure of sinking into her warm, soft bowels until he was balls deep again.

He didn't get enough opportunities to feel his full length buried inside a beautiful woman. Even with all the different pleasures he got to enjoy, many just as nice as this, it still had a unique quality all its own.

"Darkest night, you're so big inside me," the vampire moaned. She did her best to wiggle her hips in her helpless suspended state. "I'm ready, ruin me."

He withdrew to the tip, gathered some more of her flowing arousal to lubricate his shaft, then pushed in again harder. And harder. Yanking her hips back against him as he thrust, then pushing them away when he pulled out.

She thrashed against her bonds, whimpering in rapture as she came again and again, squirting his thighs once, twice, and finally a third time. And all the while she begged for more.

Dare savored the incredible pleasure, pushing harder, deeper, invading her bowels and fucking her in the most primal of ways. What pushed him over the edge was when he finally felt Veressa go limp with a languid moan, sphincter relaxing completely around his girth as she panted, "You sexy boy, you did it. You pushed me to my limits. For the first time in a very long time I can say I'm satisfied . . . go ahead and finish when you're ready."

With a groan he emptied his balls inside her bowels, filling her with his seed in intense waves of pleasure. Then he pulled his wilting erection free and sprawled on his back on the bed. "Wow," was all he could say.

"I'll say. You used every hole, and used them well." The vampire sighed contentedly, and with a twitch of her limbs the vines binding her gently lowered her to the bed beside him, then pulled free and slithered back into the wood they'd emerged from, leaving the floor almost as it had been with just a few scuff marks.

Phoenix

In spite of the roughness with which the bindings had held her and yanked her around, her skin was smooth and perfect, with not even a pinkness from being pressed against; apparently she knew how to be gentle with her vines.

He almost regretted that he wouldn't have the chance to let her have the shoe on the other foot, with him bound on the bed. That could be fun.

Veressa lay limp, wrung out and fully satisfied with his seed leaking out of her holes, an almost silly smile on her face. "That was far more than I could've expected, Dare," she said, kissing his neck. "And believe me, my expectations are always high. Your consorts did a good job teaching you how to please a woman, and I envy them the fun they must have with you."

"Too bad we won't get to try it again," he said wistfully. "Although I think we'll be great adventuring companions."

"Yes, we do seem to get along." With a sigh of regret she climbed out of bed and reached for a towel on the dresser, beside a full pitcher of water and a bar of soap. She began to clean herself off. "So should I join your group for the rest of your stay in Redoubt, or do you want to meet up when you leave? Or I guess I could travel to Terana separately."

"Absolutely not, we're companions now and we should travel together." He reluctantly joined her and began cleaning himself off as well. "How about we meet up after tomorrow's trials, and I can introduce you to my fiancees and Head Maid and Lady Marona."

"Tomorrow?" His new companion laughed outright. "It's a few hours to dawn."

Dare looked at the window, where the darkness did seem to be lighter, and groaned. "I need to get some sleep before then, or the trials are going to be brutal. Should we just toss the sheets aside and sleep on the bare mattress?"

"Mmm, that's probably a bad idea," she said, a bit regretfully. "I'd love to cuddle with you until morning, and we'd probably sleep fantastically. But your consorts have to be wondering where you've gotten to. Besides, that sort of intimacy would blur the lines when we're now strictly platonic adventuring companions."

She was probably right. Still, he took one last lingering look at her gorgeous body before he mentally shifted to stop viewing her that way.

Or at least as best he could; he was only human.

"Speaking of dawn, what exactly happens to vampires in sunlight?" he asked as he pulled on his undershorts and reached for his clothes.

Veressa grimaced. "We don't burst into flames or shrivel up like a raisin, if that's what you mean." She idly ran her fingers along her ultra fair skin. "You have a redheaded consort, so you should know they sunburn easily and have a very hard time getting a tan. Well we sunburn even more easily, and can never get a tan. We usually wear gloves and hats to protect us from direct sunlight, like a proper lady protective of her complexion. Or we use a potion or spell that has that effect."

"So I imagine winter is your favorite time of year with the reduced sunlight."

She laughed. "You'd think so. You can actually get a sunburn in winter too, including from sunlight reflecting off snow and ice so it's even harder to protect your skin. Also I hate the cold." She patted his arm. "Although I'll be there to root for you during the trials."

Dare finished pulling on his clothes and with a yawn offered his new companion his hand. "I'll see you soon, companion."

She shook firmly. "To a glorious and completely sex free future together." She grinned. "Good thing we got it out of our system."

Chapter Thirteen
Valor

Less than two hours later, Dare was back in the proving grounds with the other prospective knights. Needless to say, he hadn't slept a wink.

Although considering the fun he'd had, he wasn't sure he minded; maybe it was the excellent body Sia had given him, or the fact that he was still a teenager, but the lack of sleep wasn't hitting him as hard as he'd expected. Not with the adrenaline of the upcoming trials pumping through him.

Today was colder than yesterday had been, but that hadn't stopped the thousands of people in the crowd from returning to watch the event. If anything it just meant they pressed closer for warmth, becoming a seething, cheering mass.

Again, he couldn't see his fiancees or Marigold in the crowd, or Veressa either. Marona was up in the nobles box as expected, and she gave him a brilliant smile when he looked her way.

Just as the rising sun peeked over the horizon the Lord Judges made their appearance, same as they had yesterday. They entered the proving grounds with much pomp and circumstances, basking in the adulation of the excited crowd, and climbed up onto the judging platform.

Duke Valiant's face appeared as a fifty foot illusion overhead, and his voice was carried by air magic to boom over the field and the boisterous crowd, quieting them. Mostly.

"There remains one trial for knighthood," the duke called, raising his arms theatrically, "the Trial of Valor!"

The crowd went nuts; obviously if they'd enjoyed yesterday's events, they looked forward to today even more.

The duke raised his hands with a broad smile, speaking over the audience as they continued to cheer. "It will be split into two events. A single combat double elimination tournament for the damage, defender, and crowd control support classes, as well as any healers and damage mitigation support that wish to try their hand. The second event will be a survival challenge for the healers and mitigation support, testing how long they can last against a determined enemy of similar level."

The crowd had mostly fallen silent, listening to the rules as laid out. As was Dare; he knew them already, but he wanted to make sure there weren't any surprise last minute changes.

"As expected," Valiant continued, "the combat will be done with blunted tourney weapons, and spellcasters will use usual tourney rules with damage mitigation support assisting their opponents. Damage will be calculated as the average damage each prospective knight is capable of, taking into account armor and resistances, and their hits counted until they have exceeded the hit points of their enemy. No abilities that increase the damage of your attack are allowed."

That ruled out Burst Arrow, although that was fine.

The duke finished firmly, "Last of all, the standard tournament rules apply! No targeting the head or the groin. Cheaters will be eliminated and barred from knighthood for the remainder of their days. May all fight honorably and well, and the greatest among them win!"

The crowd roared eagerly for the upcoming spectacle.

Dare almost felt bad for the prospective knights who'd be facing him, and that wasn't arrogance. He had Fleetfoot to give him a major advantage in both movement and attack speed, was higher level than just about everyone there, and as a Hunter had more survival and movement abilities that were ideal for individual combat. Not to mention that as a ranged class he'd obliterate melee classes, even with their own movement speed improvement, movement speed debuff, and distance closing abilities.

Although in the interest of fairness it was agreed that ranged classes were at a disadvantage if they started at melee range, and melee classes were at a disadvantage if they started out too far away. So a balance was reached where the starting distance favored both as much as possible.

But not for him, it seemed.

Dare was a bit surprised when he had the honor of going first. Against a Level 37 Berserker bearing two hand axes almost long enough to be battleaxes, giving them enormous reach. The giant of a man wielding them swung them with ease, roaring eagerly at the prospect of carnage.

The axes were padded, but even so they could break bones. Dare felt a bit outmatched as he accepted the blunted arrows he'd been provided.

Especially when Valiant raised his hands for quiet before the match began. "While Darren of Nirim Manor is a ranged class, it has been decided that with his exceptional speed melee opponents are at a disadvantage at the usual starting range, or with the larger field. We will use a melee dueling square and he will begin at melee range."

The fuck?

The melee squares were only 30 feet to a side, about half again the size of a boxing ring. Which seemed pretty big until you got in there and tried to shoot a bow, while a massive barbarian lookalike with movement speed abilities did his best to hack you apart with two huge honking axes. In that space even Dare's speed wouldn't be enough to consistently stay ahead of his enemy.

Apparently the fights wouldn't be so unfair in his favor after all.

As they both took their positions in the square the Berserker clashed his axes together, activating a few abilities in preparation for the fight's start. Dare, wary of the Lord Judges further screwing him by delaying the fight until any abilities he activated wore off, but were still on cooldown, waited with his spear ready.

If he was starting out at melee range, he might as well make the most of it.

Redoubt

"Ready!" Valiant shouted; Dare thought he heard a hint of smugness in the man's voice. "Steady! Fight!"

Dare activated Cheetah's Dash and dove forward. The Berserker, expecting him to dodge away, had charged while swinging his axes wide to either side in case Dare tried to evade. The huge man stumbled off balance as he discovered his enemy had dropped and gone forward instead.

That gave Dare just enough time to Hamstring his opponent before activating Roll and Shoot, drawing his bow from his back as he slammed up against the fence circling the square, with the ability automatically bringing an arrow to the string and shooting it at the big man's chest.

One. By his calculations he needed eleven to "kill" the Berserker. Assuming he had enough space to shoot any more even with his speed.

The big man used Leap to close the distance and reengage, and this time he swung his axes lower, in case Dare tried to roll again. He must not have seen Dare's performance with the hurdles during the foot race.

Dare jumped and twisted over the lefthand axe, activating Rapid Shot in midair to bring four arrows to his bow hand. As he landed in a stumbling run he ran sideways away from the Berserker, fitting an arrow to the string and loosing it. Then another.

Three.

Then he slammed up against the encircling fence again, and his opponent wasn't far behind him. The Berserker had activated some sort of spinning whirlwind attack, axes flashing, and stuck in the corner Dare found himself facing injury at last.

Not sure if he was bold or insane, he pushed off the fence in a flying corkscrew spin straight for his enemy.

Time to see if Prey's Vigilance could work for him for once.

It did, after a fashion. Since he was midair, the automatic movement 100% guaranteed to evade an attack could only make him twist and contort his body. He somehow managed a feat he wouldn't have been able to deliberately duplicate, with superhuman grace twisting and curling in such a way that he dodged the axe headed right for him so it whooshed by just beneath him.

The Berserker's whirlwind ability was very effective at making his axes go pretty much everywhere in all directions around him, so it was incredibly hard to dodge. But he was also committed to the motions, so once Dare dodged the first axe he flew right past the man.

Unfortunately, just as he landed he got hit by a spinning backhand that sent a numb throb through his entire chest and sent him flying again.

Fuck, even with blunted weapons he couldn't take many hits like that.

He forced himself up to his feet in spite of a sharp pain growing in his ribs and a difficulty breathing, and shot an arrow at the spinning Berserker, threading the needle between his flashing axes. The big man was starting to spin his way, but now he was the one in the corner and Dare had some breathing room.

If only he could actually breathe.

He loosed another arrow as he ran to an adjacent corner, trying to goad the Berserker into going straight for him so he could flee to the next corner in turn. But the man wasn't a fool and instead made for the center of the square.

Then he Roared, sending Dare briefly to his knees, stunned.

Dare watched the Berserker come out of his whirlwind attack and charge, both axes raised overhead. In desperation he shot a Strobe Arrow to try to distract him.

It worked, the man stumbling to a halt. "Cheater!" he roared. He wasn't the only one, either, as many in the crowd and even on the judge's platform similarly raised the cry.

Jind's voice boomed over the uproar. "The ability is Strobe Arrow, adding a strobing light effect to the arrow. It does zero extra damage. Fight continue!"

Dare used Roll and Shoot to throw himself into the other corner,

Phoenix

narrowly avoiding a swinging axe. His free shot hit the Berserker in the solar plexus, making him grunt irritably.

Seven. And eight, as he got in another shot while the man closed the distance.

Trying to bolt past with all the speed of Cheetah's Dash, which had almost run out, proved a mistake as he took an axe to his side, again throwing him away with a grunt of pain and likely more broken ribs.

Taking a trick from his fight with the Darkblade a while back, as he returned to his feet and ran away again he used Snap several times in quick succession, while waving his free hand in a confusing pattern. The big man flinched and crossed his axes in front of him as if fearing a magical attack, an instinctive response.

He should've known Dare had no magical attacks, or if he did then a damage mitigation support would be on hand to provide a barrier for them.

That bought Dare enough time to loose a ninth arrow. Then, throwing caution to the wind, he activated Rapid Shot and loosed a tenth arrow even as his opponent chopped both axes down at him with a triumphant bellow.

Prey's Vigilance came off cooldown just in time to twist him aside, and he loosed his eleventh arrow at the man's side from point blank range.

A whistle blew, signaling the fight was over.

Although the Berserker didn't seem to get the memo. Face purple with rage and eyes literally glowing red, he backhanded Dare with a ferocious bellow, hitting him square on the chin with the heavy axe he gripped adding extra weight to the blow.

Dare felt his jaw dislocate from the crushing backhand with a numb sense of wrongness as he went flying again. He tumbled bonelessly, fighting to stay conscious, and in a daze watched his out of control opponent rush forward again, axes raised to swing down right on his head with enough force to shatter his skull even through the padding.

Redoubt

The Lord Judges were bellowing for the man to stop, and doubtless people were rushing forward to intervene, but it would be too late. Dare desperately dug into his pouch and pulled out his legendary chest, dropping it beside him. "Grow!" he shouted, although with his broken jaw it came out more like, "Gawh!"

The enchantment still activated, the chest popping up to full size just in time to catch the hafts of the axes as they descended, stopping the padded blades inches from his face.

A moment later the earth erupted under the Berserker, trapping him up to his neck. He also cried out and screwed his eyes shut in pain, maybe from a Blinding Light spell like Ireni could use. Or maybe actually her spell.

Within the next few seconds vines shot out from the wooden fence to further wrap the berserk prospective knight, and water splashed over it all and froze it solid.

Dare rolled onto his back with a groan of pain. Everything hurt, and healing couldn't come quickly enough.

* * * * *

Ironically, in the ensuing uproar the Berserker nearly caving in Dare's skull wasn't the issue the judges debated.

Everyone seemed to conclude that that was par for the course for the class, a risk that came with dueling them. Although heads definitely rolled for the slowness of the response in subduing the wild man once the fight was called.

The Berserker himself actually acted suitably abashed about his loss of control. He wasn't happy about losing the fight, sure, but he seemed a decent sort and definitely hadn't wanted to hurt or kill anybody.

He apologized profusely as Dare was healed, and then formally shook his hand and congratulated him on the win. "Maybe I'll see you again when I win the losers bracket," he said with a grin.

Dare sincerely hoped not.

In any case, the big hubbub over the fight's chaotic end was Dare

Phoenix

using the chest to defend himself. Apparently such a thing had never been done before, but Valiant, Zor, and a few of the other Lord Judges were furious about him using an outside item in the fight.

They were so enthusiastic about pushing their agenda about this breach of the rules that they were deaf to any arguments. It took Jind and Bero a few minutes to get through to them enough to point out that Dare hadn't used it until the fight was over, and then only to save his own life because the moderators overseeing the proceedings had dropped the ball.

"Frankly, I'm just happy to see someone using their head in these fights, rather than resorting to brute force and rote abilities as is so often the case," the slight lord added cheerfully. "The use he got out of that parlor trick ability Snap makes me rethink its value, and whoever thought of using an enchanted chest as an emergency barrier to hide behind?"

Maybe it was Dare's foul mood after being clobbered and nearly killed, but he felt like most people should've.

Being so publicly proven wrong in front of the crowd didn't do much for Valiant's or Zor's mood, but there wasn't much they could do aside from grudgingly drop the matter, giving Dare a limp warning not to use the chest in any further bouts.

He headed back to rejoin the other prospective knights, getting grudging congratulations from some. Although the Berserker seemed to have taken a liking to him, because he stuck around with him to watch the rest of the preliminary bouts. He even shared a huge gold-chased horn filled with mead, which turned out to be a family heirloom carved from a wyvern horn.

Having killed a wyvern, Dare thought it was genuine.

The big man turned out to be Lorkai Ralia, third son of Viscount Ralia of the Northwestern Marches. Pretty much as far from Terana as could be, but it never hurt to have another friend. Or at least drinking buddy.

The bouts were all interesting in their own way, although none stood out as particularly spectacular. As Bero had pointed out most of the prospectives seemed to rely on abilities, with only basic evasion or pursuit tactics.

It actually pointed to a huge flaw in the ability system, where having the abilities do things for people made them lazy and unimaginative. On Earth a swordsman or archer might train for years to become competent, and carefully consider their strategy in a fight so they were prepared for any surprises.

Here a person just needed to pick a class and start whacking monsters with the abilities and basic attacks.

The sad thing was that, as Ilin and the Monk class proved, it *was* possible to become far more dangerous with training and careful honing of the body. Most just didn't bother.

Melee versus melee seemed to be based mostly on level and gear quality, with slight class differences providing advantages in certain situations. With those things being pretty much equal the usual deciding factors for less skilled combat were what you'd expect: Size, strength, reach, and speed.

Ranged bow versus ranged bow was more interesting, but less impressive, because most people couldn't dodge an arrow and hadn't learned to anticipate a coming shot to even try. So it was basically just a slugfest with the allowed abilities until the one with higher damage and health won.

Dare actually thought he'd have a distinct advantage even beyond other considerations, since his most useful damage cooldown, Rapid Shot, didn't affect damage but speed, and so was allowed.

Also he wanted to try dodging arrows; Fleetfoot's speed and reflexes combined with Cheetah's Dash's speed and agility boost for movement might make the difference. Not to mention Prey's Vigilance and Roll and Shoot.

The magic user fights were potentially the most interesting, although in reality they weren't much different from the bow fights. Spells were just as hard to dodge as arrows, and operated in much the same way when it came to aiming.

Phoenix

The only real novelty was that there were multiple schools of magic used, so he got to see lots of spells. And also with the damage mitigation support casting barriers, the various spells splashing over them made a pretty display.

Ranged versus melee largely depended on speed and luck. If the ranged could stay away and get off their arrows or spells they won, flat out. If the melee could close the ranged usually couldn't get enough space to do any more damage, and without adequate survival abilities quickly lost.

Unlike Hunters, Archers and Marksmen didn't have good melee weapons like spears. Archers could use short swords and daggers, while Marksmen could only use daggers.

Not that Dare would've wanted to go toe to toe with a pure melee class with his spear. But at least it gave him options.

The clear favorite to win it all, aside from Dare himself, actually wasn't some big burly warrior in plate. It was a medium height, somewhat pudgy Spellwarder. Not only did was the man Level 39, the highest level there, but his class was uniquely suited to duels with its combination of offensive spells and defensive barriers.

In a party or raid when the damage was flying thick and heavy against a tank, damage mitigation and healing were roughly the same. But in a fight for your life, being able to stand behind a barrier and cast spells uninterrupted was unquestionably stronger than having to find an opening to heal as well as cast offensive spells.

The Spellwarder obliterated the Marksman he was up against in the first round. Although he had to move forward a bit to get in range of the longest distance bow class besides Snipers.

The Marksman could've capitalized on that by kiting, but he didn't. He just stood there trying to brute force down his enemy by shooting arrows as quickly as possible. Which was exactly what the pudgy, not exactly athletic Spellwarder wanted. The slugfest was very one sided, and while the Marksman eventually figured that out and tried to switch things up, it was too late.

Dare was going to need to take lessons for when he went up

against the magic user, which seemed likely.

The most interesting fight turned out to be a healing class versus a tank. The healer, a Level 33 Shaman, could've participated in the healer challenge, but apparently his balls were too big for that. His class seemed to focus around healing and melee damage, an interesting combination, and he wore leather and ringmail.

Unlike most of the others, the Shaman actually seemed to have learned more than the basics when it came to combat. Maybe because as a hybrid healer he was weaker in combat than others, and so he'd done the obvious and smart thing and improved beyond the ability system.

He wielded a combat pick, like a carpenter's hammer except with a wicked spike instead of the claw end, which looked as if it was just made for punching through armor. He also bore a small buckler on either forearm.

The tank in his plate armor was too slow to pin down the Shaman, even with his movement abilities. The shaman kept turning aside the heavy blows on his bucklers, which was brutal on his arms and on the small shields themselves, and then slipping around to the tank's unprotected side and hammering in with his pick.

Which of course was blunted and didn't actually do anything, but the judges counted the armor penetration of the weapon when tallying the damage.

It was closer than it had any right to be, especially when the Shaman pulled a cheeky move and managed to get away long enough to get off a heal, which was allowed same as damage mitigation would be from a support class.

Even so, eventually the tank got in the necessary hits. Especially when the judges announced one of the Shaman's shields shattered and he was forced to remove it. In spite of that, after the Shaman lost he got a boisterous round of applause for putting on such an unexpected show.

The other interesting fight was the single crowd control support class versus a Mage. Dare was surprised to see that the crowd control prospective knight was the only woman who wasn't among the healers and damage mitigation support. And, he was bemused to see, her class was Succubus.

Which seemed like it would be a lot more useful, or at least more dangerous, in social situations.

The fight was a long and clearly frustrating one for the Mage. The Succubus kept incapacitating the man and then draining his mana. She wasn't high enough level to drain health yet, or use some of the more powerful crowd control options Dare had seen from Ashkalla, but drain mana was all she needed.

Eventually she managed to empty the Mage's mana pool, at which point he had no option but to charge her and fight hand to hand. Which led to a somewhat amusing battle between her with a whip and him with his staff, with her incapacitating him whenever the fight got bad for her, or when he regenerated enough mana for a spell so she had to drain it again.

The entire crowd was jeering by the end of the fight, which didn't do much for the Mage's temper. Especially when he ultimately lost, cursing up a storm. He needed to use expensive mana regen items just to be ready for his upcoming fight in the loser's bracket.

Dare had a feeling the Succubus was going to be in big trouble against pretty much anyone but a spellcaster, but if nothing else she'd hold out for a while.

Or not. In the second round of the competition she ended up against Dare for the first fight, and as soon as the fight started immediately forfeited. That put her in the loser's bracket, but he didn't think she'd fare much better there.

It was a shame since she could be a useful addition to a party, but in a single combat format her true talents wouldn't be allowed to shine. Hopefully her performance wouldn't be weighed too heavily against her by the Lord Judges.

Although based on what he'd seen from that venerable panel so far, he doubted they'd be openminded.

The rest of the second round of bouts went faster, since there were half as many prospectives. The loser's bracket had their bouts at the same time, and Dare noticed that both Lorkar and the Shaman made it through.

The third round was the quarter finals, and Dare was put up against a Level 34 Mage. He got to enjoy trying not to flinch behind a barrier as the man flung water at him to soak him, then tried to freeze him solid, in between flinging ice spikes.

The fight would've been different if he was actually taking damage from the attacks, but as it was he dropped the Mage in six shots, which were mostly accomplished within the first moments of the fight with Rapid Shot and Roll and Shoot.

He even dodged an ice spike, which drew some applause.

The semifinals had him up against a Level 36 Flanker, a frustrating fight because the man was quick enough to chase him around the fighting square. Which he was once again stuck in since he was against a melee class.

But while the tank was able to take more hits than Lorkar, he didn't have the reach of the Berserker's axes or his purely offensive abilities. Dare was able to keep ahead of him for most of the fight, putting his speed to work much to the Flanker's obvious frustration.

Unlike with Lorkar, Dare didn't even take any injuries that needed healing.

Speaking of the Berserker, the finals had him up against the winner of the loser's bracket, which meant Lorkar again. A fight he'd been expecting but hadn't been looking forward to, especially since now the man was more aware of his abilities and tricks.

He was right to dread the fight, because in spite of his best efforts the constraints of the fighting square finally defeated him. The Berserker did a better job of hemming him in this time, and staying on top of him when he used his defensive abilities.

Dare only got seven hits in before the man battered down his imaginary health pool and the fight was called in the Berserker's favor.

Although his real health pool took a beating too, since Lorkar's

Phoenix

axes once again left wicked bruises and even broken bones, forcing him to get more healing.

Dare congratulated the Berserker and formally shook his hand, then clapped him on the back. "Can I buy you a drink when you're announced Grand Champion?"

Lorkar roared laughter and offered him a drink to take the edge off his pain. "I don't know, I've still got to face a Level 39 Spellwarder." He thumped Dare on the shoulder sympathetically. "And unlike you, he gets to be out on the open field."

True. The Spellwarder had been smashing through his duels. Not as interesting as some of the others, but he'd been soundly defeating other ranged classes and completely obliterating melee.

"You've got him," Dare said. "He's not exactly a sprinter, and you've got the damage to batter through his barriers before he can do anything."

"I'm counting on it." Lorkar clapped him on the shoulder again and left to prepare for the grand final.

Dare joined the other defeated prospectives in watching the final bout, and was pleasantly surprised when some of the ranged classes expressed sympathy that he'd been so hobbled in the tournament. The Succubus also flirted with him a bit, although he wasn't sure he wanted to risk fooling around with someone who'd chosen a class based entirely around mind controlling people, or using them as puppets.

The grand final turned out to be closer than anyone had expected. And, contrary to Dare's expectations, Lorkar eventually took his last hit on the verge of his own victory, giving the Spellwarder the win.

As the crowd roared their approval of the final bout, and cheered the victor as the Lord Judges showered him with accolades, Dare began searching for his fiancees in the crowd. He wanted to try to find Veressa, introduce her to the others, and invite her back to the inn as his guest.

But the Lord Judges caught them all by surprise by calling for silence. Then Bero of all people stepped forward. "By majority agreement, the Judges call for a vigil this year."

Fuck.

Dare wasn't the only one pissed, either; a collective groan passed not just through the prospective knights but from some members of the crowd, too.

"That antiquated bullshit?" the Succubus groused. "They haven't done that for years."

The Shaman nodded sourly. "With how much of a spectacle they've made the trials, I'd thought they'd completely lost interest in a trial the prospectives have to do in private."

It wasn't exactly that Dare hated the idea, he just hated the idea. The vigil called for 24 hours of seclusion in the Chapel of the Deities. In cold, bare stone cubbies with not even a chair, where they were expected to fast and pray the entire time. To purify their minds and hearts for their coming judgment on whether they'd be invited into the Order of the Northern Wall.

Not an impossible task, but it was going to suck.

With that announcement the prospective knights were all rounded up and marched "triumphantly" to the Chapel of the Deities, where they were turned over to the clerics of the chapel who led them down into the basement.

Which meant that after a sleepless night, then a day of fighting with only hurried snacks and water breaks here and there, Dare now had to fast for 24 hours and sleep in a cold room without so much as a pallet or blanket.

Fuuuuuuck.

Chapter Fourteen
Vigil

Dare followed an elderly cleric down a dank hallway in the basement, until finally he stopped at a small door. "Your vigil chamber, prospective," he said politely.

Dare looked inside to see a small round chamber all of stone, with alcoves in the walls in which the shrines of deities were arrayed. Probably not all of them, but at least the most well known ones.

There wasn't even a rug on the floor or tapestries on the walls to blunt the chill. Grimacing, he stepped into the room.

The cleric blocked the doorway behind him. "The door is not locked," he intoned. "Nor is it guarded. You may leave at any time. But know that if you do, the path to knighthood is barred to you forevermore. Likewise should you disgrace the vigil . . . this is a time for prayer and fasting, denying the desires of the flesh."

"I understand," Dare said. "Thank you."

The older man inclined his head and departed, shutting the door behind him with a creak. Leaving Dare to look around the spare round chamber, the stone floor before each alcove smoothed from generations of kneeling petitioners.

His home for 24 hours.

He searched for the Shrine to the Outsider, hoping it would be there. To his relief it was, although the floor before it didn't look as worn as the others.

He made his way over to it, inspecting the stylized globe of Collisa circled by a comet in orbit. "Well, here we are," he told Sia, bunching up the bottom of his cloak to provide some cushion so he could sit with his back against the pedestal holding her shrine. "If you're following my life for entertainment, I'm afraid you're going to be bored for the next day. Probably a good time to catch up on busywork, unless you want to be bored with me."

As it turned out he was wrong, although not immediately.

First things first, since Dare was absolutely exhausted he wrapped himself in his cloak and tried to doze on the cold, hard stone. It was as miserable as he could've guessed; he woke up periodically, shivering and body aching from sleeping on hard stone. But all he could do was shift position, pull his cloak tighter around him, and try to go back to sleep.

He probably got four hours of rest total during an eight hour period. It just left him feeling even more exhausted when he finally gave up and got up to walk around the chamber, shivering and pressing his gloved hands into his armpits.

But awful as his night was, it was by far the most pleasant part of the vigil.

Time passed slowly when you were bored and confined to a small room. But when you were also exhausted, cold, hungry, and agonizingly thirsty, the day crawled by from one moment of pure discomfort to the next.

Dare spent most of the time talking to the Shrine of the Outsider, or more accurately Sia in case she was watching. Although of course Ireni wasn't here so the goddess didn't respond no matter how much he spoke to her.

The hours passed and after a while he tried dozing again, then gave up after a brief fitful slumber and relieved himself in the waiting chamber pot. Which meant he got to enjoy the smell on top of the other discomforts.

His hunger and thirst were becoming acutely uncomfortable, especially thirst, to the point his throat frequently felt dry and he had to swallow often.

And on top of it all Dare was bored out of his mind. To pass the time he wandered the chamber, looking at the shrines to the other gods and goddesses. Some he recognized, but he was embarrassed that even after about nine months on Collisa he knew fewer than he should.

He should probably buy a few books on religion and remedy that. Especially since he was Noticed and might find himself interacting with some of these beings or their followers in the future.

After an interminable time in his vigil, he judged maybe twelve hours, the door creaked open and a slender shape in a dark cowled cloak slipped furtively into the chamber, carrying a basket. The figure lowered the hood to reveal a strikingly beautiful young woman with shimmering brunette hair framing soft features and incredibly wide eyes.

She crept over to him, smiling shyly. "Well met, my Lord," she whispered, hefting the basket. "I thought you might be hungry." She blushed prettily. "And that maybe you were cold and lonely in here all by yourself and might like some company to keep you warm."

This was so obviously a test that a part of Dare wondered if it was possible it actually wasn't. Either way, he wasn't about to bite. "Well met, miss," he said politely. "I'm sorry to correct you but I'm not a lord, merely a humble servant of Bastion cloistered in vigil."

The beautiful woman giggled and slipped off her cloak, revealing a slim, graceful body clad only in a light shift. It was a bizarrely strange choice in the chilly chamber and she immediately began shivering, but she tried to maintain her seductive front as she lifted the cloth on her basket, filling the room with the tempting scent of meat buns.

"Even humble servants must eat." She bit her lip and blushed some more. "And if the room has chilled you, as it chills me, perhaps we could warm each other."

Dare gave her a polite but firm smile. "You're very kind, but I'm afraid I must refuse. I am in vigil, and can neither eat nor drink. Nor can I enjoy your fair company, for I must kneel in prayer to the gods until my vigil is ended."

Without waiting for a response he knelt in front of the Shrine of the Outsider and focused on the globe and circling comet. *I guess you found some entertainment in this vigil after all, Sia,* he thought. *I'm not tempted, of course, but holy shit is this girl hot. And also freezing her ass off, poor thing.*

Redoubt

He hoped she'd give up and go away soon, for her own sake.

Instead the woman folded up her cloak to sit on, an unfortunate glance showing that her crosslegged position gave him a clear view beneath her shift; she wasn't wearing panties. He hastily turned his eyes back to the shrine, doing his best not to be distracted.

Over the next half hour she tried to talk to him, tempt him with various poses, and at one point even knelt beside him as if joining him in prayer, pressing her slim leg against his. Although honestly she seemed more interested in his body heat than anything amorous as she shivered, teeth chattering.

She even outright asked to be his consort, and promised to show him right then and there what she had to offer.

Dare wondered if anyone was ever beaten by this obvious temptation. Most prospective knights wouldn't reach the minimum required level of 30 until they were in their 30s, old enough for the raging hormones of the teenage years and young adulthood to settle. Old enough to know better and have developed some discipline.

Although the most painful temptation was when his visitor started eating the meat buns in front of him. That was just cruel.

Finally the girl huffed, gathered up her cloak and basket, and stormed out of the chamber. He could admit it was a relief when the door closed behind her. Although ironically, now that she was gone the lingering scent of those meat buns was giving him serious hunger pangs.

He supposed the judges felt like they needed to cover their bases, because after that they sent a young man, as handsome as the girl had been beautiful, carrying a jug of wine and similar offers. He wanted to be Dare's squire and hinted at what he'd do for the position.

That was no temptation, since while Dare fully supported people finding love and intimacy with whatever gender they desired, he just didn't have any inclination in that direction. Although when the guy downed half the jug of wine in front of him, spilling several splashes on the floor, that was more difficult.

Redoubt

Dare was getting desperately thirsty.

The man finally left, thankfully; it had been pretty awkward.

Dare eventually fell asleep again, exhaustion overpowering discomfort. He wondered if he was getting soft, since he'd spent so many months roughing it in the wilds before moving to Nirim Manor.

But no, this just sucked. Also most of his time camping in the wilds he'd had Zuri's warm, soft body pressed against him, then eventually Pella's. And it had been during the summer, when nights were downright mild even in Bastion.

So the best he could manage was a fitful doze, drifting in and out of confused dreams and shifting position frequently to ease his aching muscles. He didn't think he ever slept heavily enough to be unaware of his surroundings.

Which was why he was so startled and confused when he was awakened by a bright light in his face, far more than the few fat candles dimly illuminating the chamber.

Dare jolted up to a sitting position with a sharply indrawn breath, squinting past the light to see Duke Valiant looming over him. He immediately rose to one knee and bowed his head. "Your Grace." Was the vigil finally over?

Apparently not.

Valiant settled into a comfortable chair a servant must've carried in for him, scrutinizing him with clear distaste. "You're never going to be a knight, Hunter," he said bluntly. "The very fact you're trying is an embarrassment . . . I could enjoy seeing you humiliate yourself, but your parody of a petition brings mockery to these ancient and sacred proceedings. That I cannot tolerate."

Dare wasn't sure what he could even say to that so he kept silent, head bowed.

The duke snorted in disgust and, with a clinking sound, tossed a fat purse next to Dare's fist pressed to the floor. "That's fifty truesilver pieces. Five thousand gold. It galls me to pay off scum like you to prevent you from doing something you shouldn't be allowed to do anyway, but for the sake of the Order of the Northern Wall I will."

He kicked it closer to Dare, carefully controlled voice breaking angrily. "This is better than you deserve for the pain you caused my nephew, ultimately driving him to reckless choices that led to his death, but the offer is there. Take it and get out of Redoubt. Don't come back. Don't embarrass us all by trying to be more than you are."

If this was a test, it was far more convincing than those other two. But test or no, if Valiant thought Dare's chances were good enough to try to pay him to give up, that was heartening.

Dare silently picked up the purse and proffered it in both outstretched hands, keeping his head bowed.

For several brittle seconds the governor of Bastion said nothing. Did nothing. Then with a furious growl he snatched the purse out of Dare's hands. "Get blown by a viper, you little shit," he snapped, stalking to the door. On the way he passed the chair and kicked it across the room.

Moments after he left a servant crept into the chamber, not glancing Dare's way, and retrieved the chair before leaving and closing the door behind him.

Dare settled back down on the stone floor, trying to go back to sleep. He failed, the duke's words ringing unpleasantly in his ears as the cold seeped through the cloth to chill him.

To his vast relief, his ordeal ended not too much longer after that. The elderly cleric returned and bowed. "Your vigil is done, prospective. Please, come with me."

Dare groaned and pushed up to his feet, swaying as his body protested. It was incredible how just lying on a cold hard floor for hours shivering could leave him feeling like he'd been beaten thoroughly.

He followed the cleric to a larger room in the basement where, blessedly, a few braziers filled the space with heat. The other prospective knights were already there, huddled around the braziers gulping water from clay mugs while robed acolytes stood nearby with pitchers to make sure they had as much as they wished.

All of the other prospectives were there; he'd been the last to be fetched.

He joined Lorkar at one of the braziers and accepted a full cup from an acolyte, downing it in two gulps and holding it out for a refill. Then another. That one he sipped more moderately as he let the warmth of the brazier seep into his bones.

None of the prospectives seemed talkative; they were obviously as exhausted and worn out as he was and just wanted to find some food and a bed and sleep. Although they found some energy to straighten and salute when the Lord Judges swept into the chamber.

"Your vigil is over," Valiant intoned without preamble. "Go now to deserved rest. On the morrow you will stand before us and be judged worthy or unworthy of entry into the Order of the Northern Wall."

He swept out, although the other lords stayed to chat with the prospectives.

Dare bowed as Jind approached and clapped him on the back, then wrapped an arm around his shoulders and guided him towards the door. "You look dead on your feet, lad. Let's get you back to your inn."

"My thanks, my Lord," Dare said.

They emerged to find the sun setting. With his nose super sensitive from hunger he caught the scent of food from distant street vendors, and his feet unerringly took him in that direction.

Guessing his mind, the Marshal grinned knowingly. "So which temptation during the vigil did you most struggle with?" he asked as they walked, nudging him with his elbow. "I suppose I shouldn't have to ask, when you have a harem of beautiful women . . . a man after my own heart."

Dare smiled wryly. "Considering the stakes none of the temptations really were. Although Duke Valiant was definitely the most intimidating and convincing."

The Marshal blinked, laughter dying. "The Duke?" he repeated blankly.

Ah, so that hadn't been one of the "temptations". It really had seemed too genuine. "Let's just say he invited me to walk away."

Jind shook his head. "The things we do for family," he murmured. He glanced around and leaned close, gripping Dare's shoulder. "Best keep that tidbit to yourself, my friend. It would embarrass an enemy, sure, but that's holding a snake by the tail and you could easily get bitten. At best he'll deny it, and go from being your enemy for the sake of duty to your enemy because he hates your guts."

Dare had sort of figured Valiant wouldn't try a stunt like that if it could blow back on him. "We're encouraged not to speak of what transpires during the vigil, aren't we?"

The older man chuckled and clapped his shoulder. "Indeed we are." His smile widened. "On the subject of the fair maiden, if she caught your eye she was hired from the Blooming Rose, down in the red light district. You wouldn't be the first prospective knight to stave off temptation, only to indulge it at a more appropriate time."

That was definitely a possibility to consider. "Good to know."

Ironically, the first stall they passed sold meat buns. Probably even the same ones the girl had tempted Dare with. As it turned out they were every bit as delicious as they'd smelled, tender beef and diced vegetables swimming in rich gravy that spilled over his fingers with the first bite.

He devoured six.

Jind kept him company for the first few minutes, less messily eating a couple of the buns himself. Then, with a final slap on the back, the man wished him good luck with the next day's judgment and strode off into the crowd.

Dare avoided the temptation to stuff himself on an empty stomach and made his way purposefully to the inn, although he did stop at another vendor to buy a waxed paper horn of wine. It was sour and tasted like piss compared to the vintage Lily loved, but with his thirst he enjoyed it every bit as much.

Back at the Gilded Chalice he found everyone waiting anxiously for him. Including Veressa, he was pleased to see, who'd taken it upon herself to become acquainted with his fiancees and Marona's entourage while he was in vigil.

From what he could see, the women seemed to welcome the vampire warmly. Although of course they didn't know she was a vampire; hopefully she'd feel comfortable sharing that secret eventually.

Most of his lovers among the group, Marigold and Lily especially, seemed to be a bit confused about the Lifetangler's policy of not sleeping with adventuring companions. But while they joked that it seemed like missing out on a good thing, they accepted it.

Dare could admit that he paid closest attention to Ireni's reaction to Veressa. He had decided to trust the vampire, but he figured if anyone would have an instinct about her then the High Priestess of the Outsider would.

As well as Sia, if she decided to weigh in on the issue.

As far as he could see Ireni seemed fine with the tall, slender woman, treating her as warmly as any of the others. That made him feel a bit better.

Almost as soon as he stepped into the inn he found himself whisked to a private dining room. At which point he was glad he hadn't stuffed himself on the way home, because Marona had arranged for a feast.

They all gathered around the table to eat delicacies and delicious dishes, drink, celebrate the end of the trials, and cross their fingers (figuratively, since that wasn't a thing on Collisa) on tomorrow's judgment. Dare was showered with affection, suffusing him in a pleasant fog as his full stomach lulled him to give into his exhaustion.

As he nodded off he was fuzzily aware of the women he loved helping him out of his seat and guiding him to Marona's room. Working together they undressed him, bathed him with warm water,

Phoenix

soap, and their soft hands, and tucked him in.

He drifted off to the heavenly sensation of soft warm bodies pressed against him, gentle fingers brushing through his hair and caressing him, and loving voices soothing him to sleep.

*****

Dare woke up feeling incredibly refreshed and recovered from his vigil. Not to mention more appreciative of the sexy naked bodies cuddled against him.

Marona and Ireni seemed to have claimed the closest spots, draped over him so their soft thighs rubbed his stirring morning wood on either side, their warm sexes pressed against his hips, and their small soft breasts mashed against his chest, hard little nipples poking him.

They were both stirring awake with some very delightful motions, and he realized that what had awakened him, and the women he held, were soft wet sounds, moans, stifled giggles, and playfully stern shushing sounds.

It sounded like Lily and Leilanna were already awake and playing with each other. Dare craned his neck to look over Ireni and saw the two women grinding their pussies together in a tangle of writhing limbs, tongues wrestling in a passionate kiss as they toyed with each other's breasts.

If he hadn't already been hard, that would've had him solid as blue steel.

Marona seemed to agree, lifting her head to look as well, then gasping in appreciation of the sight. Without a word she spat on her hand, rubbed it between her legs as if she couldn't wait for natural lubrication, and climbed on top of him.

"I've been too busy to enjoy having you here with me," she said as she glided her petals against his tip, adding his precum to her spit. Then she shifted position, hands planted on his chest to hold herself up, and began lowering herself onto his shaft, moaning as he spread her open.

Redoubt

"And goddess virtuous, I've missed this," she panted as her soft pink walls wrapped around him inch by inch. Her nectar had begun to flow, easing his entry, and soon he bottomed out and she began rocking backwards and forwards so his girth could stimulate all her sensitive spots.

Dare lay back and let his noble lover ride him to her heart's content, running his hands over her soft skin and appreciating her mature beauty. Her belly showed a gentle but distinct swell from her pregnancy, and he rested his hand on it and marveled that his child was growing inside her body.

Ireni lifted onto her knees so she could tenderly kiss Marona, small hand gently stroking her breasts. Leilanna and Lily were continuing to pleasure each other while they watched the baroness mount him, movements becoming more urgent at the sight.

Marona moved more urgently as well, breath coming in soft gasps. Until finally her tight walls caressed him lovingly as her arousal flowed in a gentle but intense climax, Ireni holding her in a tender embrace. Dare heard Leilanna and Lily both cry out in a shared orgasm, and that was enough to empty himself inside his noble lover.

She sighed in satisfaction at the sensation. After they both came down from their climaxes she climbed off him to cuddle against his side again, kissing him tenderly. "I love you," she murmured.

Dare stroked her silver-streaked dark hair, returning her kiss before looking into her enchanting dark eyes. "I love you. More than you can imagine."

She laughed lightly. "I don't need to imagine anything, I can see it in your eyes."

The others all wanted their turn atop him, and either by coincidence or planning they mounted him by order of urgency. Ireni was next, gently lowering herself onto his manhood, and made love to him in the slow and deeply intimate way she loved.

In spite of that she must've been excited because she climaxed more quickly than usual. So unexpectedly, in fact, that the surprise

Phoenix

and pleasure of it triggered his own orgasm as well, and with an eager groan he released inside her warm, welcoming tunnel.

As his redheaded fiancee climbed off him to cuddle against his side again, Leilanna practically climbed over her to get on top of him. The curvy dusk elf's skin glistened with perspiration from her fun with the bunny girl, and with Dare's cock softening from coming twice in fairly quick succession she determinedly rubbed her lush body against him until he was hard again.

Then she rode him with far more enthusiasm than his two previous lovers, big firm breasts bouncing so tantalizingly that he just had to play with them as she squealed and moved even more frantically. Her entire body tensed and flopped down on him as she came, soaking his crotch with her arousal, and he held her as she trembled in pleasure and made the most delicious whimpering sounds.

To his surprise she climbed off after that. "Save your shot for the next girl," she teased with a giggle. "You might be able to go all day if we give you a chance to rest, but you've got two more women to please and it's not fair to make them wait."

Two?

His unspoken question was answered as Marigold clambered up his legs to impale her tiny body on his shaft, squeaking in delight. He had no idea when the pink-haired gnome had arrived, but she definitely made her presence known as her crushingly tight pussy slid down his length.

Since Dare could bottom out in her with half his length still outside, the maid gripped the rest of his shaft with her small hands, squeezing and rubbing hard as she rode him with wild abandon.

He always did his best to make sure his lovers came at least once before he did, but her relentless and pleasurable assault on his cock overwhelmed him. He could never hold out long inside such a viselike pussy anyway and soon tensed, grabbed the plump gnome's wide hips, and held her as he filled her up.

Which just left Lily, who'd been working herself into a frenzy watching the other girls. To the point that her love scent's pure and overpowering need hit him like an avalanche.

His wilting cock didn't stand a chance against that sort of arousal, and hardened again to super-sensitivity as she urgently rubbed her plump, sopping lips against the underside, beautiful body glistening with perspiration and eyes glazed with lust behind her adorable nerdy glasses.

Dare actually cried out as she mounted him, the sensitivity of his tip the most glorious pleasure he'd ever experienced, pushing him to his limits on the verge of discomfort. Her tight pussy milked him from the start in orgasm, squirting arousal all over his crotch as he bottomed out in her. Although she pushed through her climax to keep going, striving for greater heights as her love scent washed over him in waves.

The next few minutes were intense as the incredible pleasure from his hyper-sensitivity warred with the fact that he'd just come three times. For a moment they struck a balance, and then the stunningly beautiful bunny girl pressed her body against him, diamond hard nipples scraping against his chest, and kept bouncing up and down on his cock as she nuzzled his neck, then nipped it hard as she cried out in overwhelming ecstasy.

With a groan he grabbed her perfect ass with one hand and her adorable cottontail with the other, pulling her hard against him as he released inside her quivering tunnel. He felt almost dizzy as the surging pleasure joined with her love scent in a blurring haze.

Panting through her own powerful climax, Lily kissed where she'd nipped him. "How does this compare to vigil?" she teased.

Dare laughed and ran his hands through her silvery hair in cute pigtails. "I'd go through it again to enjoy this the next morning."

His lovers all laughed, and with a few final affectionate kisses and gropes unanimously agreed to take this to the bath so they could clean up.

He was given time to recover before getting another workout amidst a press of soft soapy bodies, and the bath lasted for almost an hour before they all dressed and headed to the private dining room for breakfast.

Sadly, Marona had to leave after eating, back to her meetings with the Council of Lords. Although the proceedings had been bogged down by several of the members busy being Lord Judges overseeing the trials, so the first half of the week was practically a joke.

"As always," she said with a sigh. "Still, even if it's mostly a waste of time I can't get out of it."

Since Dare again needed to stay close in case he was called before the Lord Judges, and wanted to be even more ready this time because he was awaiting their decision, they stuck around in the inn that morning. They cuddled in the newly turned over bed, Lily reading them passages from her current romantic book as they all listened contentedly.

Belinda joined them after while, which was nice since he'd mostly just enjoyed wild sex with the beautiful dragon girl. It was a pleasant change to enjoy holding her and stroking her soft scales as they listened to the bunny girl read.

"I can play the lute," Belinda abruptly said, surprising them. "Want me to get it?"

"Ooh, and I play the flute!" Marigold said, perking up. "Let's play together! We can be a lutist and flutist."

The dragonkin playfully swatted the little gnome. "It's pronounced flautist."

Marigold boldly swatted her back. "No it's not, and I would know since I play it." She eagerly grabbed the other maid's hand. "Come on, let's go get them so we can play for everyone!"

To Dare's disappointment, or perhaps nervous excitement considering the circumstances, he didn't get to stay to listen to them play. A runner arrived from the palace to inform him that he was expected before the Lord Judges at his earliest convenience.

Or in other words right fookin' now, as Celissa or Elyssa had joked last time.

Redoubt

Dare bid everyone a hasty goodbye, and with their well wishes following him bolted out of the inn. He rushed through the streets to the palace fast enough that people stopped and stared, but he ignored them as he reported to the guards at the gate.

As before, a servant led him to the circular chamber with the ornate double doors. And as before, after rushing he was forced to wait for almost an hour before he was finally called in.

It wouldn't have surprised him if he was the last person judged. Actually, he was sure that was the case.

Once again he took his place in the center of the room, facing the curving table of judges looking down at him sternly.

Maybe there was usually some sort of ceremony, a few last questions or speeches or something. But it seemed like with him the Lord Judges wanted to get right to it.

"As stands before us this man," Valiant intoned, "do we deem him worthy to enter the ranks of nobility, and bear the title and reputation of Knight of the Order of the Northern Wall? What say ye, my brothers?"

"Sure," Bero drawled. The duke glared at him until he smirked and amended, "I say aye."

Good; looked as if the slight man had told the truth about dealing fairly even without the bribe.

"Nay," the lord next to him said.

"Aye," Jind said.

"Nay!" Valiant said forcefully.

"Nay," the lord next to him said.

"Aye." That came as a surprise, because it had come from Herren, who'd seemed to have a chip on his shoulder about Dare this entire time.

There were only two lords left with the votes tied. Lord Zor was next, and he spent almost a full minute inspecting Dare thoughtfully before an impatiently cleared throat from the duke made him stir. "Nay."

272

Not much surprise here. The fact that it had taken him so long to decide on his vote was the only unexpected thing. Unless he'd just been dragging it out for suspense.

Dare felt his heart pounding as he looked to the last lord, the elderly Level 56 Phasewarper who had the exact sort of long flowing white hair and beard you'd expect from a wizard. He'd been mostly quiet in meetings and deliberations before now; no way to guess what was going on behind those impassive features.

Thankfully the man didn't leave him in suspense long. "Aye."

Dare's breath left him in a whoosh, although it was too early to start celebrating yet. The votes were tied, and there was every chance the tie breaker would be decided by the Governor of Bastion.

In which case he was screwed; he wished he'd asked Marona before now what happened in a tie, which seemed a high likelihood with an even number of Lord Judges.

Valiant glared at the men who'd cast their votes for Dare as if wondering what was wrong with them, then reluctantly faced forward again, looking over Dare's head. "As we are divided on this matter, we look to the gods for their wisdom." He turned to the elderly Cleric of Henor.

The man stood with his head bowed, in prayer or in thought, for even longer than Zor had taken. Finally he stirred and spoke, head still bowed. "Henor takes Note of this man, and deems him worthy by deed, by ability, and by intent. Aye."

If the duke had been irritated before, he was furious now. To the point that he spoke through gritted teeth. "Then it is decided. Darren will be inducted into the roll of the Knights of the Northern Wall. Darren, by what surname will you and your family be known henceforth?"

Dare had thought this through, and discussed it with his family. In the end, though, the choice had been clear: he already had a surname, his last tie to his parents and little sister back on Earth, and all his family before them. "Portsmouth."

There was a somewhat baffled stir among the Lord Judges.

"Portsmouth?" the old wizard-looking noble repeated.

"That's right, my Lord."

"In spite of the fact that there are no ports in Bastion, particularly anywhere near your land."

"If the Lord Judges will permit it, my Lord, the name holds special significance for me."

There was the unspoken equivalent of a disinterested shrug from the gathered lords, and Valiant snorted impatiently. "There's certainly no contest for the name from any noble in Haraldar. Congratulations, Darren Portsmouth. The ceremony will be held tomorrow evening."

One of the courtiers immediately ushered Dare out into the hall.

He allowed a servant to guide him out of the palace, departed through the gates, and strode down the street at a dignified pace until he was out of view. Then with a whoop he activated Cheetah's Dash and bolted towards the inn, weaving through the bemused crowds.

He was a knight! Or at least he would be tomorrow, assuming Valiant didn't find some way to screw him over beforehand.

Dare burst into the inn, startling the staff and drawing some huffs from the wealthy patrons, and pounded up the stairs to Marona's room. Through the door he could hear the merry sounds of flute and lute harmonizing in an upbeat melody, which seemed like the perfect setting for his announcement.

He threw it open with a grin. "Introducing Sir Darren Portsmouth!"

The girls went nuts, swamping him in hugs and kisses and filling the room with delighted squeals. He grinned like an idiot the entire time.

With the day reasonably fine for early Ged, Collisa's equivalent to January, and since there was no more reason to stay in the inn, they all agreed to a picnic lunch outside. They hadn't had a chance to visit the grand park in the center of the nobles' district yet, but the maids assured them it was beautiful year round.

Phoenix

In fact, in the winter they hired water Mages who'd honed their skills as professional sculptors to make snow and ice statues around the topiary bushes, and a pond in the center of the park became a skating rink.

Marigold ran down to the inn's kitchens to arrange the food, while they all bundled in their winter clothes and gathered the musical instruments and a few books to pass the time. Apparently skates that could be attached to their boots were rented out at the pond, if they were interested.

Dare had only been skating a few times, but he thought it would be fun.

Marona returned for lunch just in time before they set out, and her weariness at the morning's duties vanished at the prospect of an outing. Not to mention her joy at hearing his good news about the Lord Judges' decision.

Soon he found himself walking with a group of eight beautiful women. Along with his fiancees and Marona, Marigold, and Belinda, Veressa had also accepted their invitation to come, dressed all in black robes with a crimson cloak. And last of all Marona's beautiful blonde maid, whose name turned out to be Celise, joined the party to attend her lady since the other two maids seemed to be occupied.

Although from the way she did her best to walk close to Dare and brush against him, all while giving him bedroom eyes whenever he met her gaze, he had a feeling she was reminding him of her previous announcement that Belinda and Marigold weren't the only maids interested.

He returned her flirting in full, eager at the prospect. And fully aware of the knowing smirks, giggles, and hushed whispers among his lovers.

If Zuri had been there he was certain she would've done her best to make sure he got with the beautiful maid if he was interested. Although he couldn't help but notice that Sia took the fore, and she and Lily pulled Celise aside to whisper conspiratorially, shooting him furtive glances.

Redoubt

Okay, it looked as if the prospect was becoming a likelihood. Given the wicked giggles that kept escaping the group, which included two of his most adventurous and insatiable fiancees, he had a feeling it was going to be something else, too.

Marona and Veressa walked together, having hit it off in the short time they'd known each other. Which Dare supposed wasn't a big surprise, since technically they were the closest to each other in age in spite of the vampire's youthful features. And certainly closest in temperament, with their refined grace.

It looked as if they weren't the only ones who'd had the idea of visiting the park, because they soon joined a stream of finely dressed people making for the gates in the tall wrought iron fence surrounding the place. Two city guards flanked the entrance, presumably there to keep out the riffraff.

The park was every bit as beautiful as promised, with the garden plots carefully sculpted with snow and ice to make it a winter wonderland. The only sign the place wasn't pristine was that the snowy lawn where people were allowed to walk and picnic was trampled and showed grass in places.

Children built forts and had snowball fights, filling the air with laughter and shouts, while couples walked the paths cuddled close for warmth and intimacy. A group of ladies sat in collapsible chairs (his design had become surprisingly prevalent), having had the same idea of a picnic lunch. And farther down the lawn several young men were playing some sport with striped sticks and a hard wooden ball.

And on the frozen pond in the center, just about all groups were represented skating on the ice.

They found a good spot not far from the picnicking ladies, and the maids bustled about laying down a thick soft blanket and arranging the baskets. They had more blankets for everyone to sit beneath for warmth, and Dare found himself under one with Marona on one side and Sia on the other. Although Marigold boldly wiggled beneath the blanket to plop down on his lap, in case he had need of the services of his Head Maid.

Phoenix

They shared hot steak and cheese sandwiches, mulled wine and hot cider (non-alcoholic for the pregnant women), buttery garlic bread that steamed as the foil wrapping was opened, and a wide assortment of desserts.

As they ate Sia leaned up to his ear. "You've been neglecting Celise," she whispered playfully.

Dare blinked. "I didn't even know she was interested until a few days ago," he protested in a low voice.

She mock scowled at him. "Even so, you'll have to be punished for that. I thought we taught you better. You know we want you to make every woman who's interested as happy as you make us."

Marona shot them an amused look. "You wouldn't happen to be talking about my handmaiden, would you?" she murmured, glancing at the beautiful blonde. He felt his face flush, and she laughed. "Celise will eat you alive," she warned with a playful nudge. "She's close friends with Helima and they share the same tastes, if that tells you anything. Good luck."

He swallowed. Helima was Captain of the Guard in Terana, who he'd inadvertently stood up enough times that he had a feeling she was annoyed at him. And at one point she'd hinted she used manacles in the bedroom.

He wasn't sure whether to be excited or terrified.

Chapter Fifteen
Adventure

The group spent an enjoyable afternoon picnicking, walking the beautiful park, and playing in the snow.

Dare finally managed to convince a few of the girls to try ice skating with him. Ireni, Marona, and Marigold demurred, which was probably for the best in their pregnant state. Although Leilanna confidently announced she'd join him since she was in no danger of falling, which was doubtless true given her elvish grace.

Veressa also chose to stay behind chatting with the baroness, which left Lily, Belinda, and Celise to go with him and Leilanna. They made their way down to the pond and rented skates, complicated contraptions of metal and leather straps that could be bound to a shoe or boot, with wickedly sharp blades that could've been a weapon.

After figuring out how to put them on, they all climbed out onto the ice together, joining the crowd of people of all ages stumbling and sliding about.

Dare's experience of rinks had people going around in circles so they didn't get in each other's way, but the skaters here didn't seem to have figured that out. So there were numerous collisions and mishaps, usually resulting in laughter as people in heavily padded winter clothes hit the ice.

Although he noticed a healer was on standby, probably in case one of those accidents involved the skate blades.

In spite of her previous inexperience, Leilanna was soon gliding over the ice as gracefully as, well, an elf. Lily similarly got the hang of it quickly, her natural athleticism and agility making it simple. And with her bunny girl speed she was soon weaving around people on the pond, laughing delightedly.

Phoenix

Dare wanted to describe some ice skating moves to her and see how long it took her to figure them out; he'd love to see her try a triple Axel. He also desperately wanted to activate Cheetah's Dash and see if he could keep up with her.

But Belinda and Celise were complete novices to skating, and lacked the traits serving his fiancees so well. So they clung to him for support as they moved across the ice.

Doubtless being a maid involved a lot of grace and poise, but the learned skill didn't transfer over to ice skating.

He supported them as best he could, giving what little advice he knew about skating. He thought keeping your toes together was a thing. Or was that skiing? Either way, they all moved together in an awkward clump until the two women got the hang of it.

The dragon girl made use of the time to also shamelessly flirt and subtly cop feels, as well as pressing against him more often than strictly necessary. But surprisingly, in spite of Celise's evident interest in him, after her talk with Lily and Sia she'd dropped the flirting entirely.

She laughed and joked with him, sure, but it was all friendly and companionable.

Finally the two beautiful women were confident enough to hold each other's hands and skate together, giggling at near mishaps and occasionally clutching each other for balance. At their insistence Dare left them and tried some more daring moves, catching up with Leilanna and goosing her through her thick winter clothes, then laughing as she furiously whirled with her hands glowing with blue flames before she realized it was him.

"Having fun?" he asked as he skated beside her.

His beautiful dusk elf fiancee smiled fondly. "I am. It reminds me of playing in the snow when I was younger. We used to skate on the ice with our shoes, although these skates are much better for it."

Lily swooped past them skating backwards, laughing gleefully, and Dare couldn't resist the urge to activate Cheetah's Dash and give chase.

Redoubt

It was as futile on the ice as any other time, but he had a blast zooming around the pond, weaving through shouting and pointing skaters, as he tried to get close enough to his bunny girl fiancee to tug her teasingly bobbing cottontail.

When it was presented to him, that was; she spent most of the chase going backwards, giggling at his attempts to keep up. Her pale cheeks were rosy with the cold and her excitement, and her eyes sparkled with joy behind her wire frame glasses.

At one point she almost backed right into a child careening clumsily past, and without missing a beat tucked into a graceful backflip right over the wide-eyed boy, landing in a spray of ice chips and continuing on her way.

Looked as if she'd be good at figure skating, like he'd guessed.

Dare managed to flag Lily down and describe the sport to her, and her excitement reached new heights as she began trying out the moves he remembered from watching figure skaters. She soon drew a crowd of onlookers all watching in amazement, clapping and cheering.

Although she tended to get nervous in large crowds, right now she was loving the attention. She posed and blew kisses as she flipped, jumped multiple times in succession, spun multiple full rotations through the air, and skated on one foot while curving and looping and even turning to go backwards.

An hour or so passed on the ice in a pleasant blur, and then Marigold called to them from the edge of the pond to let them know that the rest of the group was packing up to leave. Lily looked crestfallen at that news, so Dare offered to stay with her for a bit longer as the others headed back to the inn.

She rewarded him with a sound kiss on the lips, which oddly also drew some applause and cheers, before laughing gleefully and taking off again, throwing herself into a quick series of flips and twists that had the audience gasping in wonder.

The wonder turned to concern when she stumbled at the end of it and went sprawling across the ice, sliding a dozen feet. Dare

Phoenix

worriedly started towards her, but he hadn't gone more than a few feet before the bunny girl gracefully did a kip up back onto her skates, holding her arms out to show she was unhurt.

Although apparently she decided she'd had enough fun, because she skated over and cuddled up to him as he wrapped his arms around her. "Ready to go back to the inn?" she murmured.

"Ready to go, at least." He grinned at her. "The Adventurer's Guild isn't far from here, and I thought we might check it out. See what's available to do there, and also what it would look like to recruit adventurers from there to fill out our party if we need more people."

"Ooh, I haven't been to an Adventurer's Guild before," she said excitedly.

Dare laughed sheepishly. "I haven't really either, actually. Just a brief visit once to sell some trophies. But I figure it's about time."

Lily grinned up at him. "I guess so. You *are* almost Level 40, and you'll be a knight soon."

They returned the skates, then walked arm in arm out of the park and down the streets to the Redoubt Adventurer's Guild.

It was by far the largest he'd ever seen, although he hadn't checked out the one in Kov which might've been even larger. It was an old building, probably one of the first ones built when Redoubt was a frontier outpost, and although it showed signs of recent innovations the stonework on the original structure remained.

They stepped through the heavy oak doors that served as the main entrance, into a large room that seemed a combination of a meeting place, common room, and venue for doing adventuring-related business. A few dozen men and women filled the room, most dressed in cloth, leather, chainmail, and plate armor and ranging in level from the high 10s to low 30s.

A grizzled adventurer immediately hurried forward to greet them. The old Warrior's gaze was unsurprisingly drawn to Lily, ethereally beautiful and as a bunny girl rarely seen in cities, and he was almost to them before he finally glanced at Dare.

Redoubt

At which point his eyes widened as he recognized him. "Prospective," he said, saluting. "How can the Redoubt Adventurer's Guild serve you?"

Dare offered the man his hand. "Dare."

The man hesitantly returned the handshake, and looked even more taken aback when Lily also offered her hand. "I, uh, Grolin, Master Dare."

"Well met, Master Grolin." Dare looked around the bustling guildhall. "I haven't visited the Adventurer's Guild here before. I was wondering if I could trouble you to give me a tour and tell me what services you offer."

The grizzled adventurer looked further surprised and pleased. "It would be my honor, prospective."

The man led them through the big main room, awkward at first and not seeming to know exactly what to talk about. So he mostly babbled about the origins of various trophies, as well as introducing them to various other guild members and usual fixtures at the guildhall. Mostly other retired adventurers.

Most of those introduced joined them, and they soon had a crowd of friendly veterans sharing tales of past valor and glory. Dangerous hunts, treacherous dungeons, ravening monster hordes. Even venturing beyond the border to brave the true wilds.

Lily seemed to be enjoying just listening to all the tales, looking right at home among the rough company, who were soon treating her as one of them. Dare enjoyed the stories as well, but tried to stay on topic and turned the discussion to practical details about the Adventurer's Guild and what it had to offer.

The place certainly had jobs available: Monster hunts, mercenary and bodyguard work, and caravan and home guard openings. As well as what seemed like borderline thuggery, like debt collection and item retrieval. There were also opportunities to form parties with other similar level adventurers.

There were even a few quests, which he and Lily accepted in case they might be able to get to them later.

Phoenix

But ultimately the guild, friendly as its adventurers were, was a disappointment. Joining them required a more restrictive and slow paced style of adventuring than Dare was used to with his friends and fiancees, and especially leveling solo.

They also asked for a hefty cut of earnings.

Granted, most adventurers probably wouldn't dare level at spawn points or take on quests without the guild's information, so it no doubt saved lives. But with his Adventurer's Eye the only real benefit he'd get from the guild was that they could point him to exactly where to go, so he didn't have to wander around scouting.

There was some potential in the matchmaking services for adventurers, but even there the process was so lengthy and involved he wasn't sure it would be his first choice.

More promising were the notices and wanted advertisements for more long term jobs north along the border. Most were urgent, and some seemed borderline desperate as they offered high rates to anyone willing to help fight back the ravening monsters and wild tribes.

At least somebody seemed keen on bringing peace and order back to northern Bastion. Dare wondered if he should head up there as his next step; he certainly didn't want his home region to fall to invasion.

He even saw a recruitment poster for the Marshal's Irregulars, offering generous recruitment bonuses that went up depending on level. They especially seemed to need high level healers, support, and well geared tanks.

Just like everyone always seemed to in multiplayer RPGs; this world really was similar to the games he'd loved on Earth in a lot of ways.

Finally, he concluded he'd seen everything he needed to. Lily looked as if she would've been happy to stay and chat longer, until he reminded her that it was getting close to dinnertime and the others would be waiting. So she reluctantly let herself be drawn away, although not before going around to all her new friends and shaking their hands, as well as throwing her arms around an embarrassed but pleased Grolin.

"Do you think the Adventurer's Guild in Terana is this great?" she asked as they stepped out onto the street and started for the Gilded Chalice.

"I hope so, because I plan to visit there next," he said as he wrapped an arm around her waist. "That's where we'll probably find long term companions to adventure with us and Veressa, anyway."

"I hope they're all as great as Veressa," his bunny girl fiancee said happily. "She-" she cut off abruptly with a surprised sound, looking past him.

Dare turned and jumped slightly when he realized a small figure was walking beside him, swathed in a heavy cloak. "Answer to my prayers," a soft voice murmured in greeting.

It was the mousy Healer who'd helped him kill Ollivan. "Thorn," he said, smiling. "It's good to see you."

"Is it?"

The awkward question didn't seem to invite a response, and with it hanging in the air he cleared his throat uncomfortably. "Um, this is my fiancee and adventuring companion, Lily."

"Hi!" Lily said. "You're the one who helped protect our family from that monster!" She enthusiastically offered her hand. "Thank you!"

Thorn looked taken aback as she uncertainly returned the handshake. "You're kind," she said stiffly, "but my motivations were not so altruistic."

The bunny girl looked sympathetic. "I know. Dare told us how Ollivan ruined your life like he was trying to ruin ours. I'm so sorry."

The Healer looked around uncomfortably at the passersby. "It's best not to talk about it, Miss Lily."

"Oh. Okay."

Phoenix

Redoubt

The uncomfortable silence settled again as they walked down the street for a few dozen paces. Finally Dare cleared his throat. "How do you fare?" He wanted to ask if she'd been able to put the pieces of her life destroyed by the corrupt knight back together, but wasn't sure it was his place.

"I live." Thorn shot him a quick glance out of the corner of her eye, looking torn, then continued in a neutral tone. "Before we parted, you offered me a place in your home. I assumed it was charity, but if you're seeking out the Adventurer's Guild then perhaps you have work for me?"

Oh? Dare gave her a keen look. "Can I be blunt, Thorn?"

She laughed quietly. "We're co-conspirators, I should hope so."

"All right. I can level alone, but there are party rated monsters I can't kill by myself, and raid rated monsters as well if I find them in my travels. More than that there are dungeons I'd like to explore and conquer."

"You have knowledge of the location of dungeons?" the Healer asked, surprised. "That is very valuable information."

"Not just knowledge, we've seen them!" Lily interjected eagerly. "They look like they'll be really fun!"

Dare couldn't help but grin. "And challenging. We're eager to try them." He continued resolutely. "The adventuring life isn't for everyone. Other than Lily, most of my fiancees have decided their future doesn't lie in leveling. While they might join me in some adventures, it's not really what they want. I'd like dedicated adventurers who want to level as much as I do, and are willing to devote their lives to it. People I can count on to explore dungeons, take on powerful monsters, or even just explore the world with me. Not just now but into the high levels."

"Hmm." Thorn glanced at him again. "You've gained five levels since I saw you last."

"And I'll continue to gain levels swiftly." He slowed to a stop, turning to her. "I'm not asking you to come to Nirim Manor out of charity. I want you to join my party, and I'm offering you equal share of the loot and a home base where you'll be safe and welcome."

"That is . . . more generous than most party leaders offer. And certainly better than the Adventurer's Guild."

Dare shrugged. "I'd be party leader solely for the responsibility of leading excursions. We'd be equal companions otherwise." He took Lily's hand and smiled at her. "Right?"

"Exactly! And Dare's a great leader, too. He knows exactly what to do in a fight, and even when things get chaotic he's always calm and calling out attack phases and responses and stuff."

"That's . . . good to hear." The mousy woman stared down the street, expression bitter. "I'll be honest, Master Dare, I'd probably be inclined to accept your offer even if it was far less generous, so I thank you for that."

"Then you'll join us?"

She nodded, pain joining her bitterness. "I have no future here. My wastrel of a husband has turned my family, his family, all of our friends, and even my own children against me. I cannot intervene with my children without becoming a fugitive, even if they would come with me. My reputation is irreparably tarnished, and even with Ollivan gone the Guild won't take me back."

She spat off to the side. "There was a time when adventuring drew me only for the support I could provide my family. But now it's all I have left. And I want to become stronger. Carve a new place in the world. Show all those who turned their backs on me that they judged me unfairly."

Thorn held out her hand. "So yes, Master Dare, if you would have an outcast like me as a companion then I would like to join you."

Dare returned her handshake. "Then welcome to the party, Thorn."

She smiled faintly. "Carilina."

"Welcome to the party, Carilina!" Lily said, bouncing eagerly. "Can I hug you?"

Redoubt

Carilina looked surprised and a bit nonplussed. "I, um, guess so?"

The bunny girl wrapped her arms around the smaller woman. "I think we're all going to be great friends and have lots of grand adventures together."

The mousy woman stood stiff in her arms. "I would settle for a life that wasn't bitterness and ashes," she murmured.

Dare motioned down the street. "We were just heading to our inn for dinner. You're part of our company now, so please join us. I'll arrange for a room, too."

She paused, need obviously warring with pride. "I won't refuse, thank you," she said.

Lily wrapped an arm around her shoulders and guided her down the street. "I can't wait to introduce you to Veressa. She's our crowd control. And we have a tank back home! That's a good solid party right there."

"I'm sorry, tank?" Carilina said.

"That's what they call defenders where he comes from. And damage dealers are DPS and crowd control is CC." The bunny girl filled the air with excited chatter as they walked, arm around their new companion's shoulder the entire time.

Dare was a bit worried that Carilina would be overwhelmed by her friendliness, but instead it seemed like the Healer relaxed as the stream of warm conversation flowed over her, and even leaned against Lily a bit.

As they got closer to the inn he noticed tears in her eyes, although he did his best not to draw attention to them; after what she'd been through, she deserved some safety and friendship with people she could trust.

They found everyone in the private dining room eating appetizers before dinner. There was some surprise about him bringing home yet another adventuring companion so soon, but when they learned that Carilina was the woman who'd helped him stop Ollivan she became an instant hero.

Phoenix

Ireni actually went so far as to wrap her arms around her in a tight hug, whispering something in her ear. Whatever she said, there were tears in both women's eyes as the petite redhead led their new companion to a seat beside hers.

Lily took Carilina's other side, of course, clearly determined to break through the woman's thorny barrier with sheer friendliness.

Veressa looked a bit lost with all the details flying past, but she seemed happy their party now had a healer. She briskly took the mousy woman under her wing, and before Dare could even consider renting a room for Carilina the vampire insisted on sharing hers.

Surprisingly, the stiff, aloof Healer seemed relieved by the offer.

Dinner was pleasant, everyone eating their fill of the delicious food. Then all of Dare's lovers, including Belinda and Marigold, bid Veressa and Carilina goodnight and dragged him to Marona's room.

They still had to celebrate his elevation to knighthood, after all.

* * * * *

Given the late night with its strenuous but very enjoyable activities, Dare ended up sleeping in.

He woke around midmorning to find Marona already gone, taking Belinda with her. Ireni and Lily were also nowhere to be seen. That left him in bed with Leilanna and Marigold, their soft warm bodies draped over him. At some point the little gnome had found his cock to grip in her small plump hand, and even while sleeping deeply she continued to hold it.

Not the worst way to wake up.

As he felt himself begin to stiffen, anticipating some morning fun, the door opened and Lily and Ireni, or no wait Sia, crept in. Expressions eager with anticipation, they beckoned to him.

Dare gently disentangled himself from the sleeping women, carefully pulling Marigold's hand away as he slipped off the bed. The little maid murmured plaintively and rolled where he'd been, cuddling up to Leilanna instead. Her questing hand found the dusk elf's large breast, and she held it contentedly as she drifted off again.

Redoubt

He dressed and followed his goddess and bunny girl fiancees out into the hallway. "What's going on?"

Lily bounced up and down in barely suppressed eagerness. "Celise will see you now."

He perked up, the last of his sleep haze vanishing. "She will?"

Sia smirked and took his hand. "This way, my beloved."

His bunny girl fiancee took his other hand, and the two led the way down the stairs one floor and to the end of the hallway before stopping at a door. "She's waiting for you in there," Sia said.

Dare looked uncertainly between his two fiancees. "Wait, you're not coming with me?"

The goddess laughed wickedly, and Lily grinned. "Oh hell no," the bunny girl said. "That woman scares the pellets out of me." She gave him a playful nudge towards the door and retreated down the hallway. "Good luck."

Sia gave a complicated knock on the door and then darted after Lily. "Good luck!"

The door creaked open ominously, revealing a completely ordinary room that appeared to be empty; Celise must be behind the door.

He cautiously stepped inside and turned to face the door as it abruptly slammed shut, revealing the petite blond handmaiden. Rather than her familiar French maid uniform she was dressed in a simple white smock, fine but nothing exceptional, her feet bare and luxurious blonde hair hanging loose to halfway down her back in ringlets.

She looked invitingly cute and innocent, and he couldn't help but smile. "So-"

Celise strode forward and planted a flat palm against his chest, turning him and shoving him back against the wall with surprising strength for her small size. He could've easily resisted, of course, but he went along with it, wondering what was going on.

Phoenix

She looked him up and down as if eyeing a rubbish heap, delicate features cold. "You'll do."

"Um-"

She pressed harder against his chest, her manner shockingly confident and in control. Nothing like the demure handmaiden he'd seen so often attending Marona. "Out in the world I know my place, as do you. But in this bedroom I am the Mistress, is that understood?"

Ah. Okay, so that's where this was going. Dare felt himself relax. "Yes, Mistress."

"Good." The strikingly beautiful woman stroked his chest, not so much lustfully as the way she might pet a faithful hound. "A good mistress/pet relationship requires absolute trust, Darren Portsmouth." She looked up at him with utter command in her big, pale green eyes. "Do you trust me?"

To his surprise he found that he did. And not just because she was Marona's trusted maid. The total confidence and sincerity in her eyes offered no other alternative. "Yes, Mistress."

"Very good." She abruptly pinched his nipple, making him gasp. "A good Mistress tests the limits of her pets for their own good. That is where a pet is happiest, pushed to their limits. What will you say if I exceed your limit, pet?"

Dare relaxed even more, letting himself enjoy this. He'd never done this sort of thing so it wasn't exactly familiar territory, but he'd certainly heard plenty about it.

Or at least, he wouldn't call his time with Ashkalla anything like this, because there'd been no trust involved.

"Pebble, Mistress," he said.

"Pebble," Celise repeated, lip curling. "That's awfully lofty, considering you should be grateful to be viewed as dirt under my heel."

The petite maid grabbed his shirt with both hands and pulled him away from the wall, twisting him around as he went. Then she gave him a forceful shove, making him stumble until the backs of his legs hit the bed and he plopped down into a seated position.

Dare wasn't sure where she'd produced the riding crop from, but there was definitely no horse in the room. He gulped as she slapped it casually against her palm. "I've been told you're getting too brig for your britches, worm. A head that's only grown more swollen with your elevation to knighthood."

Celise loomed over him in spite of her small size, eyes full of dire warning. "Do you think your station matters in this room, pet?"

"No, Mistress."

"And you realize that no matter how great you grow, a part of you knows."

He frowned in confusion. "Knows what, M-"

The riding crop came down on his leg with a sharp *smack*, not hard enough to do more than sting a bit. But it definitely made him jump. "Since when does the pet speak out of turn?" she said in cold affront. "Are you even housebroken, pet, let alone properly trained?"

Dare ducked his head. "Yes, Mistress."

Celise held up a delicate bare foot. "Then show me. Be a good pet and wash your Mistress's feet."

He dropped to his knees on the wooden floor. Her skin smelled faintly of soap, obviously just washed. Definitely better than Ashkalla's dirty feet.

He began cleaning it with his tongue, thoroughly licking over every inch and between the toes, even the bottom. Then he switched to her other foot and did the same.

It was more enjoyable than he'd expected; she had really nice feet, small and cute, and her skin was very soft.

When Dare finished he leaned back and looked hopefully up at her imperious face; she looked just as achingly lovely from below as from above. She favored him with a brief smile and stroked his head. "Very good, pet. Perhaps there's hope for you yet. Not all my pets have been so obedient."

Her eyes abruptly narrowed. "One of my most difficult was

Helima. I believe you know her? She had a very stiff back that needed to be bent. You're going to learn more quickly than Helima, aren't you pet?"

"Yes, Mistress."

Celise sniffed. "And yet ultimately she has become one of my most obedient and faithful pets. I am very fond of her. And I take care of my pets."

Uh oh.

Her riding crop slapped against her palm again, and her voice cracked just as sharply. "Drop your trousers and bend over the bed, worm!"

Dare actually felt his cheeks heating as he turned, pulled his pants down around his knees, and knelt beside the bed bent over it. He looked over his shoulder to-

"Eyes forward!"

Snapping his gaze back down to the bedspread, he could only kneel there, feeling vulnerable and exposed, and listen to the light padding of Celise's small feet as she strode back and forth behind him, smacking her riding crop into her palm.

Every time she did he jumped slightly in spite of himself.

"Helima is a faithful servant of the city and a brave and sweet woman. She looked forward with great anticipation to getting a drink with *someone*," her crop slapped her hand more sharply, "and was disappointed more than once. Do you not think that *someone*," again the sharp slap, "should be chastised for his rudeness?"

Dare swallowed. "Yes, Mistress."

He jumped and tried not to yelp as he felt the crop smack sharply against his left cheek. Just hard enough to sting lightly. "Is that punishment sufficient, dirt?" Celise demanded.

"Not even close, Mistress," he said, bracing himself.

She smacked him again on the right cheek, then again on the left. Light, sharp smacks that made him jump and smarted a bit, one after the other.

Phoenix

He wouldn't say he enjoyed it, but he wouldn't say he *didn't* enjoy it either. As evidenced by the fact that by the time Celise was done, he realized he was sporting a half chub.

"There, pet," she said, a touch of warmth in her voice. "You bravely accepted your chastisement. Now I believe I can trust that the next time Helima makes plans to share a drink, she will not be stood up?"

"No, Mistress."

"Good. Although perhaps I should be on hand to make sure my pets get along. Would you like that, pet?"

Dare couldn't help but feel a surge of excitement at the prospect. "If you wish, Mistress."

"Good. You realize that my wishes are all that are important." He jumped slightly, then relaxed and enjoyed it, as her small soft hand began tenderly rubbing where she'd smacked him, soothing him. "I believe you will be a good pet after all."

His cock stiffened further as she moved to rub his other cheek, her touch better than any balm. He found himself hoping she'd reach between his legs and soothe another part of him.

Instead Celise abruptly drew her hand away, and he heard light footsteps retreating. "Dress yourself, pet. You are dismissed."

Wait, what? That was it?

In spite of his disappointment Dare worked to stuff his rigid cock back into his pants, lacing them. He knew that teasing and tantalizing were part of the enjoyment, and seemed to recall that initial sessions with this sort of roleplay usually didn't get right to the fun stuff.

Still, as he turned to look at the beautiful blonde maid, who was standing by the door with an imperious expression on her delicate face, he couldn't help but wish it had gone on a little longer. Which was odd since all she'd done was have him lick her feet and then spanked him.

He hadn't realized he was into this sort of thing. But maybe she was right that it was good to be taught a bit of humility every now and then.

He bowed low. "Thank you for letting me serve you, Mistress."

Celise simply stood, all confidence and control as she stared at him, waiting for her order to be carried out.

Dare strode to the door and opened it, stepping outside.

"Wait."

He didn't think he'd ever heard a more glorious word. Turning perhaps a bit too quickly, he looked at her expectantly.

She motioned to the door in silent command, and he stepped back inside and closed it. Then he waited in tense anticipation as she stared up at him for what felt like an eternity. "You expect a treat for your service. But that is not how this works. You serve because I am the Mistress, and my desires are paramount. Any reward I give is because it pleases me to make my pet happy. Or because I wish to enjoy you as is my right. Am I understood?"

Dare bowed his head. "Yes, Mistress."

"Good." He couldn't help but notice that in spite of Celise's up to now perfect control and commanding presence, her cheeks were just the slightest bit flushed and her voice perhaps a touch strained. "In that case strip."

Now she was talking. Trying not to grin, he quickly pulled off his clothes, freeing his still hard cock. Although he did his best not to look too eager as he waited for her next order.

As it turned out, it went in a way different direction than he'd expected. She pointed under the bed, eyes hard. "There is a tarp there. Spread it out."

Oh. Ooooh.

Dare quickly pulled out the rough waterproofed canvas and spread it on the floor beside the bed. Then he looked to Celise expectantly.

She began pacing around him, slapping her riding crop against her palm with every step. Including once uncomfortably close to his raging erection, making him flinch. "You are still too big for your britches, it seems. Still ignorant of your role as my pet. I suppose the only thing that's going to teach you is a demonstration of your abject lowliness. I call you dirt, and so all you are good for is soaking up filth."

The petite woman pointed her crop at the tarp. "Lie down on your back, worm. Do not move an inch. Let us see if you are so lowly and eager to please that even humiliation from your Mistress is a delight."

He complied, lying flat on the slightly rough tarp with his erection standing proudly to attention. Celise stepped over so one delicate foot was planted to either side of his chest; from this position he could see her shapely legs all the way up to where they joined, and was surprised to find she wasn't wearing panties.

Had she anticipated this?

Again, Dare caught a crack in her commanding facade in the fact that her gorgeous plump labia were glistening with arousal.

Sneering at his cock straining eagerly in the air, she crouched to hit his inner thigh with her riding crop, making him jump at the sharp sting. "As I thought, you think anything that flows from your Mistress is the nectar of the gods. In that case who am I to deny you? I take good care of my pets."

Celise squatted until her beautiful pussy hovered just inches from his stomach, lifted her white smock, and he watched in awe as her plump lips parted and a stream of pale yellow urine sprayed out, splashing his abs and chest with warm wetness.

She must've really been holding it in, because the stream continued as she shuffled backwards, until her delicate little pussy hovered right over his raging erection and her fountain of pee splashed all over it.

Her teasing paid off, because the eroticism of the moment and the warmth of her urine was enough to set him off. With a groan he twitched his hips and began shooting jets of come into the air, landing all over his abs and chest.

Celise tsked and slapped his thigh with her crop again, even harder, as her warm stream continued to flow all over his pulsing cock. "So undisciplined. We will have to work on that, pet. You only have your release when your Mistress permits it."

Dare groaned in enjoyment as his twitching cock shot out a few last dribbles, washed away by her pungent torrent as it gradually petered out. His Mistress sighed in relief as the flow slowed to a trickle and finally stopped, leaving her flushed petals glistening with arousal and a few dewdrops of pee.

Without shaking, Celise shuffled up his body still in a squat until her glorious pussy hovered over his face. "I believe you know what to do, pet?" she said imperiously as she lowered herself to his mouth.

Remembering her order to not move, he used only his lips and tongue to clean her glistening sex, tasting a hint of clean urine along with her heady nectar. He started around her lips, then eagerly plunged his tongue between her folds to gather more of her arousal.

She tasted delicious.

His wilting cock started to stiffen again, and he stifled a groan of disappointment as she abruptly straightened, stepped away gracefully, and lowered her smock.

The beautiful blonde woman's face was more pink than before, breathing quick, but her commanding composure didn't crack a hair. "Look at you laying in filth and loving it, worm. Most shameful. Clean yourself up, then clean the room. And next time a woman expresses interest don't string her along. My pets are trained better."

Graceful and prim, as if she hadn't just peed all over him in the lewdest of ways and then had him clean her with his mouth, she turned and disappeared out the door.

She left it open, and Dare scrambled up to shut it before someone walked past; he wasn't sure how exactly he'd explain this scene.

Which left him soaked in Celise's pee, with a sizable puddle of it on the tarp to clean up.

Luckily he always brought one of Zuri's Cleanse Target scrolls with him, just in case, or this might've been much more awkward. He retrieved it from his belt pouch, then lay back down in the cooling puddle and cast the spell, converting the mess all to clean water.

There were towels, soap, and a pitcher of hot water on the dresser by the door. He wiped himself down and soaked up the clean puddle on the tarp, then wiped it dry, folded it, and put it back under the bed. Last of all he wrung the towels out in the washing bowl and dressed.

Opening the door, he nearly jumped out of his skin when he saw Lily standing there, long ears stiff with curiosity and expression eager. "How was it?" she asked excitedly. "Was in fun? What did you do?"

Dare felt his cheeks heat. Honestly the adventurous bunny girl probably wouldn't bat an eye about what had happened during his session with the beautiful blonde maid. In fact she'd probably think it was fun.

Truthfully, all of his lovers were understanding like that.

Still, he was in the mood to tease her after she'd ditched him earlier, probably with full knowledge of what he was getting into. "Oh, you want to know what happened after you left me to the wolf?" he said, playfully rubbing her velvety white ears and ruffling her silvery hair.

His beautiful fiancee pouted. "Oh come on, you know you had lots of fun. I can tell by the way you're grinning like an idiot."

He laughed. "I did. But if you really wanted to know what happened you should've stayed to watch."

"But she said we couldn't . . ." she started to complain, then brightened as she looked behind him. "Celise!" she squealed, darting past him. "How did it go? What did you do?"

Dare turned to find the beautiful blonde maid back in her pristine black and white ruffled uniform, not a hair out of place, demurely gliding down the hall with an armful of clean towels. "Your pardon, Mistress Lily," she said with a curtsy. "Part of maintaining trust is keeping what goes on in private sessions in confidence. Perhaps you should ask Master Dare."

With another curtsy she stepped into the room Dare had just vacated. Then she paused, obviously surprised.

"Oh you're no fun." Lily stuck out her lower lip. "You really aren't going to tell me?"

He grinned at her. "Let's just say that if you were Pella, you'd know exactly what happened in there."

If he thought that hint was mysterious enough, he was wrong. Apparently the girls talked more than he'd realized, because his bunny girl fiancee's eyes widened with delight. "Oooh!" she blurted, bolting down the hall. "I need to tell Sia!"

Damnit. Although honestly Sia already knew, even if she made it a point to not talk about his sex life.

Dare stepped into the room after Celise, who was looking around as if checking to make sure everything was in order. "You came back with towels," he observed. "I thought you wanted me to take care of this mess myself."

She kept her eyes on the floor, all professionalism as she curtsied. "Your pardon, Master Dare, but you're my Lady's paramour. What goes on in a session is one thing, but I would be failing in my duties if I allowed you to be embarrassed."

He smiled at her. "You keep your two roles very clearly defined, don't you?"

The beautiful maid simply curtsied again and continued checking the room. Although as he turned to follow Lily and see just what she was telling everyone, he heard her add under her breath, "Besides, a good Mistress cleans up her pet's messes. After she swats his nose with a newspaper for being a bad boy, that is."

Dare couldn't help but grin as he walked away. He had a feeling his relationship with Celise was going to be interesting.

Chapter Sixteen
Noble Knighthood

Dare and his fiancees, as well as the rest of Marona's entourage, spent a relaxing day close to the inn. They went out a few times to browse the high end shops, but mostly enjoyed the opportunity to wind down after a busy few days.

Finally, though, Marona returned from the day's meetings and they all prepared for the big knighting ceremony, dressing in their finest. Then they piled into her carriage to make the trip to the palace, joining a stream of other coaches and carriages full of Redoubt's wealthy and influential.

At the gates, however, they ran into a snag. Or a wall.

"Your pardon, my Lady," a courtier with a list who was checking all arrivals said apologetically. "You are of course invited and expected at the ceremony, and of course prospective Darren must be there. But I regret to say his consorts are not on the list, and only those on the list may enter."

"Since when are consorts of a newly raised knight barred from watching him achieve that honor?" Marona demanded, looking the closest to losing her composure he'd ever seen from her in public; she was genuinely upset for Ireni's, Leilanna's, and Lily's sakes.

The man hunched his shoulders. "I cannot speak to his Grace's reasons, my Lady, only his orders."

"And what if I refused to enter as well in the face of this insult?" Dare demanded, struggling for calm. Marona caught his arm and shook her head, but the words were already spoken.

"Then I suppose you would not become a knight, prospective." The courtier bowed and hastily made his escape to the next carriage, leaving the guards to bar the gate until those not invited were dismissed.

Redoubt

Once he was out of earshot the baroness huffed angrily. "One last snub. He can't prevent you from gaining your knighthood, so he insults your consorts. What a small man he's become in his decline."

"But I wanted to see you become a knight," Lily said, genuinely crestfallen. "You worked so hard for it."

Dare had wanted her to see it, too; it was just the sort of romantic event she would've cherished. And he grieved that Ireni and Leilanna wouldn't be able to share that honor with him after all their hard work helping him prepare.

If Valiant was going out of his way to make enemies of everyone Ollivan had wronged, no wonder his support base was crumbling. What a stupid, hateful bastard.

Ireni patted his knee. "There's nothing for it. We'll go back to the inn."

"Are you sure?" he asked.

"Well you're certainly not throwing aside a chance for knighthood over this," Leilanna said. "Go already."

Dare reluctantly stepped down from the carriage, offering Marona a hand down. The driver shook the reins and the carriage turned away from the gates, heading down a side street to return to the inn.

"I look forward to being home," the baroness said with a sigh as he offered her his arm and they started for the palace on foot. "Where I'm not surrounded by loathsome spiteful toads every day of this interminable Council."

"Redoubt certainly offers few reasons to return, at least among the rich and famous," he agreed.

At the doors Marona was announced and made her way inside, while a servant led Dare to an anteroom at the side of the grand hall, where the others who'd been invited into the Order of the Northern Wall waited.

He was pleased to see Lorkar there, along with the Spellwarder and the Shaman and a couple of the tanks. There were also the healers and support who'd dominated their portion of the Trial of

Valor.

Of the twenty prospectives who'd made it only half seemed to have done so through pure merit, while the others were lower level and as far as Dare could remember had done nothing to distinguish themselves. Probably due to nepotism, family ties, or bribery?

Either way, he was just glad he'd made it through merit. And probably far more help than he even knew from Marona and her allies working behind the scenes.

"Well here we are," Lorkar said, clapping his back hard enough to make him stumble. "The big event."

Dare grinned at him. "So what next for you? Back to the north?"

"Aye." The Berserker became uncharacteristically sober. "With my new rank I'll raise a banner and gather adventurers and mercenaries, lead them to push back the flood of monsters and wild tribespeople. I only pray to Brollt that things haven't taken a drastic turn for the worse in my absence."

"As do I, my friend."

Lorkar chuckled and scratched at his jaw. "I couldn't convince you to come along, eh? You'd be handy to have in a fight."

Dare gave it serious thought. "Perhaps. I need to get home and be sure everything's running smoothly there. And my betrothed gave birth to twins just before I left . . . I need to get back to them, and my other children."

"Fair enough. Family is all important." The Berserker sighed. "I just hope the north can hold out until the south finds its ass and sends aid."

"What about Haraldar's heroes? Still raiding that ruined city?"

Lorkar snorted derisively. "Last we heard they'd struck farther into the wilds, chasing rumors of other treasure troves. As always, "hero" is a generous term."

A courtier hurried in, announcing that the ceremony would begin soon. The prospectives could watch the proceedings through a screen that looked out over the great hall until it was their turn; the man had a list for the order they'd be sent out in.

Dare was last, of course.

Lorkar was first, which was a bit of a disappointment since he'd miss the man's company. From the sounds of it the ceremony was lengthy, and there were twenty prospectives to knight.

As the son of the Viscount of the Northwestern Marches was called and strode out onto the wings to present himself to the duke, Dare moved to the screen to watch. It was all very grand and elegant, the room packed with richly dressed people and everything gleaming like a dream beneath the glow of the massive chandeliers.

It all rang a bit hollow for him, though, since Leilanna, Ireni, and Lily weren't there. Although he did spot Marona with the other nobles, which heartened him a bit.

Apparently there was no tapping shoulders with a bared blade for knighthood in Haraldar. Lorkar strode forward and knelt before the Cleric of Henor, God of Fair Dealings, to swear an oath to ride out in defense of Bastion, particularly against incursions across the northern border. And also to uphold the virtues of knighthood.

Which, Dare couldn't help but notice, didn't involve protecting the innocent. Which sort of made him wonder what the point of them was.

The cleric dripped a few drops of holy oil onto the Berserker's head, intoning some solemn chant in an ancient language. Then a novice stepped forward to comb the oil into the new knight's hair, singing words of that same language in a high, sweet voice before leaning down to kiss his brow and back away.

After that the big man knelt before Duke Valiant, who solemnly declared him a knight of the Order of the Northern Wall. With great pomp and circumstance he placed a gold-embroidered dark blue tabard on the new knight, bearing across the chest and back in gold thread the sigil of half a dozen armored men bracing huge shields in a wall, presumably to hold back a ravening monster horde.

Then the duke draped a dark blue cloak over Lorkar's shoulders and fastened it with a gold clasp in the shape of one of those armored men hunkered behind a massive shield.

"Sir Lorkar Ralia, Knight of the Order of the Northern Wall!" Valiant roared, and the crowd roared back with surprising ferocity, whistling and raising fists in the air. Grinning hugely, the Berserker bowed to the worthies of Bastion and moved to join the nobles gathered at the front of the room.

Each new knight was called out in turn to repeat the ceremony, with almost zero variation. And as predicted it took almost two hours for the other knights ahead of Dare to receive their honors and be officially recognized.

Finally at the very end, when the gathered crowd of Bastion's worthies were shifting impatiently in boredom, hunger, or the need to relieve themselves, it was Dare's turn.

Whether saving him for last was intended to be a slight or not, he noticed that the crowd perked up when they realized it was him, murmuring amongst themselves. Dare did his best to keep his shoulders back, eyes up and gait smooth and steady, as he walked along the dark blue carpet and knelt before the cleric.

The elderly man looked down at him gravely. "Darren of Nirim Manor. As Bastion is your home, as a knight of the Northern Wall will you ride out against all invaders, and hold fast the integrity of Haraldar's northern border?"

"I so swear," Dare said solemnly.

"And will you uphold the virtues of your exalted rank, to safeguard the dignity of the nobility of Haraldar in word and deed? Will you be fair in your dealings with your peers, never resorting to trickery or dark tactics? Will you comport yourself at all times to protect the reputation of the noble born of our fair kingdom?"

Dare couldn't help but think that they could at least try to pretend they weren't utterly self serving. "I so swear."

"And will you uphold the laws of our kingdom and impose peace and order wherever you may travel within Bastion?"

That at least was more palatable. "I so swear."

The cleric looked him over gravely for a time. When he'd done the same with each of the other new knights the pause had felt brief, but now that Dare was beneath that intense scrutiny it felt like it lasted an eternity.

Finally the man stirred. "Henor finds you sincere. Go to your destiny, Darren of Nirim Manor." He leaned forward with the ewer of holy oil, chanting in that strange language. The drops touching Dare's head felt surprisingly thick and heavy, warmly sinking into his hair.

Then the novice stepped forward, enchanting voice filling his ears as she gently slid the comb through his hair, the gold teeth feeling cool as they massaged his scalp. When she leaned forward to kiss his brow Dare could've sworn her soft lips lingered longer than with the others.

He also didn't think he'd seen her speak to anyone, but she did to him, mouth moving close to his ear for a few moments. "Heliora smiles upon you," she whispered, then backed away with her head demurely bowed.

Dare hadn't expected that. He stared after her, startled, until a sharp clearing of the throat from Valiant made him jump slightly.

He hastily moved the few short feet to where the duke stood with a few advisors and attendants, kneeling before him with his head bowed.

Bastion's governor didn't quite look at him, speaking over his head. "Darren of Lone Ox." Great, so the man had scrolled through his list of titles and picked the most mundane. "Having been found worthy by the Lord Judges of the Order of the Northern Wall, with the acclaim of the commons, and under the grace of the God of Fair Dealings, you are elevated to the nobility of Haraldar as a knight of Bastion.

"Henceforth your descendants will carry your noble blood as members of the House Portsmouth, with all the attendant duties and privileges. May the gods shine upon your line until the end of days."

Dare was a bit surprised the man hadn't tried to pull some last minute bullshit to disqualify him. Maybe the duke's position in

Bastion really was that weak. Or he just didn't care about his nephew enough to deal with the fallout of openly messing with an ancient and sacred tradition.

Either way, as Valiant presented the tabard Dare lowered his head so the man could settle it over his shoulders. Then he straightened as the duke draped the dark blue cloak over him, fastening it on one shoulder with the clasp of the Knights of the Northern Wall.

Finally the man lifted him to to his feet, bearing an expression of such practiced gravity that only his eyes showed his intense dislike. He ceremoniously straightened Dare's new tabard and cloak, fiddled with the gold clasp, then with a pleased grunt clapped him on both arms and turned him about. "Esteemed guests and peers of Bastion, I give you Sir Darren Portsmouth, Knight of the Northern Wall! Long may he serve our land in honor and glory!"

There was some polite applause, which was better than nothing. Marona clapped more warmly, eyes shining with happiness for him, and she was the only person there Dare really cared about. He saluted her and the assembled worthies and departed along the carpet.

He was a knight. A real live knight. Not in a game, some title he could show off that meant nothing, an actual real live knight.

The Lord Judges were waiting at the end of the carpet to solemnly congratulate him. Maybe they were conscious of the hundreds of eyes on them, but each and every one of them was cordial and affable as they clasped forearms and slapped his shoulder.

Even Zor put up a jolly front, although his eyes were calculating.

With the formalities over with the festivities began. Musicians in the corner struck up a lively tune at some unseen signal, and servants began filtering through the crowd offering drinks and delicacies. The more structured grouping of attendees by rank, influence, and wealth blurred as people mingled and chatted, and the new knights found themselves mobbed by well-wishers.

Redoubt

Even Dare drew more than a little attention, maybe because he was standing beside Lorkar, the third son of the Viscount of the Northwestern Marches, and their camaraderie was clear.

Young men invited him out hunting or to private card games, dignified lords and ladies invited him to various events or even to visit their estates. And blushing maidens gave him slips of paper inviting him to private rendezvouses, eyes smoky and full of promise.

Marona soon joined him, to his relief, and he introduced her to Lorkar. Although as it turned out the two were passingly familiar with each other. As expected for nobles moving in their circles, even with living on opposite sides of the region.

With the baroness on his arm they worked the room, greeting her friends as well as more well-wishers. Dare actually found he was enjoying himself, liking the feeling of his new rank and the fact that he was more welcome in this esteemed company now that he had a noble title.

He wasn't blind to the shallowness of that welcome, of course. But even if he didn't think much of many of these people, it was human nature to want to be accepted.

Although the only acceptance that really mattered to him was that of the beautiful woman on his arm, and his fiancees and lovers. He wished they could be here with him.

After a while the baroness was called away to a late night meeting, responding to some major news from the north. With her gone Dare realized he had little desire to remain, unless of course he wanted to accept one of the invitations to a card game or a secret assignation with a young noblewoman.

He would rather be with his loved ones, especially when they'd been barred from this gathering. So he found Lorkar and the few other new knights he was friendly with and bid them good evening, then excused himself.

Making his way through the brilliantly glittering grand hall, he headed for one of the side passages in search of a more private exit

Phoenix

than the very large and visible front doors. Although as he started down what looked like a servant's hallway a voice called from behind.

"Leaving the celebration so soon?"

Dare did his best not to tense as he turned to face Zor, who'd apparently followed him. "I am, my Lord."

The man frowned. "You'll lose favor with the nobility."

Dare couldn't help but laugh. "I don't believe I can lose something I don't have."

"Then you'll fail to gain it."

"I'll have to take that risk. My consorts were not invited to this event, and I'd prefer to be celebrating with them."

The Paladin chuckled, giving him a knowing wink. "I'm sure you would be."

Dare fought back a frown at the innuendo; they weren't friends to make those sorts of jokes. "Is there something you needed, Lord Zor?"

The man's smile faded. "I figured that now that you've joined the nobility, we should clear the air about the unpleasantness that occurred during my raid."

"You mean the "unpleasantness" of Ollivan trying to kidnap and rape my fiancee, while you stood there holding your dick?" Dare snapped. He knew he shouldn't lose his cool, but this son of a bitch had let Ollivan go unpunished after what he'd done, then spent the entire trials trying to fuck Dare over.

And now he was, what, trying to curry favor? Ensure they wouldn't depart as enemies even if they'd never be friends?

"That's not how the matter was presented to me," Zor said with forced calm.

"Oh, you mean when you walked up to the scene of my tent with a huge slash in the back of it, Ireni bruised and battered, and you decided to kick us out of your raid for defending ourselves?"

The man grit his teeth. "You fail to mention that I also walked up to Ollivan on the brink of death, his squire beaten unconscious."

Dare bit back a curse. "You want to clear the air? At least acknowledge what Ollivan and Dorias did. At least tell me that you don't approve of them raping women in your own camp, but your hands were tied because you didn't have the political clout to act against them."

"I'll not speak ill of a friend," Zor growled.

"Loyalty to a friend is one thing, but defending a rapist and arsonist, an attempted murderer even, is another thing entirely."

"What does it matter now?" the Paladin demanded angrily. "He's dead."

Dare fought to rein in his own mounting temper. "Your pardon, my Lord, but what does his death matter to whether you're willing to denounce his crimes? As a Paladin you've sworn to champion the cause of justice."

The man flushed. "He was drunk during your fight, and you know how drink affects the inhibitions."

"He was drunk when he cut into the back of my tent, gagged my consort, and tried to drag her away to gang rape her with his squire, then beat her when she resisted," Dare said coldly. "Your pardon, but no matter how drunk I became, I would not do such a thing. I sincerely hope you can say the same."

"Have a care for your words," Zor growled. "Recall you were drunk as well, and it is your word against his."

"And was Ollivan drunk when he raped Baroness Marona's maid while a guest in her home?"

The man hesitated. "He insists she was willing."

Dare looked at him coldly, thinking of what Ollivan had done to Carilina. "No doubt he says that about all the women he rapes."

The Paladin reddened further. "You'd best remove your blinders, knight. Now that you're nobility yourself, you should be warned that there are no shortage of women who'd falsely accuse us. Hired by an enemy to discredit us, perhaps, or in hopes of gaining coin in recompense."

"So whenever a woman accuses a noble she's automatically assumed to be lying?" Dare pressed harshly. "How convenient for you. You speak as if Ollivan has been accused before. How many times does he have to be accused by his victims before it no longer becomes his word against theirs?"

Zor looked away. "Be that as it may, you know nothing of what a defender goes through. Facing the agony of grievous injury from monsters again and again, healed but still bearing scars, both outwardly and inwardly. It takes its toll."

"Then other defenders become a danger to others?" Dare asked. "I've heard nothing to suggest that."

The Paladin slammed his fist into his palm. "Enough! This is in the past, and you'd be best served in considering how things will be moving forward. I don't like you, Portsmouth, but I respect your competence and the loyalty you instill in your friends. I even believe you to be honorable, in your own way."

He stepped forward, thrusting an armored finger at Dare's chest. "But you gain nothing by antagonizing me. We will never be friends, I fear, but you need not have me as an enemy."

Dare took a breath. "I have no desire to be your enemy, my Lord." Zor started to smirk until he continued. "But I will not, and cannot, forget that when the woman I love was brutally assaulted by that animal, you stood on his side. And you do so still."

He bowed, then turned and strode away without waiting for a response. And whether or not his words had had any impact, none came.

He was twenty or so yards down the hall, about to turn a corner, when an amused voice spoke quietly from behind him and to the side. "Very well spoken, young man."

Dare jumped and spun to see the wizard-looking Phasewarper walking beside him. "I-"

"Didn't realize I was here?" the man said, clear blue eyes twinkling. "Few do." He offered his hand. "We were never formally introduced, I don't believe. Earl Hormot Valarins."

Dare took it, bowing. "An honor, my Lord. Thank you for your support during my judgment."

"You're quite welcome, although I merely acted in the interest of fairness." He stroked his long white beard. "Although you continue to surprise . . . I wouldn't have expected you to spurn Zor's limp attempt at a peace offering."

"Do you think it was the wrong choice?"

Hormot snorted. "Standing by your principles is never the wrong choice, although you may often find yourself beset by hardship for it. But wrong or not, I enjoyed seeing Zor turn purple as a grape . . . the man is a strutting peacock who's always been far more attentive to his noble reputation and peerless image than actual truth or justice. He looked the other way when it came to Ollivan's crimes because the Warrior was an effective defender and well connected politically."

The old man tsked. "Somewhat of a fool, though, to keep claiming friendship with a man of such sullied reputation. Perhaps he still hopes to curry favor with the Governor through that tie. If so I fear he's backing the wrong horse."

Dare was curious. "Your pardon, but did the Governor also refuse to see what his nephew was?"

Hormot smiled grimly. "Oh no, I'm sure he saw. And took quiet steps to try to rein the vicious brute in. None of which turned out to be effective." He shook his head. "Although in the end Ollivan's own vile actions proved his undoing. As is often the case."

"Not often enough, it sometimes feels," Dare said. "Far too many evil people are never punished in this life, while far too many innocents suffer and are never given help or justice."

"I wish I could say you are wrong." The old man looked sad. "But then again, other times a kindhearted woman ignores the advice of a friend and joins the party of an evil man, only to be dragged into his tent and suffer unspeakable abuse for days. Until finally in answer to prayers she receives the aid she needs to take back control of her life and see justice done."

If Dare had been surprised by any of this, that shocked him; Hormot was friends with Carilina? He looked at the mysterious lord with new eyes. "I am sorry your friend suffered so. I owe a great deal of gratitude to Miss Carilina, and I would wish she had been spared such a horror."

"As would I." Hormot shook his head with a sigh. "A pity you didn't kill the man that night when he attacked your betrothed, although I fear it would've ended badly for you if you had." He patted him on the shoulder. "In any case, know that your willingness to stand up against such men has not gone unnoticed. And do look after Miss Carilina in her new life . . . I think moving away from this place and its bitter memories will do her much good."

He turned away, and with a shimmer in the air vanished.

Dare continued down the hallway, eventually finding an exit that led out to the palace grounds. He left the place behind and trotted down the streets back to the Gilded Chalice, where he was touched by the scene in the common room.

His fiancees, the maids, and his new companions were all celebrating his elevation to knighthood. The room was full of warmth and laughter, musicians playing and everyone dancing, even the serving girls.

As soon as everyone spotted him at the door he was pulled into the center of the festivities, and immediately decided it was far better than the celebration at the palace could even pretend to be. He felt a surge of love for the women in his life, feeling fortunate beyond words to have each and every one of them.

It was almost midnight before the party wound down. The girls were all ready to go to bed, many sleeping on each other's shoulders in their seats. Marona still hadn't returned, and Dare decided to stay behind to wait for her, waving the girls on without him.

They might've been a bit disappointed, but they also fully agreed with that idea.

Already more than a bit buzzed, he nursed an iced fruit juice as he settled into a booth. After a few minutes he regretted not having a book, but he didn't want to disturb the girls to get one. Instead he spent the time considering their situation and making plans for the future.

And missing his fiancees and children back home. He ached to hold Gelaa, to look down at her sweet little face with its adorable expressions and listen to her soft cooing sounds. And he'd barely had a chance to hold Nic and Rellia at all and missed that opportunity. And Eloise, still nestled in the ground waiting to grow.

He wanted to be there with them, to watch his children grow. To hold Zuri and Pella and their babies, and Se'weir.

Exciting as the last few weeks had been, he was ready to go home.

Marona finally arrived around one in the morning, asleep on her feet and assisted by her carriage driver. Dare hurried to take over for him supporting her weight, although at her insistence led her to the booth he'd been sitting at. Where she unabashedly grabbed his fruit drink and downed it in a few deep gulps.

"Thanks," she said with a sigh, leaning back against him. "We were all so focused we didn't think to call for refreshments."

"What was it you were called for?" he asked, wrapping his arms around her.

"An urgent meeting for grim tidings," his noble lover said wearily. "Pelanos, the town closest to the border, was conquered by a band of wild tribes calling themselves the Outcasts of Balor. Mostly orcs and goblins, with a few dozen bovids and a handful of dragonkin."

Her weary expression tightened. "According to the reports we received they've murdered or enslaved all the elderly, men, and children, and have divided the women between them to suffer lives of unspeakable brutality."

Dare grit his teeth, protectively holding her closer. "What's being done?"

His lover sighed. "Marshal Jind is marching north with every member of his company in Redoubt, as well as all the adventurers and mercenaries he can recruit on short notice. He'll also be recalling more units of Irregulars from the border to join him on the march there."

"Should I join him?" he asked. He didn't want to be away from his family at Nirim Manor any longer than he had to be, but if these Outcasts of Balor were rampaging then they needed to be stopped.

She smiled tightly. "He actually anticipated you might offer, and asked that you return home and prepare for a fresh influx of refugees, as well as seeing to those who'd already have arrived or soon will." Her smile became more genuine. "And he also wants you to be there for Linia until she gives birth. I believe he's genuinely fond of her."

While Dare didn't like the reminder of that tangle he was out of it now. The two could be together however they wished.

Honestly, even though his offer had been genuine he was relieved to be going home. Although he wondered how long he'd be able to enjoy his time there with his fiancees and children before he was called north, if the situation there kept deteriorating.

"This might be a silly question," he said wryly, "but where the hell have the so-called heroes of Haraldar and their Royal Guard escort disappeared to? I was there to watch them arrive and saw 70 people ranging from Level 40 to Level 66. Seems like they'd be useful right about now."

Marona gave him a grim smile. "Actually, it's a very appropriate question because they *have* seemed to disappear. Last we heard of them they were venturing farther north chasing rumors of another raid dungeon, and then all contact ceased abruptly. Just a couple weeks ago, in fact. All our messengers sent to contact them have also disappeared, and our scryers are turning up nothing."

Dare swore softly. "Should I be worried that there might be a threat up there capable of beating a bunch of the kingdom's most powerful people?"

"I certainly am." She slumped against him wearily. "But let's

Redoubt

stop talking about this for now. I'm already so tired and dispirited."

"All right," he said, kissing her neck then getting to work rubbing the tension from her shoulders. "You'll rest better when we get you home, away from scheming lords and time wasting councils. How many days will we remain in Redoubt?"

She sighed and relaxed into his hands. "Two more days of council, assuming this most recent crisis doesn't bog things down. If things go as planned then we can set out for home on the eighth of Ged." She smiled and kissed his hand. "That'll give you time to rest and relax a bit."

"I feel like I've already rested and relaxed plenty on this trip," Dare said. "Maybe I'll run out with Lily and see if I can get her a level before we depart for home."

"So energetic." The baroness laughed and eased back against him, closing her eyes. "Your time is yours, I suppose, but I'd be sad not to see you at all before we leave. You're one of the few enjoyable parts of this trip."

"Then I'll stay," he said, kissing her neck again as he rested his hands on the gentle swell of her belly. "I don't feel like I've been able to get enough time with you, either." With a playful chuckle he moved his hands farther down, running them over her hips and thighs. "Speaking of enjoyable company, is there anything I can do for you right now?"

She moaned softly, twisting in his arms to kiss him lovingly. "Hold me while I sleep, Dare. I'd like to do more, but I have to be up early in the morning and I'm not as energetic as you."

"As you wish, my Lady." Dare gently stood and lifted her into his arms, carrying her towards her room where the others slept.

Marona looked up at him, dark eyes full of feeling. "Thank you, Dare."

He smiled. "You're most welcome. I savor every opportunity to hold you."

She shook her head, expression intent. "I mean it. For everything. When I asked you to try to use your high fertility to give me a child, and maybe take you as a sometime lover, I never expected what we'd have. What I thought I'd never have again after Orin's death."

She cupped his cheek with a soft hand, smiling. "It feels like you've given me a second life. I was so lonely after my husband died, just me and my maids in my grief, channeling all my drive into governing Terana. You and the girls pulled me out of it, reminded me I was still alive and what made life wonderful."

Marona's eyelids drooped sleepily, but she still held his gaze lovingly. "Even more than that, you gave me your love. And I realized I still had room to love in return." She laughed. "I just hope you can forgive me if I can't always keep up with you."

Dare leaned down and pressed his lips to hers. "I'll always follow your pace, Marona."

She rested her head on his shoulder, closing her eyes. "I don't say this lightly, Dare. A woman my age can't be careless with her words. But I'm coming to love you very dearly."

His heart warmed at her words. "I'm coming to love you very dearly too. I'm blessed to have you in my life."

"Then let's make the most of it," she murmured, breathing deepening. Moments later she was asleep.

The girls had left a spot for them between Lily and Ireni. Dare gently undressed Marona, undressing as well, then cuddled up with her as Ireni woke up just enough to sleepily snuggle against his back, kissing his shoulder.

As he drifted off he quietly savored the feeling of being a Knight of the Northern Wall. Although their business in Redoubt wasn't quite finished, he was already looking forward to going home and being reunited with Zuri, Pella, and Se'weir.

And his children. His last thoughts before sinking into sleep were of their precious little faces, their tiny hands gripping his finger. Of holding them in his arms and looking down at them in the wonder of knowing he was a father.

He'd been away from them for too long.

Chapter Seventeen
Going Home

There was little to say about the last two days in Redoubt.

Dare and the girls who didn't have other duties spent the time touring the city, enjoying the various parks and other attractions, and shopping for more items for the manor. Veressa and Carilina were there for some of it, although they were busy preparing for their move to their new home.

Surprisingly, the two women seemed to have hit it off and tended to stick together even when they were with the group. Which he was happy to see, since he wanted his party to be tight-knit. He did his best to spend time with them as well, and encouraged Lily to do the same.

Which was hardly a chore for his friendly fiancee, who seemed become quick and firm friends with just about everyone she met.

Speaking of Lily, he finally found a time to take her to the Crate when it wasn't crowded but the stage was still hopping. The adorable bunny girl had a great time throwing silvers to the dancers as they stripped, giggling the entire time about the silliness of the idea.

When the beautiful elf serving girl took the stage, Lily grabbed Dare's hand and pointed it urgently up at the ceiling, squeaking in excitement as she jiggled her coin purse. He was pleasantly surprised when the strikingly beautiful platinum blonde high elf immediately vacated the stage with an inviting smile.

Maybe she was interested in the rare and spectacularly beautiful bunny girl. Or she'd seen the Northern Wall clasp on his cloak. Or maybe she thought he was cute. Possibly all of the above.

Either way, he was just as eager to bed the gorgeous high elf as Lily was. His initial dream when coming to Collisa had been to be with an elf, and the plain fact was that the serving girl almost perfectly fit the image he'd had of the elf he fantasized being with.

Phoenix

Redoubt

Leilanna was more wonderful than he could've ever imagined, and he was deeply fortunate to have her. She was far more than some dream woman he'd pictured in his head, and he loved her with all his heart.

Still, he couldn't pass up the opportunity to be with the platinum blonde high elf.

Which was how he finally found himself up in the opulent rooms the Crate rented by the hour. A closer look of course revealed that the gold was paint and the fine carpets were threadbare, the sheets faded from multiple washings.

None of it mattered, though, because as he watched the high elf do her own private dance for him, finally baring her perfect body to his gaze, she was the only thing in the room he wanted to look at.

The serving girl was a true professional, managing to settle on a suitable price without taking away from the sensual atmosphere. Possibly because she was grinding on his lap at the time while making out with Lily, as the bunny girl played with the beautiful elf's perfect breasts and teased her dark pink nipples.

The sex wasn't particularly adventurous, the serving girl starting things off after a bit of foreplay by lying on her back with her legs spread, revealing her glistening petals. Still, Dare fully enjoyed thrusting into the beautiful elf while watching his fiancee ride her face, panting and moaning in pleasure at whatever the other woman was doing with her tongue.

He took it as a challenge to make the courtesan orgasm as many times as he could, teasing her pearl with his thumb and tweaking her eraser-thick nipples. He also shifted the angle of his thrusts to hit her everywhere, although his sheer size stretching her was enough to have her squealing all on its own.

He came the first time after her back arched with a muffled cry of rapture and she squirted all over his crotch, her walls milking him until he gave in and shot inside her. Her fragrant nectar reminded him of roses and honey, and he regretted not getting a taste before mounting her.

Lily was more than happy to, though, continuing to urgently ride the high elf's face as she lowered her own to where Dare and the serving girl were joined, lapping up their combined sex juices.

"Nature's bounty, you two taste good together," she panted, urgently reaching between her legs to rub her clit. It didn't take long before she squealed and squirted all over the blonde high elf's face, then slumped over to sprawl on the bed with a satisfied grin.

The serving girl gave him a sultry look, coyly teasing her plump pink lips with her fingers. "Come clean me up, handsome?"

Dare eagerly leaned down and cleaned Lily's fragrant nectar from her face with his tongue, then passionately kissed the elf as his bunny girl fiancee got to work between her legs.

Thanks to their efforts the high elf climaxed at least half a dozen more times, reaching higher and higher peaks until her eyes rolled back in her head and she went limp in languid satisfaction.

About that point she reluctantly announced that their time was up soon, and pulled herself to her feet on trembling legs to get to work cleaning them up.

"My name's Inaria, by the way," she said as she lovingly ran a soapy cloth over his semirigid cock. "I live on 38 Broad Street, upper apartment 3." She winked. "Come visit me during the day sometime and we'll have some more fun as lovers, not patrons and courtesan."

"Okay!" Lily said, kissing her warmly. "Thanks for the fun time, Inaria."

They didn't get a chance to visit the beautiful high elf before leaving, but that wasn't the only sex they had. Of course.

Another highlight was when Leilanna surprised Dare by arranging a visit to the brothel where his vigil temptress worked. She'd apparently been very taken by his accounting of the event, and was clearly excited as she led him into the room where the beautiful young woman waited. In the exact same garb as he'd seen her in that night, including the basket of tantalizing meat buns.

The vigil temptress was a great actress, probably why she'd been selected for the job, and continued her role as the innocent but eager maiden as she completed her task of seducing him while his dusk elf fiancee watched and rubbed herself.

His vigil temptress certainly wouldn't have been worth sacrificing knighthood for, but her soft body and tight pussy felt incredible as he fucked her to multiple orgasms in a few different positions and came in her twice. Then as their time ran out she cleaned him off with her sweet mouth, took him deep down her slender throat, and swallowed a final load of his seed.

"Come back any time, Sir Dare," she said in her demure maiden persona as he and a very pleased looking Leilanna left the room.

Out on the street Dare gathered his dusk elf fiancee into his arms and kissed her soundly. "Thank you," he told her.

She grinned up at him. "I wouldn't want you to return from this trip with any regrets about what could've been." She leaned up close to his ear. "Now take me home and fuck me silly while I'm still hot from watching you."

He was more than happy to do just that.

When Dare and the others weren't touring the town they were up in Marona's room at the Gilded Chalice, having fun together. Dare got a thorough workout, and did his best to give all the girls as much attention as they wanted.

Particularly Marona, when she could spare time from her duties. She wanted to cuddle or hold hands on long walks through the city as often as make love, but he enjoyed his time with her all the same. As did the other girls; Marona enjoyed watching more often than participating, usually while cuddling one of them after they came down from a climax.

But they all had fun with her.

He was a bit disappointed that Celise didn't join them. Apparently the petite maid wasn't interested, at least not yet. Although he did have another session with the dom where she put a leash and collar on him and taught him tricks. Then she had him pull down his pants, took him over her lap, and spanked him hard for every mistake he made.

Finally Celise spent a few minutes soothing his sore bottom by spreading lotion over it with her soft hands, while his rock hard cock throbbed between her thighs against the smooth cloth of her innocent white dress.

That was the extent of that session, leaving him to seek out a more than eager Lily to help him find relief, but he still found himself oddly enjoying it.

To his amusement his bunny girl fiancee begged Marona's handmaiden to do a session with her as well, which she returned from walking gingerly and blushing an adorable pink. She wouldn't talk about what they'd done, but she must've enjoyed it because she arranged for another session next time she was in Terana.

"Maybe we can do one together sometime!" she panted as she rode him relentlessly afterwards, obviously working off pent up arousal with him same as he had with her.

Dare thought of his impending double session with Helima and couldn't help but grin. Looked as if more fun with Celise was on the horizon.

Now it was the morning of their departure, and the Gilded Chalice's stable yard was a flurry of activity. Marona's entourage, including all her maids, wagon drivers, animal handlers, and guards, were bustling around her carriage, their mounts, and a few baggage and passenger wagons, packing things up and making last minute repairs and adjustments.

Dare's own group's preparations to leave were more modest but no less energetic, readying their mounts and packhorses and making sure nothing had been left behind.

While his group would be traveling with the baroness, including invitations to ride in her carriage if there was room, they still gathered around him as they prepared to set out. The group included him, Ireni, Leilanna, Lily, Veressa, and Carilina.

A surprise addition was Marigold, who'd been formally dismissed from Marona's staff to officially become Nirim Manor's

Head Maid for the journey back. The tiny gnome bustled about with twice as much energy as any of them, pink hair down to her ankles pulled into a tight braid and tucked beneath her cloak so it wouldn't get in the way.

She was determined to start off her duties as perfectly as possible, and put even Ireni to shame as she expertly organized the loading and personally checked to make sure nothing had been left behind.

Marigold remained just as determined that her duties were to take care of his sexual needs as well, because amid the bustle of activity she managed to sneak him behind the stables. Once there she wasted no time ducking into his cloak, which hid her while she freed his cock and gave him an enthusiastic, sloppy blowjob.

She was obviously in a hurry and jacked him furiously as she worked, and between that and the feel of her soft, warm mouth he soon grabbed the plump gnome's head and unloaded down her throat with a moan of pleasure, while she made muffled sounds of pleased enjoyment.

After cleaning him up she popped back into view, hurriedly fixing her clothes and mussed pink hair while beaming up at him. "Was my service satisfactory, Master?"

Dare couldn't help but chuckle. "Exemplary, Head Maid."

Marigold made a pleased sound and bustled away to get back to the preparations to leave.

He made his own adjustments and stepped out into the stable yard, then paused when he saw that all preparations had ceased and everyone was warily looking towards the street, where Bero and a few attendants stood.

"Ah, Sir Darren!" the slight lord called brightly, ambling over to join him. "Well met."

"Lord Bero," Dare said, offering the man his hand. "I wasn't sure I'd see you after the knighthood ceremony. Good of you to come see us off."

"Of course, lad, always a pleasure." The slight man gave him a subtle smile. "I hope you enjoyed your stay in Redoubt. Do visit again sometime."

There was just the slightest emphasis on the word "visit"; Dare hadn't forgotten the man's warning about keeping his nose out of Redoubt's politics and business. "I imagine I will, when time allows. And if I do I hope to see you again."

Bero snorted. "Charmingly naive." He bowed to Marona, who was standing a cautious distance away. "Pleasant trip, my Lady. Do be careful on those winter roads . . . travel can be hard this time of year, especially while expecting a little bundle of joy."

The baroness inclined her head. "How kind, my Lord. Until next we meet."

The slight lord glanced around the stable yard, gave a cheery wave, then rejoined his attendants and disappeared down the street.

"Well, there's our formal farewell," Marona said, slipping an arm through Dare's. "Will you ride in the carriage with me and your fiancees for the first part of our trip?"

"I'd be delighted to." He helped her, Leilanna, Ireni, and Lily into the pleasantly heated carriage and joined them inside, where they dined on small honey cakes while the final preparations were made and the caravan was lined up in order on the busy street.

Finally Miss Garena gave a curt order from the head of the caravan, and after a brief pause the carriage lurched into motion.

The girls all had a window seat and leaned out to get one last look at the sights of Redoubt. Seated between Marona and Leilanna, he settled back and pulled out his book on Collisa's history, or at least the fragment of the world's ancient past that the writer knew of.

At the urging of the others he began to read aloud, beginning with the mythos of Collisa's creation as a vast blank slate, and the arrival of the deities to work their will on it, each in their own way.

Some to shape the terrain and create the breathtaking landscapes of rugged mountains, lush valleys, awe-inspiring canyons, great waterfalls, and other wonders. Some to fill the oceans and seas and make the rains fall and the seasons change. Some to paint the sky with marvels to dazzle the eye and inspire the imagination.

Then some to create plants, some to create the creatures of land and sea, some to create monsters. Shaping, changing, refining, as ancient mythical beasts and indescribably vast leviathans struggled for survival in a swiftly changing landscape as the gods continued their work around them.

Last of all how the Creator of Collisa, who'd made the blank slate for the others to work upon, began populating the world with the first intelligent races, the event so lost to antiquity that none could say which they were. Although most of the races of the world insisted they were one.

And how the gods, enchanted by these new beings, and excited and inspired by them, began creating their own races. And how other races formed of the unions of those that had been created.

A vast, wonderful, ever changing pattern as the races began to take charge of their own destinies, and the gods agreed to step back and let them. Then the collaboration between the greatest deities to create the world system, and implement classes and leveling and abilities, and plan monster spawn points. Not to mention seeing to all the balancing.

Dare noticed that Sia had taken the fore and was listening with a look of clear amusement. "How's the book doing?" he asked wryly.

The goddess glanced at Marona, and with chagrin he remembered that they had yet to tell the baroness anything about Sia being the Outsider or Dare being from another world. "We can know only what the gods tell us about such a distant past," Sia said cryptically.

"And not even they seem to agree on the details," Marona said with a laugh. "But it's interesting to read the variations. Please, go on."

Nodding, he settled back and continued to read.

* * * * *

Dare made it three hours outside of Redoubt before he decided

Phoenix

he just couldn't stand the pace of Marona's entourage. Or, for that matter, the awful springs on her carriage.

So as much as he wanted to spend time with her, he decided he could only endure an hour or so at a time before had to get out.

Thankfully she was understanding about it when he announced he was heading outside. "Orin could never stand to sit still either," she said with a laugh. "And given how much you love to run, being cooped up in here has to be torture. Go on, stretch your legs."

Once he was outside he found that riding ahead to scout the road, or to look at interesting landmarks, soon began to chafe at him as well.

The adventurer in him wanted to check the nearby spawn points and see if any were worth farming. Which, if they could give him any experience at all, or for that matter his fiancees and new adventuring companions, were as an alternative to crawling along the road.

So he returned to the caravan and asked if anyone wanted to do some leveling.

Lily accompanied him, of course. She seemed determined to be his adventuring companion and never passed up a chance for experience so she could catch up in levels. And also because once they were alone she was usually in the mood to get frisky.

Veressa and Carilina of course also wanted to come along. Veressa would've happily rode in the carriage with Marona, and did at times, but the adventurer in her was ready to get out and make things happen.

Not to mention it gave the vampire opportunities to slip away and catch animals to feed on.

As for Carilina, she was eager for any scrap of experience she could get. She'd obviously been dead serious when she said she wanted to get powerful and prove her detractors wrong.

Dare was pleasantly surprised that Ireni also accompanied them, which made the leveling easier and safer. But the biggest surprise was Leilanna; in spite of her bitter complaints about the cold, she usually came along as well.

When he teased her about it she just glowered and pointedly rubbed her rump. "If it's a choice between the cold or those hard benches and damnable springs, I'll pick spending time with you in the cold."

He scratched his cheek thoughtfully. "I wonder if introducing better springs would get me Noticed 3. Leaf springs or maybe even coil springs."

His dusk elf fiancee literally grabbed him by the lapels and shook him. "If you can do better than what's on that grain wagon, you sure as hell better," she growled. "I am *not* riding around in that thing if there's an alternative."

He laughed. "I can't do it here on the road, so you'll just have to put up with it." He playfully swatted her bottom. "Besides, with that sexy thick ass of yours you should be complaining the least out of all of us."

Blue flames whooshed into life around her hands, and her pink eyes glinted. "What was that again?" she asked sweetly.

"As a veteran traveler who's lived your life in caravans, you're most well suited to the discomforts of the road," Dare corrected, deadpan.

Leilanna sniffed and made the flames disappear. "Better." She crossed her arms beneath her luscious breasts. "Now tell me more about how sexy you think my ass is."

He grinned and nodded towards a nearby copse of trees. "How about we find some privacy and I show you instead?"

Of course Lily wanted to tag along, but Ireni insisted she stay to continue clearing the spawn point they were at, which was only suitable level for the bunny girl. If barely.

The week passed more quickly than Dare had expected. Or maybe feared, given their sluggish pace. They spent each night in Marona's luxurious tent, and aside from brief stints in the carriage to keep the baroness company they rode out every day to level.

Dare and Lily usually left early in the morning, him so he could

Phoenix

run out and check monster levels in the spawn points for the others when he wasn't around, her to keep him company. And also to just run full out for the sheer joy of running, the icy wind whipping past as they sped across the fields, through the forests, and over the hills of Bastion.

The spawn points they found weren't optimal, and only a few were high enough level for Dare to even benefit from, so he usually stayed out of the party so the others could get more experience. On top of that the party changed day to day and even hour to hour as his companions came and went from the caravan.

All in all their experience and loot gains were only modest, but everyone seemed to enjoy their time. It was a good opportunity for Veressa and Carilina to get to know them better, and get used to how they did things.

They reached Terana midafternoon on the eighth day, and while Marona invited them all to spend the night at Mondshadow Estate Dare had to refuse. He was itching to get home, to see his children and his beloved betrothed. Also he was worried about the refugees the Marshal had been sending his way, and wanted to make sure there were no issues there.

"I'll visit soon," he promised his noble lover as he kissed her goodbye. "Thank you for being such a wonderful host on this trip, Marona."

She chuckled. "Thank you for being such an engaging guest. You and your lovely betrothed." She looked almost wistful. "I'll admit, a part of me wishes I could have your ring on my finger as well."

He bit back the flippant remark that he'd be honored to make her one. "Not politically expedient?"

"That is one consideration." Marona smiled gently. "I care very deeply for you, Dare. But Orin was the love of my life and the only man I'll ever call husband."

"I understand." Dare kissed her again. "I hope to see you soon, Marona."

Redoubt

His party made a few purchases in the market, mostly necessities since they'd already bought so many gifts for their family and friends in Redoubt, as well as amenities for the home. Ireni also loaded down their packhorses with food and supplies for the refugees, and even went so far as to purchase more horses to carry more. She also talked to the crafters about more building supplies for the ongoing construction projects.

He was again glad his redheaded fiancee was so on top of things, because he hadn't even considered doing so. Although once he did he made a few purchases himself in the crafter's section, making sure the new Melarawn village would be able to address potential sewage and hygiene problems.

Including commissioning some toilets for a public privy. And it looked as if Morwal would be getting more work digging out a hole for another septic tank, as well as a drainfield.

Once the purchases and arrangements were made they set out for home, keeping up a brisk pace.

Camp that night was more subdued. Everyone was eager to get home and see the others, and also weary from the long trip. Only Lily seemed in the mood to get frisky, and even she dozed off on his chest after a few minutes of sleepy lovemaking.

They set out early the next morning and pushed hard for home, coming in sight of Nirim Manor in the afternoon. Dare saw nothing amiss in the goblin village, aside from maybe a few more houses than he recalled. Farther in the distance the meager beginnings of the new Melarawn village had developed into a dozen longhalls, in various stages of construction.

Speaking of Melarawn, Linia was riding out the gate at their approach, probably headed there to check up on things. Although at the sight of them her face lit up with delight and she nudged her horse into a gallop towards them.

"You're back!" she shouted, sliding out of the saddle to waddle the remaining distance, arms outstretched. She was much more visibly pregnant now, and Dare realized she only had a couple more weeks before the baby was due.

Phoenix

At the sight of the orange catgirl's obvious joy he felt a pang; she still didn't seem to understand.

Instead of accepting her hug he dismounted and offered his hand for a handshake.

The catgirl stopped fast, looking at him in surprise. "You're still mad at me?" she asked in a confused voice.

"No," Dare said gently. "I understand you are how you are, Linia. I wish I'd understood sooner, but now I do."

Linia bit her lip. "What does that mean? For us?"

Dare took a moment to collect his thoughts. "We'll be raising the baby together and I want us to be on good terms. Let's call ourselves friends and keep it at that."

Her expression fell. "And that's all? No hope of anything in the future?"

Dare shook his head, hurting but determined. Although in a way committing to this course and making sure there were no further misunderstandings was like a weight off his chest.

"No," he said firmly. "I want to devote my time and love to my harem, the women who've given me their love and commitment. It wouldn't be fair to them, to you, or to myself to do anything else."

He looked at the tears dripping down her cheeks and steeled his heart. "I'd be honored to have you as a friend of the family, Linia. And I'm sure the others all feel the same. But that's all we can be."

Linia nodded and wiped at her eyes with the back of her hand. "I'll miss you, but I understand." She hesitated. "Or, well, I wish I understood this attachment you and the others feel, and why it means so much to you. I love you in my own way, but I can move on if needed."

She abruptly squared her shoulders, voice becoming businesslike as she offered her hand. "Okay then, here's to our friendship."

Dare shook firmly. "Our friendship."

The petite catgirl gave him a pained smile. "All right, friend, then if we're done here . . ."

Redoubt

She ran past him to Ireni, giving her a huge hug. "It's great to have you back too, Ireni! You have no idea what a mess it's been with you gone. We have over a hundred new refugees we're trying to get settled, with more arriving every day. Without you sorting out the details it's been absolute chaos. Lady Amalisa and Ilin have been doing their best, but none of us have the experience managing big projects that you do."

"Hey, I can help with that too." Dare moved to join them. "Come on, let's go get all this straightened out."

"My hero," the catgirl said with a laugh.

"Hey, I wouldn't have said no to a welcome home hug," Leilanna groused.

Lily giggled and pulled the curvy dusk elf into an enthusiastic hug, kissing her fiercely. "Welcome home." She giggled again, a bubbly sound of delight. "And to me, too. Our home together!"

Dare had only gone a few steps before Ireni tugged on his elbow. "Leave this to me, my love," she murmured. "You can get involved once things settle down, but right now you have two newborn babies you've only had a chance to see for a few hours, as well as an older daughter. Not to mention three women who've missed you fiercely."

He hesitated, looking between Linia and the packhorses. He should at least help with unpacking. And make sure Veressa and Carilina were settled in and had everything they needed.

Marigold tugged on his other elbow. "Go on, Master. Leave arrangements to your new Head Maid."

"Oh go on," Linia said, playfully batting at his shoulder. "Whatever challenges we're facing, it's nothing serious enough to stop a father from seeing his children after a long trip."

With a laugh he gave in. "All right, thank you." He activated Cheetah's Dash and sprinted away, listening to the warm laughter of his loved ones behind at his eagerness.

Going across the yard he paused only to blow a kiss in Eloise's direction before bursting into the entry room. He startled several women in the process of laying out lunch, some of whom he recognized from Linia's group and others who were strangers.

They gave him bemused looks as he nodded politely before zooming past, bounding up the stairs five at a time and tearing down the hallway to the master bedroom. He paused only a moment to compose himself before quietly opening the door and stepping inside.

He found Pella sitting up in bed against some pillows, nursing Nic while Rellia cooed in a bassinet nearby. He couldn't help but stop and stare in wonder at the peaceful scene of the woman he loved and their children safe and happy.

His dog girl fiancee had obviously heard him coming, because she greeted him with a radiant smile, tail wagging furiously against the pillows. "Dare!" she whispered. "I heard your return. I was hoping you'd come to me soon."

"Very first thing," Dare said solemnly. "I missed you and the babies every second I was gone, and wish I could've stayed with you."

She smiled warmly and patted the bed beside her. "How about you pick up your daughter and we can cuddle for a while as I feed them?"

He couldn't think of a more perfect thing, and quietly moved to the bassinet to tenderly lift Rellia into his arms. He cradled her close as he scooted onto the bed to sit beside Pella, gently stroking his baby girl's little raven-furred ears as she yawned hugely and waved her tiny hands inside her swaddling.

"She looks just like you," his fiancee said, smiling tenderly as she brushed Nic's cheek with a delicate finger. "They both do."

He grinned at her as he leaned down and kissed his daughter's head. "I was going to say they inherited every bit of their mother's beauty."

His dog girl fiancee sighed contentedly and leaned her head against his shoulder. "They haven't grown so very much in the weeks you were gone, but at the same time so much more than I would've thought. So many delightful firsts. I'm glad you're here

Redoubt

now to share them with me."

"Speaking of firsts," Zuri whispered from the doorway, stepping into the room cradling Gelaa, "look!"

As Dare watched eagerly his goblin fiancee set their daughter down on a blanket on the carpet, where she yawned sleepily and stared up at the ceiling.

He beamed down at his firstborn daughter waving her tiny pale green arms and legs. She'd be around four months old now and had grown so much, and yet she was still barely bigger than her little brother and sister.

But she was definitely growing up. To his delight, as he watched she began rocking back and forth, making little cooing sounds, then with obvious effort began to roll over. Moments later she was on her tummy, happily kicking her little legs against the floor.

"She rolled over!" he said. "Good job, Gelaa! You're such a big girl!"

Zuri beamed with pride. "She's on the verge of crawling, too. She's a quick learner, our daughter."

He leaned down and kissed Rellia's head. "You see your big sister, Rellia? Soon you'll be rolling over too, and she can show you just how it's done."

His daughter yawned and smacked her lips in response, making little sucking motions; she was obviously getting hungry. Luckily Nic seemed to be finished nursing, because Pella handed Dare his son and took their daughter from him to lift to her breast, where the baby eagerly latched on with contented noises.

Zuri picked Gelaa up and climbed onto the bed to cuddle in against his other side. "How was Redoubt?" She playfully poked his cloak clasp. "That looks an awful lot like a knight's pin to me, Sir Dare."

He grinned. "Yes, I earned knighthood. Although it was a close thing."

"Ooh, are we having a cuddle party?" Se'weir blurted from the door. She climbed onto the bed and lay on her back across his legs, resting her head on his lap and staring up at him lovingly. "Aside from a reunion where we did more adult things, this is exactly what I hoped for."

Dare tenderly rested his hand on his hobgoblin fiancee's cheek, stroking her soft skin. "Me too. I've missed you all so much while I was away. And I thought about the kids constantly." He lowered his hand to her belly, which was clearly showing her pregnancy.

As he would've expected; she was almost 4 months along, which for a 6 month pregnancy was the equivalent of 6 months. She'd be bearing his child soon, a thought that filled him with excitement.

He settled in with his beloved fiancees and children, savoring the chance to be with them after weeks of separation. "I'm going to take a week off," he abruptly announced.

The three women looked at him, surprised. "What do you mean?" Pella asked, shifting Rellia to her other breast. "A week off what?"

Dare offered Nic to Zuri, taking Gelaa in turn and kissing her sharp little cheek. "Away from leveling. After the months of preparation before going to Redoubt, then everything there, I just want to spend some time at home with my family."

His fiancees all brightened. "Really?" Zuri asked. "A whole week? Isn't that too much?"

"If anything it isn't enough." He leaned over and tenderly kissed her. "You deserve so much more."

"Mmm." She leaned against him, gently stroking Nic's ears while the baby's eyelids drooped sleepily as he began drifting off, full and contented. "My beloved, you've given me more than I ever could've hoped for. More than I even believed was possible."

"And me," Se'weir agreed. "I expected to be given as a mate to a chieftain or great warrior, to be bred and raise his babies. Perhaps never even to have a real conversation with him other than grunts of pleasure." She lowered her hands to tenderly cup her belly. "I didn't even know it was possible to have a relationship like this with a mate."

"And me," Pella murmured, tenderly stroking Rellia's soft cheek. "I was raised to be a pet, but you showed me the wonder of true freedom and independence. You helped me resolve things with my old master's family, and welcomed me into yours. Ours. The chance to share a life with you, to feel your deep love and have the children I've longed for. With you, the man I love with all my heart."

Her eyes glimmered with tears as she leaned in and kissed him, then licked his mouth with a giggle. "Although I won't say no to a week of you staying with us, too. There's so many things I want to do that we haven't tried yet." She sniffed, then brightened. "And not just with you but with Lily and Marigold."

"You proposed to Lily!" Se'weir squealed, clapping her hands. That startled Gelaa, who began to fuss, and the hobgoblin's pale green skin blushed pink in embarrassment. "Sorry."

Zuri laughed as she traded her daughter back from Dare, soothing her. "It's all right, that's how I responded inside. I'm so happy for both of you."

"I'm so happy for all of us," Pella said, tail straining to wag against the pillows she lay against. "Our family's getting so big, with so many wonderful people." She giggled. "We're going to have to get a bigger bed. Especially when Trissela gets here."

Dare frowned. "Won't Trissela be sleeping in her pool?" Which actually raised the question of how he was going to sleep with her, since he obviously couldn't breathe underwater. Unless he could get his hands on a spell or enchantment that did that; that might actually be a pretty pleasant experience, like a sensory deprivation tank.

That he got to share with a beautiful mermaid. So sensory deprivation aside from all the best sensations.

Pella grinned at him. "I bet she could spend a little while out of it to play with us."

"Shh," Zuri said gently. "I look forward to lots of fun in the future, but for now let's just enjoy this moment."

That sounded perfect to him, and he contentedly settled back in his familiar bed, cradling Nic in his arms and marveling at his son's

Phoenix

perfect little face as he slept peacefully.
    He was home.

Epilogue
New Adventures

Two weeks later Dare found himself in the parlor seated in one of the overstuffed chairs by the fire, tensely sipping mulled wine while Linia's caterwauls filled the house.

She was giving birth to his child in one of the first floor guest bedrooms, and in typical catgirl fashion letting the experience be loudly known.

Ilin sat across from him, while Veressa and Carilina shared one of the couches. On the other couch sat Bradis, who'd come at Dare's invitation to adventure with the new party and was now looking uncomfortable about being there. A few of Linia's male friends from among the refugees were also there to pay their respects.

Her female friends and the women of the household were all crowded in helping with the birthing, or at least staying close to offer their support.

Dare had asked what he could do, and been told he could wait. As he'd probably have to do with most of the births of his children, given the view on Collisa that childbirth was fully the domain of women and men had no place anywhere near it.

He wasn't in the mood to talk to his friends, so with not much to do besides wait he found himself thinking of all the women carrying his children, whether deliberately or by accident thanks to the snafu with his high fertility.

It was a surprising number, one which would've been shocking back on Earth and raised a few eyebrows even here, although usually in approval and admiration.

As far as he knew from the timing and what he knew of how long pregnancies lasted for the various races, the only lover besides Linia due to give birth around now was Ellui back in Lone Ox. He assumed, or at least hoped, that she didn't even realize the baby was his, since he'd pulled out and she didn't know about his high fertility.

It wasn't that he didn't want to take responsibility for the child, and he certainly worried for its welfare. But he didn't see how he could do anything without blowing up Ellui's and Brennal's marriage, toxic and unstable as it was, and causing hardship for their other children.

Maybe he should talk to Ireni and see if she had any ideas.

In any case, that was a worry for another time. Right now his focus was all on his catgirl friend down the hall giving birth to their baby right here, right now.

After what felt like an eternity, longer than the other births he thought, although that might've just been because time dragged on interminably as he waited in tense silence, Linia's caterwauls turned from pain to joy. Everyone in the room perked up and Dare shot to his feet, setting down the wineglass and listening intently.

Everything went quiet, and another eternity passed that was probably two or three minutes before Ireni bustled into the room, smiling broadly. "Congratulations, my love," she said, wrapping her arms around him and resting her head on his chest, "you have a new felid daughter. Melinia."

Dare's breath went out of him in a delighted whoosh, and he hugged his fiancee tightly as the others in the room gathered around to slap him on the back and shake his hand. He barely noticed, grinning like an idiot as he looked towards the stairs. "Can I see her?"

"Soon," Ireni said placidly. "Linia wants to compose herself and feed the baby. It'll be about an hour."

That was understandable, he supposed, although he couldn't help but feel disappointed. He was eager to meet his new daughter, and to tell Linia what a wonderful job she'd done.

Ilin chuckled at his expression. "It's not so long, my friend. A reasonable, customary wait."

"Aye," Veressa agreed with a warm smile. "Most fathers aren't so eager to rush into the birthing room moments after the child is born. They might risk seeing something they'd rather not see, and the mother would rather them not see. Childbirth is a beautiful and joyous process, but it can get a bit . . . messy."

"And that's more than I care to hear," Bradis cut in hastily, standing. "Some mysteries I'll happily leave the domain of women. I'm going to go check on my horse."

As Ireni hurried down the hall again Dare settled back into his chair and pulled out a book, impatiently waiting for an hour to pass. He wished he could get his hands on a clock so he could track the time, but Bastion had a dearth of clockmakers and getting one from Haraldar's capitol usually required a custom order and great expense.

Which hadn't stopped him from ordering one anyway, although it would take months to arrive.

He found himself just staring at the words on the page, listening to try to hear what was going on down the hall. So it was a relief when Zuri, Pella, and Se'weir came in after a while, carrying Gelaa and the twins.

Dare moved to a couch with them and took turns holding his babies, while his fiancees reassured him that Linia was fine and Melinia was absolutely precious.

He couldn't wait to meet her.

Time passed much more swiftly after that, and finally Amalisa came in to let him know Linia was ready for him. His fiancees came with him, bringing the babies so they could meet their new sister, and they made their way to the guest bedroom.

Linia sat propped up against pillows on a small bed, glowing with joy as she cradled a little bundle wrapped in a super soft blanket. She beamed up at him with fierce pride. "Meet your new daughter Melinia, Dare."

Grinning like an idiot, he stepped forward and gently lifted his baby girl into his arms. Her velvety cat ears and the fuzz on her head were a shimmering black, and she looked up at him myopically with big blue eyes; she'd taken after her daddy. Although she had all of her mother's delicate beauty.

Dare stared at her in wonder for what felt like an eternity before looking at Linia, tears in his eyes. "She's beautiful."

"So beautiful," the orange catgirl agreed in weary but wholehearted joy. She patted the bed beside her. "Come on, my friend, come sit down and spend time with your new daughter."

He nodded and carefully settled onto the bed, stroking the baby's silky ears in quiet delight. "My baby," he whispered. "My little Melinia."

Dare looked around at his family and their friends as they gathered around, beaming at this precious moment.

*****

"So this is Gurzan's Last Hold?" Bradis said, holding his torch up high and peering around curiously as the light faded to dark emptiness, in all directions but the tunnel they'd just entered through. "Didn't expect it to be so big."

He laughed as if he'd made a joke, probably the juxtaposition of short dwarves and large underground caverns. Although any doubt was dispelled as he continued. "Think they're compensating for something?"

Veressa smirked as she stepped past him, dull silver eye squinting into the darkness. "It must be quite the compensation." She turned to Dare. "Can you do your fancy flickery arrow and give us an idea of what we're looking at?"

"I can at least give you a better appreciation of the sheer scale of this place." Chuckling, Dare drew an arrow from his quiver and set it to the string, activating Strobe Arrow and sending it flying into the gloom. It revealed the vast cavern in brief flashes for hundreds of yards with no other walls in sight before hitting the ground, skipping a few times, and winking one last time as it rolled to a stop.

Lily whistled. "Every time I see it the *size* of this place blows me away. It makes my burrow seem like a hole in the ground in comparison."

Their Fighter scratched his jaw. "Technically isn't that exactly what both of these are?"

The party lined up facing the darkness, looking around as if they could see anything. For this venture Dare had managed to talk Ireni and Leilanna into accompanying them, as well as what he was tentatively coming to consider his core party of him, Lily, Bradis, Veressa, and Carilina.

An unexpected addition was Bradis's lover: Estellis, the Invigorator who'd been in their party in the fight against the monster horde. She was at best a buff dispenser, with her only real combat ability a regeneration spell that would serve as a form of healing.

And Dare loved the idea of having her along.

Crunching the numbers, it would take at least 6 other people in the party with her for her buffs to equal the contribution she could provide if she was a different class. But after that it was all benefit for each added person in the party or raid. Better yet, she could sit outside of the fight in a safe spot, maybe tossing her regeneration spell on healers or ranged DPS as needed, and contribute with one less person having to be in danger.

Her buffs also ranged across the entire gamut of usefulness, from providing added health and defense, added strength and stamina, added agility and speed, and last of all added mana regeneration, lingual nimbleness, and dexterity, which both affected cast times.

Only one buff could be active on a person at a time, but pretty much the entire raid could be served by a single Invigorator.

And it certainly didn't hurt that the buff that was most ideal for Dare, agility and speed, allowed him to run even faster. Still not quite as fast as Lily even with her unbuffed, but close enough that he could sometimes reach out and brush her fluffy white cottontail.

As for her, when she got the buff her speed was just insane.

After half a minute or so of admiring the lack of a view in the darkness Estellis cleared her throat. "The dungeon is up one of those pillars you illuminated?" she asked.

Phoenix

Redoubt

Dare nodded. "The one on the right. But I figure in a place this vast, where there's one dungeon there might be others. And hopefully we'll have a guide."

As if the words were a summons, at the corner of his vision the shadows created by the flickering torches resolved into a ragged goblin, smaller than most he'd seen, and scrawny and wizened and more than a little dirty on top of it.

Bradis jumped and started to draw his sword with a curse. Dare caught his hand, shaking his head. "Considering how many goblin friends I have around here," he said mildly, "I hope you'll think twice before drawing your blade on any you encounter."

The Fighter flushed. "It's not that he's a goblin, my friend, it's that he popped out of the damn shadows like a revenant."

The goblin watched them warily with overlarge, unblinking eyes. "Abovegrounder," he said in an even, flat tone.

Dare nodded at him. "When last I saw you I offered to hire your people as guides. Have you considered my offer?"

The subterranean dweller bowed politely. "We are at your service. But food would be better payment than silver. And the trade with the surface you offered?"

He glanced at Ireni, who cleared her throat and offered the goblin spokesman a parchment Zuri had written for her in Goblin, and which she'd transcribed in Haraldar's common tongue. "Formal treaties with the Avenging Wolf tribe, Melarawn village, and Nirim Manor. Present this at any of them and you will be treated fairly."

The goblin accepted the paper almost reverently. "Haz'u'dirik, spokesman for the undermountain goblins," he said with a bow.

"Well met, Haz," Dare said solemnly. "I'm Dare. I don't suppose you have a map of these tunnels?"

"Nay, abovegrounder. But I've brought my scoutmaster." Another goblin shimmered into view, coming out of Stealth; a Stalker.

Dare nodded to the newcomer. "I'm looking for tunnels that have been blocked off or collapsed, as well as ones infested with

Phoenix

monsters you can't get past."

The Stalker glanced at Haz, who nodded. "Many collapsed tunnels, abovegrounder," the scoutmaster said in a voice that was high pitched even by the standards of goblins. "Some blocked off." He paused thoughtfully. "Seven with monsters."

The collapsed ones would take more effort than they could probably manage, especially if Haz's tribe hadn't already managed the feat. It might be something to leave to the dwarves once Dare told them how to find this place.

And after he turned the dwarvish records they'd found here over to their proper owners; the goblin transcribers had finally finished the work, now he just needed to get in touch with the dwarvish contingent of the Irregulars and find out who he was supposed to talk to.

The blocked tunnels were an option, but again the goblins would've gotten through them if they could. "Show me the ones with monsters," he told Haz.

The ragged goblin saluted and led the way into the darkness, his scoutmaster hugging his heels. Dare and the others followed, torches raised.

The first tunnel Haz led them to had the same monsters Dare had encountered in the one at the top of the column, party rated Level 52 and 53 monsters that looked like hideous mushroom creatures. He immediately called for them to turn back.

The second and third tunnels didn't have mushrooms, but the monsters in them were also in the low 50s. But then in the fourth tunnel the monsters were Level 30-31.

And they weren't party rated.

Dare scratched at his jaw, staring at the giant centipede-like creatures skittering over the walls and ceiling as well as the floor. "They're not party rated," he told his companions. "Is this not a dungeon?"

Veressa sucked in a sharp breath, pale skin flushing with sudden excitement. "An underground spawn point," she said. "The only place those exist underground are in Molzog's Delvings." She paused doubtfully. "Or so I've heard. A dwarf would know better."

"Or a goblin," Haz said with a huff. "The other three tunnels with monsters are far deeper below the ground, after passing through vast caverns with wide abysses where other monsters and underground dwelling plants and animals can be found."

"In Molzog's Delvings," the Stalker added helpfully, in case they'd missed it.

Dare frowned. "You said there were only seven tunnels with monsters. What about these caverns you speak of?"

The two goblins stared at him blankly. "They're not tunnels we can't get past," Haz finally said.

Of course. Dare shook his head and turned to Veressa. "I saw Molzog's Delvings mentioned a few times in the dwarvish records. And I've heard a bit about it. It's some sort of underground world with denizens of its own?"

"So I've heard," she repeated. "Molzog is God of the Deeps, who is said to always be expanding his domain with ever more extensive systems of tunnels, caverns, and chasms. Until finally either the latticework of supports will grow so fragile that an earthquake will send the surface collapsing down upon his Delvings in mutual ruin, or magma from below will rise to fill everything with new stone."

"Let's hope for the latter," Bradis said dryly.

Dare snorted in agreement. "So it's a world of its own with spawn points. A place where we could level?"

"If you dare, no pun intended," Veressa said to a few chuckles among the group. "Molzog's Delvings is the domain of his children, the dark elves. As well as other dangerous and aggressive races. They'll keep to their caverns for millennia, and then an interloper might suddenly stir them to boil forth in fury."

"Like what happened to Gurzan's Last Hold," Lily mused.

The vampire shrugged. "If you say so. In any case Molzog usually gets around to connecting his Delvings to any large underground civilization. In almost all cases they serve as the connection between the underground world and the surface."

And there was an entrance to the Delvings, and all its denizens, within a day's walk of Nirim Manor. Shit.

Ireni seemed to be thinking along the same lines. Or reading his mind, as she often was able to. "Maybe we should try to buy another legendary chest so we can rig up a way to collapse this entire place if needed," she murmured.

Dare nodded. "On second thought, let's not use Molzog's Delvings as a convenient place to find spawn points for leveling, as well as exciting new opportunities for exploration. I don't want to stir any denizen of the deeps."

"Wise," Carilina said. "Dark elves are said to be warlike and fearless, throwing themselves at unknown spawn points even if it means death, so those who come behind can know the monsters' strength. They get to dangerously high levels, especially as they tend to be as long lived as any elvish race."

"In that case let's plan on the dungeon when we get high enough level, and get the hell out of here," Bradis said cheerfully.

Most seemed to wholeheartedly agree and hastily turned back. But Lily and Veressa lingered, expressions wistful, and Dare found himself hanging back with them.

His heart yearned to explore the deep places of the world. Fight its monsters, see its strange and unique animals, witness its breathtaking wonders. Meet the races of the underground and see if the terrible rumors of them were true, and maybe romance some of them.

It seemed incredible that Collisa, already such a vast world full of potential, had an entire other world below. A world that called to him for its sheer alienness, unlike anything that could be found on Earth.

But Molzog's Delvings would have to wait until he grew stronger. And perhaps not even then; he didn't want to disturb people just living their lives in their own home if it would lead to conflict.

Redoubt

"Come on," Dare said, taking Lily's hand and reluctantly turning away. "Let's get to the next good spawn point on the surface. We've got a lot of leveling to do if we want to beat these dungeons."

"And find everything else that's waiting for us out there," she agreed happily, leaning into his side. "Wonders we'll discover together. Adventures we'll share."

He couldn't wait.

End of Redoubt.
The adventures of Dare and his family
continue in Brighthill, seventh book of the Outsider series.

Phoenix

Thank you for reading Redoubt!

I hope you enjoyed reading it as much as I enjoyed writing it. If you feel the book is worthy of support, I'd greatly appreciate it if you'd rate it, or better yet review it, on Amazon, as well as recommend it to anyone you think would also enjoy it.

As a self-published author I flourish with the help of readers who review and recommend my work. Your support helps me continue doing what I love and bringing you more books to enjoy.

About the Author

Aiden Phoenix became an established author
writing stories about the end of the world.

Then Collisa called, a new and exciting world to explore,
and like the characters in his series he was reborn anew there.

Printed in Great Britain
by Amazon